'Forensic scientist Rhona MacLeod has become one of the most satisfying characters in modern crime fiction – honourable, inquisitive and yet plagued by doubts and, sometimes, fears . . . As ever, the landscape is stunningly evoked and MacLeod's decency and humanity shine through on every page' *Daily Mail*

'Lin Anderson is one of Scotland's national treasures . . . her writing is unique, bringing warmth and depth to even the seediest parts of Glasgow. Rhona MacLeod is a complex and compelling heroine who just gets better with every outing' Stuart MacBride

'Vivid and atmospheric . . . enthralling' *Guardian*

'The bleak landscape is beautifully described, giving this popular series a new lease of life' *Sunday Times*

'Greenock-born Anderson's work is sharper than a pathologist's scalpel. One of the best Scottish crime series since Rebus' *Daily Record*

'Inventive, compelling, genuinely scary and beautifully written, as always' Denzil Meyrick

'Hugely imaginative and exciting'
James Grieve (Emeritus Professor of Forensic Pathology)

Time for the Dead

Lin Anderson is a Scottish author and screenwriter known for her bestselling crime series featuring forensic scientist Dr Rhona MacLeod. Four of her novels have been longlisted for the Scottish Crime Book of the Year, with *Follow the Dead* being a 2018 finalist. Her short film *River Child* won a student BAFTA for Best Fiction and the Celtic Film Festival's Best Drama award and has garnered more than one and a half million views on YouTube. Lin is also the co-founder of the international crime-writing festival Bloody Scotland, which takes place annually in Stirling.

By Lin Anderson

Driftnet
Torch
Deadly Code
Dark Flight
Easy Kill
Final Cut
The Reborn
Picture Her Dead
Paths of the Dead
The Special Dead
None but the Dead
Follow the Dead
Sins of the Dead
Time for the Dead

NOVELLA
Blood Red Roses

Time for the Dead

to have their revenge . . .

LIN ANDERSON

PAN BOOKS

First published 2019 by Macmillan

This paperback edition published 2020 by Pan Books
an imprint of Pan Macmillan
The Smithson, 6 Briset Street, London EC1M 5NR
Associated companies throughout the world
www.panmacmillan.com

ISBN 978-1-5098-6624-3

1 3 5 7 9 8 6 4 2

A CIP catalogue record for this book is available from the British Library.

Map artwork by Hemesh Alles 2019

Typeset in Meridien by Palimpsest Book Production Ltd, Falkirk, Stirlingshire
Printed and bound by CPI Group (UK) Ltd, Croydon, CR0 4YY

For
Blaze fae Skye, Border Collie,
who inspired this story

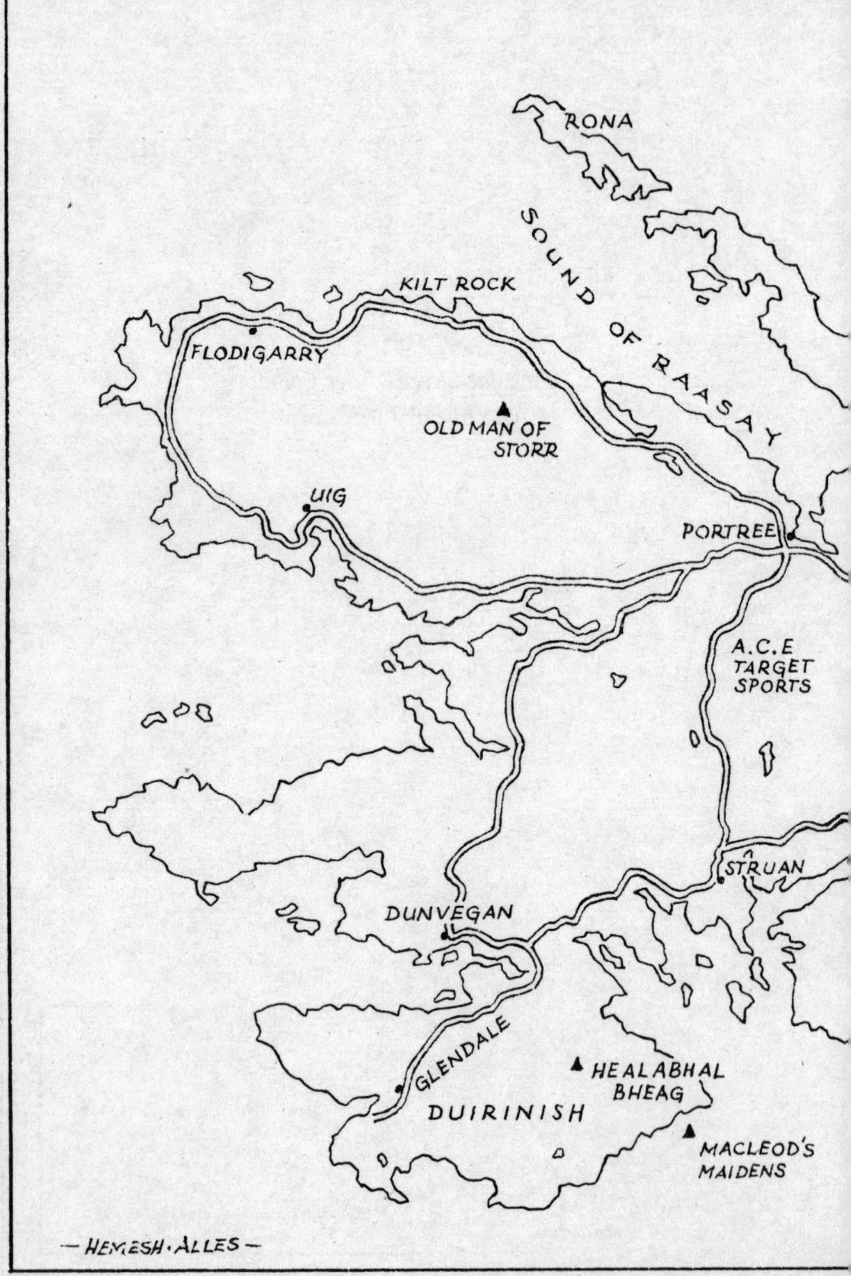
RONA
SOUND OF RAASAY
KILT ROCK
FLODIGARRY
OLD MAN OF STORR
UIG
PORTREE
A.C.E TARGET SPORTS
STRUAN
DUNVEGAN
GLENDALE
HEALABHAL BHEAG
DUIRINISH
MACLEOD'S MAIDENS
—HEMESH·ALLES—

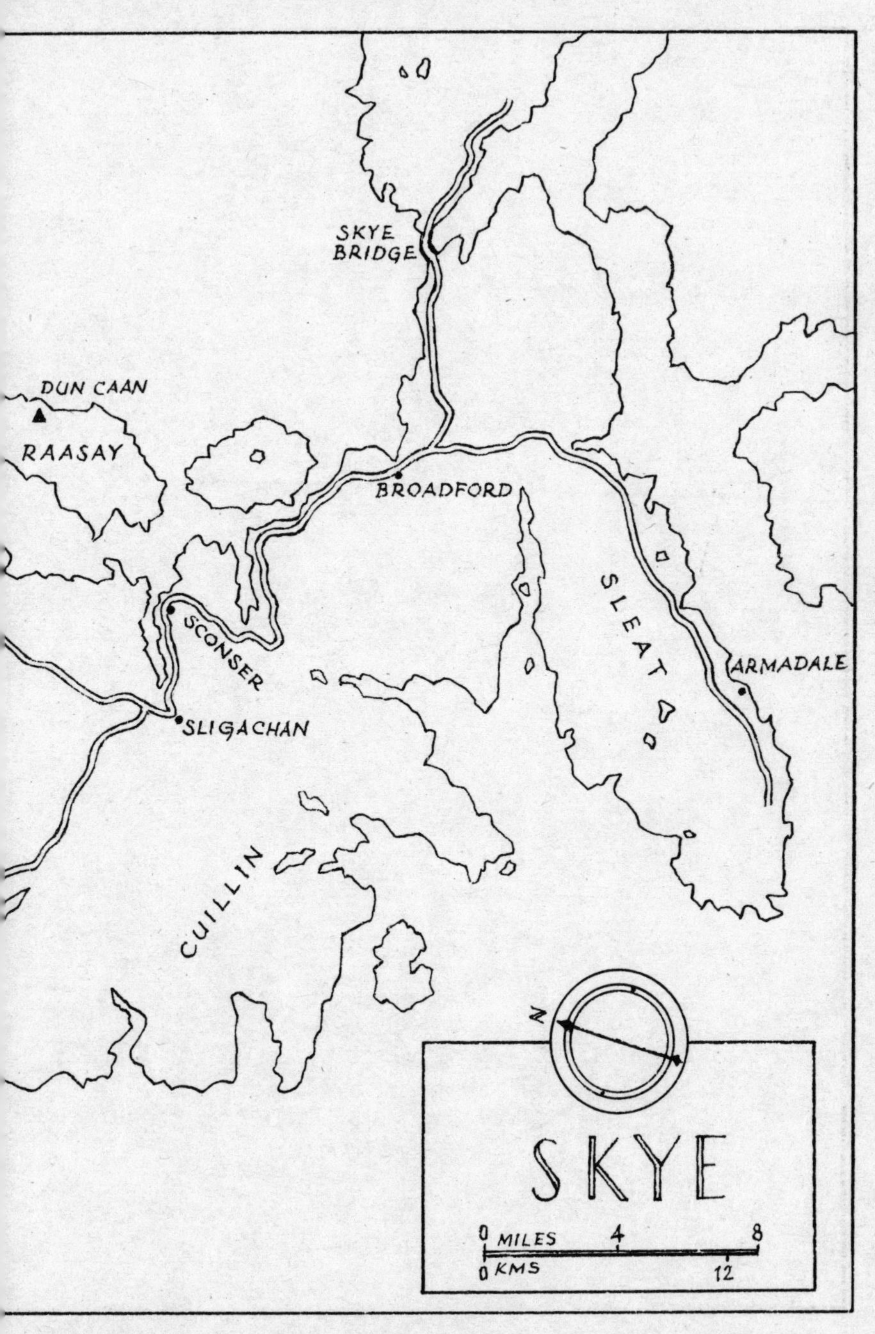
SKYE
BRIDGE
DUN CAAN
RAASAY
BROADFORD
SCONSER
SLIGACHAN
SLEAT
ARMADALE
CUILLIN
N
SKYE
0 MILES 4 8
0 KMS 12

All the Gods, the Heavens and the Hells are within us.

The dog stirred, ears pricking up, positioning themselves like radar. The night was full of noise for the Border collie, not so for his owner slumbering only inches away.

The crackle and spit as a log settled in the stove, the hoot of an owl, the rustle of trees in the wind, the chatter of the burn that ran behind their caravan. All those the big collie heard and dismissed.

But not the other sound.

Raising his head, he listened, searching for what had awakened him, the memory of which troubled the dog, because he sensed that the sound had been made by a human. One in distress.

The dog jumped up, certain now of what he should do and how quickly he would need to do it.

A loud bark brought his bleary-eyed master to open the door, his words at having been woken so abruptly sharp on the air.

A blast of icy wind swept in, together with a flurry of wet snow as the dog jumped out, oblivious to the order to be quick.

He caught the smell of human almost immediately. More than one. Only a limited number of humans visited his home site during the winter months, and at least one of the scents he picked up now he recognized.

How far away was the fear, and in which direction?

The dog paused to sniff the ground, catching perhaps the trail deposited earlier. Into the trees now, his swift run disturbed other creatures that lived on the twelve-acre site, causing them to flee before him. A white hare rushed past and the dog almost lost concentration, until his training kicked back in.

Find the human. Follow their fear.

He was circling, radar ears turning, nose to the air, aware that as the group had moved in circles in their earlier game, he too might do the same, never to reach his goal.

The dog stood stock-still, every hair on his shaggy body bristling.

The new smell came to him then on the wind, making his shiny black nose twitch in anticipation.

It was one he knew well. A scent that emanated from his usual prey.

The blood smell of the kill.

1

Run. Breathe.

She could smell her own sweat, feel it trickle inside her gear, despite her breath condensing in the freezing air.

She paused to catch her breath and check the thump of her heart. Sniffing the air like a dog, she sought a scent of the others.

People thought that all perspiration had the same smell. It didn't. She knew what each member of the group smelt like. In the midnight darkness of a desert hideout, she was able to distinguish each one of them by their footfall, by their breathing pattern as they slept and by the scent of their bodies.

She knew when they were at peace. When they were afraid, which was most of the time, and when they were aroused.

Like now.

Her ears attuned, she instinctively knew where the others were with respect to her own location. She knew exactly where *he* was. And that was close behind her.

Very close.

She could hear the faint rumble of the burn, swollen with melting snow, but not yet see it. In Afghanistan they'd had their night-vision goggles. Not here. Here they had to rely on their own eyes and their instincts.

She would stop, she decided. She would wait for him to come to her, as she knew he would. Her heart beat like a marching band and her sweat mingled with the tang of wet birch as she awaited his arrival.

As it was, she caught the stink of his body before she saw him.

Then a shaft of moonlight escaped from behind the sleet-laden clouds, to find his outline. Tall, broad, his body dense and tense. She knew what he would do when he reached her. Crow his success. Look for his reward. Take it.

She knew real fear then and longed to turn and run.

Spinning suddenly, she took off again, denying him his prize. He gave a shout of anger. Despite her quick getaway, he would be on her soon. Now she could smell what he wanted. Something she was unwilling to give.

2

The temperature had dropped again overnight. Rhona watched as her breath condensed above her, then pulling the cover over her head once more, rejoiced in the warmth below the duvet.

It was, she decided, the coldest winter she'd ever experienced on Skye.

Not that she had spent many winters here to judge.

Summer had been her time for visiting as a teenager, apart from a week last November just before the case that had called her to Sanday, one of Orkney's most northerly islands.

Thinking about work stirred her properly awake. She had spent the time since the sin-eater case blanking her mind of all things related to that subject. And since work normally consumed her for most hours of the day, that had been a difficult thing to achieve.

An impossible thing to achieve.

So, she had compensated by studying past unsolved cases she hadn't been involved in, together with new developments in the field of forensics. And she had spent time reading, working her way through every book she'd found in the cottage, before joining the travelling library and requesting more.

She'd taken a daily swim until the weather had got too

cold even for her wetsuit. She'd climbed and walked, and walked and climbed, since Skye was a perfect place to do both.

In all this endeavour to forget, she'd enlisted the help of Jamie McColl, who had shared her teenage summers on the island. Jamie had stayed behind to run the family undertaker's, while Rhona had gone to Glasgow University initially to study medicine, then switching to forensic science. A member of the local Mountain Rescue Team, Jamie also knew the hills better than anyone, so was the perfect guide when she required one.

He was also easy company and they never discussed his work or hers, or even why she'd forsaken it.

Throwing back the duvet, Rhona rose and, grabbing a jumper, went to check on the stove. Entering the sitting room, she found it still warm from the dying embers of the fire. Had she remembered to build it up with peat before falling into bed, the rest of the cottage would have been equally warm.

Used to gas central heating in her Glasgow flat, and the instantly available fire in the sitting room, her biggest adjustment in coming here had been how to stay continuously warm. Only now did she fully appreciate the work involved in doing that.

Rhona opened the stove and threw in some more wood, after which she headed for the kitchen. Filling the coffee machine, she then grabbed her coat, pulled on her boots, opened the back door and stepped outside. Despite having done this every morning since her arrival, the sight that met her never failed to fill her with wonder.

This was why she'd come here and this was what might save her.

In the darkness of despair, in the blackness of her incarceration, this was the image she'd tried to remember when she closed her eyes.

The tide was out, leaving glistening pools among the grey rocks. The Sound of Sleat was as calm as the sky above it. Something that didn't happen very often. A blue sky belied the cold that sent a shiver through her body, although the distant peaks of the mainland told the truth, coated as they were in a white mantle.

Bathed by the warmth of the Gulf Stream, the west coast of Scotland experienced plenty of rain, but wasn't renowned for snow cover. Winter climbers rarely visited Skye and the Cuillin to challenge themselves on snow or ice, but this winter had been different.

This winter had brought more snow and lower temperatures than usual, and, Rhona thought, made this part of Scotland even more beautiful for its presence. She stood breathing in both the scene and the sharp air, before the scent of the freshly brewed coffee beckoned.

Heading inside, she found the fire ablaze and the chill in the remainder of the cottage definitely diminished. She opened the stove and, laying on some peat blocks, turned the damper down, as she should have done overnight.

Pouring a cup of strong coffee brought a fleeting image of DS Michael McNab, her colleague, friend and, briefly, former lover. With that came the memory of the moment McNab had turned his Harley-Davidson Street Glide into the rough track that led to the cottage, with her riding pillion.

The trip itself by motorbike had been an eye-opener for Rhona. She'd travelled the same route before, many times, by car. On a bike it had been totally different. Surprisingly so. Still traumatized by her recent experience, she'd found herself able to smile again as she observed the Highlands with new eyes.

McNab had been quick to note the change, and had suggested she might like to embrace freedom and buy a bike of her own.

By the time they'd reached Skye, Rhona was beginning to consider doing just that.

McNab might have opened her eyes to a new way of travelling through the Highlands. Rhona, on the other hand, hadn't succeeded in opening McNab's eyes to the pleasures of living there. His first words as he'd approached the cottage had in fact been, 'You're planning to stay . . . here?'

He'd tried, she remembered, not to sound too horrified at the thought.

McNab, as an urban warrior, had no desire to be anywhere other than his beloved Glasgow and its 'mean streets', the countryside being anathema to him.

Yet he agreed to bring me here despite his misgivings.

'You'll lose the plot,' he offered as he drew up outside. 'No Chrissy, no Sean. No shops. No pubs.'

Rhona, choosing to ignore any reference to her mental state, however throwaway, said instead, 'There's a very nice pub not far from here. And I can have my food delivered just like in Glasgow.'

McNab hadn't looked convinced by that.

'Internet?' he'd countered as she'd unlocked the blue, salt-streaked front door.

Rhona couldn't lie. 'I hear it's better than it was.'

'Better than on Sanday, I hope?' He'd shaken his head, as though even the memory of their incarceration on that particular remote island still caused him pain.

'I'll adjust,' Rhona had assured him, wondering if she would, or even could.

Still, anything was better than being in the Glasgow flat at the moment. Or maybe ever again.

McNab had checked out the tiny cottage as though it were a crime scene, before unlocking the back door and stepping outside.

'Jeez,' he'd said, noting how close they were to the water. 'You're nearly in the fucking sea.'

'The tide doesn't come past those rocks,' Rhona had assured him. 'Even when it's stormy.'

She'd watched as McNab cut off whatever he'd been about to say in response, although Rhona had been able to read every line on his face. He was worried about her, although trying desperately not to say it out loud. Something that wasn't easy for him.

The journey west had gone well, mainly because he'd loved riding his motorbike on such open roads. Now they were actually here, he'd had to face up to the fact that he felt like he was abandoning her 'in a foreign land'.

'It's not foreign,' Rhona had laughed at that. 'This is where my adopted parents came from. This is where I spent a large chunk of my childhood,' she'd reminded him.

The box of groceries she'd pre-ordered had been left in the back shed as she'd requested. 'See,' Rhona had said as she'd lifted it out. 'Tonight's tea.'

She'd lit the fire then, while McNab selected something to eat and set about warming it up in the microwave. Fed and weary after the long bike ride, they'd settled companionably in front of the fire, Rhona with a whisky, McNab choosing a beer.

McNab had looked slightly askance when she'd poured

herself a malt from the cabinet rather than open the bottle of white wine delivered with the groceries.

'I'm not ready for white wine . . . yet,' she'd said, remembering too well its significance.

'Same for me with whisky.'

Rhona had left McNab in front of the glowing fire nursing his beer and gone to make up the beds. Hers in the double bedroom that had once been her parents' room and McNab's in the single room that had once been hers. They'd parted company around ten, but she suspected McNab had got as little sleep as she had.

In truth, Rhona had been glad to see McNab leave the next morning. He was so much a part of what she'd been through that his presence there merely served as a reminder of what she was here to forget.

Nevertheless, she'd surprised both McNab and herself by giving him a hug goodbye, recalling the scent of his skin and the feel of his bristled cheek against her own.

'Give Ellie my love,' she'd told him as he'd hugged her back.

'I will,' he'd said, his look of affection bringing a swell of emotion Rhona could hardly contain.

As the motorbike reached the main road, he'd turned and waved his last goodbye, and at his departure, Rhona had felt so lost and alone that she'd gone quickly inside and locked the door.

3

Rhona stared at the front door, key in hand.

If, or when, she felt able to leave the door unlocked, she would, she realized, have reached a definite signpost on her road to recovery.

This isn't Glasgow, she reminded herself. *This is Skye, where everyone knows your business and your whereabouts.*

Her parents had never locked their door when going out and neither had she in past times. No one around here had locked their doors. What if a visitor arrived, cold, wet or hungry, and couldn't get inside?

Perish the thought.

Perhaps, though, things had changed. There were more strangers about. The local population of 10,000 was now dwarfed annually by over half a million tourists. And Skye wasn't an island any more. It had a bridge to the mainland. Plus, there was crime, although rarely major. And, unlike on Sanday, there was a police station.

All these excuses for her urban-style behaviour caused Rhona's hand to hover two inches from the keyhole.

McNab would blow a fuse if he knew she was even contemplating leaving the door unlocked. As would Sean.

Conscience assuaged, Rhona slid in the key and turned it. Then, as recompense for her lack of faith in the people of Skye, she put the key under a nearby stone.

Jamie's borrowed jeep was coated in a spidery film of snow, although last night's light fall had already melted into the muddy car track.

Rhona checked her watch as she joined the main road. She had agreed to meet up with Jamie in Portree, but before that she had to face her appointment with the trauma counsellor. Despite her protestations that she had no need of such support, DI Wilson had continued to insist. 'If you'd agreed to go to Castlebrae, this wouldn't be necessary,' had been Bill's exact words.

Castlebrae was a treatment centre for police officers, injured physically or psychologically in the line of duty.

'I'm not a police officer,' Rhona had reminded him. 'But I am due some time off. And I plan to spend it on Skye.'

Bill had backed off then, but Rhona had known he wouldn't give up. And he hadn't. She had finally agreed to a meeting with a psychiatrist, more because of Chrissy's constant urging.

'What harm can it do?' her friend and forensic assistant had told her. 'And it'll get Bill off your back, and mine.'

So for Chrissy's sake at least, Rhona had eventually agreed to today's meeting.

Besides, she liked the hour-long run from Armadale to Portree, which lay roughly halfway up the east coast of the island. Most people visiting Skye for the first time had no conception of just how large the island was, and how little of the landmass was accessible by road.

When she'd shown McNab the large framed map on the sitting-room wall of the cottage, he'd been openly surprised, both by its size and the fact that it was covered with Gaelic place names.

In fact it had been that which had prompted his 'foreign land' remark.

'Try looking at any map featuring land north of the central belt,' she'd told him. 'It's all in Gaelic.'

'It wasn't on Sanday,' he'd reminded her.

'That's because Orkney and Shetland are Norse. Didn't they teach you anything about Scotland in school?'

He'd laughed then. 'I went to a Catholic school, remember? It was all about the conversion of Scotland.'

She was almost at Sconser and the ferry terminal for Raasay. Her favourite view of Raasay was from Portree, but it was here that her most lasting memory of the island began. It had been earlier in her career. Not long after she'd found her son, Liam. Or he had found her.

A fishing boat had netted a severed male foot in Raasay Sound, a month after another fishing boat had gone down in the vicinity. Tempers had been running high among the locals since it hadn't been the first time a submarine on manoeuvres on the west coast of Scotland had snagged a net and sunk a boat. The forensic trail on that investigation had led Rhona to Raasay via Santa Monica, USA, uncovering a conspiracy that had gone far beyond a clumsy attempt by the Ministry of Defence to shut down the story of the foot.

Today, the ferry was halfway across the Sound, and seeing its steady path to Raasay, Rhona thought she might like to revisit the island sometime during her stay on Skye. Perhaps call in on Mrs McMurdo who'd run the post office back then, and given her a place to stay.

The long length of Loch Sligachan travelled, she now passed the large family-run hotel at its head, then began the steep climb up towards the intermittent plantations that lined the road leading into Portree. The best views on this road were undoubtedly in the opposite direction because of the exciting glimpses of the Cuillin. Something she could enjoy on the way back.

After she got this meeting over with.

Checking her watch, Rhona realized she was going to be late. Something that was entirely down to her reluctance to set out in the first place. As luck would have it, the Dunvegan Road was this side of Portree and she soon spotted the sign for Am Fasgadh. Sweeping into the small car park outside the one-storey building, Rhona swiftly abandoned the jeep and hurried inside.

'Dr MacLeod?' a voice called her name on entry.

The man who stood at reception had his hand outstretched, as though certain that she was the person he sought. When Rhona indicated that he was right, he introduced himself.

'Dr Mike Bailey. I was beginning to think you might have got lost,' he added with a smile. He waited for a moment, as though expecting an explanation, which Rhona had no desire to give. When this became obvious, he said, 'If you'd like to follow me through, Dr MacLeod.'

Moments later Rhona found herself in a pleasant room with an equally pleasing view of the surrounding woodland.

'Welcome to The Shelter,' he said as he offered her a seat.

'I know what Am Fasgadh means,' Rhona heard herself answer testily.

'Ah.' Her belligerent tone had seemingly left him unmarked. 'So you have the Gaelic?'

And that smile again.

'A smattering,' Rhona said, as annoyed by her own behaviour as Dr Bailey's irritatingly kind manner. Gathering herself, she settled back in the chair, at the same time wondering just how much Dr Bailey had been told about her experiences during the sin-eater case. Whatever it was he knew, Rhona had no intention of expanding on it.

She'd turned up here, as requested. *No, ordered*. That was enough.

Rhona now began her evaluation of Dr Bailey.

He was Irish, by the accent. Probably Dublin, because he sounded a little like Sean, although that was where the likeness ended. No black hair, no blue eyes and probably no saxophone.

'Where are *you* from?' she said, keen to be first in the conversation.

'Dublin,' he confirmed.

'My adopted parents were from Skye, but I've spent more time in Glasgow than on the island. Are you based here?' she asked, before he could get in with a question of his own.

'Inverness. I do a surgery in Portree once a week.'

'So you're kept busy?'

He nodded, beginning to look a little put out by her string of enquiries.

'So,' Rhona said, 'why am I taking up your obviously valuable time?'

'You tell me,' he offered.

'Because I refused to follow procedure and go to Castlebrae. I preferred a holiday here on Skye instead.'

'So your stay here is a holiday?'

'Yes,' Rhona said with certainty.

'I understood from DI Wilson that you'd recently had a traumatic experience.'

'I process and analyse violent death for a living, Dr Bailey. Some would say that every day could be considered traumatic.' She waited, wondering where that remark would take him. Eventually she learned.

'But you're not often a victim yourself.'

Rhona took her gaze to the window and thought herself outside again, with the air blowing in her face. With the smell of the sea. With a view of the Cuillin.

'I am not a victim. A young man and a young woman died on the case I'm assuming you're referring to. I did not. I'm a survivor and the only reason I'm here now is because I was given no choice.'

'I see.'

Rhona followed his quick glance at the clock above the door. She suspected he was registering how little had been achieved in the last fifteen minutes.

'I have to meet someone. So if we're finished here,' she said, rising.

Rhona thought by his surprised expression that Dr Bailey might dispute this, but wisely he did not.

'Same time next week, Dr MacLeod?' he offered instead.

Rhona gave a brief nod, although she had no intention of ever coming back. To her mind, she had done what was required of her.

They shook hands again. His was warm and dry. Her own, she noticed, was cold and damp.

Registering the increased beat of her heart and her trembling hand as she unlocked the jeep, Rhona took a deep breath and fastened her gaze on the mountains to remind herself that she hadn't been buried alive again in Dr Bailey's questioning eyes.

Now outside the funeral director's, which was minutes away from Am Fasgadh, Rhona was counselling herself against going inside, the meeting with Dr Bailey having stirred up memories of a certain Glasgow undertaker's and what had happened there.

Which was why dwelling on the past was not a good thing.

When Rhona rang Jamie's number, he answered immediately.

'Are you on your way?'

'I'm here already.'

'Great. I'll be right out.'

He was as good as his word. Rhona watched as his tall figure emerged and felt her heart lift at the sight of him. With Jamie she could relax because he wouldn't ask her how she felt and why she was here.

Rhona climbed out of the driver's seat. 'I think you should drive. It's your jeep after all.'

Jamie took her place behind the wheel, while she buckled herself into the passenger seat.

'She's running smoothly for you?'

'I really like her,' Rhona assured him.

'I didn't want to use one of the funeral cars, not where we're going.'

'And where is that exactly?' Rhona said as they set off.

'A.C.E Target Sports to book a stag do for my mate. I'm the best man so it's my job to organize it all.'

'Okay . . .' Rhona said. 'But you don't need me to tag along. I can walk into Portree. Have a coffee.'

'I want you to try out some of the weapons.'

'Weapons?'

'Axes, knives. That sort of thing.'

'You are joking?'

'Nope.' Jamie grinned. 'It's just up the road a bit. In this weather it'll be muddy. How's your footwear?'

'Sturdy.'

'Good.'

He headed towards Portree before turning right into the Struan Road.

'And how are you with dogs?'

'Fine . . .' Rhona ventured, somewhat puzzled by the question.

'Then you'll enjoy meeting Blaze. He basically runs the place.'

4

Stavanger, Norway, the previous day

Inspector Alvis Olsen watched the snow-dusted coast of Scotland approach from his window seat. They said that whatever weather you left behind in Stavanger, you met it again in Aberdeen an hour later.

On this day, the saying was proving to be true. Rising early this morning, he'd found the sky still heavy with snow clouds from an overnight fall, the picturesque wooden buildings of old Stavanger draped in white.

By the time he'd set off for the Commissariat de Polis on Lagårdsveien, the snow underfoot had already turned to slush, though the brightly lit giant winter cruise ship tied up in the harbour still glistened like a frosted, tiered Christmas cake.

His usual route took him from his apartment on Kirkegata through the park at Breiavatnet and along the western flank of its shallow lake, after which the pedestrian walkways gave way to cars as he crossed the road to Lagård Gravlund.

Just as every other day, Alvis entered the graveyard and, turning left, made his way to the quiet rear of the cemetery. Here the usual cypress trees and grey headstones had their own frosting of snow although underfoot the path was clear.

Reaching his wife's grave, he sat down, ignoring the fact that the bench too had been exposed to the elements. Composing himself for what he wanted to say to Marita, he remained silent for a moment, wondering when or if the urge to speak to his dead wife would ever be satisfied. It was verging on three years now since she'd died in the Cairngorm Mountains of Scotland.

Since that time he'd managed to revisit the place of her death, even made a sort of peace with it. In fact he'd planned to go back there today for a week of winter walking, had it not been for the phone call he'd made yesterday to Scotland.

Calm now, the words ready, Alvis explained why he wouldn't be going where he had planned, but somewhere else entirely.

'Remember how much you loved the Isle of Mists, Marita? Although in truth during our short time there we didn't encounter mist. Rain, yes, and wind. Remember when we walked to the Coral Beach and you could hardly stand up against the wind?'

Alvis laughed, as though he were joining the tinkling laugh he had known so well.

Her silent *why* drove him on.

'I called to tell Rhona I was headed back to Scotland and would likely visit Glasgow, but she wasn't at the lab and apparently hasn't been since her last case. Chrissy said she's gone back to Skye.' He halted, remembering Chrissy's voice as she'd tried to explain why Rhona wasn't at work. Why she hadn't been at work for some time.

'So I thought, rather than Cairngorm, I might head back to Skye, walk a bit there instead, say hello to the island for you. Check on Dr MacLeod.'

For a long time after Marita's death on that mountain, he could hear her speaking to him, all the time wondering why no one else could. Now the voice had become internal, almost like a thought, but Alvis still knew what her message was.

He nodded, satisfied with her silent reply. 'Of course,' he answered in return. 'Of course, I will.'

Alvis rose from the seat and, with a swift nod to the neighbouring child's grave, acknowledged that he hadn't been able to tell Marita that during the darkness of her incarceration Rhona had suffered a miscarriage, because even now the memory of his wife enduring the same loss was still raw in his mind.

The drive from Aberdeen to Inverness passed uneventfully. The fields were white, but the road a glistening black. He was aware that the majority of the snowfall had visited the west coast of Scotland, something unusual in itself, and that the roads into the west from the capital of the Highlands might not be as clear. And according to the weather report, Skye too had had a heavy fall.

Immediately after he'd ended the conversation with Chrissy, Alvis had set about cancelling his previously booked accommodation in Aviemore and then phoned the hotel he and Marita had stayed at before in Portree, only to discover it was shut for the winter season.

Checking online for an alternative, he suddenly remembered a pub, the Isles, in the main square where he and Marita had spent a great evening, listening to live traditional music. According to the webpage it also had rooms and was open during the winter months.

A quick call there set him up with a place to stay.

According to the address Chrissy had given him, it was about an hour away from Rhona's cottage. He'd already decided to play his visit to the island as though it was nothing to do with Rhona's situation, something Chrissy had strongly advised.

'If Rhona gets wind that you're there because of what's happened, you'll be lucky if she even agrees to see you.'

'That bad?' he'd queried.

'That bad,' Chrissy had said.

Alvis had picked up food in Inverness and, checking the weather and road conditions, headed off by way of the Great Glen. Snow accompanied him en route, but more of a benign presence than a threat, falling softly and intermittently. The great expanse of water that was Loch Ness made him feel at home, although the sides were definitely not fjord-steep.

Passing the Cluanie Dam, he entered the golden pass of Glen Shiel. Alvis had experienced it all before, but his breath still caught in his throat at the sight of the white-topped river, the nearby crags carved during some prehistoric era, and the sadness of the tumbledown ruins of its past inhabitants, in many cases driven from their homes.

As the jagged pinnacles of the Five Sisters of Kintail rose before him in their snow-covered splendour, Alvis decided that one day he would return to climb the classic ridge walk that took in three Munros.

But not this week.

Loch Duich followed as the west coast opened up before him. Looping through the lovely village of Dornie, he spotted the much-photographed Eilean Donan Castle. Arriving where the bridge should be, he found it mysteriously hidden in a thick mist, causing Alvis to mouth his surprise to Marita as he ventured across the hidden arch to re-emerge on dry land again.

The journey had taken just over the statutory three hours from Inverness, and during that time he had thought carefully how he might approach any meeting he would have with Dr MacLeod. They had previously worked well together on the joint investigation between his office and Police Scotland, but that too hadn't been without trauma.

Alvis flinched at the memories it had left behind, some of whose scars still ran deep in his heart. It had begun with his discovery of the bodies of two small refugee children, frozen in the ice on Norway's northern border with Russia. Things had only got worse after that and Dr MacLeod had been his mainstay in all of it.

Now it was his turn to be hers.

5

The dog was observing Rhona with large, intelligent eyes. A big black-and-white Border collie, it looked very much the proprietor of the place, just as Jamie had suggested.

'You must be Blaze?' Rhona said.

Approaching, the dog sniffed at her proffered hand.

The collie's deep bark had greeted the jeep's arrival and had also alerted the human inhabitants of the centre, one of whom now introduced himself as Donald McKay.

Rhona ruffled the collie's ears. 'Are you his owner?'

'I suspect he believes he's mine,' Donald said with a bemused grin.

Next up was Matt, who, spotting Jamie, gave a whoop of success. 'I thought you'd bailed on bringing the stag do here?'

'No way,' Jamie said. 'Although it took a bit of negotiation on my part.' He rattled off three guys' names. 'Who,' he said, 'spent a lot of time in the pub last night discussing how exactly they planned to kill one another.'

'Nothing gets killed here, except the male ego,' Matt said, smiling at Rhona.

Jamie obligingly introduced her. 'Rhona is a Skye MacLeod, although currently residing in MacDonald country.'

'Ah,' Matt said, with a knowing look. 'You're based in Sleat?'

Rhona smiled a yes, knowing full well the turbulent history between the MacDonalds and the MacLeods of Skye. 'My parents' cottage is there, where I spent most of my summers. That's when I got to know Jamie.'

'I heard our Jamie was a bit of a lad during his teenage years?' Matt raised a questioning eyebrow.

'He most definitely was,' Rhona agreed.

'With a little help from you, Dr MacLeod,' Jamie added, before throwing Rhona an apologetic look, realizing he'd let the cat out of the bag.

'*Dr* MacLeod,' Matt said with a look of surprise. 'So, you've moved back home to look after our health?'

'I'm not that sort of doctor,' Rhona said. 'And I'm only here on holiday.'

Matt and Donald exchanged glances which Rhona couldn't interpret, although she suspected they thought her extended stay might be about Jamie. Something she made no effort to contradict.

Let them think that. It saved her an explanation.

'So, do you fancy having a go at one of the target sports while you're here?' Matt said.

'What's on offer?' Rhona said, glad to change the subject.

'How about trying your hand at axe throwing?' Matt suggested.

'I get to throw an axe at a target?'

'Not a human one, but yes.'

'Bring it on,' Rhona said, feeling her mood definitely lifting. She might not have a human target but there was one face she might like to visualize as one.

Blaze, who'd seemed to be intently absorbing their conversation, now set off towards a nearby sheltered range.

'He knows the routine?' Rhona said as they all trooped after the collie.

'Blaze effectively runs the place,' Donald told her.

Matt selected an axe from a stand and offered it to Rhona.

'It's really modelled on a tomahawk,' Matt explained. 'Lighter than what most people think of as an axe and the head isn't fixed to the body.'

Rhona liked the shape of it, the pattern on the handle and the weight of it in her hand. It didn't feel heavy and nothing like the wood-chopping axe at the cottage.

'Throwing this type of axe is not about strength,' Matt told her, 'but technique. At the right distance, and thrown in the correct manner, the axe should turn once in the air before meeting the target head-on.'

He showed Rhona how to hold the axe, then swing it back over her right shoulder.

'You're going to bring it forward and simply release it.'

Rhona rarely handled anything that might be described as a weapon, if you omitted the tools she used to do her job. But then again, anything might become a weapon in an emergency, she thought. At which point a flashback hit her with surprising force and for a moment her hand held, not the tomahawk, but a bloodied slither of glass from a broken wine bottle.

Rhona stared down at her hand, remembering . . .

'You okay with this?' Matt whispered under his breath.

Rhona dispelled the memory of the last time she'd tried to stab something. 'Tell me one more time.'

Matt guided her hand back so that the axe would begin

its flight from just behind her right shoulder. 'At this distance when released it will turn once, then embed in the target. And remember,' he reminded her, 'it's not about strength.'

Rhona took a deep breath and relaxed, then followed his instructions exactly.

It was over in a second, followed by the whooping of all three men as her axe embedded itself firmly in the top of the target.

'Very few get it first time,' Matt said, fetching the tomahawk. 'D'you want another go?'

'I think I'll quit while I'm ahead,' Rhona said, slightly overcome by her success.

Matt handed her an ace of spades card. 'For an ace axe thrower.'

As Rhona stepped back to allow Jamie his turn, Blaze began barking at her and running back and forth towards the woods.

'He wants you to go with him,' Donald said. 'Show you around.'

Rhona looked to Jamie.

'I could be here a while,' he said as his first attempt bounced off the wooden backdrop and fell to the ground. 'Maybe better if the ace player doesn't watch. And Blaze seems pretty insistent.'

'Okay,' Rhona told the collie. 'Take me for a walk and spare Jamie his embarrassment.'

According to Matt, the twelve-acre site where the airsoft games were played was thickly covered in birch trees, rising to open ground higher up. At first the dog followed a clear path through the lichen-covered trunks, where, on either side, the interwoven bare branches appeared impenetrable. At ground level it was obvious by the thick russet tangle that in spring and summer bracken would grow to waist height.

Overhead, the light was already beginning to fail as the midwinter solstice approached. Any snow that had fallen here had since melted, although through the spidery branches Rhona could still see the white-topped mountains.

All was silent apart from the panting of the dog as it ran a little ahead, turning frequently to check on Rhona's progress. She passed two small clearings set up with wooden barriers for the pursued to hide from their attackers during airsoft games. At the top of the hill the trees parted to reveal a grassy clearing in the middle of which stood a wooden fort, where the defenders made their last stand.

At this, the highest position among the trees, the defenders might survive a concentrated attack from below, in much the same way that Scots had defended hilltops over the centuries. Rhona halted here to climb on the palisade and stare down into the skeleton trees, until Blaze barked at her to indicate she hadn't yet reached her required destination.

With the path petering out, the dog now made off into the trees to the right of the fort, its bushy tail swaying.

Trying to follow, Rhona was immediately met by a web of interlocking branches which necessitated ducking and weaving, even as she stumbled over rocks buried under mounds of dying bracken.

If you're chasing a rabbit or a deer, Blaze . . .

As Rhona paused for breath, she spotted Blaze a little distance ahead, standing to attention, the shaggy coat glistening with moisture from the undergrowth. The dog was looking towards her, obviously waiting for her to come and join him. Whatever Blaze wanted her to see, it seemed they had reached it.

Rhona began to force her way upwards through the undergrowth.

They had reached a small break in the tree cover. Rhona registered the sound of a burn running somewhere close by. A bird rose with a hoarse call that startled her, raising her heartbeat.

As she drew alongside the dog, it turned to lick her hand, whining a little.

'What is it, boy? What's wrong?'

Everything, the answering whine told her. *Everything about this place is wrong.*

'Show me, Blaze. Show me what you've found.'

A worried Jamie met Rhona at the gate. 'We thought you'd got lost!'

'No, although Blaze did take me a fair distance into the woods.'

'Is something wrong?' Jamie asked, taking note of her perturbed expression.

Rhona didn't know what to tell him, because she wasn't sure herself if anything was wrong.

'I need to speak to Matt and Donald.'

'They're in the office.'

'What's up?' Matt looked up from his laptop when Rhona appeared in the doorway.

Rhona got straight to the point. 'Did someone get hurt recently in the woods?'

'You mean during an airsoft battle?' Matt said, with a

worried expression. He looked to Donald, who shook his head, as puzzled it seemed by her question as Matt was. 'We're dead quiet at the moment. Just one group yesterday. Soldiers on leave. They really went to town, but they all left unhurt. Why?'

'Blaze took me directly to a spot in the woods he was obviously interested in, just like a police dog would.'

'He catches game. Might he have killed something up there? He's dragged me to a couple of places he's made a kill and buried it for later,' Donald offered. 'Oh, come to think of it, he did ask to be let out late last night.'

'That could be it,' Rhona said, to ease their concern. 'But I'd like to come back with my forensic bag. Take a proper look.' She'd said this almost to herself, then realized that Matt and Donald were looking at her, slack-jawed.

'Forensic bag?' Matt repeated, stunned.

Jamie came in then, speaking directly to Rhona. 'Do you want to talk to Sergeant MacDonald? We could call in at the station on our way back.'

Rhona wasn't sure she did. 'I'll take another look first. Check if it's human blood.'

'There was blood?' Matt repeated, horrified.

Rhona ignored his panicked expression. 'I'd like to protect the area until tomorrow morning,' she told him. 'D'you have a tarpaulin I could use?'

Jamie was silent when they eventually exited the site after stretching and securing the tarpaulin, although Rhona knew he really wanted to question her further. The problem was she had nothing to tell him, nothing concrete anyway. Just an informed feeling about the scene.

'You really think something bad happened there?'

Rhona tried to make light of it. 'I think I'm maybe missing my work.'

Jamie's face broke into a relieved grin. 'And that's good, isn't it?' When she nodded, he said, 'You didn't half scare the shit out of Matt, though.'

Rhona changed the subject. 'Did you organize the stag do?'

'I did.' Jamie seemed pleased to talk about something else. Then a worrying thought occurred. 'Will your investigation be over by next weekend?'

'It will,' Rhona assured him.

As they drew into the square at Portree, Jamie asked if she wanted to eat with him at the Isles before heading home.

'I have to get back,' Rhona said. 'I'm expecting a Skype call.'

'Chrissy?'

'DS McNab.'

Rhona had felt it necessary to give Jamie some explanation for her extended time on the island, although he'd never questioned her himself. And he was no fool, nor was he off-grid. Therefore he had to be aware of the sin-eater case and at least the fact that she'd been involved in it.

Rhona tried to make light of things. 'McNab asks how I'm doing. I tell him fine, which is true. Although I suspect if I don't agree to such calls, he may well get on his motorbike and head back here.'

'He's that protective of you?' Jamie said.

'He'd be the same with Chrissy,' Rhona told him. 'Her wee boy's called Michael after McNab,' she said to illustrate. 'And not because he's the father.'

Jamie drew into the square and turned off the ignition. 'Are you sure you don't want to run your suspicions about the site past Lee MacDonald?'

'I'd rather wait and see if there's anything to tell him first,' Rhona said.

'D'you want me to come back with you tomorrow?' Jamie looked so worried for her when he said that, Rhona almost laughed.

'I specialize in hidden and buried bodies, remember?'

'At least we have the burying bit in common.' He gave her a half-smile. 'You'll let me know?'

'Of course,' Rhona promised.

The sky was a brooding grey mass as she crossed into Sleat. The pleasure she normally took in the long stretch of road was missing tonight, replaced by the recurring image of that small clearing in the woods.

In most cases you knew you were entering a crime scene, but not always. Like the time she'd been called to the Shelter Stone cave on Cairngorm to view the bodies of three dead climbers. Death had many guises on the mountain, the majority being the result of the weather and the terrain. Not in that particular case, though.

Studying a body and the context in which it was found eventually told death's true story.

There had been no body in the woods, but there had been enough to suggest there had been, if she respected her instincts . . . and those of the dog.

She'd seen enough police dogs in action to know their response to the discovery of human blood. According to Donald, Blaze had been trained like a rescue dog and the collie had all the instincts of one.

Someone had lain injured there. That was all she knew . . . until tomorrow.

As she turned down the track that led to the cottage, Rhona realized that she had a visitor, although who might have arrived here in a black SUV, she had no idea. A horrible thought that it might actually be McNab entered her head momentarily, but the vehicle was an unlikely match for the detective sergeant.

So if it wasn't McNab, who was it?

6

'Rhona,' Alvis said in obvious surprise as he appeared round the side of the cottage. 'What are you doing here?'

'I could say the same thing to you,' Rhona said, suspicion already forming in her mind as to why Inspector Alvis Olsen of Stavanger Police should be standing on her doorstep.

'I'm on a climbing holiday. Arrived yesterday afternoon and decided to start easy with a walk today to the Point of Sleat. I remembered you talking about the cottage, so I thought I'd check out if you were right,' he said brightly.

'Right about what?'

'You told me it had the best view on Skye, remember?'

Rhona did remember. Her suspicions abating a little, she said, 'Was I right?'

'Most definitely.'

They stood for a moment in awkward silence. *What to say next?* Rhona knew it would seem odd if she didn't ask Alvis in, but she wasn't certain how long she could keep up a pretence of normality. And he was sure to ask why she was here.

The suspicion re-formed. *Or maybe he knew already?* She could of course say she was on holiday, like him, but then he might suggest they do some walking together.

In the absence of a decision, Rhona retrieved the

key from below the stone and proceeded to open the door.

'I thought you said no one locked their doors on Skye?' Alvis jokingly reminded her.

'Times have changed,' was all Rhona could muster in response.

The cottage was warm, the fire still lit. Rhona busied herself stoking it and putting on more peat.

'How long are you here for?' she said as she moved to set up the coffee machine.

'A week,' Alvis told her.

Squashed together in the small kitchen, Alvis seemed taller and broader than Rhona remembered. But his voice was the same. The clear concise English, with a touch of humour. Standing so close, she also recalled his scent, and with it came a rush of memories from the night they had spent together in the Aberdeen hotel room, where they had tried to forget, however briefly, the terrible world their case had led them into.

'How have you been?' Rhona found herself saying the words she didn't want to hear from him.

'Okay.' He sounded slightly unsure.

'Last time I saw you was—' Rhona began.

'At Loch A'an,' he finished for her.

They shared an unspoken memory that brought a fleeting look of sorrow to his eyes as Rhona recalled watching Alvis walk off into the hills to finally revisit the place he'd lost his beloved wife, Marita.

'How's Detective Sergeant McNab?' Alvis said swiftly, perhaps to change the subject.

At McNab's name, Rhona remembered. Checking her watch, she said, 'He's about to Skype me.' She glanced at her laptop sitting open on the small dining table.

'If you want to talk privately I can go outside and admire the view again,' Alvis immediately offered.

'No. He'll be pleased to see you,' Rhona said, realizing that spotting Alvis's presence would alter what McNab planned to say, which would have undoubtedly referred to her appointment that morning.

Rhona carried both mugs to the table and, pulling up a chair alongside, suggested Alvis join her. Not usually known for his timekeeping, McNab had been more than punctual on his arranged calls up to now. He had been adamant about this regular method of keeping in touch before he'd agreed to leave her here, 'alone in the Highlands'. Rhona had accepted his conditions, all the while assuming that eventually pressure of work at home in Glasgow would let her off the hook.

The sound of the sing-song Skype ringtone indicated that it hadn't.

And there he was, a little rough and ready, the reddish stubble just a bit too long, the eyes in need of sleep. McNab's face broke into that characteristic smile as he spotted her. 'Dr MacLeod. It's yourself – or should I say *Tha thu fhèin*?'

Rhona ignored his attempt at Gaelic and swivelled her laptop so that he might see Alvis. 'And look who's with me.'

McNab's face now presented a picture, and not a pretty one, before he swiftly assumed a less gobsmacked look.

'Inspector Olsen. What are you doing there?'

'Good to see you, McNab. I'm on holiday, just like Rhona. How's Chrissy and DI Wilson?'

'Okay,' McNab finally managed, his expression betraying the thought processes going on behind it.

'Please give them my regards.'

Rhona's initial suspicions regarding Alvis came into full bloom at this interchange.

Alvis knows. He must have called the lab for some reason and Chrissy told him I was here and probably why. But she didn't tell McNab about that call.

Rhona broke into the conversation and said in a bright voice, 'Tell Chrissy my holiday's about to be over.'

'You're coming back?' McNab said in delighted surprise.

'Not exactly.' Rhona described the possible crime scene, embellishing it a little for effect. 'I plan to take a closer look in the morning.'

'You're having us on?' McNab said in disbelief.

'Can I come with you?' Alvis said with obvious enthusiasm, which didn't please McNab, by the look on his face.

'You're on holiday. Remember?' Rhona reminded him.

The conversation ground to a halt after that. She knew McNab was itching to find out if she had gone to her appointment with Dr Bailey that morning, but there was no way he could bring himself to ask her in front of Alvis. Eventually, Rhona brought the stilted interchange to an end, but not before McNab got the next date set up.

'I'll see you then,' McNab said, meaning *I'll question you then*.

'Over and out,' Rhona said and switched off the video link on his determined expression.

After Alvis had departed, Rhona walked down to the shore. She and Alvis had talked a little after the Skype conversation with McNab, but not of the true reason why either of them were here on Skye.

He'd spoken of where he might walk tomorrow. That he

was staying at the Isles on the square in Portree. That he planned to call in at Portree police station, and make his presence on the island known. Before she'd had a chance to ask why, he'd said, 'Sergeant Lee MacDonald's a member of Skye and Lochaber Mountain Rescue Team. I met him in Aviemore when Marita . . .' He'd tailed off at that, knowing Rhona didn't require any further explanation.

Rhona looked across the wide and now smooth expanse of the Sound of Sleat towards the snow-capped mainland. This part of Scotland appeared vast and empty, yet the myriad connections between the people who lived here were as intricately spun as a spider's web and stretched even as far as Norway.

Alvis's cover had been good, Rhona had to grant him that. He may well have come walking here as an alternative to Cairngorm. But it hadn't been coincidence that he'd visited the cottage. Chrissy had undoubtedly had a hand in that.

Rhona thought of the worried face of her forensic assistant. After McNab, Chrissy knew her best. Even thinking that made Rhona feel a little guilty, because that put Sean at number three in the list, maybe even four if she brought DI Bill Wilson into the frame.

Bill had been her mentor since she'd started on the job. He'd been there that terrible night in the dingy little room that had smelt of sex and death, when she'd examined the teenage victim of a sexual predator and thought that it might, just might, be the son she'd given up for adoption seventeen years previously.

And yet . . .

It had been Sean who'd encouraged her to find her son. Sean who'd persuaded her that Liam would like her. Sean who'd made the mother-and-son meeting possible, even a success.

In the quirky nature of things, here on the shore behind the cottage was where she got the best signal. She'd spoken with Chrissy, with Bill and with McNab since she'd come here. What she hadn't done was speak to Sean.

Rhona brought up his number. There was something she hadn't told Sean. Something he of all people ought to know.

Whether she felt free of her prison and could say the words, Rhona didn't know.

7

Afghanistan, six months earlier

They call the robes the women are forced to wear the Blue Prison, with its little barred window to look out on the world. I am wearing one now. Beneath it, I am naked. Sweat runs in rivulets down my body, the biggest and most free-flowing between my breasts. My hair is clamped to my head, the sweat there mixed with sand and blood under the blue hood.

The view I have of the world is through a cobweb. Almost blind, I have grown to rely on my other senses. Smell has been the strongest. I know each of my guards by their scent.

I don't think of smell in the same way any more. I think of it in a hundred ways. I know when they're fearful, angry, depressed, sexually aroused. The last one is the scent I fear most.

Night has fallen with a depth of darkness that is difficult to describe. Strangely now, in the coldness of the night, I wish for the sweat to flow free again, trickling moisture on my lips. But the sweat has solidified in the cold, sticking to my body like a second layer.

The door suddenly clangs open and, through shouts, they propel *him* into the room.

I can smell his blood and realize they must have re-opened old wounds, or made new ones. A light outside frames the faces now pressed against the barred opening on the door.

His head is covered with a sack, but I know who it is, because I recognize his smell. The fear, the blood and the lust.

This one will do in the dark what is ordered. Not to save his life or mine, but because he wants to.

8

It was dark when Alvis drew up outside the police station. He had planned, as he'd told Rhona, to meet with Sergeant MacDonald in the morning, until Rhona had bizarrely revealed her decision to forensically search a possible crime scene in the woods behind a place called A.C.E Target Sports.

He'd been as taken aback as McNab by that, and probably for similar reasons. He'd hoped to spend longer with Rhona after the Skype call had ended, maybe learn a bit more about this strange turn of affairs, but she'd made it pretty clear that she wanted him gone and she'd avoided arranging to meet him again during his week's visit.

Despite his conversation with Chrissy about the sin-eater case, Alvis definitely hadn't been prepared for the Rhona he'd found here.

She looked thinner. And fragile – a word he could never have imagined using to describe Rhona MacLeod.

Alvis parked up and headed inside to discover he wasn't the only visitor at this hour. What appeared to be a noisy family gathering was giving the PC on reception a hard time. By the raised voices, he made out that an elderly and confused relative had taken a car and could have gone off the road anywhere between Portree and Osmigarry. They were being very precise about Osmigarry.

At that point Sergeant MacDonald appeared and urged Alvis inside the station proper. Once in the relative quiet of the inner sanctum, they shook hands.

'If you're busy . . .' Alvis motioned towards reception.

'There's a patrol car out looking for Jake Ross. He's eighty and he's done this before. He'll likely head for Osmigarry.' Lee repeated the destination mentioned outside.

When Alvis made a questioning face, he said, 'That's where the Flora MacDonald statue is,' as though that supplied the answer. 'So,' Lee went on, 'how are things in Stavanger?'

'Cold and snowy, like here,' Alvis obliged.

'And you've come to climb?'

Alvis nodded. 'I had been planning Cairngorm but . . .'

'You heard what happened and wanted to check in on Dr MacLeod?'

Alvis regarded the kind face of one of the men who had searched so long and so hard for Marita in the snowy wastes of Cairngorm.

'Yes, but I don't want her to know that.'

'Probably best. DS McNab also asked us to keep an eye on her.'

'He's that thorough?' Alvis wondered why he'd ever thought otherwise.

'You bet.' Lee paused. 'Rhona's been in a few times. More to placate McNab than anything else. She seemed okay . . .'

'If you don't know her well,' Alvis said with conviction.

Lee nodded. 'I wondered. But it takes time. You and I know that.'

'I also know that cutting yourself off from colleagues and friends doesn't help. And neither does running away.'

They both fell silent at that.

'So, what can I do, if anything?' Lee said.

'I wondered if anyone other than Jake has been reported missing?'

Lee looked puzzled by Alvis's question. 'No. Well, not in the last few days, but it does happen fairly regularly. Climbers, of course, but more often vulnerable folk like Jake. Why are you asking?'

Alvis explained about Rhona and her supposed find in the woods.

'At Matt's place?' Lee said in surprise. 'We've never had a problem at A.C.E Target Sports, even with stag events. Matt's a good guy. I visit often to check on safety. If someone got hurt there, he would have reported it.'

'The dog Blaze apparently took Rhona to a spot in the woods, and she detected signs of a scuffle and blood which she thinks may be human.' Alvis explained what Rhona planned to do. 'She didn't intend to call you unless she was certain.'

'We get plenty of punch-ups on Skye. Mainly domestics and drink-fuelled fights, but they don't normally take it into the woods and we usually hear about it. News travels fast here.'

'Might it be drugs-related? Over a stash maybe?'

'We've taken a couple of big hauls of cannabis and cocaine recently. But no indication of internecine wars over it. Most visitors bring it with them, if they're so inclined.'

'Where does the general supply come from?' Alvis said.

'The nearest distribution centre, Glasgow, although Inverness is fast catching up, and we have the coastline. Fishing boats and yachts coming and going.'

'We have the same problem in Stavanger,' Alvis nodded.

'Well, Dr MacLeod doesn't strike me as someone who would be easily mistaken,' Lee said thoughtfully. 'I'll make some enquiries. Check the hospitals here, Fort William and Inverness, and let you know.'

9

When Rhona stopped at the edge of the clearing to don her kit, indicating that Blaze should come no further, the collie did not demur, but sat down to observe whatever it was this white-suited woman was planning to do.

On first inspection the evening before, she'd looked for any indication of something being buried nearby. Although back then the dog hadn't made a point of digging anywhere, and Rhona had picked up no scent of decomposition.

Walking the area again, Rhona could find no evidence of disturbed earth and no discoloured vegetation. A buried body would have produced a sinking in ground level as it decomposed. Plus, she suspected, Blaze would have led her straight to such a point of interest.

She now approached the tree that had caused her disquiet the previous night. The contact environment round the mature birch consisted of exposed soil. And it was this area that had so excited Blaze. Blood could leave behind a change in the microbial community and in the volatile organic compounds which emanated from the soil. Police recovery dogs hit on blood in soil and got excited. Just as Blaze had done.

Then there was the compressed vegetation . . .

Rhona adjusted her camera, taking multiple shots of the

contact area, more convinced than ever that a body had lain here, a body that had definitely been bleeding.

Now she turned her attention to the tree.

She'd detected blood at around five feet from the ground on her last visit. Now a phenolphthalein test confirmed her suspicions, suggesting someone's head had hit off the bark. She used a magnifying glass to take a closer look.

The maturity of the birch tree had caused strips of silver bark to peel back. She could see the tree's insect inhabitants scurrying out of sight of her prying eyes, except at one particular spot.

An area they obviously had no desire to leave.

At first she assumed it was blood, rich in nutrients and a veritable feast, but closer inspection suggested something more. Rhona used tweezers to extract the material.

A hair, blood-soaked but probably blond in colour, was attached to what definitely looked like scalp tissue.

So someone's head had hit the tree trunk with enough force to cause a scalp wound or maybe even a skull fracture?

Even minor cuts on the head often bled heavily because the face and scalp had many blood vessels close to the surface of the skin. Judging by the blood on surrounding soil, this one had too. From the compressed vegetation, it appeared that the injured person had been sufficiently traumatized to end up on the ground.

So maybe more than a scalp abrasion?

The average thickness of a man's skull was 6.5 millimetres. Women's skulls were thicker at an average of 7.1, although in back-to-front measurement and width, male skulls won the size game. She couldn't tell here if the material in her hand belonged to a male or a female, but she could say it had come from a human.

Having drawn the tarpaulin back into place, Rhona gathered her samples. Realizing she was finished with whatever she'd been doing, Blaze sprang up to lead her back to the camp. But Rhona wasn't ready to go there yet.

Whoever had been injured here had either walked out, aided or unaided, or else they'd been carried. Either way they had to have left tracks. Tracks she might be able to follow. But if not her, then certainly the dog that had brought her here in the first place.

10

McNab stared at the big bloke across the table from him. Beside him, DS Clark maintained a calm expression, although he knew her well enough to know her blood was at boiling point.

'Fucking pair of tits ordering me about.'

It wasn't clear if the punk's utterance referred to the female detective before him or the girl whose nose he'd 'allegedly' broken.

'Tell us again what happened,' McNab said.

'Just like she told you. She fell.'

'She fell just like that?'

'Tripped over the fucking dog. Silly bitch. Banged into the door.'

McNab had often wondered what it was that doors and door frames had against the female population of Glasgow. They seemed to take a perverse delight in banging into them, with no provocation whatsoever.

'Jess tells a different story.'

The smug look shifted a little, then resettled, fear quickly dispensed with.

'Jess would never—'

'Never say never,' McNab offered with a knowing smile.

Some words were said under the radar, the punk's lips

barely moving. He went back to focusing on Janice, or on her breasts to be exact.

McNab thought of the young woman next door, and whether she would find the courage to do what he had just said. If not . . .

Outside the interview room now, McNab made for the coffee machine for his caffeine fix, a silent Janice alongside.

'We won't get him on the domestic,' she offered as he put in the money and selected a double espresso. 'She tells the same story,' she reminded him, 'regarding the door.'

'Fucking doors.' McNab banged at the coffee machine to hurry it up. 'Misogynist bastards all of them.'

Janice gave a laugh and its sound reminded McNab of why he'd once nursed the notion of a pairing with DS Clark.

'You've become quite the feminist,' she offered. 'Is this Ellie's doing?'

'I've always liked women,' McNab countered.

'Mmmm,' Janice said in a not altogether believing tone.

McNab experienced something he realized might be hurt feelings.

'I'm surrounded by capable women. What's not to like about that?'

'At least you don't stare at my breasts,' Janice offered.

McNab was tempted to say, 'That's what you think,' but wisely didn't.

Janice changed the subject. 'Any word about Dr MacLeod returning to the fray?'

'Nope.' McNab grabbed his espresso.

'Will she be able to go back to her flat after what happened?'

McNab hated hearing Janice voice the question he'd been asking himself for some time.

'There are other flats in Glasgow,' he heard himself say.

'Have you spoken to her recently?'

'Is this a fucking interrogation, DS Clark? Would you like me to accompany you to the interview room?'

His tone had both offended and worried her. McNab almost said sorry, but knew that wouldn't wash. Better to be honest. After all, that's how Janice dealt with him.

'She's working an investigation on Skye.'

Janice's eyes opened wide. 'Officially?'

How could he say he thought it imaginary? That every time he looked at Rhona's face on Skype he grew more concerned for her well-being. As for her latest revelation about a crime scene in the woods. *Fuck's sake*.

Everyone knew DI Wilson had been pressuring Rhona to see a counsellor. Everyone knew she'd refused to go to Castlebrae. They were all acquainted with staff who'd been traumatized on the front line. As the Chief Constable said, the officers at the top weren't the heroes of the force. The heroes were the guys who turned up never knowing what an incident might hold for their own safety.

McNab had met with DI Wilson first thing, keen to offload his concerns about what was happening on Skye. The boss had matched McNab's disquiet. Apparently during the fifteen-minute consultation with Dr Bailey, Rhona had made it clear she was there on sufferance.

'They scheduled another appointment for next week, but Dr Bailey doesn't think Dr MacLeod is likely to turn up,' had been the boss's worried response.

'You could go and see her?' Janice offered, after McNab had related the story.

McNab shook his head. 'She doesn't like seeing my mug on Skype. Turning up at her door wouldn't go down well.'

'Get Chrissy to go then,' Janice suggested. 'Rhona won't turn her away.'

She'd waited until McNab, the caffeine addict, had got what he needed; now she pressed for hers.

'So, it doesn't look like we're going to get McNulty on his latest domestic,' she said.

'It was a way to get him in here.'

'But not what we really want him for,' Janice said, reminding McNab what this morning's performance was really about. 'You ready?'

Checking his watch, McNab nodded. 'Okay, let's go.'

The room was packed. All were observing the board, the title of which was:

From Kabul to Glasgow

McNulty, a small cog in a big wheel, was up there along with his more important associates. In the centre was a circle with the title *Sandman*. Surrounding the unidentified head of the operation were three names or pseudo names. Glaswegians had a penchant for entertaining nomenclature. *Wee Malky*, one Malcolm Stevenson, *Sparky*, suspected title for Norman Watts, and last but never least, Stephen *Bawbags* McClusky. None of whom had yet been brought to court for drug trafficking.

DI Wilson was doing the intro. McNab only half listened, because he knew the story already. Glasgow had the highest percentage of heroin deaths in Europe. The path to

Glasgow from Afghanistan was well trodden. Afghanistan produced over 94 per cent of heroin on the open market and production was at its highest for a decade. Afghanistan was the forgotten war, but only to uninformed Western populations. The USA had a minimum of 17,000 troops still there. The UK was about to up its contingent above the 9,000 mark.

The heroin now produced was 46 per cent purer than what many of Glasgow's addicts had started out on, laced as it was back then with paracetamol. Hence one of the reasons for the current rise in deaths.

'We can't stop it being trafficked from Helmand province. We can try and stop it reaching Scotland's streets, and locating the Sandman, as he's known, is our key to this.'

McNab thought back to McNulty with his pasty face and tattooed knuckles. They had nothing on him apart from the fact he wasn't a proponent of marital bliss.

He was suddenly aware that the boss was looking straight at him.

'Well, Detective Sergeant?'

McNab made a guess at the unheard question. 'McNulty's still with us, sir, plus his partner, Jess.'

'And?'

'Things are progressing, sir.' McNab's lie brought a small expulsion of air from Janice.

'Any mention of the Sandman?'

'I've yet to bring that into the conversation, sir. Didn't want to spook him.'

McNab was pretty sure he heard a 'Fuck's sake' from Janice, and he hissed back, 'So, you answer next time.'

Thankfully the heat had moved on and someone else

was now in the firing line. McNab breathed a sigh of relief.

'I suggest we talk to Jolly Jess again,' he said. 'You take the lead this time. Woman to woman. Maybe she's heard of the Sandman.'

11

The Isles bar, Portree, the previous night

The pub was busy, with a group of young local musicians playing fiddles and uilleann pipes being the draw. For a while she imagined it would be okay. The games had all gone well earlier. She'd excelled at the knife and axe throwing, mostly because she'd carefully followed the instructor's advice. The dog, too, had helped her feel at ease. She smiled at the memory of the big Border collie and its herding of her towards the target range. In the bar tonight, it had already come over to say hello to her and Sugarboy.

They had been their usual bullish and combative selves at A.C.E, laughing and mocking each other's attempts at axe and knife throwing, but all the while gracious about her success.

They were, she realized, treating her with kid gloves.

She was trying not to study them openly, but joined in with the alcohol-induced camaraderie, all the while imagining what might be going on in their heads.

In his *head.*

They'd all had to undergo counselling after the event. *The event.* What a fucking way to describe it. The others had never openly discussed their supposed rehabilitation. At least not with her. She wondered, now, if they'd discussed it with each other.

If they'd talked about her.

Is that why we're here, she thought? To check her out? Find out how much she'd revealed of what had happened?

She lifted her drink, more to stop herself catching anyone's eye.

And she didn't know the whole story, she reminded herself. Isolated as she'd been in her blue prison, she had no idea how bad it had been for the others after they'd been captured. One thing she did know. There had been seven alive before the attack. *The magnificent seven.* And now there were only five.

In her mind she made the group whole again, adding in Mitch with his crooked smile and deftly moving hands. The Stitcher, they'd called him, because of the speed he dealt with wounds. And big Gordo, who'd professed to having only one testicle, having lost the other one, or so he claimed, to a sniper's bullet.

More likely gnawed off by a dissatisfied fuck, according to Mitch.

Strained by trying not to study them, she closed her eyes, listening as they talked and laughed over their pints, easily pinpointing each of their voices. In that moment she felt a wash of something resembling love, in a way that can only happen when you've faced death together.

The sound was innocuous at first. Tucked in the corner seat between the window and the wood stove, she registered it only subconsciously. Then Sugarboy jumped up and shouted in a raucous voice.

'Fucking chopper, boys. Get ready. It's the fucking chopper.'

And . . . she was back in the hospital tent with the cloying smell of disinfectant and blood, the relentless beat of an approaching helicopter sending them, like the swirling sand, into a paroxysm of activity and excitement, mixed with the accompanying guilt at their pleasure at that sound.

They had a job to do, but in order to do it, someone had to have been hurt. Shootings, maimings, explosions, roadside devices that shattered bodies. They treated everyone that came their way. The children had affected her most. Blinded, wounded, terrified. Nothing, she knew, had prepared her for the real casualties of war.

All four of them were standing, cheering on the chopper as it flew over the pub, bound no doubt for the hills and some missing climber.

She stayed seated, conscious of all the eyes upon them, especially those of the tall blond man at the bar. Seeing she hadn't risen, *he'd* been the one to grab her arm and drag her to her feet. She smelt him then, the beer, the sweat, the heat, his agitation.

As the sound diminished, so too did the mood of excitement.

'Fuck that,' Sugarboy said, heading for the bar.

Minutes later he was back with a bottle and five shot glasses.

'A few of these. And some snow.' He tapped his trouser pocket. 'Straight, I should say, from Sand Land. Then we rumble for real,' he said, throwing her a secret smile.

12

Emerging from the trees, Rhona noted a single-track road below her, which according to the map should be the route that ran past A.C.E Target Sports, albeit a mile at least further west. So, whoever had been in the woods must have left their vehicle somewhere around here. On her nearside was a deep ditch, designed to take the run-off from the hill she'd just descended. On the other side was flat ground.

Crossing the single-track road, she looked both ways. Before she could decide which direction to check first, the dog did it for her, leading her back towards the sports site. Rhona wondered briefly if Blaze was just heading for home, but no, he was definitely following a scent, the source of which she eventually saw for herself.

It would have been difficult for her to spot blood on the muddy grass, but not on a patch of snow.

Hunkering down beside the tell-tale red, she did her best to take a sample, then straightening up, she studied the churned ground immediately ahead.

So, whoever was injured had been heading here.

It wasn't clear by the tread marks from which direction the vehicle had come, nor which direction it had headed when it left. Portree was minutes away, but had it gone the other way, it would eventually have reached Bracadale, where it could have headed north towards Dunvegan, or south to Broadford.

The dog, having led her there, was now looking quizzically at her. If Rhona could have interpreted what Blaze was saying, it would have been, 'So what now, partner?'

'We head for home,' Rhona told him. 'Or your home at least.'

Rhona looked back to the hillside track that had led her here. She'd done her best to mark it on the map as she'd walked, all the while taking photos and soil samples. Not for the first time did she wish she had a soil scientist with her, like her friend and colleague Dr Jen Mackie, who'd been instrumental in the sin-eater case.

Checking her phone, she realized firstly that she had no signal, and secondly that she'd been absent long enough for concern. The likelihood was that either Donald or Matt would already be out looking for her.

Rhona set off at a brisk pace, accompanied by her new forensic assistant. She smiled, thinking of Chrissy's expression when Rhona told her she'd been replaced by a Border collie.

The rain came on minutes later, light at first then falling in sheets. The midwinter light had turned everything grey, and the surrounding hills were wrapped in mist. Rhona imagined the downpour washing away all remnants of the possible crime scene not protected by the tarpaulin.

To the north, intermittent headlamps signalled cars on the A87, the road Donald had described as leading to the Fairy Glen. In this light, in this place, Rhona could almost believe in fairies.

Head down against the onslaught, she didn't register the approaching vehicle until Blaze gave a warning bark.

Drawing up alongside her, Donald rolled down the window.

'Come on, hop in,' he said.

Blaze waited patiently as Donald saw Rhona inside, before having the back door opened for him.

'Thanks for coming to look for me,' Rhona said as Donald sought a place to turn the big 4x4.

'I suspected if you hadn't come back via the woods that Blaze would have taken you to the road. Did you find what you were looking for?' He eyed her obviously laden back-pack.

'I did,' Rhona said.

'I could take you straight to Sergeant MacDonald?' Donald offered. 'The sergeant and Blaze go way back,' he smiled. 'In fact Blaze has been behind bars for toast steal-ing. Isn't that right, Blaze? And we have photos to prove it.' He tossed a tennis ball into the back, which the collie deftly caught.

Rhona knew Donald was trying to lighten the tension, which didn't make it any easier to turn him down.

'Thanks. But I'd rather pick up the jeep first and head down there myself.'

'Fair enough.' Donald nodded, having suspected, Rhona thought, that that would be her answer.

The site eventually appeared in the headlights. As soon as Donald eased the vehicle into the car park, Matt appeared at the door of the container and waved at them to come inside.

'Can you explain to Matt?' Rhona said to Donald, head-ing instead to the jeep. 'I should get this stuff to the police station.'

Rhona felt bad about abandoning Matt and Donald

without further explanation, but the same would have happened at the discovery of any potential crime scene. Her responsibility was to report her findings to the police and let them decide how it should be handled.

13

Portree was huddled under a laden sky. As she approached, a shaft of lightning split the dense rain clouds, followed swiftly by a thunderclap. Around her, house lights went off, suggesting the power surge had flipped a few trip switches.

The rain turned to hailstones cracking against the bonnet and roof of the jeep as she drew into Somerled Square. The Isles Inn too had had a power outage, although the image of flickering lights suggested candles were being lit.

As she parked, she noted the presence of Alvis's vehicle, covered now in ice pellets. Wherever he'd walked today, she was relieved to see he was safely back. Emerging from the vehicle, Rhona made a dash for the police station even as its own lights flashed back on.

Entering the station, it was obvious by the moans around laptops that in the few seconds between the power going off and the backup generator kicking in, a few folk had lost whatever they'd been typing.

The desk duty officer tried to speak to her but was suddenly drowned out by a bellow of thunder directly overhead.

'Sergeant MacDonald in?' Rhona shouted back.

He nodded and waved her through.

Lee looked up from his laptop as she entered. 'Rhona, you're brave venturing out in this.' He glanced at the full backpack. 'Ah,' he said.

'Alvis told you what I was planning?' Rhona said.

'He came by last night.'

From Alvis's expression as he'd left, Rhona had suspected that was exactly what he would do. She didn't blame him for that. Had their positions been reversed, she might well have done the same.

'I bet McNab called?' she said.

When Lee gave an apologetic nod, Rhona laughed.

'And I thought I could get away from it all if I came to Skye.'

'You should have known better,' Lee offered.

'Well,' Rhona said. 'Someone was definitely injured.'

She brought out the evidence bag with the sterile container. 'In here is scalp residue which I retrieved from a tree trunk. It needs to be kept cool and sent as quickly as possible to my forensic assistant. She'll organize a DNA profile. The soil samples too. I'll email Chrissy and tell her they're on their way.'

'I checked Portree and Broadford hospitals, then Inverness,' Lee said. 'No emergency admissions from Skye, except for a climber with a broken leg picked up last night.'

'What about Glasgow or Edinburgh?' Rhona offered. 'It's further than Inverness, but if it was a holidaymaker, perhaps they headed home.'

'I'll contact them too. What do you want to do about the site?'

'I sectioned it off with tape and the tarpaulin's back in place. I've taken photos and soil samples from the exit route path. I also located and photographed tyre tracks where we met the B885 and some blood traces.' Rhona showed Lee where on the map. 'The ground's churned up, I couldn't be sure of the direction taken when they left.'

She glanced at the window, still rattling under an onslaught of hailstones. 'Any evidence not covered by the tarpaulin will likely be washed away by tomorrow.'

'Any idea if a weapon was used?'

'The head hit the tree with substantial force, that's all I can say at the moment. And there was no sign of a weapon in the immediate vicinity. A proper search would be needed for that.'

'Are we looking for a body?' Lee said, his face serious.

'I wouldn't rule it out.'

14

As she crossed the car park, Rhona realized her mood had lifted.

If it felt that good to work a possible crime scene again, did that mean she was ready to return home to Glasgow?

Her mind immediately revisited her flat, walking her through it, replaying terrifying images she'd thought she'd managed to subdue. Yet here they were again, in all their original intensity.

Even the sight and sound of the gushing water in the nearby gutter recalled the stream she'd encountered during the sin-eater case. A stream, she tried to remind herself, that had helped save her life.

She halted by the jeep, registering the light from the windows of the Isles bar. It looked and sounded as though they were back in business. She thought of going inside, having something to eat, maybe talking to Alvis. Running it over in her mind, it didn't seem too bad a proposition. Alvis and she had been through a lot together. He deserved more than her evasive brush-off of yesterday.

Decided now, Rhona walked quickly across to the entrance.

On opening the door, music and warmth quickly enveloped her. Rhona had been here before with Jamie, who'd introduced her to the bar staff. She now knew that Donald worked here part-time too behind the scenes.

The L-shaped bar with its roaring fire held many faces, but no Jamie in his usual spot, nor any sign of Alvis. Despite having come in with the intention of engaging with Alvis, Rhona found herself a little relieved about that. She turned towards the restaurant area and the scent of food made her realize just how hungry she was. She quickly decided that eating here was preferable to heading home in the storm to prepare a meal.

'Has Jamie been in?' Rhona ventured as she was shown to a table.

'Not yet,' the waitress told her with a smile of recognition. 'He'll likely be in later, though.'

With a quick glance at the menu, Rhona gave her order of fish and chips.

Seated now, she was conscious of the various foreign voices surrounding her in the small restaurant. Americans to her right, probably Californian, she thought. Ahead of her was a party of four French people. On her left, Italians.

It seemed tourists came to Skye whatever the time of year. And whatever the weather.

'Rhona?' Suddenly Alvis's tall, smiling figure came striding towards her. 'Are you about to eat? If so, may I join you?'

'Of course,' Rhona said. 'I was going to text you to let you know I was here.'

Not strictly true, but yet . . .

Alvis smiled as though he might believe her.

'How did it go today?' he asked as soon as he'd ordered his own meal.

'I processed the locus and handed the evidence to Sergeant MacDonald for transfer.'

'So, do we have a crime on our hands?'

Rhona repeated her explanation of what she'd found, before pointing out that she hadn't given that amount of detail to Donald or Matt.

Alvis nodded. 'So someone did get hurt, but you have no idea who?'

'Matt said the only folk they'd had in the last few days were army personnel and they left unscathed.'

Alvis looked interested by that. 'Was there a female among them, do you know?'

Rhona had no idea. 'Why?' she asked.

'There was a group in here the night I arrived. Four blokes and a girl. Medics who'd served in Afghanistan together.'

'That could be them. Are they still around?'

'They were heading for the hills, survival training, or so they told the barman.' Alvis glanced at the window. 'It's definitely not camping weather. Still, if they're service personnel they'll be used to rough conditions.'

15

Afghanistan

I have lost all sense of time. I sometimes try to piece the broken past together. To view the jigsaw between then and now. At first I attempted to count the days by the sun's movement across the dirt floor. And focusing on the light means I can see the other non-human occupants of my cell.

My greatest fear has been of the scorpions who love to shelter in stone walls like the ones that surround me.

I perpetually scan for the most dangerous ones, those with thin pincers and thick tails. I've treated soldiers who'd encountered them when they'd used walls for cover, or when they'd hollowed out dugouts. I've watched them writhe and scream from the neurotoxic sting. Dressed an arm as raw as a third-degree burn from the cytotoxic poison of the *Hemiscorpius lepturus*, for which there is no antivenom.

The spiders frighten me less. Out to forage in the dark, the danger is that they will crawl into my blue prison while I sleep and I will inadvertently crush them, forcing them to retaliate.

How many hours did I spend spraying the sandbags encircling the medical tent and our sleeping quarters to prevent scorpions entering? How often did I move beds as far away from the inside walls as space would allow, imagining that despite our care, a life might be taken inadvertently in the night?

As for our own sleeping quarters, the others would make fun of my efforts. They weren't scared of a wee spider, they told me.

While all the time, a scorpion was already among us.

16

'Who?'

McNulty's expression was a mixture of feigned surprise, guile and, without a doubt, self-satisfaction.

McNab wondered if Janice had registered the fact that McNulty much preferred to be questioned about his possible connection to a drug cartel, rather than for beating up his partner.

'Jess questioned you about the Sandman. That's why you hit her,' Janice said.

'You've got no chance on the domestic so you're switching to some geezer called the Sandman?' he laughed, his big belly shaking against the table.

'Once the word gets out . . .' Janice said in a voice that suggested he should be worried about his welfare.

A flicker of animal cunning sprang to life in McNulty's eyes.

'The tits tells jokes. Ha fucking ha.'

McNab realized he was grinding his teeth. He forced his mouth open a little and sat back in his seat, curbing his desire to cut in on Janice's questioning.

'You're supplying. Jess was making things difficult. So you shut her up. Knocked two teeth out in the process and broke her arm, which unfortunately meant an A&E visit.'

McNulty was the one now gritting his teeth.

'A bit embarrassing to be put away for hitting a wee lassie when you're such –' she moved her eyes to the bulging belly – 'a big man.'

McNab watched as the curtains came down on McNulty's eyes. It was all over, for the moment at least.

'Why the fuck does she stay with that bastard?' McNab said as they emerged from the interview room to breathe in air that wasn't filled with the stink of McNulty.

'Because he'll kill her if she leaves,' Janice told him.

'We could definitely get him on that,' McNab said, only half in jest.

'Yeah. Let's get a woman killed, so we can get our man.' Janice shot him a look that suggested Ellie wasn't working hard enough on his feminist transformation.

McNab couldn't bring himself to say sorry, but tried to look it nonetheless. Thankfully his mobile rang at this precise moment.

'Sergeant MacDonald, thanks for getting back to me.' He gestured to Janice that it was a call from Skye, and made himself scarce. 'Well?' he said, once out of earshot.

'Dr MacLeod was right. Something did happen. Enough to embed the skin from someone's skull in a tree trunk.'

McNab found himself mightily relieved at the news that Rhona wasn't imagining things.

'Rhona asked me to send the evidence to Chrissy for processing.'

'Any sign of the victim?'

'None. We've checked the local hospitals and Inverness Raigmore for any recent head injuries and got nothing. Rhona suggested we check Glasgow.'

'I can do that,' McNab offered, glad he could take on any role in the Rhona-inspired investigation.

'Severe scalp abrasions, blond hair. Chrissy will have blood and scalp samples as soon as.'

'So, you could be looking for a body?'

'More blood was found near vehicle tracks at the suspected exit point from the woods.'

McNab imagined for a moment the area that might have to be covered if they were looking for a body. The Orkney island of Sanday had been bad enough, and it was flat and a manageable size, plus no one could get on or off without it being noted.

Skye was an island, but way bigger, and with a bridge to the mainland. Still, if it was anything like Sanday, local folk were a good resource for anything suspicious happening.

'No word of anything locally that might have led to this?' McNab tried.

'Not so far.'

As he rang off, McNab's immediate and cheering thought was that Rhona was back at work.

17

On moving through to the bar after their meal, they'd discovered Jamie seated with the big collie next to the fire.

'Blaze is my forensic assistant,' Rhona explained, after introducing Alvis. 'It was Blaze who drew my attention to the locus in the first place.'

'And I heard you found something?' Jamie said.

'From Donald and Matt?' Rhona said.

'From several people, including Archie McKinnon, who captured you and Blaze via his drone. You were apparently approaching the road with what looked like a full rucksack.'

'I was spied on by a drone?' Rhona said, wide-eyed.

'Archie's gathering aerial views for the Skye tourist website. You just happened to emerge from the woods as his drone was heading for home. He checked with Donald and was told what you were up to.' Jamie was laughing. 'And now everyone knows your real occupation, Dr MacLeod.'

'If folk are aware that something happened in the woods, maybe we'll find out who was in there,' Rhona said.

'If it was locals, I suspect the word will be out soon,' Jamie said. 'I assume you can't discuss what you found?'

'You assume right.'

Alvis, perhaps to back her up on this, swiftly changed

the subject. 'Have the police located the elderly man who was missing? Jake Ross, I think Sergeant MacDonald said his name was?'

Jamie's face clouded over. 'Not yet. Old Jake's done this before but he's usually been picked up by now.' He glanced at the window as another flash of lightning briefly lit up the darkness. 'He's unlikely to survive a night out in this. Lee's got together a search team. I'm out with it first thing tomorrow with the Mountain Rescue Team and the helicopter.'

Almost in unison, Alvis and Rhona asked if they could join the MRT.

'Sure thing. Blaze will be there. Won't you, boy?' he said, ruffling the collie's ears.

Rhona felt her mobile vibrate in her pocket. She hadn't expected a response from Chrissy tonight but there was always a chance. Checking the screen, she saw it was Lee.

'Rhona? I see your jeep's still in the square. I take it you're at the Isles?'

'I am.'

'Just to tell you there's been an accident on the A851 and the road's currently blocked. Lochaber and Skye Police Twitter account is posting updates.'

'Thanks, Lee.' She mentioned tomorrow's search.

'I'd appreciate your help. We hope to find Jake alive, but if not, having you early on the scene to record the circumstances would be good.'

As she rang off, Donald appeared from the back and repeated what she'd just learned.

'Road to Armadale's closed until further notice. It's up on Twitter.'

'Lee's just phoned to warn me,' Rhona told him. 'Is there a room vacant here by any chance?'

'Sorry, as far as I know we're full of French, Americans—'

'And Italians,' Rhona finished for him.

Alvis looked flustered for a moment, and Rhona realized he might well be about to suggest she take his room, so she turned to Jamie.

'D'you still have that spare room you offered?'

'I do, and it's yours if you need it.'

Rhona avoided looking at Donald, knowing her swift request, just as quickly agreed to, would probably further fuel the speculation that she and Jamie were an item.

'You can leave the jeep here,' Jamie said. 'I'm only along the road.'

'Which means I can now drink something stronger.'

18

A text to Chrissy had established that she would meet him at the jazz club after work, but only briefly.

McNab was aware that Chrissy's mother looked after his namesake, wee Michael, and that Chrissy was always home in time to put him to bed. He thought, not for the first time, of his godson, and how close to death he'd been that night outside the Glasgow casino.

The memory always brought a sharp pain to McNab's back, as though the bullet he'd taken while shielding a pregnant Chrissy might still be in there.

Since Ellie had inked a skull over the scar, McNab would imagine the bullet shattering the skeleton head. He wondered sometimes if this was his subconscious reminding him that he should never have got the biker tattoo in the first place.

Pushing open the door of the jazz club, he headed downstairs. The place was busy with after-work drinkers, but he soon spotted Chrissy in her usual place at the bar.

McNab had never hit on Chrissy, nor she on him. It seemed the best male–female relationships were formed in such a way. Or so Chrissy often reminded him.

'Rhona's back on the job,' she said with a smile. 'There was an evidence delivery at the lab.'

'Sergeant MacDonald told me.'

'He's your spy in the Skye camp?'

'Him and now Norwegian Inspector Alvis Olsen,' McNab said with an accusing look.

'He called to say he was coming back to Scotland. I told him why Rhona wasn't here to speak to him,' Chrissy said defiantly.

'Did you suggest he went to Skye?'

'No, but I hoped he would. He and Rhona faced some real shit together.' Chrissy glared at McNab. 'He might be the one to persuade her to come home,' she said hopefully. 'And now that she's working again . . .' She tailed off, a question in her eyes.

'I have the feeling Dr MacLeod prefers island life, and her friends there.'

Chrissy was examining his expression, unsure if he was joking or not.

'Maybe it's that bloke Jamie she was pally with back in the day.' McNab paused for effect. 'Let's face it, things haven't been great with Sean since . . .' He halted, trying to look suitably worried, which he undoubtedly was.

'Fuck. Rhona has to come back and soon. Or I need to find another job.'

'What's wrong with Derek? He seems an okay guy.'

Chrissy bit back whatever she was about to say about Rhona's temporary replacement. 'What the hell do we do?'

'If you went out there,' McNab ventured, 'Rhona might be more likely to come back.'

'If she thinks I've come to persuade her?' Chrissy didn't look convinced. 'You know what she's like.'

'Well, let's hope they do find a body in suspicious circumstances. Then you have the perfect excuse.' Even as he said this, McNab was conscious that he'd now wished death on two people in order to achieve his current desires – the identification of the Sandman and Rhona back in Glasgow and on the job. But catching a thoughtful look in Chrissy's eye, he decided he'd sown the seed of her possible trip to Skye and would have to await its hopeful germination.

'Okay, I'm off,' Chrissy said, glancing at her watch.

McNab said his goodbyes, then called the barman over. There was someone else he needed to speak to. As he was served his order, he asked if Sean Maguire was about.

The Irishman doesn't look so good, McNab thought as Maguire slid onto the stool beside him. They exchanged greetings. Always guarded, even more so now, since the sin-eater affair.

Maguire had acknowledged McNab's role in helping Rhona in her darkest hour, but hadn't forgiven him for his other transgressions.

God, we Catholics don't half do guilt well.

Maguire nodded to the barman and two measures of whisky slid along the bar to them.

'*Sláinte,*' Maguire offered.

McNab took him at his word, and chinking glasses returned his offer of good health.

'I assume you've heard from Rhona?' Maguire was saying.

'We keep in touch regularly via Skype. The boss insists on it,' McNab added as though it had nothing to do with him. He waited, wanting to ask if Maguire had heard from her, but not sure whether the enquiry would be welcomed or answered in the affirmative.

'I haven't heard from her,' Maguire said, after swallowing the whisky. 'Not yet anyway.'

McNab nodded, aware that showing sympathy would not be welcome.

'Have you tried calling?' McNab tried.

'She asked me not to,' Maguire shot back at him. 'When she left for Skye. I'm respecting her wishes.' A sharp edge of pain crossed his face as he gestured to the barman that they would have a refill.

'She attended the counselling session the boss set up for her.' McNab offered what might be a crumb of comfort, although he already knew that Rhona hadn't stayed long enough with the doc for a meaningful interchange.

He thought back to his own experience with trauma counselling after the shooting. How unwilling he had been. The only reason he'd gone through with it was because he had to, seeing that he was holed up in a police safe house and couldn't avoid the psych visits.

Who could blame Rhona for not wanting to relive her own experience?

'There's something Rhona isn't telling me.' Maguire eyed McNab. 'About what happened to her that night. I know that much.' He said this as though he suspected McNab was aware what that might be.

'You know what I know,' McNab declared, hoping that was true, but suspecting it might not be.

Maguire was sampling his refill. McNab had a sudden and overwhelming desire to tell him not to drown himself in drink, but that would be way too ironic, even for him.

Noting McNab hadn't yet touched his whisky, Maguire said with a wry smile, 'I see *you're* on the wagon?'

'Trying.'

Maguire drew McNab's glass towards himself. 'Better not tempt you then. How's Ellie?'

'Fine,' McNab said.

Maguire finished both McNab's whisky and his own. 'I'm on shortly, so we'll say goodbye, Detective Sergeant.'

As Maguire stood up, McNab said, 'It seems Rhona's back on the job. Doing some work for Skye and Lochaber police.'

That caught Maguire by surprise. 'You think she's planning to stay there?' He looked worried.

'I doubt it,' McNab said cheerily. 'Not enough criminal activity to keep her busy.'

Maguire was watching him, aware there was something else he wanted to say.

'It's a good sign, though,' McNab went on. 'And Chrissy's planning a trip out there. If anyone can get Rhona to come home, it will be Chrissy.'

Maguire gave him a lopsided smile. 'And all the time I thought it would be you, Detective Sergeant.'

19

'Coffee or a nightcap?'

'Maybe both?' Rhona said.

'Talisker good?'

'Perfect.'

Rhona sat back in the sofa next to the fire. Her decision to spend the night at Jamie's had seemed an even better idea during the short but wild walk back to his place, although there had been little choice with the road to the cottage still closed.

Despite her recent time spent in Jamie's company she hadn't until now visited him at home. In fact he hadn't invited her to do so. Just mentioned he had a spare room if she ever needed to stay in town. Rhona wondered, as he disappeared into the kitchen to make the coffee, how she would have responded if Jamie had made a move.

They had joked with Donald and Matt about she and Jamie as wild teenagers together. It wasn't strictly true, although there had been feelings between them back then. A teenage romance even, but she was never going to stay on the island and Jamie was never going to leave. Since she'd returned, Jamie had behaved towards her like a platonic friend, although Rhona didn't think his feelings were that exactly. A more likely explanation was that Jamie believed that was the way she wanted to play it and was respecting her wishes.

And he'll continue to behave like that, until I give him cause to think otherwise.

Through the open door to the kitchen, Rhona watched as he prepared the coffee and poured two generous measures of Talisker.

As he re-entered with his tray, she found herself asking him why he'd never married.

If Jamie was surprised by the sudden question, he didn't show it. Setting the tray down on the coffee table, he handed Rhona a glass of whisky and offered her the water jug. Once she'd added a little to her glass, he did the same, then sitting alongside her, he gave his answer.

'I almost did get married.'

Rhona waited, hoping he would tell her why he hadn't. After sampling the Talisker, he did.

'Trina met someone else she liked better. They're married now and living over by Plockton. They have a son, Finn.' He met Rhona's eye. 'What about you?'

She could have said, *I'm married to my work*, which was for the most part true, but she didn't. Maybe it was the power of the Talisker, on top of the whisky she'd had in the pub. Or perhaps it was because it felt unfair not to answer Jamie's question, as he had answered hers.

'I got pregnant in my second year at university.' She paused to collect herself. 'That's why I didn't come back that summer. I didn't tell my parents about the pregnancy or about my baby son, who I gave up for adoption.'

Jamie didn't look surprised, just thoughtful, as though she'd answered a question that had puzzled him for some time.

'The guy you brought here that first summer after you

went to university. The one with the sports car. Was he the father?'

Rhona nodded. 'Edward Stewart. When I discovered I was pregnant he wanted me to have an abortion. I wouldn't. We didn't last long after that.' Rhona took another sip of whisky. 'He found someone he liked better. He and Fiona have two teenage children.'

'And your son?'

'Liam Hope. I tried to find him, but in fact he found me.' She remembered how freaked she'd been back then. How guilty she'd felt all those years at having given him up. 'It wasn't easy to meet him, but Sean was . . .' She halted, realizing that having mentioned Sean's name, she would have to explain more than just how good he'd been with Liam.

'Sean?' Jamie prompted gently.

'Sean Maguire. He plays saxophone at the club Chrissy and I go to,' she said, finding herself avoiding Sean's actual role in her life.

Now Jamie did look surprised. 'You're talking about Sean Maguire, the Irish saxophonist?'

Rhona was used to people recognizing Sean's name in Glasgow, but she hadn't imagined he would be known on Skye.

'You've heard him?' she said.

'He played here at the Aros Centre a few years ago. He's very good. I think they've been after him to come back.' Jamie paused for a moment, then seemed to decide to ask the question Rhona had been trying to avoid.

'Are you and he an item then?'

Rhona hesitated. 'Sean and I have tried, on occasion, to live together, but . . .' She ground to a halt.

'It didn't work out,' Jamie finished for her.

'No, it didn't.' Rhona chose to stop there. How could she explain, even to herself, the ups and downs of her relationship with Sean, especially the most recent reason for their split?

Jamie, sensing her reluctance to go further, tried to lighten the situation.

'We should have made an arrangement, you and I, that if we reached a certain age and no one else would have us, then we would rescue one another,' he joked.

'That may yet be necessary,' Rhona said with a relieved smile that the subject was over.

They fell quiet after that, but it was a comfortable silence, as though having confided in one another, they could go back to the way things had been.

Minutes later, finishing her whisky, Rhona suggested she would like to head for bed.

'Sure thing.' Jamie sprang up and indicated that she should follow him upstairs.

At the top of the narrow staircase was a small landing with three doors.

'The middle one's the bathroom,' Jamie told her. 'I'm on the left, you're on the right.' He opened the right-hand door for her.

Rhona had no idea what to expect, but was quietly surprised by the obviously female bedroom.

'My wee sister sometimes comes to stay,' Jamie explained. 'I keep it ready for her. If I didn't I'd have hell to pay.'

'Thank you. It's great,' Rhona said.

'I'm not sure if there's a nightgown or pyjamas,' Jamie apologized.

'A warm bed's all I need.'

'Great, well, goodnight, Rhona. I'll give you a shout in the morning for the search party.'

She thought for a moment he might kiss her on the cheek, but if that had been his intention, Jamie stopped himself and, turning, headed back downstairs.

Entering her room, Rhona closed the door with a definite feeling of relief.

She was, she decided, okay about telling Jamie about Liam. He knew now that her parents had never learned about their grandchild. That she had kept his existence from them. Something that could no longer be fixed, however much she wanted to.

If her revelation had changed Jamie's opinion of her, he hadn't shown it. Maybe some day she would bring Liam to Skye and introduce him to Jamie. The idea of doing that lifted her spirits.

She took off her shoes and, stripping down to T-shirt and pants, retrieved her notebook and map from her backpack and spread it out beside her on the bed. Had she managed to reach the cottage, her plan had been to write up her notes from this morning's examination. Now she was alone, she could do just that.

Studying the map, she could see no reason for the mystery vehicle to continue on the B885. Lee had suggested the same, especially if whoever was driving was looking for medical help. According to the Ordnance Survey map, the single-track road wound westwards to Loch Bracadale, from where you could head north to Dunvegan or return east to join the Uig road, leading back to Portree.

But if they were seeking medical help, Portree's minor injury unit was only minutes away in the opposite direction. If the injury had been too severe for them to treat, the patient would have been sent on to Broadford hospital or taken by road or even air ambulance to Raigmore.

So why head in the opposite direction, unless you had a reason not to report the incident? That seemed to Rhona the most likely scenario.

Completing her notes, she laid aside her notebook and, snuggling down, tried to go to sleep. The lightning storm had passed, as had the rain, and moonlight now shone down on her through the attic window.

Hearing Jamie come upstairs to bed, she realized she was glad of his benign presence across the landing, which then reminded her of the nights Sean had stayed over at her flat after coming back late from playing at the jazz club.

How often she'd woken to find Sean's arms about her, his warm breath brushing her neck.

I miss him, she thought. *More than I'm willing to admit, even to myself.*

20

Ashton Lane was deserted in the rain; anyone with any sense was staying in the various drinking establishments that lined the cobbled alley. McNab stood for a moment in the doorway, wondering where he should go next.

The meeting with Maguire had been necessary, but not altogether satisfactory. McNab had been keen to know if Rhona had been in touch with Maguire, and how the Irishman had felt about her state of mind.

God knows why I thought he would reveal such a thing to me.

One thing he had learned was that Maguire wasn't in a good place right now. And that had a lot to do with Rhona.

Their interchange had also planted a seed of doubt in McNab's mind. Maguire thought Rhona had kept something from him, something McNab knew about. Now McNab fretted as to what that could possibly be.

Had something even worse happened to Rhona that he wasn't aware of? That no one knew about, even Chrissy?

Across the road, a door, caught by a sudden gust of wind, abruptly slammed shut. The bang burst in his brain like a gunshot and McNab instinctively turned as he had that night outside the casino in order to shield a terrified Chrissy, only to find a puzzled girl trying to leave the jazz club.

Muttering an apology, he stepped aside to let her pass.

Scent, the PTSD counsellor had told him, would stay the longest. After that, specific sounds. For soldiers who'd been on the front line, anything resembling gunfire or even the innocent beat of an approaching chopper might send them back to their darkest place.

If his recall could still be triggered by a door slamming shut, what the hell was it like for Rhona?

Exiting the lane, McNab made for Hillhead underground station, his thoughts moving from Rhona to Ellie. He'd told the Irishman that Ellie was fine and it was true enough, although it was difficult to judge, considering how little time they'd spent together recently.

Along with her work at the Ink Parlour and her part-time position at the Harley-Davidson shop, Ellie had taken on a bar job at the Rock Cafe three nights a week, she'd said to help her save for a new bike.

If McNab wanted to see her tonight, that was where he had to go.

The platform was quiet, and when the train arrived it was almost empty. Despite the vacant seats, McNab chose as usual to remain standing next to the door, a habit of his, acquired when he'd joined the force. That and the inevitable scan of the passengers, always on the lookout for recognizable faces.

Emerging at St Enoch's, he walked west, the dreary and incessant drizzle speeding him along Argyle Street, keen now to get inside the Rock Cafe. Passing Pizza Hut, he was almost drawn in by the smell, his stomach groaning with hunger.

Crossing the road at the Celtic shop, he noted a guy in a sleeping bag propped at the foot of the steps that led into House of Fraser. A quick scan of the face told McNab he too was an unknown. Not that he could know every face that haunted the streets of inner Glasgow, looking for a sub for life's necessities or a bed for the night.

By the time he'd entered the tunnel that ran under the glassed edifice of Glasgow Central station, he'd passed two more guys with the same hopes and the same cry of 'Any small change, pal?'

McNab, like most Glaswegians, hadn't grown immune to the ravages of fate on his fellow men and women, but still he had no desire to provide the Sandman and his associates with a steady income stream.

Pushing open the bar door, he stepped inside, meeting a wall of music and warmth. Easing his way through the chattering clientele, he headed downstairs, where a surprising rush of emotion hit him as he caught sight of Ellie behind the bar, laughing at some comment a punter had just made to her.

The top she wore showed off a lot of her artwork, and McNab marvelled again at the inked glory of intricacy and colour. Noting the punter who'd shared a joke didn't look intent on leaving his spot at the bar, McNab decided it was time to encourage him to do so.

Ellie turned as he approached and gave him what he interpreted as a *what the hell are you doing here?* look.

'When's your break?' McNab said, elbowing his way past her latest admirer.

'I could take five minutes now,' Ellie offered, obviously perturbed by McNab's intense expression.

McNab motioned her out from behind the bar and, taking her hand, led her away.

'Where are we going?' she said with a laugh, sensing now he was up to something.

'I'm rescuing you from the arse at the bar.'

'I don't need to be rescued,' Ellie protested.

They'd reached the corridor that led to the fire escape. Coming to an abrupt halt, McNab gathered Ellie in his arms and kissed her.

Eventually he let her come up for air.

'What was that all about?' she said, a smile playing on her lips.

'When do you finish?' McNab said.

'Eleven.'

Her voice, he thought, sounded a little husky.

'Then I'll wait.'

'But . . .'

'And take you home, and we'll get to know one another a little better.' He bent towards her again, catching her bottom lip lightly. 'You can even ink me in a place of your choosing,' he offered.

She smiled. 'You're talking about the snake? The long curling one that winds itself round your—'

McNab put his hand over her mouth. 'If that's what it takes, then yes.'

Ellie laughed and he knew that he'd won her back, for the moment at least.

Ten minutes later, sitting at a table with a very good view of Ellie, awaiting his burger and curly fries, McNab had decided his evening was turning out better than expected. That was until he spied a face he recognized near the pool table.

One of the problems in his line of work was how many scumbags you encountered and, even worse, how many you remembered. McNab wasn't a super recognizer like his mate Ollie in IT. He couldn't pick out folk he'd arrested from CCTV recordings, especially when they were hooded, with only a partial view of their face on offer. But McNab didn't need Ollie tonight to tell him that the guy waiting his turn at pool was none other than one Malcolm Stevenson, a suspected major player in the Sandman case, whose mug-shot had taken pride of place in the incident room earlier.

The clientele at the Rock Cafe were a mixed bunch, the common factor being atmosphere, a love of rock music, decent food and drink. It was popular, especially with folk heading for the nearby music venues, but McNab wouldn't have placed it on Wee Malky's radar.

Yet here he was.

As McNab contemplated this, a guy deposited a plate of burger and curly fries in front of him.

'That bloke with the forehead tattoo at the pool table and the flashy ring,' McNab asked him. 'Is he a regular in here?'

The guy glanced surreptitiously at the said Malky. 'Why? D'you know him?'

'Do I want to?' McNab countered.

The young man was studying McNab more closely now. 'You're Ellie's . . .' He hesitated, wondering what to call him.

'Bodyguard?' McNab offered.

A swift glance from both of them found Ellie more than holding her own at the bar.

'I don't think she needs one,' he told McNab with an attempt at a joke.

'But might she need one to protect her from him?' McNab waved his fork in the direction of Stevenson.

'He comes in sometimes to play pool,' he offered grudgingly.

'And that's all he's here for?'

The guy, having given a non-committal shrug, made off, which caused McNab to suspect that Stevenson was there to deal, or more likely pick up his local dealer's takings. This was the problem with being a policeman and trying to have a night out in Glasgow. The underworld couldn't just pass him by.

McNab toyed with his food, knowing that he was eventually heading over there, whether he thought it wise or not.

What was he planning to do? Request a game of pool?

He checked on Ellie again, as though she was the anchor, holding him in his seat. In half an hour they would go home together and play whatever game she chose. The thought stirred him, and he could smell again the scent of her when they'd embraced earlier.

But still the gremlin on his shoulder urged him on.

McNab pushed aside the partially eaten meal.

Fuck it.

As he rose, he realized Stevenson's eyes were upon him and had probably been so for a while. A smile was playing at the corner of his mouth as he waited to see what McNab would do next.

McNab had nothing to accuse him of. Nothing at all. So why approach?

'You leaving, pal?' a voice said at his ear.

A couple who'd obviously hankered after his table had now presented themselves right in front of McNab.

'Sure thing,' McNab said and sidestepped them, only to spot Stevenson making for the corridor he and Ellie had visited earlier.

So he's heading out. I wonder why?

If the bastard was running, then he was in possession of something he thought McNab might be interested in.

The crowd round the bar had suddenly multiplied with the arrival of half a dozen biker-clad males, hampering McNab's ability to thread his way through. His bludgeoning attempts pissed a few folk off and the last thing he saw was Ellie's exasperated look.

By the time he reached the corridor it was empty, the fire door swinging open. Swearing his annoyance, he went for a look outside, knowing he was likely too late.

The rain was still falling, pinging off the empty metal beer barrels against the back wall. A yellow street light found the alley deserted except for himself and . . .

McNab stepped out onto the cobbled back lane. Ahead of him, a hot-air vent under an overhang was providing a warm, dry place of refuge for a rough sleeper. Approaching, McNab noted that the slumped figure looked like the guy from the steps at House of Fraser.

McNab prodded him with his foot. 'Did you see a blond guy pass this way? He had a tattoo on his forehead?'

With cocaine, amphetamines or marijuana, the eyes usually got very large. McNab had seen mydriasis last for days. Heroin, an opiate, was different. That caused miosis – pinprick pupils.

In this light diagnosis was impossible, but when McNab had seen him earlier, the guy had been alert and requesting money. Not any more. So maybe this was a distribution point. Maybe that was why Malky had been there.

McNab, noting the tail of the sleeping bag was getting soaked by the rain, stooped to move it back under the overhang. As he did so, a metal tag on a chain jingled onto the cobbles.

He picked it up and read it.

Now he knew the blood group, service number, surname, initials and even the religion of the poor bastard who lay comatose at his feet. The tag felt wet. In the darkness he assumed it was the rain, then his fingers told him a different story.

McNab hunkered down for a closer look, the soles of his shoes now turning the same red colour.

Fuck!

The guy wasn't in la-la land after all, he was checking out of this life as quickly as the blood that flowed from his body.

One-handed, his other pressing on the knife wound, McNab was calling 999 as Ellie's face appeared in the doorway.

'Get me towels, cloths, anything to stem the bleeding,' he told her. 'And make it quick.'

Saying nothing, but her own face drained of colour, she disappeared without a word, to reappear with a bundle of cloths.

'They're clean,' she told him.

'Get down here,' he ordered. 'Be ready when I lift my hand.'

She did as told. As he eased his hold, McNab felt the gush of escaping blood before he clamped his hand back down again, this time with the benefit of the wad of material.

A couple of faces appeared at the doorway, one of them the young guy that had served McNab earlier.

'Shut the fucking door,' McNab said. 'And keep your mouth shut or we'll have the hordes out here to gawk at the poor bastard.'

They took him at his word and closed the fire door.

'What if the ambulance doesn't get here in time?' Ellie said, her face creased in concern.

'Then he dies,' McNab said bluntly.

Kneeling down beside him, Ellie asked what had happened.

'I followed the tattooed guy from the pool table out here, and found this one lying comatose. I thought he was high until I spotted the blood.'

Ellie was examining their patient's face more closely.

'D'you know him?' McNab said.

'He has a spot at House of Fraser's steps. I chat to him sometimes.'

'And give him money?' McNab demanded. 'To buy his next fix?'

Ellie drew away a little, annoyed by his tone. 'He was a soldier. Fought in Iraq and Afghanistan. It fucked him up. Being on the front line does that to people,' she said, her eyes staring pointedly at McNab.

Catching the approaching blare of a siren and the accompanying flashing blue light, he prayed it was heading their way. In response, his cramped hand sought to release the pressure a little, despite his best efforts, until Ellie laid her hand firmly on top of his own.

21

Afghanistan

I catch the sharp metallic scent of blood. How badly have they hurt him?

He has kept his distance all through the night, despite the urgings and beatings of the guards.

As the first tentacle of light finds the opening high in the wall that serves as our window on the outside world, I sense him gather himself, making sounds as though he is just emerging from sleep. He pulls himself upright against the opposite wall, just as the first flurry of sand enters, swallowing the sunlight.

It's not the first time I've experienced a sandstorm, but it's the first in my blue prison.

I hear him splutter and cough as the sand birls about us. Watch as he tucks his head between his drawn-up knees for protection.

The sand is coarse, and will pistol-whip his nakedness as well as force entry to every crevice and opening in his body.

I call out to him, urging him to come to me.

My pleading is swept away by the swirling sand, now dense as soup, but he must have heard, because he's crawling across the stony ground towards me.

I pull him close and, lifting the tent of the blue prison, welcome him under its protection.

22

She'd been woken at dawn by Jamie's urgent knock at the bedroom door.

'Lee's been on the phone. They need you out at Kilt Rock.'

Rhona's heart skipped a beat. 'They've found Jake?'

'They've spotted something at the base of the cliff,' Jamie told her. 'The MRT's there already.'

'I'll be right down.' Rhona flicked on the light and, rising, quickly pulled on her jeans and jumper.

Downstairs, Jamie handed her a thermos of coffee and a bacon roll. 'Not sure when we'll next be fed,' he said.

'I'll eat it on the way,' Rhona told him, grabbing her jacket from the hall. 'And I'll need to pick up my forensic bag from the jeep en route. And Alvis from the Isles.'

'He knows we're on our way.'

Jamie was driving the MRT vehicle with caution, his fog lights barely puncturing the thick, swirling mist. Skye, this morning, was living up to its Gaelic nickname of Eilean a' Cheò, the Misty Isle.

As far as Rhona could make out, having left Portree they were now heading north, although in truth they could have been anywhere on the island or even driving towards a cliff edge for all that she could see.

Sitting in the back, she'd listened as Jamie had given Alvis an update on the situation.

'An Italian tourist took a series of photographs of Kilt Rock from the Mealt Falls lookout point yesterday. This morning, going through them, he spotted what might be a body on the shore and contacted the police.' Jamie passed Alvis his mobile. 'Here's the photo.'

Rhona had already viewed the image. The black basalt cliffs which, she knew, got their name from their folded appearance, were skirted by a shoreline of equally dark rocks split and fallen from the cliff face. In the photograph that had so troubled the tourist, there appeared to be a different-coloured shape amongst the stones, which, with a little imagination, might be the crumpled form of a body.

'The Coastguard have the search and recovery remit, but the Stornoway station's currently fog-bound,' Jamie told Alvis. 'Looks like we might get a chopper from Glasgow instead. Sergeant MacDonald and my MRT teammates will meet us at the viewpoint. For speed they'll be first responder.'

'Any forecast for when the mist will clear?' Alvis said.

'Word is, it will thin out soon. Enough for us to descend the cliff face, I hope.'

For the moment, driving through what resembled grey soup, that sounded more of a hope than a reality.

It was a testament to Jamie's knowledge of the road that he didn't miss the sign for the viewpoint. As they entered the car park, other vehicles loomed out of the haar. Plus a food truck, apparently open and selling coffee and breakfast to the assembled Mountain Rescue Team and police officers.

As they approached the crowd round the van, a concerned Lee came to meet them.

'Rhona. It's good to have you here, but let's hope you're not needed.'

'You still don't know if it's a body?'

'It's not been confirmed as yet, but it wouldn't be the first one we've retrieved from the base of the cliff. Some folk don't heed warnings and get too close to the edge.'

Lee gestured along the clifftop, barely distinguishable in the mist. 'A couple of the MRT are on their way down via the gully.' He turned to Rhona. 'If it proves to be a body, do you want to view it in situ?'

'Definitely,' Rhona told him. 'How do I get down there?'

'The gully's pretty tricky for non-climbers.'

'Is there another way?'

'You could wait for the chopper and get winched in or . . .'

'Or what?' Rhona said.

'Have you any experience of abseiling?'

That she hadn't expected.

'Once, for charity. Chrissy and I went off the Erskine Bridge,' Rhona said, trying not to remember exactly what she'd felt about that little escapade.

'If you're needed and willing, Jamie could take you down and the chopper could lift you off afterwards when the mist's cleared,' Lee suggested. 'You've been helicoptered in before?'

'Yes, with the MRT on Cairngorm and Police Scotland.'

'So, nothing to it, then.'

His radio crackled before Rhona could explain that she had neither been lowered from a helicopter nor, for that matter, winched up. Merely stepped out of the rescue chopper onto a frozen Loch A'an.

'It *is* a body,' Lee reported, having answered the radio

call. 'A young guy, so definitely not Jake.' He was looking at Rhona, awaiting her decision on how exactly she wanted to get on site.

Her mind made up, Rhona turned to Jamie. 'I'd definitely like to take a look, if you're okay with taking me down?'

Jamie, perhaps sensing her apprehension, joked with Rhona as he kitted them both up.

'So you enjoyed your first abseil?'

'I wouldn't say *enjoyed*. It was Chrissy's idea that we should do it, and she's pretty persuasive, 'Rhona told him. 'I do remember vowing never to do it again.'

'You can change your mind, you know,' Jamie offered, with a look of concern. 'Wait for the chopper?'

Rhona shook her head. Her insides didn't relish the prospect of dropping 180 feet down a cliff face, but her curiosity about the body on the beach currently held the upper hand.

'Besides, I trust you not to drop me,' she said, as much to convince herself as to reassure Jamie. 'What about my bag?'

'We'll lower it down after you.'

The mist enveloped them. Unable to see how far she had to fall was, Rhona decided, somewhat reassuring. And Lee was right when he'd said how sheltered the Kilt Rock was.

'Unless, of course, we get high winds from the west, when the waterfall next to the lookout is simply blown away, never reaching the ground.'

Rhona tried not to envisage herself in such a situation as she began her descent, firmly gripped in Jamie's arms. And for the moment, thankfully, there was little movement in the air, just the damp fingers of mist on her face and the sound of the sea breaking on the black rocks below.

As her feet eventually touched the ground, the mist began to thin and, glancing up, Rhona realized just how far she'd descended.

'Okay?' Jamie said as he released her.

'Thank you for my life,' Rhona said with a relieved smile.

'I was really looking after my own,' Jamie joked back.

Freed now from her harness, Rhona took stock of where she was.

Looking up and to her left, she could just make out the lights of the rescue vehicles behind the railing that encircled the viewpoint. To her right, Jamie had explained, lay the steep gully used by the MRT to access the foreshore.

'The way I brought you down was easier, and quicker,' he added.

Having orientated herself and retrieved her bag, Rhona now followed Jamie across the jumble of rocks to his two teammates.

Introduced by Jamie as Scott and Allan, they in turn led her to the cordon they'd set up around the body.

'We've taken a 360-degree recording and checked for ID but the pockets we can reach without moving him are empty,' Scott told her. 'There's no evidence that he abseiled down or planned to climb the cliffs, although his outfit and boots suggest he was prepared for a walk at least.'

From where she now stood, the crumpled and twisted body was partially visible between the black rocks. Rhona glanced upwards again, trying to visualize where he may have fallen from.

'They'll have secured the possible fall-off area for you to take a look at,' Jamie assured her.

Outer jacket removed, a forensic suit now encasing her body, Rhona stepped over the tape.

Although the MRT guys had already recorded the scene, Rhona did it now for her own purposes. Jamie had assured her that the remains lay above the high-water mark, unless and until a storm brought surging seas to Staffin Bay. The ongoing weather forecast apparently didn't indicate such a possibility, but that could change as swiftly as the weather on the Cuillin, according to Jamie.

Rhona noted that the body, now in full view, didn't appear swollen or waterlogged, as it would have been had it been washed ashore. Instead, the broken shape immediately suggested a high-impact fall. None of the limbs held their basic shape, but were twisted back on themselves where they'd hit the boulders.

Landing on his front, the victim's left cheek and partial forehead were visible, as too was the back of the head. The hair was blond, the facial features too battered to be recognizable.

The victim's height Rhona estimated as close to six feet. His build was lean and muscular, much as she imagined a rock climber who might tackle these cliffs would be, but as Scott had indicated, there was nothing on or near the body to suggest the victim had fallen while climbing the cliff.

'How long will you need?' Jamie called out to her.

'As long as it takes,' Rhona told him.

23

'We last met when you were heading to Sanday with Dr MacLeod,' Neil, the observing officer stationed in the rear of the Air Support helicopter, reminded Chrissy.

'When you promised we would land on a beach,' she accused him in return. 'Which we didn't.'

'You'll have to get sent to Barra for that,' Neil told her above the beat of the helicopter blades. 'Although I can't imagine there'll be a big call on your services out there in the Western Isles.'

'That's what we thought about Sanday,' Chrissy said. 'Turns out we were wrong.'

'So what's it this time?' Neil asked.

'A body at the foot of Kilt Rock. Dr MacLeod's on the scene. Luckily she was on Skye when it was discovered.'

Neil threw Chrissy a sympathetic look as though he already knew the background to Rhona's presence on the island, which wasn't surprising. If Scotland was a village, Police Scotland was a big family, and not always a happy one.

'Where will you put me down?' Chrissy said.

'As near as possible to the lookout point on the clifftop. By the time we get there, the mist should have lifted.'

Looking down on a beautiful clear view of the snow-covered western Highlands, it was difficult to imagine a mist-bound Skye.

'How do I get onto the foreshore?' Chrissy said.

'That's for the MRT guys to decide,' Neil said with a mischievous grin.

Chrissy chose not to imagine how that might be exactly. She'd googled Kilt Rock after McNab's morning phone call, but a quick glance at the scary black cliffs was all she'd managed before getting ready for her helicopter ride to Skye.

She'd been feeding wee Michael at the time. Seeing McNab's name on the screen had sent her into a paroxysm of worry after last night's conversation about Rhona. In fact she'd already discussed with her mum whether she would keep wee Michael and let Chrissy drive to Skye on the coming weekend.

'This is your chance to see how Rhona really is,' McNab had told Chrissy. Hearing her hesitation, he'd laid it on even thicker. 'Rhona's likely to be with the body for most of the day. She would welcome some help, according to Sergeant MacDonald at Portree.'

'Does Rhona know DI Wilson's sending me out there?' Chrissy had asked.

'It'll be like Orkney all over again,' he'd urged, not answering her question.

'I *was* thinking of driving over this weekend,' Chrissy had admitted at that point.

'Perfect,' McNab had declared, before swiftly ending the call in case she should change her mind.

'We're almost there.' Neil broke into Chrissy's thoughts. 'There's the bridge ahead.'

Chrissy had never been to Skye. Sanday had been the first Scottish island she'd visited. Back then she'd taken a vow to visit more of them. Like many city dwellers, previously she'd thought more of seeking the sun when she had time off, rather than heading north or west.

Above the landmass now, Neil pointed out various places as they passed over.

'The long island on the right is Raasay,' he told her. 'The flat-topped mountain in the middle is Dun Caan. And ahead is Portree.'

Portree, she saw, was clustered round a bay with a pretty little harbour. If this was a population centre, it wasn't very big.

'There's a police station in the main square with the sheriff court alongside. Sergeant MacDonald, who you'll meet soon, is based there. We're heading a bit further north to Ellishadder. That's where the lookout point for Kilt Rock is.'

They followed the road, departing from the coastline to pass above a string of dark lochs. To the left rose a sharp pinnacle of rock, which Chrissy was told was the Old Man of Storr.

'They had a big electrical storm on Skye last night,' Neil told her. 'Knocked out the power for a while.' He pointed ahead. 'And there's Kilt Rock.'

Chrissy craned her head for a better view of the pleated rock formation, which looked even more daunting in real life. Her stomach somersaulted at the sight of it.

'Shit! Rhona's at the foot of that?'

'One hundred and eighty feet down, the pilot assures me. Hope you have a good head for heights,' Neil said brightly.

As they began their descent, Chrissy spotted a car park busy with police and MRT vehicles. Plus what looked suspiciously like a burger van.

'Is that what I think it is?' she said, her spirits lifting.

'The Black Sheep food truck,' Neil assured her. 'And I intend visiting it.'

Chrissy only realized the full extent of her hunger when she was offered her haggis roll. This morning's early start avoiding the lab had meant missing her usual copiously filled roll and coffee breakfast, which she and Rhona had liked to indulge in.

On the way here, she'd resigned herself to a locus out in the wilds with no food on hand. A common enough problem when out on the job. At least in Glasgow they could send a young obliging uniform to the nearest chippy.

Chrissy certainly hadn't imagined finding such an outlet here in a car park in the middle of nowhere.

Already in receipt of her coffee, she now gratefully accepted the loaded haggis roll she'd ordered and proceeded to add some tomato ketchup to it.

'I'll need another one of these,' she said after the first bite. 'Chances are I won't get anything after this for a while.'

The young woman nodded with a smile.

'Oh, and do you know if any food's been sent down to Dr MacLeod on the shore?'

'I don't think so,' the girl said.

'Then make that two more haggis rolls, and stick some bacon on them too.'

Armed with her second breakfast, Chrissy turned to find a black-and-white Border collie waiting next in the queue.

'Hi, Blaze,' the girl in the van was saying. 'The usual?'

The dog seemed to indicate by a single bark that that was indeed the case.

Impressed by this interchange, Chrissy greeted her new acquaintance.

'So you're the famous Blaze I've heard so much about.'

She held out her hand, not expecting the dog to deliver the high five that it did.

'And you're clever too,' she said. 'What else do you do?'

A deep male voice answered her question.

'Blaze has a full repertoire which you can view nightly at the Isles Inn, or alternatively daily in the square at Portree outside the police station.' The guy held out his hand. 'Hi, I'm Domhnall MhicAoidh, or in English, Donald MacKay. Blaze's owner, although I'm sure he probably thinks he's mine.'

'Chrissy McInsh,' Chrissy offered. 'Rhona . . . Dr MacLeod's forensic assistant, although I've heard on the grapevine that Blaze here might be after my job?'

'I think he may well be,' Donald said with an apologetic look. 'Good to meet you, Chrissy McInsh.'

'And you.'

'I take it you're here to join Rhona on the shore?'

'That's the plan. How did Rhona get down?' Chrissy asked.

'She abseiled with one of the MRT guys.'

Chrissy mouthed a *fuck*. 'Well, if that's how Dr MacLeod got down there.' She glanced around at the milling personnel. 'So who's to be the lucky guy?'

Donald gestured to a tall bloke near the barrier on the clifftop.

'Jamie McColl. He knows Rhona from way back on Skye. Come on, I'll introduce you,' Donald said, giving Blaze a share of his breakfast roll.

24

Studying the dead brought you closer to them. Everything Rhona recorded here would help paint a picture of the living, breathing person, who now lay lifeless before her.

She was the first mourner. The first to study the body. The first to contextualize the end of their life.

In an autopsy, the body would be recorded in minute detail, focusing on the forensic nature of the wounds and inner organs, but the pathologist wouldn't be here on this rocky foreshore, with the basalt cliffs towering behind, amid the cry of the gulls and the rush of the breaking waves.

The locus of the body wasn't necessarily the place where the victim had died. Bodies might be moved after death, disposed of by a perpetrator in order to conceal their death or at least disguise the way they had died.

A hanging disguised as a suicide.

A murder masquerading as an accident.

So when did this young man die?

According to Jamie on their way down the cliff face – he had kept her talking to keep her mind off the descent – the Italian tourist had arrived at the viewpoint on a minibus around 3.30 yesterday. He hadn't liked standing too close to the railing, especially when he'd heard the weird moaning sound the barrier made. So he basically pointed the camera, clicked a few times, then headed back to the bus.

'Were there any other photographs taken that showed the body?' Rhona had asked.

'According to Lee, there were at least four tour buses here yesterday. They're trying to get in touch with the companies involved.'

So it seemed the victim had been on the cliff path sometime before 3.30 p.m. yesterday.

Jamie must have been reading her mind, because he'd said that the call had gone out for any possible witnesses in the area of the cliff around that time.

'Lots of folk follow the Skye and Lochaber Police Twitter feed. Chances are someone will have seen something, since the alert was already out for Jake.'

Rhona turned, as a sudden shout from behind appeared to call her name.

To say she was surprised by the person currently being disengaged from Jamie's harness was the understatement of the century. But Rhona's surprise wasn't as great as her delight at seeing Chrissy McInsh stumble across the intervening rocks towards her.

'I've brought food.' Chrissy waved a bag. 'A haggis roll. Can you take a break?'

They were now seated on a large boulder within sight of the locus. Along with the rolls, Jamie had requisitioned more hot coffee to be lowered down in a flask. After depositing Chrissy, he'd moved to discuss how to take the body away with his fellow MRT colleagues, either by stretchering it up the cliff face or, alternatively, bringing in the lifeboat and taking it out by sea.

'So.' Chrissy was regarding Rhona as she now scoffed the food she hadn't been aware she'd needed. 'Who's the dishy guy you knew from before? And why was I never told about him?'

For the first time in what seemed like months, Rhona laughed. Not the polite or restrained version she'd been using, but a real laugh. One that almost made her choke on the haggis and bacon combination.

'God, I've missed you, Chrissy McInsh.'

'And I you,' Chrissy said with a grin. 'It took me ages to stop buying an extra filled roll of a morning. I put on weight by eating yours along with my own. And, by the way, if you don't come back soon, I'm likely to get my jotters.'

'They'll never give you the sack.'

'You haven't met Derek.' Chrissy's graphic description of Rhona's replacement would have provided a stand-up comedy routine on a par with Frankie Boyle in terms of expletives.

Rhona held up her hands. 'Stop, please.'

'So when are you coming back?'

'Soon,' Rhona said, wiping her hands and replacing her gloves. 'Let's deal with the body, then I'll tell you everything that's been happening here,' she promised.

Rhona and Chrissy watched as the RNLI rib, having secured the body on board, set off in a burst of engine and froth towards the harbour at Portree. Rhona had given Chrissy the option of going with the lifeboat, but she'd chosen instead to be lifted by the recently arrived coast-guard helicopter, so that they might work the scene on the cliff face above together, before time ran out on them.

The light would fade soon, and although a couple of SOCOs had been examining the area deemed most likely to have originated the fall, Rhona was keen to view it herself.

As it was, perhaps immunized by her recent cliff descent, being lifted by the coastguard and deposited in the field next to the car park hadn't raised Rhona's heartbeat too much. As for Chrissy, she was beyond excited, insisting she had her photo taken during the transfer. Rhona could see the image being on show at the jazz club on her return to Glasgow. There and everywhere else Chrissy might interest someone in her 'rescue'.

Waiting for their lift, Rhona had brought Chrissy up to date on the incident in the woods behind A.C.E Target Sports.

'And you suspect the dead guy may be linked to that?'

Rhona couldn't say that exactly, but time-wise it might fit. The state of decomposition of the body on the beach could certainly place the death in that time frame. She explained about the head injury and the material she'd collected from the tree trunk. 'The majority of the shore victim's injuries were from impact as he landed on his front. But there was a sizable older wound on the back of the head.'

'Which may provide a match for the material you found in the birch tree?'

'And the blood deposits,' Rhona had added. 'Has anything come back on those, and the soil samples I sent?'

'God, I forgot to tell you, Jen Mackie came back on the soil. Seems she did find evidence suggesting cocaine. Something about benzoylecgonine?'

Rhona knew it would have been unlikely to find cocaine

molecules in the soil. The natural water content would have metabolized the cocaine quite rapidly. Jen would have had to look for the cocaine metabolites, the predominant one being benzoylecgonine, its presence indicative of cocaine having been there.

'And you detected cocaine on your faller?'

It'd been one of the first tests Rhona had done on the body.

'According to Sergeant MacDonald, it's increasingly the drug of choice for both visitors and locals and it's available on the island, despite all their efforts.'

'Maybe the victim got high and went too near the edge?' Chrissy had suggested.

'Or maybe,' Rhona had said, 'that's what we're supposed to believe.'

Crossing the stream that left the small loch to tumble over the cliff face, Rhona, led by Blaze and followed by Chrissy, took the path that wound its way along the headland. The wire fence between them and the sheer drop was a grim reminder of just how easy it would be to stray too close, especially in the thick mist of earlier.

When Blaze had indicated he wished to accompany them, Rhona had been happy to agree.

'He's safe on the cliffs?' she'd asked Donald.

'He's mountain-trained,' Donald had told her. 'And very cautious.' He gave Rhona a selection of the dog's commands. 'But if you tell him to *stay*, remember to release him, otherwise he'll stay in that place forever,' he warned them with a smile. 'I left him in the pub once. He hasn't forgotten.'

Rhona's 'walk on' had sent Blaze a little ahead of them. Her 'here to me' brought him swiftly back.

'Hey,' Chrissy said. 'You're bossing him about just like me.'

Cresting a small hill, they found an area sectioned off by police tape, an officer on duty, although it looked like the SOCOs had already departed.

The crime scene manager turned out to be Jamie's friend, the one who was due to have his stag do the forthcoming weekend. Introducing himself in a London accent as Sergeant Frank Duns, he told them he'd transferred to Skye from the Met five years ago.

'I used to climb here on holiday once a year. Now I can climb whenever I like,' he told them. 'And the murder rate's a lot lower,' he added with a wry smile.

'Did the SOCOs find anything of interest?' Rhona said.

'A few footprints, but folk wander up this way from the car park all the time. Good thinking on Blaze, though.'

Freshly kitted up, Rhona and Chrissy entered the enclosed area. Rhona then produced the swab she'd taken from the victim and offered it up to Blaze.

If the collie could detect blood in the woods behind the sports centre, he was equally likely to pick up where the victim had been on the clifftop.

Donald's instructions had been clear. 'Use "Go find it" and if Blaze is in close proximity to what he's meant to be looking for, you call "Good boy" and he'll do a detailed search of about a five-yard area.'

Blaze took a while sniffing the swab, then, on her command, he took off. Rhona's biggest fear in trying this was that Blaze might pick up the faller's scent around the cliff edge.

She was wrong in that. The dog was circling the area, but if the faller had walked this section, it seemed he had left no trace.

Chrissy turned to Rhona, disappointed. 'Could this be the wrong spot they've identified?'

Having crossed and recrossed the sectioned-off area, Blaze now passed under the tape and moved further afield in his search.

'Maybe he's looking for a rabbit?' Chrissy said.

'I thought that in the woods,' Rhona told her, 'and I was wrong then.'

The dog had come to a halt and now stood waiting, the brown eyes fixed firmly on Rhona.

'Looks like Blaze has found something he wants us to see,' Rhona said.

25

Afghanistan

Back before this happened, according to Sugarboy, the guys had decided that at home in Glasgow, I'd be a 4-10-4. But out here, I was way higher, a 6-10-6, maybe even a 7.

Lack of women, he'd added, with a grin. *Changes the odds.*

So *Seven* became my nickname, a compliment of sorts. The Scottish male version of a compliment.

I'd laughed anyway.

I didn't give a fuck what screwing score they gave me. I knew what my scores for them were. I knew who I'd want stitching me up and who I needed if the skin fried on my body. I knew who would restart my heart and who would be quickest at staunching the flow of blood. Even who I wanted near if the scorpion with the fat tail dropped from the canvas onto my body during the night.

And, best of all, who would make me laugh when everything seemed at an end.

And that was Sugarboy.

I am laughing now, despite the choking red sand that swirls about our blue prison, seeking entrance to it, and us. The cloud that seeks my tight-shut eyes through the prison mesh, and my mouth open from laughing.

Sugarboy joins in, and we laugh the way we'd done back then, before the world as we knew it ended.

It was Sugarboy who had wakened me that fateful night.

'There's a fucking big spider! Quick, Seven. It's on your tits.'

'Fuck off,' I'd said, and rolled over.

Then I'd caught the sweep of the beams and heard the unmistakable sound of the chopper. Something or some-one was coming in.

We were up and ready, hearts beating wilder than the chopper's blades, but cool and calm inside. At that point I'd have scored us all at a 9.

The boy appeared first, alone, limping and crying, the tears streaking through the blood on his face. I waved Mitch away and took charge of him, because kids are less frightened of a woman, even in uniform.

I led him to a bed and started to clean him up, trying to work out whose blood was on him. His or someone else's.

Then the first stretcher appeared, Gordo and *him* carry-ing it.

'A roadside fucking bomb,' Gordo said. I remember at that moment thinking the streaks on his face made by red sand and sweat looked like rivulets of blood.

The stretcher was weighed down by a soldier in full protective gear, which hadn't saved him from the blast. I registered the missing leg and arm, the gaping chest wound . . . and stepped in front of the boy to shield him from the horror, just as the next stretcher arrived via Ben and Charlie.

The shape on it was so fucking small I thought it was another kid, then I registered it was a blood-soaked sniffer dog.

That's all the dying soldier cared about. With his last words he begged us to save his fucking dog and Sugarboy took his remaining hand and promised him that we would.

I'd wiped the boy clean by then, finding only superficial wounds, cuts from stones, not shrapnel. I should have searched him, checked he'd come in via the chopper, but he was just a wide-eyed kid. Wasn't he?

When you think of it that way, *he* was right and it was all my fault it happened.

But back to the dog . . . right front leg looked a goner, but Sugarboy wouldn't hear of taking it off. We set to work, and during that time the boy did what he was there to do.

The chopper never took off again, blown to bits when the boy threw a grenade.

Just far enough away from the blast, Sugarboy, myself, Ben, Charlie . . . and the fat-tailed *scorpion* survived. Gordo and Mitch weren't so lucky.

Or maybe they were the fortunate ones.

The deafening blast hit the tent like a whirlwind. After that, the first thing I remember when I forced my grit-filled eyes open was the boy pointing down at me, a triumphant smile on his face.

Seems I scored a 7 with the enemy too.

'You didn't rape me,' I say as the sandstorm ends and everything becomes quiet again. 'Not even when they threatened to cut off your balls.'

He reaches up and touches my face. I can smell blood on his fingers.

'And I'll kill any bastard who does.'

I know he means it.

26

'What is that?' Chrissy said.

Rhona placed the oval gemstone in the palm of her hand so that they might both take a proper look. Set in an intricately worked metal tin casing, the jewel was a clouded dark blue-green. On one side it was linked to a similarly fashioned but smaller triangular metal piece, without a stone.

'It looks Arabic, like part of a necklace,' Chrissy said.

When Rhona held it up by the short chain, the parts jangled together.

'Not the victim's then?'

It seemed unlikely, but it had been dropped here on the churned-up ground that the dog had led them to. Rhona took a picture of it then dropped it into an evidence bag.

'We're out of time to do this properly,' Chrissy said, glancing at the swiftly darkening sky.

They'd photographed the ground and the footsteps found there. Rhona had counted maybe four sets of boots, of individual sole patterns and sizes, which had imprinted deeply on the moistened ground. None matched the soles of the victim's boots.

She'd also taken soil samples, noting the presence of Sitka spruce needles, some of which she'd also found on the victim's clothing. *Picea sitchensis* wasn't a native conifer.

Introduced to Britain from North America, it was grown in commercial plantations all over the Highlands and, it seemed, also on Skye.

'We'll come back tomorrow, at first light,' Rhona said. 'Look for where the footprints came from.'

The area Blaze had brought them to was apparently the only location that held the victim's scent. After leading them there, the collie had spread his search far and wide, but nowhere else had elicited the same excitement.

'Our victim must have flown over the edge,' Chrissy said, exasperated, as leaving the site in Sergeant Duns's capable hands, they'd begun their trudge back to the car park. 'Or maybe he was carried there?'

That thought had been also in Rhona's mind, but it was a thought only, not a conclusion.

'Maybe Blaze missed the trail near the edge,' she said. 'The rock's exposed there and the rain and snow could have diminished any scent he left behind.'

As if in response to such thoughts, a sleet shower decided to accompany them to the car park, where they discovered that the burger van had shut up shop, much to Chrissy's dismay.

'We'll eat in Portree,' Rhona promised. 'Then head back to the cottage, where I'll no doubt get a check-up call from McNab.' She gave Chrissy a piercing look. 'But then you'd know all about those, wouldn't you?'

'You were the one who chose to become a hermit on Skye,' Chrissy told her testily.

Blaze had gone on ahead and was already reunited with his owner.

'How'd he do?' Donald said as they came in behind the dog.

'Very well,' Rhona said. 'Thanks for the help.'

Donald nodded, aware that Rhona wasn't in a position to give out information.

'We're going to take another look in the morning.'

'D'you want Blaze here?' Donald said.

Rhona thought about it for a second. 'Yes. If you can spare him.'

Chrissy ruffled the dog's ears. 'See, you are taking over my job, and I don't mind a bit.'

'You headed back to the Isles?' Donald asked.

'For food, definitely.'

'Maybe see you there later,' Donald said with a grin.

'You've got a fan,' Rhona told Chrissy as Donald headed for his own vehicle. 'And I don't mean the dog.'

Chrissy threw her a look that suggested such a thing wasn't a rare occurrence, then spotting Alvis's tall figure approaching, went to meet him.

They greeted one another with a big hug, the top of Chrissy's head barely reaching Alvis's chin.

'It's good to see you again, Alvis,' she said.

'And you, Chrissy.'

Rhona suddenly remembered the first time she'd observed them together at the jazz club. McNab had seemingly taken umbrage about what he'd regarded as Inspector Alvis Olsen sticking his nose into his investigation, and Rhona had overheard Chrissy explain about McNab's 'Byronic' character traits and how he'd saved her unborn son's life.

'How is Detective Sergeant McNab?' Alvis was saying. 'I saw him only briefly when he made a Skype call to Rhona.'

This remark brought a twinkle to Chrissy's eye. 'So that's why he was so desperate that I come here. He didn't like the handsome Inspector Olsen having Rhona all to himself.'

Alvis, always the gentleman, merely smiled wryly at such an idea.

Jamie's vehicle was one of the last to leave the car park. Having arrived in thick mist, they departed in utter darkness. For Chrissy, a trip along a dark unlit road 'in the middle of nowhere' reminded her of various horror films she'd seen, which she then proceeded to tell them all about.

In response, Jamie provided them with Skye tales of strange goings-on, of fairies and witches and pacts with the devil.

A quick glance at Chrissy's face suggested at least some of his tales wouldn't be quickly forgotten.

'Your place isn't miles from anywhere, is it?' Chrissy asked Rhona. 'We're not headed for –' she lowered her voice – 'the cabin in the woods?'

'Remember the place we stayed on Sanday?' Rhona reminded her.

'Yes,' Chrissy said suspiciously.

'Well, it's more remote than that,' Rhona told her.

Chrissy groaned. 'But you do have food?'

'We'll fill you up before we leave Portree.'

On arrival at Somerled Square, Rhona indicated she would hand in the evidence she'd collected and catch up with Sergeant MacDonald on developments.

'Don't wait for me before ordering,' she added, noting Chrissy's stricken expression as she imagined a delay before she could eat.

On entry to the station, Rhona was shown through to Lee's office and immediately offered hot tea, which she gratefully accepted.

'It was pretty cold up there on the clifftop,' she admitted, nursing the mug.

'You found something?' Lee said hopefully.

'Blaze did, but not near the edge. Much further back.' Abandoning her mug, Rhona brought up the images she'd taken to show him.

'It looks like a skirmish,' Lee said.

'My thoughts too.'

'So maybe the victim didn't walk to the edge?'

'The dog didn't seem to think so,' Rhona admitted.

'The material you sent via the rib is already on its way to Glasgow with the body,' Lee told her. 'Once we log the clifftop evidence, I'll take you up to the conference room. The team's all there for a debrief.'

As she unpacked her bag, Rhona showed him the clear evidence bag with the gemstone.

Lee peered at it for a moment. 'Skye has a reputation for its jewellery, but this doesn't look local, more oriental. But you never know, someone upstairs might recognize it.'

The conference room on the upper level of the building was packed with officers, some of whom Rhona recognized from Kilt Rock. If this did turn out to be a murder enquiry, more would have to be brought in, together with a serious crime team from the mainland.

The first thing she learned on entry was that Jake Ross had been found. He'd apparently driven to Kyle of Lochalsh, where he'd abandoned the car and caught the Inverness train, eventually turning up at Raigmore hospital, where his wife had died earlier in the year.

'He'd made that journey scores of times to see her, when she was still alive,' Lee explained to Rhona. 'He just forgot that she had gone.'

It was a sad story, but it could have ended much worse, and it meant all their resources could now concentrate on the incident at Kilt Rock.

Lee confirmed that the body had been airlifted to Glasgow rather than Inverness, and that Rhona's forensic examination evidence was following.

Rhona explained about the lack of a scent trail to the cliff edge, and the previous injury to the back of the head. 'I also found evidence of cocaine use in the victim,' Rhona said. 'My forensic assistant brought the news that the soil samples from the site behind A.C.E Target Sports contained benzoylecgonine, which suggests the presence of cocaine.' She turned to Lee. 'You mentioned to Alvis that you'd taken a big haul of cocaine and cannabis recently. I wonder if what's been happening here could be linked in some way to that?'

'We're sharing info all the time on the circulation of heroin. Norway has the same problems as we have, especially the rural areas. Most often the drugs coming into Skye and Lochaber come from Glasgow, via Europe and Scandinavia, a lot of it originating from Afghanistan. We've been speaking to officers in Glasgow including DS McNab about their Sandman operation.' He paused. 'Are you planning to go across for the post-mortem, Dr MacLeod?'

Rhona didn't have an answer to that. If she did go back for the autopsy, she would be unlikely to return, and she wasn't convinced she was ready to do that, just yet.

'Last thing,' Lee was saying, realizing she wasn't going to give an answer on the PM. 'Let's show them the gemstone you found.'

Rhona, having attached her camera to the system, produced the image of the blue-green stone, which caused some interest and chatter among the officers. Eventually one young female constable raised her hand.

'You recognize this?' Lee said.

'My brother was in the army, Sarge. In Afghanistan. He said the British and American planes carpet-bombed the way to Kabul in advance of the friendly northern rebels. When the rocks shattered they revealed semi-precious stones like that one. My brother had one made into a bracelet for his girlfriend.'

27

McNab didn't like visiting hospitals, and this was his second visit in twenty-four hours to the new Queen Elizabeth hospital, or what Glaswegians had ironically named the Death Star.

Riding with the former Private H. McArthur in the ambulance, McNab didn't think the skinny wreck of a bloke lying beside him had a hope in hell of making it. But he was wrong, and mostly thanks to an NHS team who were well versed in dealing with stab wounds. One consolation for being a resident of Glasgow, once the knife capital of Scotland, although much improved in recent times.

McNab had departed once they'd wheeled the victim into surgery, and a call later had informed him that Harry, who he'd ID'd via his dog tag, had survived the operation, the knife hadn't damaged any of his vital organs and he could visit the next day if he wanted to speak to him.

McNab extracted himself from his vehicle and, remote-locking it, made his way towards the entrance. He didn't like mortuaries either, but for whatever reason, the smells of the morgue didn't trigger his PTSD.

That was more random, like the sudden bang on Ashton Lane the previous night or the sounds and scents of a busy hospital, which brought forth ghost pains, as though the bullet wound had never healed. Back when he'd been a patient, he'd understood how folk could get hooked on opiates, having pressed the feed on his morphine drip as often as was allowed.

Standing for a moment at the ward entrance, McNab tried to persuade the PTSD version of himself that he wasn't the one courting death here. That, this time, the black echo wasn't for him.

The nurse on the desk greeted him with a nod.

'How's our patient?' McNab said.

'He's conscious – not sure about lucid, though, if you're planning an interview.'

'So he'll definitely live?'

She threw him a look. 'The knife wound's been dealt with. As to the other ways he's killing himself . . .' She shrugged. 'I see he's been in the wars before.'

'He was a soldier,' McNab said.

A shadow crossed her face. 'That explains the scars then.'

The ones that are visible, McNab thought.

The uniform on duty outside the room stood up on McNab's approach.

'Any visitors or interested parties?'

'None, Sarge.'

The face on the pillow had been scrubbed up, but that hadn't altered the gauntness or the disfigurement. What age was the bastard?

According to his army record, twenty-five going on fucking eighty.

In the darkness of the alley, McNab had barely registered the face. Now he studied it in more detail. Purple shrapnel scars and burn scars pitted Private McArthur's left cheek, neck and chest. No doubt the explosion had fucked with his hearing too. Probably left him with headaches. Being hit in the head by flying shrapnel, McNab had been informed, was like having a knitting needle stabbed into your eardrum. Agonizing, unbearable and long-lasting.

The black echo.

No wonder the poor bastard had looked for a way out of that pain. And heroin, 'the joy plant', had been his saviour.

Registering that someone was in the room, the eyes flickered cautiously open. McNab watched as first confusion then fear flooded them.

'You got stabbed,' McNab said as though this was news. 'Your attacker aimed for the kidneys. You're lucky he missed.' He paused. 'I found you in the alley behind the Rock Cafe and called an ambulance.'

The bewildered look at this part of the story suggested he was perplexed as to why McNab had bothered, then a light bloomed in his eyes.

'You're a fucking cop.'

'Detective Sergeant Michael McNab. Pleased to meet you, Private H. McArthur.' McNab dangled the metal tag he'd recovered at the scene. 'H for Harry, like Prince Harry, that other famous soldier.'

The guy's face suddenly creased up and for a brief and uncomfortable moment McNab thought he would break down and weep. How he might proceed with a sobbing ex-soldier, McNab had no idea. That, he thought, was where DS Clark would have come in useful.

However, the tears did not materialize. Prince Harry instead tried to pull himself up in the bed, which was an obviously painful experience.

'Better not to do that,' McNab offered. 'I speak from experience, mate.'

'When can I get out of here?'

'That's for the doctors to decide.'

He shot McNab a worried look. 'Are you arresting me?'

'For what? Getting stabbed in an alley?'

An idea seemed to come to him and he said, 'I did it myself. Wanted it all over with.'

McNab assumed a thoughtful expression. 'You did? What happened to the knife?'

By his lack of response, Harry hadn't worked on that aspect of his story yet.

McNab carried on with his own version. 'One Malcolm Stevenson, commonly known as Wee Malky, left the Rock Cafe by the fire escape that led to the alley where you were. I followed him.'

A glimmer of recognition and fear played on McArthur's face before he shook his head. 'I was out of it, didn't see anyone.'

McNab nodded as though he understood his reticence.

'Why'd you quit the army, Private?'

The question caught him off guard, so his answer, when it came, was close to the truth – as revealed by McNab's recent enquiries.

'They chucked me out.' He pointed to his scarred face. 'Not pretty enough for their recruitment videos.'

McNab smiled. 'Didn't want to frighten the troops, eh?' He paused. 'Where are you staying, soldier?'

McArthur gave a dismissive laugh. 'Well, it's not in a home for heroes.'

'What if I found you somewhere to go when you get out of here?' McNab offered.

Suspicion snaked across the marked face.

'Like a cell, you mean?'

'Like a room. Somewhere you can recover.' McNab almost added, *and maybe hide from Malky*, but didn't.

'You think you're fucking Santa Claus?'

'Maybe Christmas just came early for you.'

McNab emerged into the night air and took a deep, cold breath.

Despite his questions, Prince Harry had stuck to his story that he'd stabbed himself and dropped the knife down a nearby stank, somewhere between his Argyle Street pitch and the alley.

Drains would have to be checked in the vicinity, of course, but McNab knew the story to be a big fat lie. If what he imagined had happened was in fact true, then McArthur was well aware that once Malky found out he was alive, he and others would come looking for him. Then he would indeed become dead meat, whether he got his next heroin hit or not.

The question McNab now asked himself was why, when he knew McNab was likely tailing him, would Malky stab McArthur on his way out?

An answer immediately presented itself.

He thought I would ignore what looked like a spaced-out junkie and, for whatever reason, he wanted McArthur dead.

The why of that was what McNab found most interesting.

It was a legal requirement that notification should be made to the MOD if any serving soldier was arrested. One who had been discharged under a cloud, the MOD weren't so interested in. Even if the former soldier had been injured in the line of duty.

If the army was a family, McNab had discovered in the process of his enquiry, it was one that was no longer interested in its son Private Harry McArthur.

McNab wondered what it was Prince Harry had done to piss them off so badly. He hadn't been jailed, as far as McNab was aware, but he'd obviously committed some sort of crime while serving. If he was already using out there in Afghanistan, and let's face it, there was an ample supply, then that in itself would have been enough. If they suspected he was involved in a supply line . . .

McNab found himself nursing a suspicion that getting to know Prince Harry better might just bring him a little closer to the Sandman.

28

Rhona crossed the silent square to the welcome lights of the Isles hotel.

The clouds had departed and above her the night sky was lit by a myriad of stars. It would be colder tonight because of it. She thought of the cottage, any heat from the stove having long ago dissipated in her absence.

Had she been back in Glasgow, the central heating would have kicked on with the timer, allowing her to arrive back to a warm flat. The thought surprised her because it was, she realized, the first time she'd recalled her home in a positive light since she'd come to Skye.

As for the cold welcome they would get at the cottage – no amount of reassurances on her part about how quickly it would heat up once the stove was lit would be enough for a shivering Chrissy.

Rhona wondered if it might be better to stay in Portree tonight, since they were heading out early again in the morning. Then there was the post-mortem to think about. They had conference facilities at the police station, and she could talk McNab into going along to the autopsy and keeping her in the loop. There was so much about the victim's wounds, especially the old one, that might help give a clearer picture of what the hell was going on here.

The revelation that the dropped necklace may have had

its origins in Afghanistan had reminded her of the party of medics, who'd seemingly left A.C.E Target Sports unhurt, only to head off into the wild places of Skye.

Lee had voiced the same thought at the end of the meeting.

'We'd better check on their whereabouts or at least if they're still on Skye. See if the Isles have info on any of them.'

Gazing round the busy bar, Rhona spotted her team close to the roaring fire and, by the satisfied expression on Chrissy's face, it looked as though they'd already been fed. Chrissy was deep in conversation with Donald, while Blaze was performing nearby for a party of tourists keen to have him catch a tennis ball in mid-air.

When Jamie spotted her, he waved Rhona over.

'We saved a seat for you. And your fish and chips will be here just as soon as I let them know you've arrived.'

Glancing round them all, Rhona noted that Alvis was missing.

'He went upstairs,' Jamie said. 'Something about checking in back home in Stavanger. Can I get you something to drink?'

'Something non-alcoholic. I've an hour's drive ahead of me.'

Now in the warmth, the idea of driving back to the undoubtedly cold cottage only to return first thing tomorrow morning seemed even less appealing. Rhona wondered if Jamie was reading her mind, because he immediately said, 'You can stay over again if you want.'

Before Rhona could say, 'What about Chrissy?' Jamie had supplied her with an answer. 'There's a sofa bed in the sitting room.'

When Rhona still hesitated, he added, 'You'd save Chrissy from a night in the cabin in the woods and –' he nodded at the hilarity coming from the corner – 'she does seem to like it here.'

She does indeed, Rhona thought.

'Okay, I'll speak to Chrissy. And thanks.'

'You're welcome, but you know that.' Jamie smiled. 'And here comes your food.'

Ten minutes later, her plate cleared, Rhona checked out the area around the bar.

Lee had requested she ask at the hotel if they had a mobile number for the medic team who'd stayed there. There was no reception area in the small hotel, both room and meal bookings being managed via a laptop behind the bar, which was currently too busy to deal with her request. Rhona decided it could wait, especially now she wasn't setting off on the hour's drive from Portree to Armadale.

Unusually for Chrissy, she'd merely waved at Rhona but had not yet made any attempt to come and engage her in conversation, which suggested she was definitely enjoying herself.

Rhona thought again how pleased she'd been to see Chrissy on the shore. Back then Chrissy's head had been encased in a parka, then in a forensic suit. Now Rhona could admire the current hair colour, which, she realized, resembled a rainbow that shone radiantly in the firelight.

Relaxing back in the chair, her appetite appeased, Rhona sampled the whisky Jamie had brought her and decided that she was indeed a fan of Talisker. That thought brought an image of McNab trying valiantly to Skype her.

Her plan had been to make contact with him tomorrow

morning, but she was sufficiently in the zone now to face him tonight. Only problem was, where exactly? It was much too noisy in here, even though there was a decent signal, and she didn't fancy heading back out in the cold to visit the police station. She could wait until she was back at Jamie's, but by the look of things that might not be for some time. She decided to head for the bar, where the queue to be served had diminished.

'Sergeant MacDonald asked me to check if you had contact details for the medics who stayed here recently?'

The girl nodded. 'The Norwegian policeman asked the same thing when he came back from Kilt Rock. They booked one night for the five of them all under one name. Pete Galbraith. He used his credit card. I gave Inspector Olsen the email used in the booking.' She paused, a look of horror crossing her face. 'You don't think . . .?'

'I think Sergeant MacDonald's just concerned about them camping in this weather,' Rhona reassured her. 'Which room is Alvis in?'

'First floor, room six.'

Rhona took off before any more questions might be posed regarding the identity of the victim. No doubt the islanders would be busy trying to work out who might have been found on the beach. What little had been released left room for speculation and Rhona didn't want to add any more.

According to Lee, 'News travels at the speed of light round the island. Speculation even faster.'

Rhona eased her way past the performing Blaze and, exiting the bar, climbed to the first floor. Listening for a moment outside room six to assure herself Alvis was inside, she knocked.

'Alvis, it's Rhona.'

There was a squeaking sound as though he'd been sitting or lying on the bed, then the creak of flooring and the door opened.

'I wondered if I might use your room to Skype McNab?' Rhona said. 'I've decided to stay over here tonight again and downstairs is too noisy for a conversation.'

Alvis hesitated but only briefly, then flung the door open wide. 'As you can see, the room's not very big,' he warned her, 'and you'll have to sit on the bed, but other than that you're welcome.'

He was right about the room. The double bed took up most of the space, even though, in his meticulous fashion, Alvis had carefully placed his belongings to allow the most vacant floor space.

'I was just checking in myself,' he told her.

'How's Stavanger?'

'Cold and snowy like here.'

Alvis began folding up the map he'd had spread out on the bed.

'I heard you were asking for a contact for the soldiers?' Rhona said.

'Lee asked me to check. They gave me an email address. I've sent a message and copied in Lee, but no reply as yet. Then again, if their intention was to go off-grid, that's not surprising. I was studying the map, wondering where they might have gone.

'Do you want me to make myself scarce while you Skype?' Alvis offered.

'No need,' Rhona assured him, texting McNab as she said it.

Minutes later, her mobile signalled an incoming Skype

call, then McNab's face appeared on the screen. He looked pleased to see her.

'Busy day, Dr MacLeod?'

'Very.'

'Heard all about it. Your body's in the mortuary. Your evidence is at the lab. How's Chrissy doing?'

'Thanks for sending her.'

'The boss's idea, but I'm happy to take the credit.'

She knew by the change of expression that McNab had just spied the man behind her. Plus, he'd probably registered the fact that she was in a bedroom.

'I'm in Alvis's room at the Isles,' Rhona said. 'The bar's too noisy to talk.'

McNab's face showed his disquiet at that information. 'So what's wrong with the cottage?' he demanded.

'It's an hour away, and since we need to be back sharp in the morning, I've decided to stay here tonight,' Rhona told him.

By his expression McNab was factoring in the possibility that she actually meant she was staying at the Isles, maybe even in this particular room.

Rhona read the look, which clearly said, *with him?* and smothered a laugh. Winding McNab up was normally Chrissy's job, but she found she was rather enjoying it.

She decided to put him right, knowing that the truth might annoy him just as much. 'I'm staying at Jamie's again.'

She watched as McNab considered the implications of that, before he came fighting back.

'I spoke to *Sean* last night,' he said, a penetrating look on his face. 'He said you hadn't been in touch with him. At all,' he added for emphasis.

She hadn't and felt bad about it, but that didn't mean it was any of McNab's damn business.

Whatever fun she'd had ribbing McNab was now over.

'I'd like you to attend the PM,' Rhona said. 'There's an earlier wound on the back of the head. Find out if it's got traces of birch tree in it. It might just be the injured party from the woods. His face is unrecognizable, pulp mostly, and his body's pretty mangled too,' she added, 'so it won't be pretty.'

This was her revenge for the Sean jibe. McNab wasn't squeamish in the field but he had no love of the mortuary and the sound of electric drills and saws.

He forced a smile. 'No problem, Dr MacLeod. I'll report back on that.'

'Also, the rocks he hit are basalt, but there might be an earlier wound in the face that the fall obliterated. Have the pathologist check for metal residue.'

'From what?' McNab sounded interested now.

'A knife, an axe.'

'Fuck's sake. It's the Wild West out there. Puts Glasgow to shame.'

'Also, he'd been handling cocaine, and with no ID on him, and the big haul they took here recently . . .'

'You and Sergeant MacDonald wondered if there might be a Sandman connection?'

'You can read my mind,' Rhona said briskly.

'And that, Dr MacLeod, is not always pleasant.'

Rhona ignored the snide remark.

'One other thing: there were some soldiers, medics, from Glasgow at the Isles hotel for a night. They've gone off-grid, camping supposedly. The card they booked under was Pete Galbraith.' She spelled out the email address Alvis handed her. 'Could Ollie check him out?'

'Glad to be of service, Dr MacLeod,' McNab said, somewhat sarcastically.

The *boing* sounded as Rhona broke the connection first. 'Prick,' she said under her breath.

Alvis, standing by the window, turned and waited silently without comment.

'Detective Sergeant McNab and I go back a long way, but he still gets on my tits sometimes,' Rhona said, exasperated.

Alvis laughed. A deep, infectious sound. Rhona found her anger dissipating as she joined in.

Alvis produced a whisky bottle from the cupboard and waved it at her.

'Shall we discuss these medics and take a look at the map?'

'One thing before we do,' she said, accepting the drink he'd poured for her. 'I retrieved Sitka spruce needles both from the victim's clothing and the area Blaze identified on the clifftop.'

'There's no Sitka spruce cover near Kilt Rock?'

'Nor in the woods behind A.C.E, which is native birch.'

'So the victim had likely been in a Sitka plantation, of which I fear there are many hectares on Skye.'

'I suggest we try and identify them,' Rhona said. 'Since that may have been the last place the victim was alive.'

29

Rolling over in the bed, Rhona reached out to douse her phone alarm. Above her the skylight window offered a vision of a red-and-blue-streaked dawn complete with scurrying grey clouds.

The night before had gone on longer than she'd anticipated, but the detailed discussion with Alvis had proved useful. They'd spent some time identifying the tracts of land laid down with Sitka spruce, which turned out to be fewer acres than they'd imagined.

Skye's landmass according to Google Earth was 639 square miles. Looking at the forest cover, they'd identified four plantations, covering roughly 5 per cent of the total acreage.

'Tightly packed, with little to no wildlife to be heard or seen, and no undergrowth,' Alvis had said. 'Most likely planted between the sixties and eighties for commercial reasons. They're not managed woodland for walking in.'

'What about this one?' Rhona had indicated the green block further along the B885. 'I think the party exited the woods just beyond Matt's place. If they headed away from Portree, that's the closest plantation to their route.'

'We could take a look that way tomorrow?' Alvis had suggested. 'Unless you're heading back to Kilt Rock.'

It was at that point Rhona had decided to leave the

remainder of the work on the clifftop to Chrissy, but when she and Alvis went back to the bar, Chrissy was no longer there to tell her so.

'She's gone off somewhere with Donald,' Jamie had informed her. 'Last I heard he was describing his favourite excursions round the island, all of which seemed to include the word fairy in the title . . . the Fairy Glen, Fairy Pools and a few even I haven't heard of. Chrissy said to tell you she'd see us later at my place.'

'Which I think I'd like to head for shortly,' Rhona said.

The next morning, showered and dressed, Rhona headed downstairs to give Chrissy her instructions for the day, only to discover the bed settee, which Jamie had made up in preparation for her forensic assistant's late return, lay unmarked by evidence that anyone had slept there.

'Coffee?' Jamie called from the kitchen.

'Please,' Rhona said. 'And some of that bacon I can smell.'

When Jamie brought through her bacon roll and coffee, she raised an eyebrow and said, 'I take it Chrissy never came home?'

'Looks like it.' He gave her a knowing smile in return.

As if on cue, the front door opened and in walked Rhona's wandering assistant.

'That smells good. Anything left for me?' She gave them a wide grin.

'Of course,' Jamie said.

When Jamie had disappeared into the kitchen, Chrissy threw Rhona an *I've got stuff to tell you* look. 'I learned a lot about Skye last night. Even managed some Gaelic.'

Rhona decided not to ask any questions. The likelihood

was, the less she asked, the keener Chrissy would be to tell her.

'I thought you could cover the clifftop this morning,' Rhona said, ignoring the gesture from Chrissy suggesting they go somewhere out of earshot. 'Jamie will go with you.'

Chrissy's expressions were getting wilder, so Rhona gave in and motioned that they should go upstairs.

Once inside Rhona's room, Chrissy closed the door.

'I stayed with Donald last night out at A.C.E Target Sports.'

Rhona's expression suggested she'd guessed that already.

'We talked about the group of medics who were game-playing up there. The ones that stayed at the Isles for a night?'

Rhona nodded. 'And?'

'Donald said one of them, the girl, was an excellent axe thrower. Also very good with a knife. He said one guy was complaining about the games being child's play for them, because they'd seen the real thing in Afghanistan. And he preferred throwing full-sized axes, rather than the tomahawk version.'

Rhona listened in silence, before reminding Chrissy that Donald had also said the group had left without a scratch on them.

Chrissy nodded. 'I know, but Donald said that later in the pub they were all drinking shots and whooping when they heard the coastguard helicopter go over. It was as though they were back in the field. In retrospect, Donald wondered if they were planning something.'

'Their camping trip, perhaps?' Rhona tried, although following Chrissy's story, it might as easily have been a return trip to the woods, to play a more realistic game.

'And,' by Chrissy's expression, she was coming to the main point of her story, 'Donald said he walked in on one of the males in the toilet. He says he was pretty sure the guy was high.'

'Has he told Lee about this?'

'He said if he told the police every time he thought a visitor to Skye was high . . .'

'Can Donald provide a good description of them?'

'I'd say so. He's an observer, likes watching people.'

'Does Donald have any thoughts on where the group might have gone?'

'He says it depends if they want to be found or not.' Chrissy paused. 'Is McNab going to the PM?'

Rhona nodded.

'Then we'll maybe know more about our beach victim after that.'

A shout from below indicated Jamie was ready to depart.

They split forces outside Jamie's place, Chrissy and Jamie taking his jeep, while Rhona asked Donald, who'd arrived in the interim, if Blaze might go with her and Alvis, instead of accompanying Chrissy.

'Sure,' Donald said, a little puzzled by this new development. 'D'you need me along?'

'Alvis and I can manage, if you're okay about being separated from Blaze. I can drop him back at A.C.E Target Sports?'

'I'll be at the Isles until mid-afternoon.' Donald hesitated. 'Did Chrissy mention the bloke in the loo?'

'She did. I think you should run that past Lee. He'll want to know.'

Donald looked perturbed by her suggestion. 'I don't

want to drop anyone in it. I didn't find any evidence that he was using. Even if he was, it wouldn't be the first time a visitor had enhanced their visit to Skye.'

'It's still important to tell Sergeant MacDonald,' Rhona said.

However much she might personally trust Jamie or Donald, she couldn't reveal the evidence of cocaine deposits in the woods behind A.C.E, and on the victim's clothing on the beach, so she would have to rely on encouragement only.

Donald was eyeing her keenly. 'Okay, I'll check in with Lee now.' He called Blaze and told him to go with Rhona. 'Same commands as before,' he reminded her, before heading in the direction of the police station.

Rhona had gained the impression that Donald would have liked to ask where she was going with the dog, probably also offer his help. The rules of engagement didn't quite work here on Skye, she realized, because local knowledge and help were essential. However, explaining why they were interested in visiting a Sitka spruce plantation would mean revealing the Sitka evidence, and she wasn't prepared to do that as yet.

McNab's mantra came to mind: *Everyone is guilty until proven innocent.*

'Apart from you,' Rhona said quietly as she ruffled Blaze's ears.

30

The boss asked about Rhona the moment McNab walked into his office.

'She's back on the job, sir,' McNab answered, hoping that was true.

DI Wilson absorbed McNab's news. 'So, she's coming for the PM on the cliff victim?'

'No, sir.' McNab tried to look unconcerned by this. 'She asked me to attend. Gave me some things to look out for,' he added for good measure.

'So, she's not actually back at work. This is more of a holiday job?'

'It's better than nothing, sir,' McNab suggested.

The boss gave a grunt that may have been positive or negative, McNab wasn't sure.

'Rhona also asked me to check out a serving army medic, name of Pete Galbraith. There were five of them staying in the Isles hotel for a night. They went survival camping after that. You'll get a request in from Sergeant MacDonald at Portree too.'

'What's the interest in these men?'

'Four men and one woman, sir, but we only have one name.' McNab paused. 'Rhona didn't say exactly, but I suspect she thinks they may have been involved in the probable crime scene behind A.C.E Target Sports.'

'Okay, Sergeant. See what you can find out about this medic.'

As McNab made for the door, another question followed him.

'How's your patient?'

The question caught McNab off guard, because he wasn't sure how much the boss knew regarding the incident in the alley, and he also had plans of his own regarding Prince Harry. Plans he didn't want to reveal as yet.

'He'll live, sir,' McNab offered cautiously.

'Has he given us anything on his attacker?'

'Claims he stabbed himself and dropped the knife down a drain.'

'Does that sound plausible to you?'

McNab couldn't lie. 'No, sir.'

'Could it be a turf war?'

'Maybe.'

'Keep me informed, Sergeant,' DI Wilson ordered, before answering the phone ringing insistently on his desk.

McNab allowed himself a small sigh of relief as he closed the door behind him. He hadn't formulated how he planned to play Prince Harry, and he didn't want any possible moves forbidden in advance.

Next visit was to Ollie, but never without offerings. McNab made a quick trip to the canteen, settling on two sugar-coated ring doughnuts for his bespectacled accomplice and two black coffees. He'd never worked out Ollie's schedule, because he always seemed to be at work in front of his screens.

As he was again today.

Catching sight of McNab, Ollie pointedly checked out the contents of the paper bag he was handed.

'How did you know?' he said with a grin.

'I have my spies,' McNab said, recalling Maria behind the counter's advice.

'The girl with the red hair?' Ollie said shyly.

'She's got a definite soft spot for you.'

Ollie blinked behind his glasses, a small flush finding his cheeks.

'Fuck's sake, Ollie, you've done nothing about it?'

'I help her with her social media, Instagram, that sort of thing.'

'Ask her round to your place next time, so she can see your big screen set-up,' McNab advised. 'But tidy the place up first. I remember the night I slept on your couch. Once I found it,' he added, thinking he was one to talk about a tidy flat.

Since Ellie had moved back to her own place, he'd let things slide. *Slide? The place was a pigsty.*

'So what can I do you for, Detective Sergeant?'

'Pete Galbraith. Here's his email address. He's supposedly an army medic on leave, currently somewhere on Skye, we think. He used his credit card to book rooms for himself and four others at the Isles Inn, Portree.'

Ollie gave a small nod. 'Has this got anything to do with Dr MacLeod?'

'It does,' McNab said.

'Then I'll start on it right away. How's Dr MacLeod doing?'

'Better, I think,' McNab said, hoping it was true.

Ollie looked pleased by that. 'She coming back soon, then?'

'I'm working on it,' McNab promised.

*

Back in the office, he located Detective Sergeant Clark and brought her up to date, specifically on Rhona, while strategically avoiding mention of Prince Harry. Unfortunately for McNab, his partner could, it seemed, read him like a book.

'What about your stab victim?'

'Recovering.'

'What happens when they discharge him?' Janice demanded.

McNab shook his head as though he hadn't given it a moment's thought.

'How long do you think the poor bugger will last on the streets?' Janice challenged him.

'Not long,' McNab admitted, wondering where exactly Janice was going with this.

'So what's your plan?'

'I haven't got one,' he tried.

Janice snorted. 'You always have a plan. Screwed-up or otherwise. As your partner, I demand to know what it is.'

McNab decided to oblige her. 'I find him a safe place to recuperate.'

'A hostel is the first place they'd look, if he does know something.' She halted. 'Or maybe our Harry was just in the wrong place at the wrong time?'

'Then we don't have to worry about him.' McNab quickly changed the subject to avoid telling Janice what he really intended doing. 'I'm off to the post-mortem on the Skye body. The boss knows,' he added, to make everything legitimate.

'You'll miss the strategy meeting,' she warned.

'Then you can tell me about it later.'

'Enjoy your post-mortem,' Janice called to McNab's retreating figure.

31

Afghanistan

The stones of my prison tell my story. A vertical scratch for each sunrise, a cross for each visitation. One scratched heart only, for Sugarboy.

He said something to me the night of the sandstorm. Couldn't remember where he'd heard or read it, but it had stuck with him, just as it does with me.

All the Gods, the Heavens and the Hells are within us.

They came for him as soon as the sand settled. By then he'd left my blue prison and sat shivering in the cold desert air against the far wall. He didn't want to give them the satisfaction of thinking he might have done what they'd demanded.

The two who came in for him were unnerved by something, jabbering wildly and seemingly uninterested in either of us. Except that as they dragged Sugarboy away, the younger one looked directly at me and said a word in Pashto I understood. Nurse.

I have seen the women walk by my prison. Indistinguishable one from another, the age and shape made one, under the blue robe. Sometimes they are together in a group, on their way to fetch water.

I know that at the water source, free from male eyes,

they will gossip and laugh together. I know this because in one of the villages we'd visited earlier, our commander had repaired their well, only to discover it had been the women who'd damaged it, because they enjoyed their walks together to the river where they could speak freely without the men.

Sugarboy gone, my only company is the black scorpion venturing out to meet the day. I greet him, savouring again the fact he is my way out of here, forever, if I so choose.

He chose the name *Scorpion* for himself, just as he'd given me *Seven*, Pete *Sugarboy*, Ben *Mountain* and Charlie *Chucky*. Not forgetting the dead, Mitch *Stitcher* and Gordo *One Ball*. I know now the nicknames weren't bestowed on his brothers through affection and camaraderie, but to remodel them to suit himself.

His own choice of name was perhaps the most apt. While I dutifully sprayed the tent to dissuade the scorpions from entering, the human Scorpion captured a prize black specimen and ran bets on it. Sugarboy, the inveterate gambler, tried hard to find a suitable opponent, only to watch them all lose the fight and die.

The door scrapes open and in they come, the young one leading the way. He drags me to my feet, shouting something I don't understand. In this moment I believe I am about to be executed. Shot or perhaps beheaded, like the Afghan women who displease them.

The sun blinds me as I exit, the mesh of my blue prison no protection for my light-starved eyes. I am not allowed to raise my head, to look on men, but I try, seeking the others. Are they to be executed with me?

I am led towards a mud building and thrust through a curtained doorway into dim light again.

I make out the white of their eyes beyond the veil, then as my guards depart, an excited babble explodes about me. A female hand touches me. Urges me gently forward. We all pass through a further curtain. In here there is a light of sorts. Suddenly all the blue burkas are discarded, including my own. I look on female faces, some bright and inquisitive, others frightened or disapproving, while they react to my blood-streaked nakedness with a high cry of 'eeee'.

I find a robe thrust into my hand and I pull it over my head. Now we are all equally clad. Their relief meets in a concentrated sigh.

The hand that directed me is owned by a girl, barely in her teens. She points to a figure on a raised platform covered by rugs, whose moans are swallowed in the rag she has stuffed into her mouth.

I translate her words as 'Please help.'

32

The road, a dark ribbon, wound out before them. Above, the sky hung grey and heavy, the quality of light suggesting dusk rather than day.

Skye has never looked more magnificently ominous, Rhona thought, *as though we are headed into its heart without permission.*

Despite the feeling of foreboding, she loved this landscape. If a dinosaur was suddenly to appear from behind a promontory, she wouldn't have been the least surprised. As it was, an Arctic hare, foraging between the patches of snow, barely cast them a glance as the 4x4 drove past, headlights blazing through the gloom. A red deer lifted its head, but only for a moment before returning to its grazing.

We are insignificant. A moving dot on a landscape that belongs to them.

'You okay?' Alvis said, casting her a sideways glance.

Rhona murmured 'fine' in response, while registering the increasing frequency of Alvis's enquiries as to her current state of mind. It seemed Alvis might be taking over from McNab as her minder.

'Stop here,' Rhona said, suddenly realizing what they were about to pass.

As a surprised Alvis drew in, Blaze gave a little yelp, perhaps in recognition of where they were.

Rhona unstrapped herself and stepped out of the vehicle. The wind, although not strong, was more than a little cold. Though no more snow had fallen overnight, temperatures had remained below freezing.

'Is this where they parked the vehicle?' Alvis asked.

Rhona nodded.

'You didn't go further than this?'

'No. Blaze and I headed back in the direction of A.C.E Target Sports by foot, then Donald picked us up.'

The muddy lay-by was churned up even more than Rhona remembered. Lee had sent out a team here as requested, who'd attempted to take tyre-track imprints. Useful, but only if they came up with a vehicle to check them against.

'We're not far from the Sitka plantation.' Alvis glanced up at the glowering sky. 'Forecast's for rain, though.'

'Let's go then.'

Rhona held the map open on her knees. From their research, she was aware that many of the marked plantations had been planted in difficult terrain in the seventies, when wealthy folk were encouraged to tax-dodge by putting their money into forestry.

Some of these forests had failed to thrive, their roots in boggy ground. Others hadn't been harvested, because extraction had proved to be too expensive.

From the map, the B885 ran through the southern reaches of the plantation they were focusing on. Two tracks led from the tarred road to a summit named Beinn a' Ghlinne Bhig. Separated by a hundred yards, both wound their way up through the Sitka plantation, the second looking more like vehicle access than a footpath.

Rhona said as much to Alvis.

'If anyone wanted to take a vehicle off-road among the trees, the second track looks like the one they would choose.'

Alvis braked a little as the road curved suddenly westwards and started to climb. Soon they left the moorland and entered the plantation, a barrier of tall Sitka towering on either side of the car. Passing the first lay-by, Rhona spotted the wall of rock she'd noted via Google Earth, signalling the entrance they sought.

Alvis pulled into a good-sized gravelled parking area, just left of a double gate.

'We're walking from here?' he checked.

'Yes,' Rhona said, jumping out and opening the back door for Blaze.

The uphill track was mostly clear of snow, although the densely packed trees alongside still wore a mantle from the last fall.

Blaze ran ahead, his nose to the ground.

Rhona held out little hope that the dog might locate the victim's scent in the vicinity, although the dog had been eager to play that game again. Everything they did at the moment was a longshot, but it was worth a try.

They trudged upwards in silence, the big collie leading the way. The closely packed trees on either side suggested straying from the path wouldn't be easy, or pleasant. This was further enforced when they reached a wide clearing hosting a small cairn that indicated a forest path to Beinn a' Ghlinne Bhig off to their right.

Staring at the densely packed branches where the path was supposed to be, Alvis said, 'I guess the sign went up a decade before this lot of trees matured?'

'Shall we check, just in case?' Rhona said.

As they crossed the turning circle, it was obvious one or more vehicles had been there in recent times. A deep set of tracks suggested one at least had sat for a while, its markings deep in the muddy ground.

'It looks like someone's had a go at the supposed path,' Rhona said, indicating the churned-up bank that led down into the trees.

Blaze, realizing their intentions, took the lead again. The going was easier for the collie, as he made his way below the branches.

'He certainly knows how to blaze a trail,' Alvis joked. 'It's times like this I wish I wasn't quite as tall.'

Rhona was already ahead, ducking in pursuit of the dog. Someone had definitely been there before them, the lower Sitka branches snapped off in their attempt to force a way through. Underfoot, there was a path of sorts, because she wasn't stumbling over the ridges and troughs normally found in a planted forest.

Still, an ordinary walker would surely have given up, Rhona thought after only a few yards, *and sought an alternative route to the trig point.*

The air, she registered, was cold and still and soundless, and the deeper she'd penetrated, the darker the way had become. She halted for a moment and tried to breathe in what little oxygen seemed to linger between the tightly packed branches, increasingly aware of what was about to happen.

The sense of being suffocated rose, flirting with her at first, although she knew if she didn't succeed in controlling it, it would swamp her. The fight was mental, yet her hands fisted themselves in preparation for the fray. Memories assailed her, playing out in smell and sound and blackness. Invisible soil found her throat and closed it. She coughed, spitting out the imagined foe. Her fisted hands found the bark of the nearest tree and beat at it, as though it was her jailer.

And still she did not let herself scream.

The physical fight back seemed to reassert the rational in her brain. She wasn't being buried alive, it told her. This episode will pass, like all the others before it. There was a sky up there, vast and endless, beyond the dense blanket of dark green.

Time, which had stretched out like an elastic band, sprang abruptly back into shape.

She registered where she was and that, thankfully, Alvis had yet to appear, so wouldn't have seen her fight her way out of the recurrent nightmare that had haunted her since her last case in Glasgow. Feeling the warm trickle of blood on her hands, she noted the damage done to her knuckles.

Something that could be easily lied about, considering the terrain.

In the interim, Blaze, it appeared, had completely deserted her. Rhona was now besieged by the worrying thought that she might have lost Donald's dog, something Chrissy would never forgive her for, never mind Donald.

'Blaze,' she shouted. 'Here to me.'

An answering bark seemed to come from ahead and to her right, although in the thickness of the forest it was hard to tell.

Hearing Alvis's approach, Rhona prepared herself, not wishing for another enquiry about her well-being. When he appeared from under a low-lying branch, she noted he too was bleeding.

'What happened to your head?'

He reached up to where she'd pointed and wiped the blood away. 'It's like walking through a maze of sharpened knives,' he said.

'Tell me about it.' Rhona showed him her own injuries.

'What were you doing?' he said, obviously taken aback by the state of her knuckles, which had begun to swell. 'Punching the trees?'

She was saved further comment by a flurry of excited barking suggesting that Blaze might well have found something. This was quickly followed by a female voice indicating surprise at the dog's arrival. Heading towards the sounds of their interchange, Rhona emerged into a clearing, housing a single-person tent and various bits of equipment, to find a young woman patting Blaze.

'You came through the plantation?' she said with a look of amazement.

'It wasn't easy,' Rhona said. 'Except for Blaze, that is.'

'I came that way too, but I had to hack a bit to get here. Then I discovered it was easier to approach from the trig point itself.' She gestured to a more obvious path on the opposite side of the small clearing.

Rhona introduced herself. 'Rhona MacLeod, and this is Blaze.'

The dog was whining now, staying close by the girl in a protective manner. When Rhona gave the 'Here to me' command, it had to be said twice. Even then Blaze didn't seem keen to leave the girl's side.

'I know Blaze,' she offered as way of an explanation for the dog's determined behaviour. 'From the Isles bar and A.C.E Target Sports.'

'You were there with the group of army medics?' Rhona voiced what she'd suspected since finding the camp.

The girl looked surprised by the question. 'Yes.'

At this point, she registered Alvis's presence. The swift glance the girl threw him moved from surprise to recognition and Rhona realized she must have spotted Alvis the night of the drinking session.

'The Portree police are keen to make contact with you and your colleagues,' Rhona explained. 'Check you're okay out on the hills in this weather. They like to take care of their tourists on Skye,' she added with a reassuring smile.

'We've all served in Afghanistan,' the girl said. 'Believe me, we can take anything Skye throws at us.'

'Sergeant MacDonald'll be pleased to hear that. Are the others about?'

The girl shook her head. 'We all split up. The plan was to do our own thing for a bit before we head back to Glasgow.'

It sounded plausible.

'Where's your vehicle?' Alvis said.

'The guys took it. Why?' She appeared a little ruffled by the questions.

Rhona decided to tell her what had happened, as much to view her reaction as anything else. 'A man's body was found on the shore at Kilt Rock. It looked like he'd fallen from the cliff. No ID on him. The police are keen to eliminate any walkers or climbers on the island.'

'Oh my God!' The girl's hand rose to her mouth in what looked like genuine distress. 'When did this happen?'

She looked so upset, Rhona had to tell her the truth. 'The body was spotted the day before yesterday.'

The girl's relief at this news was palpable. She sat down abruptly as though her legs could no longer hold her, colour rushing back into an ashen face. 'So it can't be any of the boys. They all left here yesterday.'

Rhona almost believed her.

'Are you something to do with the police? Is that how you know all this?' the girl said.

'MRT volunteers,' Alvis swiftly told her. 'Can you make contact with your colleagues? Check they're still okay?'

'We're off-grid. That's the rule when we're practising survival techniques. Mobiles are switched off unless there's an emergency.'

'When do you plan to meet up?' Rhona asked.

'Three days' time in the square in Portree.'

'Will they come for you?' Alvis said.

'I'll walk in. Portree's not far.'

While they'd been talking, Blaze had moved back to the girl, sniffing her scent.

'You've got a real friend there,' Rhona said.

A flash of what might have been concern or fear on the girl's face vanished as swiftly as it had appeared, causing Rhona to wonder if she'd imagined it.

'Can I give you my number?' she said on the spur of the moment. 'So you can let us know when you're back safely in town.'

The girl looked perplexed by such an idea. 'Okay,' she said finally, accepting the hastily scribbled number.

Rhona called Blaze to her side again.

'We'll tell Sergeant MacDonald we met you, and that the guys are okay too.'

'Thanks,' the girl said.

'You didn't mention your name?'

'Seven,' the girl offered. 'The guys call me Seven.'

'You're their lucky mascot?'

She gave a half-smile.

*

Emerging from the trees, the heather-topped hill of Beinn a′ Ghlinne Bhig presented itself.

'She was right,' Alvis said. 'That was easier.'

The rain came on as they headed down a narrow path that would take them, they hoped, to the main track.

Rhona, leading the way, didn't attempt a conversation until they met the turning circle again and could walk side by side.

'She never gave up her real name. Nor did she mention any of the others by name,' she said.

'And that bothers you?'

'Why do you think they christened her Seven?'

'Maybe there were seven in the group at one time,' Alvis said. 'Or else . . .'

When he didn't finish, Rhona said it for him. 'That was her fuckable rating among the men.'

33

McNab, fully suited now, took a final breath of fresh air before securing his mask.

Through the glass panels he could see that Dr Sissons was already at work. The second pathologist, required by Scots law, was likely Dr Walker, who'd processed the second victim in the sin-eater case.

The victim had already been stripped of his clothing by the two forensic assistants, who were currently taping his nether regions, every move of which was being photographed.

Being late to the party would be much frowned upon by Dr Sissons, who didn't like McNab anyway, so his entry, however meek and mild, would still provoke ire.

'Fuck that,' McNab muttered as he pushed the door wide and strode in.

The raised blue eyes told McNab he'd been right about the presence of Dr Walker, whose gaze conveyed a mix of sympathy and humour as they both awaited Sissons's reaction to McNab's arrival. However, the pathologist didn't even acknowledge his entry, intent as he was on examining the victim's head.

McNab, seeing they'd reached that stage in the proceedings, made his presence known and immediately set about relating Rhona's queries.

'Dr MacLeod said to say that she noticed what looked like an earlier wound on the back of the head, which may have been in contact with a birch tree.'

Sissons managed to ignore the fact that this statement had emerged from McNab's mouth and said, 'Her reason for thinking this?'

'She collected forensic evidence of what appeared to be an altercation in a wooded location near A.C.E Target Sports, Portree, prior to finding the body on the beach.'

'And she thinks the victim may be the recipient of this previous violence?'

'It's a possibility. Also she asked me to tell you that the rocks the victim hit on his way down the cliff are black basalt, but she's concerned the face wounds may have obliterated an earlier wound, maybe from a knife or a tomahawk.'

The pathologist gave a snort at this pronouncement, which might actually have been laughter. Something McNab had never heard emerge from Sissons before.

By the looks of those in attendance, the sound was causing a bout of suppressed hysteria. McNab felt for them, since he too was seized by an overwhelming need to laugh. Dr Walker turned away in order to compose himself, and one of the forensics quickly excused herself to go to the toilet.

'So we're in the Wild West now, Sergeant? "Portree Kid" country.'

McNab had no idea what the pathologist was referring to, and also didn't want to ask.

'Check out "The Portree Kid" on YouTube,' Sissons surprised McNab by saying.

McNab thought he might just do that. Anything that made the sour-faced bugger laugh should be investigated.

Calm began to descend as Dr Sissons's voice returned to its normal steely sarcasm.

'So we're looking for plant and tree residue, possibly birch, plus metal and basalt deposits. Okay, let's take a closer look at the wounds.'

McNab exited before any drills or saws made an appearance and, discarding his suit, headed out of the mortuary, intent now on checking on his patient.

En route he used Mr Google to answer his query as to what the hell 'The Portree Kid' was, and found it to be a song, written by Bill Hill and made famous by the Corries, a folk duo he remembered his mother listening to. Moving through the usual crowds in the Death Star, he stuck in his earplugs and played it, suddenly recalling his mother's smiles when watching the Corries perform on the TV.

The shock of the recall from the music was profound. He hadn't thought about his mother for a long time, and now here she was again through the words of a song. The lyrics were wry and humorous, poking fun at Scots folk in general, and Skye and Portree in particular. It was parody at its best and even made McNab smile.

And it was all thanks to Sissons. A sobering thought.

Emerging from the lift, he pocketed the mobile and brought his thoughts back to his next predicament. A decision would have to be made soon about where Harry McArthur went when he was discharged. McNab had tried a couple of hostels, but knew Janice had been right when she'd pointed out how easy it would be to find him there, were Malky intent on doing so.

'We could lock him up?' had been her final response.

'It might come to that,' McNab had confessed.

It wasn't until he recalled his haranguing of Ellie about giving Prince Harry money that the idea came to him. An idea he hadn't yet broached with Ellie.

Emerging from the lift, he headed into the ward. The safest place would be here, McNab thought, seeing the bored officer still sitting outside Harry's room, but they couldn't keep him in hospital forever.

'How's he doing?' McNab asked at the desk.

'Okay,' the nurse said cautiously. 'The methadone's helping. He has a visitor, by the way.'

'A visitor?' McNab said, instantly on the alert.

Noting his alarmed expression, the nurse added somewhat defensively, 'The officer okayed it. Says you know her.'

Who the fuck?

'He was pleased to see her,' the nurse embellished some more. 'I heard them laughing.'

Desperate to find out the identity of the woman who could make Harry laugh, McNab walked swiftly along the corridor. Without speaking to the officer, he peered through the glass. The visitor had her back to him but he knew instantly who it was.

The officer was on his feet. 'Sorry, Sarge, I know you said no visitors but . . .' He tailed off, noting McNab's expression.

Without giving a response either way, McNab stepped into the room, where Harry caught sight of him and went even paler than usual.

Ellie, on the other hand, turned to greet McNab with a smile.

'Michael, you'll be glad to hear Harry's feeling much better.'

'Can I speak to you?' McNab gave a jerk of his head. 'Outside.'

Ellie's expression didn't change, seemingly unintimidated by McNab's thundering look.

'Okay,' she said, rising. 'Will I bring you back a coffee?' she offered Harry.

McNab swore under his breath.

Once outside the room, he marched down the corridor, past the nurse, who he thought might be wearing a half-smile, and out onto the landing beside the lifts.

'What the fuck, Ellie?' he said, his tone shifting from belligerent to utter amazement.

'I told you I knew him.'

'He's a suspect, under police protection,' McNab tried.

'That doesn't mean he can't have a visitor,' Ellie said firmly.

Something McNab couldn't disagree with, although he really wanted to.

Perhaps noting McNab's momentary loss for words, Ellie quickly added, 'I think Harry should stay with me when he's discharged, at least until you're sure he's not in any danger.'

McNab was aware his mouth was hanging open, and that he had no idea how to react to such a suggestion, apart from with a string of expletives.

'It'll be temporary of course, just while we look for somewhere more permanent, because I don't want him back on the streets.'

McNab bit his tongue before he said something caustic along the lines of playing Mother Teresa, which he knew wouldn't go down well. He also knew that his own dodgy plan had involved him asking to stay with Ellie, so that he might stash Prince Harry at his own flat in the interim.

'Well?' Ellie demanded.

'It's too dangerous,' McNab said.

'Who would know he was there?' she immediately countered. 'And if you're worried about me being there, I can come stay at yours.'

When he still hesitated, she added, 'I don't need your permission to give him a place to stay.'

She didn't, but McNab had still hoped she might seek it.

A heavy silence descended before McNab eventually said, 'You don't want to get mixed up with a drug addict.'

There was another heavy moment of silence, before Ellie said, in a scarily quiet voice, 'Like my dead brother, you mean?'

Fuck. Fuck. Fuck. He'd forgotten about her brother.

'I'm sorry.' McNab tried to put his hand on her arm, but she quickly shook him off.

When she answered, McNab could hear the tremor in her voice.

'Harry was an okay guy, until they sent him out there. It screwed with him and this is the result.'

'You can't save him, Ellie,' he tried.

'Maybe not, but I can try.'

34

So often she'd watched as the dunes, aided by the wind, had advanced, seemingly intent on smothering their camp.

But just sometimes, when the sky was clear and the sand slumbering, she'd caught a view of the distant tree-covered mountains and imagined she could smell pine in the air.

She was surrounded by that scent, sweet and sharp. She'd longed for this, and yet now it tasted like the red dust of the desert.

She'd pushed her way further into the trees, to think. She knew there had to be a group post-mortem after the woman's visit and she knew who would be in charge of it.

'Seven! Come. Here. Now.'

She wanted to tell *him* to fuck off. She wasn't his to order about. Not any more. Not here. Not in Afghanistan. But after what had happened? Her throat closed in horror as she relived the moment it had all gone wrong.

Composing herself, she stood up, the closely packed Sitka spruce leaving barely enough room to manoeuvre around and through its interlocking branches.

From one prison to another.

They were waiting for her, standing together, brothers in arms. Ignoring *him,* she studied the other two, their expressions serious and concerned.

They think they're saving me, when nothing can save me now.

She brushed at her eyes, fearful that there might be evidence there of her turmoil.

'Okay, this is where we're at,' *he* was saying. 'They've got a body, but they have no idea who it is yet. They'll have detected the coke. The forensic suits were down there with him for long enough. But he's unrecognizable after the fall.'

'What the fuck, Seven?' Ben shook his head as though the enormity of their dilemma was only now presenting itself.

He interrupted before she'd even formulated a thought, never mind an answer. 'Shut up, Mountain. None of what's happened is Seven's fault.' He paused. 'We'll separate as planned. Stay off-grid. Then leave the island and report for duty.'

'And when Sugarboy doesn't turn up?' Charlie said.

'The army'll think he's gone AWOL and, when they do a little digging, they'll find out why. They believe we're all still okay?' The question was directed at her.

'The woman told me when the body was spotted. I said you were here until after that.'

'You were convincing?'

She thought back to her portrayal of relief, which had been real enough. 'Yes,' she said. That part she had got right. Still, the way the woman had looked at her, as though she was reading her mind. And the dog . . . she had covered the dog's protective behaviour by explaining that they'd met when she'd tried out the axe throwing and again in the bar at the Isles. But it was really the scent of her fear that had worried the dog.

'Why were they here in the bloody plantation in the first

place?' Charlie demanded. 'Unless they were looking for us.'

'Well, they found us,' *he* said. 'And Seven made sure we were all accounted for.'

He gave her an appraising look that made her shrink inside.

'And don't forget it was Seven who got us out of that hellhole in Afghanistan.'

His words satisfied Ben and Charlie, but then they always had. How much of the truth were they really aware of? How much did they care?

If she ever told the real story, they would be in the shit too. For what happened here and in Afghanistan. But her only witness to what had really gone on out there was Sugarboy.

His face reared up at her again, the darkness, the frantic fight, the blood, the smell.

She forced herself to focus instead on that day in the hospital tent when they'd brought in the soldier and his dog. Remembered how hard Sugarboy had fought to save the dog's life.

Seeing Blaze in the bar that night when the helicopter had gone over had brought it all back. Not for the others, but for her and Sugarboy. He'd made a big fuss of the collie, staring over at her to remind her of what they had planned and why.

Sugarboy had been high that night. High and drunk, like the rest of them. Perhaps if he hadn't been, things would have turned out the way they'd planned.

The three of them were huddled together now, discussing where on Skye each of them would go, while assuming she would stay here in the plantation.

After this, they would return to Afghanistan. Escape this horror for another one.

But what about her? If she went back with them, *he* would be there and her fear of him was worse than her fear of dying. And this time there would be no Sugarboy to protect her.

Maybe she could have a relapse, convince the psych doctor that she wasn't ready for active duty yet? But *he* wouldn't leave her at home.

What if she presented herself at a police station, told them the truth about Sugarboy's death and what had happened in Afghanistan?

She was, she knew, a loose end that needed tying off, just like the wayward Sugarboy.

He called out that they were ready to go.

'You okay staying here, Seven?'

That's what he wanted, for her to stay put.

She wondered how long it would be before he came for her.

35

Back now in the square in Portree, Rhona opened the door for Blaze, who jumped out and immediately headed for the Isles hotel.

'I guess Donald's back,' Rhona said.

Blaze gave an excited bark at the door, which was swiftly opened, and they watched as the big collie and his owner were reunited. Donald waved his thanks and the two disappeared inside.

Ushered into Lee's office, Rhona and Alvis were presented with a welcome mug of tea each.

'How'd it go?'

'We found one of the medics, the girl, camped in the Sitka plantation just north-west of A.C.E Target Sports,' Rhona told him.

'In a plantation?' Lee's face was a picture. 'Okay, she'd be out of the wind, but?'

'Blaze led us to the camp,' Rhona said. 'The girl told us the others had all gone solo and off-grid. Apparently they split up yesterday.'

'Which would eliminate them from our enquiries on the body?'

'If she's telling the truth,' Rhona said.

'And you're not sure about that?' Lee prompted.

Rhona didn't know what to say. The girl's shock seemed

genuine, but if she already knew what had happened, but didn't know when the body had been found, the timing in her answer would be crucial. Hence her obvious relief.

'I told her when it was found, which gave her the chance to give the right answer.'

She hadn't been thinking straight when she'd entered that clearing. McNab would never have made such an error. Neither would Alvis. She should have left it up to him.

Alvis, sensing her annoyance, took up the story. 'She did look genuinely shocked by the news of the body and our concern that it might have been one of them. And she promised they would call in at the station before they left the island.'

'Can we contact them now?' Lee said.

'Apparently they switch off their mobiles unless there's an emergency, although she said she would try,' Rhona said.

Lee rose. 'Okay. We'll use Twitter to alert the locals. See if anyone's spotted the other four. We'll check with the MRT, ask them to put out the word too. If they're all alive and well, we can eliminate them from our enquiries.' He focused on Rhona. 'Did you ask if they'd gone back to the woods that night?'

'No,' Rhona told him. She began to say why, then found herself tailing off, as though she couldn't explain her decision, even to herself.

At this, Lee and Alvis exchanged swift glances. Rhona had seen that look before. It was the *PTSD question* look.

She quickly changed the subject. 'How did Chrissy get on?'

'See for yourself. She's in the production room,' Lee told her.

Rhona got up and left the room. As she closed the door behind her, she stood for a moment, waiting for the conversation that would undoubtedly follow her departure. Lee had noted her bloodied hands, although he hadn't commented on them. Now she learned through the door that Alvis had seen at least a portion of her meltdown in the forest.

Rhona swore under her breath.

This was the reason she'd refused to go to Castlebrae. She wanted to deal with what had happened in her own way, in her own time. Not have endless discussions about it.

Seeing Chrissy's multi-coloured head bent over the table on which a collection of evidence bags lay brought a rush of relief. Since their first conversation on the beach, Rhona had known that Chrissy believed her to be back in the game. Maybe not fully, but definitely on the way.

Alvis, she'd hoped, thought that too, although there was still a gentle reticence about how he dealt with her. Lee had met her when she'd first arrived in Skye, traumatized and reclusive. *And* he'd been in touch with McNab ever since, so he was to be forgiven for any doubts he might still have.

Whatever they all thought, she could do nothing about it.

As the door opened, Chrissy looked up, her brows knitted.

'Oh, hi. You're back.'

'Any luck?' Rhona said.

'It's never luck,' Chrissy informed her, 'it's forensic genius.'

'So you did find something?'

'Every locus tells a story. Someone taught me that.'

Rhona met Chrissy's smile with one of her own.

'I've identified three matching sets of prints in the area near where we found the necklace. I've taken casts. The prints were deep and the pattern and depth could suggest they may have been carrying a weight between them, although Jen Mackie would be the one to decide that.'

Rhona listened quietly as Chrissy explained in more detail, using the images she'd taken.

'It was more difficult to trace where the footprints originated, although the A855 passes pretty close by.'

'What about the car park at the lookout point?' Rhona said.

Chrissy shook her head. 'I checked back that way, but lots of folk walk up from there. MRT had the barrier up quickly but with all the tourists and the wet weather . . .' She tailed off.

'Well done,' Rhona said.

'What about you and Blaze?'

Rhona described in detail their encounter with the girl in the plantation.

'She actually referred to herself as Seven?' Chrissy said in disbelief. 'You do know what that means in army terms?'

'Maybe there were seven in the group at one time?' Rhona tried Alvis's explanation.

'Aye, right.' Chrissy wasn't convinced. 'Well, if the gang left when she said they did, the guy on the beach isn't one of them,' Chrissy went on. 'Which means we've been wrong about all of this.'

'*I've* been wrong about all of this,' Rhona corrected her.

'Let's see what the PM produces,' Chrissy said. 'If there's any link between the evidence you collected in the woods and the body on the beach, that changes everything.'

36

McNab had done his best to smooth things over with Ellie. Even conceded against his better judgement that he couldn't stop her if she wanted to offer Prince Harry a room. But, if she did, he wanted her to stay at his place.

'You'll have to clean up first,' had been Ellie's final riposte before she'd departed.

McNab disliked the idea of that job, even more than the reason for it. He resolved to finally take DS Clark's advice when he'd mumped on about it earlier, and hire a one-day deep clean, whatever that was.

'It'll take four hours at least to make your flat safe for human habitation,' she'd assured him.

'How would you know?' he'd countered.

She'd raised an eyebrow at that point and indicated his cubicle, which McNab had had to admit was rivalling Ollie's workstation.

Balancing the two coffees he'd fetched from downstairs, McNab pressed the lift button taking him back up to Harry's room. The coffee was a sweetener offered by Ellie but brought by him. It would be the opener to the news that there would be a price to pay for safety and a bed at Ellie's.

The same nurse was still at the desk. No doubt the drama that had enfolded in front of her was no more or less than she encountered every day. McNab gave her a sweet smile and breezed on past.

Sadly for the bored officer still on duty outside the room, whose eyes had lit up at the sight of the approaching coffee cups, McNab passed without stopping. His gratitude was therefore overwhelming when McNab told him to take a thirty-minute break while he chatted to Prince Harry.

McNab now proceeded to take a seat next to the bed and, handing Harry the coffee, said, 'I assumed you would take sugar so I put three in.'

Harry's surprise and concern at McNab's reappearance weren't assuaged by the offer of coffee. That much was obvious. Nevertheless, McNab settled himself back in the chair and set about his own caffeine fix.

Eventually, with nothing being said, Harry did the same.

'When did you join the army?' McNab asked after a minute or so.

'As soon as I could.'

'So sixteen?'

He nodded. The shot of caffeine had turned the pasty look to something a little less pale, but the jittery nature of his voice spoke of other needs that hadn't been satisfied.

'I had mates who did the same,' McNab said. 'Three of them.'

Harry hadn't expected that.

'I thought about it, right enough,' McNab admitted. 'Learn a trade. Be a hero. All the shite they tell you.'

'It's not all shite,' Harry came back at him.

'No? So why did you leave?'

'I told you.'

McNab paused for a moment and really studied the face Harry was pointing at.

'How'd it happen?' he said simply.

The shadows moved in and Harry's eyes clouded over. He shook his head. 'Best forgotten.'

McNab rose and, taking off his jacket, threw it to one side.

'You never forget,' he said, pulling up his shirt and turning to display his back.

He heard a whispered 'fuck' as the bullet hole and its skull disguise came into view. McNab rearranged his clothing.

'Ellie did the ink work,' he said. 'She's good. I've only seen it in reflection, of course. Maybe you could get her to work on your face?'

'Turn my face into a skull, you mean?' The laugh was hollow but at least he'd laughed. 'I think I'm managing that all on my own.'

Silence fell as they both contemplated the truth in that.

'You get any help afterwards?'

Harry snorted. 'You're fucking joking. Not when they saw my record.'

'So it wasn't an honourable discharge then?'

'Fucked out of my brain a lot of the time. Afghanistan's a junkie's paradise.' He gave a laugh. 'What about you when you took the bullet?'

'I pressed the morphine button a lot,' McNab admitted. 'When I rose from the grave I went for a whisky alternative.'

'You still doing that?' Harry said, looking interested.

'Sometimes,' McNab admitted. 'I'm trying caffeine as a substitute.'

'Once an addict, always an addict.'

'Tell me something I don't know, brother.'

Harry's face clouded again. 'Two mates died when I got this. Blown to fuck. Bits of them stuck to my face.' His hand grasped at his cheek and he motioned as though scraping it clean.

McNab had been playing the role of brother-in-arms up to now, but at that moment Harry's remembered horror almost sank him. Eventually, he said the words that he didn't want to hear coming out of his mouth.

'Ellie's willing to give you a place to stay when you're discharged.'

'What?' Harry regarded McNab with astonishment.

'I don't like it, but I can't stop her.'

Harry's face was suffused with colour, as if his heart had finally started to beat.

'I can't do that.'

'Good,' said McNab.

Harry threw him a look that said he had no idea what the hell was going on.

'But Ellie doesn't give up easily. I can vouch for that.' McNab paused. 'If you were to move into a room at her place, she would move into mine. That bit I do like.'

'She's your girlfriend?'

'Correct. So maybe we might come to some arrangement that works for us both?'

37

Lee hadn't seemed keen when Rhona had announced her intention of heading home to Sleat that afternoon.

'I assumed you'd be staying over at Jamie's again,' had been his response.

'There's no problem with the road, is there?' Rhona had checked.

'Some surface water, because of the heavy rain.'

'Doesn't sound any different from Glasgow.' Rhona had attempted to add a little humour into the awkwardness.

'Is Chrissy going with you?' Alvis had ventured at this point.

Chrissy in fact had been equally discouraging when Rhona had announced her intention in the production room. It seemed her forensic assistant already had her evening planned, which included food at the Isles and time spent in Donald's company.

'You don't have to come back with me, anyway,' Rhona had assured Chrissy.

'Can't you just stay at Jamie's again? It's more convenient.'

'For what?' Rhona had said. 'Our part in the investigation is over. You should be heading back to Glasgow.'

Chrissy had looked startled by such an idea. 'I was assuming we'd stick around for a bit, at least until the results come back on the evidence we've submitted.'

'I am "sticking around" as you call it. You're the one heading back.' Seeing Chrissy's reaction to that announcement, Rhona realized that Chrissy had assumed she would be returning with her, whereas she had no intention of going back to Glasgow yet.

'I want to go home and sleep in my own bed at the cottage,' Rhona had said, trying to lighten the mood.

For once Chrissy had nothing to say in response. In fact Rhona could almost see her bite her tongue in an effort to remain silent.

So here she was, driving the dark road through the rain alone, and glad of it.

Rhona turned the windscreen wipers up a notch as the radio informed her that the west of Scotland in particular was experiencing very heavy rain and flooding in a number of locations.

'Tell me about it,' she said in return as she drove through another sheet of water.

It seemed the worst affected at the moment wasn't Skye, but the Rest & Be Thankful pass in Argyll, which was closed to traffic as two very large boulders were threatening the road, despite the fact that the extra-strong fences erected along the pass were containing the debris from the current run-off.

At least the road to Sleat was relatively flat, Rhona thought, and she wasn't being sent on a sixty-mile detour in order to get home, unlike the poor residents of Argyll.

Her thoughts returned to the track up through the plantation and the small encampment hidden among the Sitka spruce. It wouldn't be pleasant up there in heavy rain, and probably worse than during the recent snowstorms.

The girl's words, 'we can take anything Skye throws at

us', had suggested she would be unfazed by the new conditions, yet what people said and what they actually thought could be entirely different.

As I know too well.

Rhona ran over the strange meeting in the woods once again, looking for some reason other than her own state of mind for her disquiet about it. She was used to trusting her own judgement, often against the odds, but the sin-eater case had seemingly changed things and she found herself constantly questioning her ability to read people and situations.

Something had told her that the girl was frightened. Was it because she too was living on the edge of fear and not admitting to it? Was she merely transferring her own emotions onto the girl?

Rhona shook her head in an effort to dispel such thoughts. What was the point of avoiding psychotherapy if she was analysing herself all the time?

The latest episode in the plantation, she acknowledged, had unnerved her. Similar events had plagued her since her captivity, but they had been diminishing in frequency and power. Something she'd put down to her stay here on the island.

What if the resurgence had been caused by her being back on the job? If that were the case, did that mean she could no longer deal with the stress associated with her profession?

She had been fine on the beach, but if she was required to process a body anywhere more confined, that might lead to the same attack as she'd experienced among the densely packed trees.

Which meant she couldn't do her job properly.

She wasn't even sure if she would welcome being back in the lab. Something she hadn't divulged to Chrissy. Being confined in a PPI suit for long periods of time, with her mouth and nose covered? On a beach with a view of the sky that had been manageable, but . . .

Rhona rolled down the car window and let the air rush in. Raindrops splattered her face, but she didn't care. She could stop the car any time she chose, she reasoned. The car wasn't a prison even though it was enveloped in darkness.

Turning off the main road, the beams of the jeep eventually found the cottage. The surge of relief Rhona felt at seeing the reassuring steadfastness of that small white building with its blue-painted door seemed out of all proportion to its size against the expanse of grey sea and the stormy sky.

But it was there, and in and around it she knew she would feel safe.

Breathing a sigh of relief, she drew up outside and switched off the engine. The patter of rain on the roof of the jeep had ceased and now all she could discern was the rush of the sea as it met the nearby shore.

The door opened with its usual creak, wood against wood. Cold air met her nostrils, but no colder than she'd endured with the window open in the car. It seemed the temperature had risen after the rain.

She set about turning on the lamps and lighting the stove, putting on the kettle, then pouring herself a dram. The terrible sense of failure that had consumed her in the car was dissipating.

Food wasn't so swiftly dealt with. Rhona chose the biggest potato she could find, forked it, then set it in the tiny microwave, before opening a can of beans. It was never going to be one of Sean's slow-cooked meals, full of flavour, but it would satisfy a need.

Taking her whisky outside, she made for the beach and her favourite rock.

A few lights twinkled from the opposite shore, but the still heavily laden sky didn't allow a glimpse of moon or stars.

Yet they were there.

It would take time for the bad memories to fade. Although, according to Bill Wilson, that time would have been shortened if she'd agreed to go to Castlebrae.

'They know what they're doing there,' he'd told her. 'Take my advice and go.'

It had been difficult to turn down Bill, her mentor and her friend. But gut instinct had told her that constantly talking about it would make the memories more powerful. So she'd chosen instead to leave the memories behind in Glasgow, which had been working *until today*.

Glancing at her watch, she realized it was nearing time for McNab's check-up call. She could of course ignore it, but if she did, that might result in him suddenly turning up on Skye unannounced, especially if he'd been told of the incident in the plantation.

No, better to speak to him, Rhona decided.

She was barely inside when her laptop sitting on the kitchen table indicated an incoming Skype call. Rhona braced herself and answered.

If McNab had been informed about what happened today, it wasn't obvious in his demeanour.

'Dr MacLeod, you've come home,' he said, somewhat relieved, she thought, as the view behind her put her back in the kitchen of the cottage.

'I have.'

'Is Chrissy with you?'

'She's still in Portree,' Rhona said, keeping her voice light. 'Keeping an eye on Blaze, my other forensic assistant.'

McNab's laugh sounded genuine. 'And his owner, I suspect. So where are you in the investigation?'

'You haven't spoken to Sergeant MacDonald then?' Rhona said, a little suspiciously.

'I thought I'd speak to you first.'

Rhona wondered if that were true. McNab was perfectly prepared to tell an outright lie if he believed one was necessary. Despite her knowledge of his capability to do so, she still found it difficult at times to recognize that that's what he was doing.

'We found the female medic,' she said without embellishment. 'The others, she said, were out doing individual survival training somewhere on Skye. It seems they split up after the time the body on the beach was first spotted.'

'And they're conveniently off the radar so we can't check up on them?'

'You did speak to Lee,' Rhona accused him.

McNab assumed a wide-eyed look. 'You, as I said, were my first port of call.'

'Bastard,' Rhona whispered under her breath, while desperately wanting to believe him. 'Anything your end?'

'This Pete bloke seems to be bona fide. His credit card and email are okay. Not used much recently, so one assumes he was on active duty somewhere. MOD don't take kindly to questions about army clientele and where they've been. If Pete does become officially missing, and we get feedback on the body, and can't identify it by other means . . .' McNab tailed off.

'What about the post-mortem?' Rhona said.

McNab cleared his throat a little. Not a good sign.

'According to Dr Sissons, there was no birch residue anywhere in the wounds. Evidence of basalt from the rock-fall, nothing suggesting knife or axe wounds, though. He did give me an extended written treatise on what an injury is.' McNab paused here before obviously reading from Sissons's script.

'Injury is the result of tissue distortion as a consequence of transfer of energy, usually kinetic energy in mechanical injury, which in turn is related to half of the mass multiplied by the square of the velocity (speed) of the impact. The distinction between self-infliction, accident and assault is based on other evidence (witness and circumstantial), pattern of injury and common sense.' He gave Rhona a characteristic grin. 'So that's you told,' he added.

Rhona laughed. 'He's right, of course. Which is why pushing someone off a cliff is a good way to kill them and not be found out.'

'But you thought he was already injured?'

'I made the mistake of linking the scene in the woods with the scene on the beach,' Rhona said. 'And hoping they matched.'

'You don't normally make assumptions, Dr MacLeod, without careful thought.'

At that moment Rhona could have hugged McNab. Why, she wasn't sure, except for the fact that his voice told her he had courage in her convictions, even if she did not.

McNab continued, 'So we need to locate all the medics just to be sure. And –' he paused for a moment – 'someone got injured in those woods you checked out and, from your evidence, cocaine was involved. I for one would like to know who that was.'

That had been Rhona's thought too. 'The scalp residue and hair I retrieved from the birch tree needs to be compared to the body from the beach.'

'Agreed.'

When the call ended, Rhona took her whisky through to the sitting room where the stove was now burning brightly. Her mood had lifted, especially after McNab had filled her in on his own current investigation and its possible links to the cocaine trail from Afghanistan.

'The Sandman's like bloody Amazon, delivering to your door throughout Scotland. Why would Portree not be on his delivery list?'

'The medics were stationed somewhere in Afghanistan,' Rhona had told him.

Now that did interest McNab. 'As was the former soldier stabbed in the alley.'

At this point he'd revealed his plan for Prince Harry. As Rhona listened, she'd realized he was telling her something no one else knew, except Ellie.

'That could land you in trouble,' she'd said, concerned.

'Ellie doesn't take no for an answer.' McNab didn't add *a bit like yourself*, but it was there in his voice anyway.

McNab had finished by saying, 'Do me a favour, Dr MacLeod, and give Maguire a call. The poor bastard thinks I know something about your incarceration that he doesn't. I have no idea what that is, but if I was him, it would make me mad too.'

Rhona stared into the flames.

Nobody knew what she'd decided during her captivity. Not Chrissy. Not Sean. Not McNab. She doubted whether she would tell anyone. Ever. Maybe that was why she'd avoided Castlebrae and the psychologist's couch. She never wanted that pried out of her. If that meant she must live with what she recognized as PTSD, then so be it.

38

Alvis stepped out into the night air. Portree, used to rain in abundance, had dealt with the downpour as always, diverting it into its gutters and drains and sending it back out to sea.

A well-washed Somerled Square glistened in the street lights and the air smelt fresh and clean. It was, he accepted, like being at home in Stavanger. No weather flung at Norway or Scotland could ever defeat the resilience of their populations. After all, they'd had centuries of practice in surviving its extremities.

Visitors who came to walk and climb didn't let the weather put them off either, whatever the time of year. Alvis could understand why soldiers might come to Skye, to test themselves in its terrain and escape memories of Afghanistan for a short period of time at least.

His first impression of the group that night in the bar had been of a stag party. It was the presence of a girl that had put paid to that idea. From memory, the female member of the group appeared more than a little lost in thought, trying to join in the fun from duty, rather than desire.

The reaction when the rescue helicopter had flown over had exemplified that. The tall blond male that Donald may have encountered in the toilet was the one bringing the shots and encouraging everyone to toast the chopper.

The girl, on the other hand, had appeared more frightened than ecstatic at whatever memory the helicopter had evoked, although she'd successfully covered this by engaging with the big collie and encouraging his tricks.

Perhaps because the beating of the blades conjured up memories she would rather forget?

Several of Alvis's own colleagues in Police National had spent time in Afghanistan. Norway still maintained a presence there, attached to the larger International Security Assistance Force (ISAF). Ten Norwegian soldiers had already died in the forgotten war, seven of them blown up by IEDs and twenty-six injured in combat action, some badly.

Alvis had seen the fallout from this, both as a police officer and as a civilian, with friends and colleagues caught up in the aftermath. It wasn't only physical injuries that left their mark, but the forever-lurking PTSD, haunting those involved for years afterwards, just as it did among fellow officers who'd served on the front line at home.

Because not all atrocities happened in war zones.

His mind moved back to 22 July 2011 and the terrible work of right-wing extremist Anders Behring Breivik, the numbers of young people killed or seriously injured by a lone gunman still too awful to contemplate, although he, like most Norwegians, knew the totals by heart – 69 dead, 110 injured, 55 seriously, when the white extremist, dressed in police uniform, went on a shooting spree on the island of Utøya in Tyrifjorden.

He thought of the young woman in the plantation and wondered about her state of mind. Trying to preserve life, especially on the front line, could prove as traumatizing as being a combat soldier. The group was a team, that much had been obvious by the camaraderie, but the girl seemed to be, at times, a reluctant member.

The ringing of his mobile brought him out of his reverie. Glancing at the screen, he was pleased to find Rhona's name.

'You're back safely?'

'I am,' she assured him. 'I called to say I'm planning a walk tomorrow instead of coming into Portree.'

'D'you want some company?'

She hesitated a little, then said, 'No, but thanks anyway. How much longer are you here for?'

'I leave in a couple of days.'

Alvis had the strongest feeling in that moment that Rhona had called to say goodbye.

'Chrissy will be heading back to Glasgow shortly too,' she said.

'And you?' Alvis asked.

'Probably stay until Christmas. After that . . .'

'So your work here is over?'

'The PM found no evidence of foul play, according to McNab, no birch residue, no evidence of a knife or tomahawk wound. It looks like the injured party in the birch woods is unconnected to the body on the beach.' She paused, then almost as an afterthought, said, 'Do you remember roughly the heights of the medic group?'

Alvis, slightly taken aback by the question, thought for a moment. 'Average for the men, five nine or ten, except for the blond one who was closer to my height, and to the body on the beach. Why?'

'Just curious. We'll find out anyway when they eventually report to the station.'

She sounded about ready to ring off, so he intervened.

'What about the DNA evidence you collected from the woods?'

'Nothing back on that, yet.'

Her tone suggested she didn't expect there to be a match to the victim either. It sounded as though Dr MacLeod no longer had faith in her earlier connections.

'Well, enjoy your walk,' Alvis said.

'Thanks, I intend to.'

Alvis slipped the mobile back in his pocket. Across the way, it appeared the police station had shut its doors for the night. Maybe that's why Rhona had called him and not Sergeant MacDonald.

She was right. Her job here was done, as was Chrissy's, although Chrissy would be reluctant to go if that meant leaving Rhona behind.

He thought again of the recent incident in the plantation. As far as he knew, Rhona was unaware that he had seen it, hence the lie about how her hands were bloodied. Whatever she'd relived in that moment amongst the tightly packed trees had, he assumed, come from her time in captivity.

As his mood settled into one of gloom, Alvis rose and, leaving the square, made for the harbour, intent on using the scenery and the sea smells to remind him of home. Whatever he'd hoped to achieve here on Skye was over. As much as he wished good health on Dr MacLeod, he wasn't in a position to personally deliver it.

Only time might do that.

39

On opening the door, McNab was besieged by a smell he didn't encounter often in his flat: cleanliness – which, he decided, reminded him of his home as a boy. No dirty dishes stacked in and around the sink, no remains of half-eaten ready meals.

Breathing it all in, he wandered between the main room, bedroom and bathroom. The scummy sink and shower had been rendered a glistening white. Damp smelly towels removed and replaced with fresh. The bedding had been changed too. Where had all the dirty stuff gone?

McNab eventually found it in the dryer and, captivated by his new-look home, proceeded to fold everything and put it in the airing cupboard, which had also been tidied.

So this was what a deep clean looked like. It was worth it, McNab decided, whatever the price. Good old DS Clark, who'd furnished him with the number for Clean It! Enterprises and would have to be congratulated and rewarded for her efforts.

McNab grinned when he opened the fridge door to discover the basics had also been supplied. Stocking your fridge. An added extra.

Sitting on the table was a note from the guardian angel who had transformed his home, to say if he required a weekly tidy-up he should give Darren at Clean It! a call, as it would be his pleasure to pop in once a week for a refresh.

McNab now took advantage of the clean shower and the fresh towels. After which he studied the Indian carry-out menu and ordered in tonight's meal for two, making sure he chose mostly Ellie's favourites.

His conversation with Prince Harry had resulted in an agreement of sorts which would happen tomorrow when he was discharged. Ellie, somewhat mollified by McNab's attempts to get things right, had agreed to come round after tonight's shift at the Rock Cafe.

All in all, the day had improved, almost as much as his flat. McNab decided that he might celebrate a little with two fingers of whisky before the food and Ellie's arrival. Retrieving the bottle, he studied its slowly diminishing contents.

'Everything in moderation' had been his mother's watchword. If only he'd adopted it as his own earlier.

'I'm trying, Mum,' he muttered to the ceiling before measuring out his allotted amount and putting the bottle back in the cupboard.

Taking his time, he savoured the scent of the malt, which he'd bought in place of the usual easily quaffable blended version. Treat it like the French treat wine, *with respect,* he reminded himself. And the less you drink over time, the more powerful the result when you do.

That much he had found to be true.

McNab added a little water, then sniffed again. Anticipation was the name of the game, as important in drinking whisky as in having sex.

He married the idea of whisky and sex in his head, then tasted the malt, allowing a ripple of delight to combine with sexual desire. Hey, maybe the French were right after all.

The roar of the approaching Harley was timed to perfection. The question was what would come first. The food or the sex?

He watched as Ellie parked her bike below. She wouldn't have brought it if she didn't intend staying over, or that's what McNab told himself. He waited for the buzzer, forgetting momentarily that Ellie hadn't given back her key.

Hearing her footsteps on the stairs, he realized that she must have let herself in at the main door, but there was no sound of her key in the inner lock. After a slight wait, he heard her knock on the door and immediately went to open it.

She had her helmet in her hands and her backpack over her arm. When he smiled at her, she wrinkled her nose and said, 'What smells so nice?'

'Something Darren from Clean It! put in with the washing, I think,' McNab ventured.

'Darren?' Ellie said with a suggestive smile.

'No sexism here. Men can be cleaners too.' McNab pulled her inside and shut the door.

'Lemon Lenor,' she offered. 'And plenty of it.'

McNab took her helmet and bag and dropped them on the hall chair, then did what he'd planned as he'd listened to her climbing the stairs.

She eventually emerged with a gasp. 'Can I at least see the sitting room first?'

McNab let her go, albeit reluctantly, having already conjured up an image of them moving swiftly into the bedroom with just enough time before the curry would arrive.

But, it seemed, Ellie was more captivated by cleanliness than by him.

'My God. The place is unrecognizable, by sight or smell,' she said as she surveyed the main room. 'And you've even set the table.'

'Curry won't arrive for thirty minutes or so.' McNab raised a hopeful eyebrow.

'So let's have a drink while we wait.' Ellie eyed his whisky glass. 'I take it you have wine?'

Fuck. That's what he didn't have. Maybe Darren could replenish that too in future, if asked.

Ellie smiled at his discomfort. 'Just as well I brought a bottle, courtesy of the Rock Cafe.'

She left him to go through to the hall for her backpack. Flourishing the bottle of red wine on re-entry, she said with a pitying smile, 'We could take our drinks into that rather nice bedroom.'

'Thank you, Darren,' McNab whispered under his breath.

Later, it was McNab who rose and, donning his boxers, went to the door to take possession of the curry. Behind him, Ellie scurried through to the sitting room in what looked like his T-shirt.

The sex had obviously given her an appetite, because she moved to swiftly open the various cartons and murmur delight at their contents.

'You've chosen the stuff I like,' she said in surprise. 'Normally I have to beg for the mild curries and a Peshwari naan.'

Usually McNab preferred a hot curry, but his taste buds had reappeared since he'd cut back on the whisky, so he'd been okay about going for the milder choices. Something he didn't mention, of course, since he was rather enjoying the thoughtful boyfriend role he was playing.

Ellie topped up her wine. McNab, who hadn't yet finished his two fingers of whisky, decided to save it until the end.

'You have cut back,' Ellie said. 'Less booze, and a clean flat. You must have really wanted me back here.' She threw him a suspicious look. 'Or is this really about Harry?'

'He's getting out tomorrow,' McNab said. 'And he's agreed to stay at your place, if you'll have him.'

Ellie pondered that as she broke off a piece of naan.

'What did you say to him?'

McNab chose his words carefully. 'He wants to get clean. He agreed to see a counsellor. I'll put him in touch with the right folk. He's a former soldier, injured in the line of duty. He should be getting help.'

She was regarding him now in much the way that Rhona did when she was trying to work out exactly what game he was playing. McNab felt a stab of regret because he was playing her *and* Harry, and he wanted to win as always.

'What's he got to do in return?'

'Stay fucking alive,' McNab said. 'That's what you want, isn't it?'

'Will he testify as to who stabbed him?'

McNab shook his head. 'We aren't there yet. One step at a time.'

She didn't like his tone. He could see that by the raising of an eyebrow.

'If you're fucking with him . . .' She tailed off accusingly.

'I'm not fucking with him.' McNab hoped his tone now suggested honesty. 'If you're okay with him staying, I'll deliver him myself tomorrow.'

'He's not a prisoner, you know.'

'No, but he might be a victim if I don't keep an eye on him.'

Her look suggested she was remembering the blood-soaked body in the alley and their attempts together to stem the flow.

'You have to let me do my job,' McNab said. '*Semper vigilo*: Keeping people safe.'

She gave him a thoughtful look then, and McNab hoped she was remembering that he had done that on a previous occasion for her.

'Okay,' she nodded. 'You've got a key. It's clean. Maybe not as clean as here, though.'

When she smiled at him, McNab knew he had won, for the moment.

40

Rhona spread the map out on the kitchen table.

Initially she'd thought to tell Alvis that she wanted to have a quiet couple of days at the cottage, but then it had struck her that he might turn up unexpectedly to find that wasn't the case, so had decided instead to mention the walk.

And he'd bought it, she thought. Jamie and Lee would too, because she'd spent so much time doing exactly that since coming to Skye.

She hadn't called Chrissy, just sent a text saying she was safely back and to enjoy her night with Donald. Any mention of not turning up in Portree she would keep until tomorrow.

Having made up her mind, she'd then eaten her baked potato and beans and helped herself to a second whisky before setting about packing for her trip.

The girl they called Seven had intimated that she planned to camp in the plantation until it was time to meet up with the others. Rhona wasn't sure she believed her, but there was one way to find out.

When Rhona had first viewed the clearing, the girl had been patting the dog, her head bare. It was only when Rhona had come into view that she'd raised the hood on her cagoule. Nothing particularly odd about that and yet . . .

Rhona now brought up the images she'd taken when examining the locus in the woods. Her notes indicated that someone had impacted on the birch tree at around five feet from the ground. Of course, that didn't say anything definitive about the height of the person involved. The impact would depend on how far someone had been from the tree prior to connecting with it. A tall person might have fallen from a distance or perhaps been only partly upright when they'd hit the trunk.

Alternatively, the damage might have happened to someone shorter, like a blonde girl of around five feet three inches tall.

Hardly scientific, but intriguing nonetheless. If the result came back that the DNA evidence she'd extracted from the bark wasn't a match for the beach victim, might it still have come from one of the other members of the group, possibly the girl?

Had the group been visiting the assault course out of hours, having taken drugs and alcohol, the MOD would definitely not be impressed. An injury sustained in such a 'game', if treated in a hospital, would have to be reported to the police, and the police were legally obliged to inform the MOD if any serving personnel were involved.

As medics, one assumed they would treat an injury themselves, provided it wasn't life-threatening.

So wasn't it perfectly possible they'd done so?

And it might go some way to explaining her own reading of Seven's state of mind.

It was still dark when she loaded the jeep. She'd refilled the petrol tank before setting off home yesterday, keen not to have to worry about fuel for the next few days at least.

She'd only used the tent once during her sojourn on the island, always preferring to wend her way home after a long walk. This time she packed it, and sufficient supplies to keep her fed and watered for a couple of days.

After that, Seven and her fellow medics would be reporting to the police station prior to leaving the island. Perhaps too the police would have established the identity of the beach victim, maybe even the reason he'd fallen from Kilt Rock. Although deciding whether a fall was induced or accidental was a difficult thing, as Dr Sissons had indicated via his detailed email to McNab.

Her discussion with McNab had convinced Rhona that she should set aside the beach death for the moment and aim to discover what had happened in the woods. Her plan therefore was to try and meet up with Seven and challenge her on what they'd got up to after leaving the Isles bar that night. Perhaps, by doing that, one mystery at least would be solved.

However, to do so would involve another visit to the plantation, and Rhona had no desire to use the overgrown forest path again. Approaching the camp the way she'd exited with Alvis was, she decided, the safer alternative.

The heavy rain of the previous evening had settled into a light drizzle which involved using the wipers to periodically scrape at the windscreen. Irritating as this was, Rhona consoled herself with the thought that walking in drizzle would be better than in torrential rain.

It took the statutory hour to reach Portree. Approaching the scattering of wooden buildings on the outskirts that constituted A.C.E Target Sports, Rhona noted all were in darkness, including Donald's place, which gave her an excuse not to text Chrissy, just yet.

Rhona had considered asking if she might borrow Blaze for her walk, although that may have involved questions she wasn't ready to answer, but, as chance would have it, as she passed the parking place she noticed the black-and-white shaggy shape of the dog down by the stream. Blaze, she knew, wasn't averse to going off on his own exploring the surrounding countryside when the notion took him.

Rhona drew up and, opening the window, gave the 'here to me' call. The big collie, his ears obviously like radar, picked up her voice immediately and, emerging from the gate, headed up the road towards her.

She'd already heard the tale where Blaze had joined a jogger for a six-mile early run, so, promising herself she would text Blaze's whereabouts, she decided to take the dog with her. Chrissy might be suspicious of her motives for doing that, but then again, Chrissy was always suspicious.

The dog happily jumped up to join her in the jeep, seemingly unperturbed by any lies Rhona would have to tell.

'I like an assistant who says very little,' she told the dog, who gave her a winning grin in return.

By the time she'd driven up the steep forest track to the turning circle, the sun had risen and the drizzle had been replaced by a cold wind. Zipping up her cagoule, Rhona ordered the dog out and locked the jeep. The heavy rain the previous evening had reduced the turning circle to mud, and it wasn't possible to say whether a vehicle had been here since her last visit.

Blaze, thinking they must be making for the forest path, set off that way until Rhona called him back. Quickly registering her intention to climb towards the trig point instead, the dog swiftly took the lead.

Before she got into her stride, Rhona pulled out her mobile and texted Chrissy to say she was out for a walk with Blaze and would see her later. Then she turned off her phone, although judging by the diminishing signal, she was heading out of range anyway.

Within sight of the trig point, she stopped and turned. Up here, close to the hilltop, the ground cover was grass and heather, with the line of the plantation some yards below. On escaping the forest with Alvis, she'd chosen a large rock jutting out of the heather as a marker for their exit point.

And there it was.

From where she stood, there was no visible sign of a break in the trees, but, trusting to memory, she headed for the landmark anyway. The dog, who had waited patiently while she decided her route, now took off, to swiftly disappear among the trees.

Drawing closer, Rhona spotted the route the dog had taken.

A sudden flashback of that smothering green prison brought the same taste to her mouth as before. Rhona coughed and, spitting out her fear, replaced it with a deep breath, then marshalled herself to enter. Recall told her it was a ten-minute walk to the girl's camp in the clearing. *I can manage that if I move swiftly and focus only on the path.*

At this point, Blaze came running back as though he had sensed or scented her rising anxiety.

'Thank you,' Rhona said, ruffling his head in relief.

Blaze gave a little whine and, staying in front of her on the narrow track, checked back periodically to make sure she was still with him. Minutes later they were through and stepping into the clearing that held the campground.

The tent, Rhona was relieved to see, was still there, zipped up, and she now registered why the location had been chosen in the first place. It was certainly secluded, given that the few walkers making for the trig point would use the clearly marked path that led up directly from the turning circle.

It was sheltered, the cold wind that had harassed her as she'd climbed unnoticeable here. To the east was a small stream for fresh water. A place had been marked out for cooking, but there was no evidence of a fire having been lit, so presumably Seven had been using a gas stove.

One thing she hadn't noted on her first visit, focused as she had been on the girl, were the probable marks of other tents, at least three of them. Suggesting the likelihood that the others had also camped at that spot at some time.

As she took this in, Blaze remained beside her, apparently awaiting instructions, his lack of agitation suggesting the girl wasn't in the vicinity. Rhona tried anyway.

Her call of 'Seven, are you there?' brought forth a couple of startled ravens to rise from the treetops, cawing their escape, but no human response.

As her second attempt faded and died, Rhona approached the tent.

Entering would be an intrusion, but one she deemed necessary. The dog too had begun snuffling and whining, pawing the ground at the entrance. If Blaze was interested in what was in there, then she should be too, Rhona told herself as she reached for the zip.

41

Ordering the dog to stay, Rhona unzipped the tent flap and crawled inside.

In here the dimness of the winter light was exacerbated, and she put on her torch to view the contents more clearly. A winter sleeping bag was rolled at the back, with a few items of clothing folded nearby including a pair of trainers, with a single soiled anklet sock lying next to them. Hanging above all this was a drawstring bag.

There were kitchen utensils stacked together with a small gas stove, plus a pile of what looked like British Army ration packs. Checking out the menu, it appeared Seven had no intention of going hungry.

There was, however, no backpack, first-aid kit, outer garments or walking boots, so it was safe to assume that Seven was out walking somewhere, and intended to come back here to sleep.

Rhona eyed the drawstring bag. Made of canvas, it looked like it might also be an army issue. Curious as to its contents, she lifted it down and, loosening the cord, tipped them out. She wasn't sure what she expected to discover – a piece of equipment most likely or maybe even toiletries.

Instead she found a torn and stained piece of mesh-like blue cloth. A neck cord attached to a pendant fashioned from what looked like a black scorpion encased in acrylic.

The lifelike quality of the three-dimensional insect was so good, Rhona found herself moving back, just in case the scorpion flickered into life. The final item was a metal tag with the name 'Rex' attached to a fragment of an ornamental chain. There were none of the usual army details of number, date of birth or blood type on the tag, so it wasn't for a human.

Were these mementos of her time in Afghanistan?

As Rhona spread them out and took a photograph, a wave of guilt swept over her at the thought that she was rummaging through Seven's private things. Quickly returning the items to the bag, she hung it back up, wondering if Seven would know instinctively that someone had been here and feel violated by such an intrusion.

A feeling Rhona knew only too well.

Keen now to be out of the tent, Rhona made a decision. She could either linger about the camp area and wait for Seven to return or she could go looking for her, and for that she might need Blaze's help.

Rhona lifted the discarded sock and, crawling to the open flap, offered it to Blaze to take the scent.

'Go find it, boy.'

Seven had been moving around the campsite, and this was obvious by the initial criss-crossing pattern of the dog. Rhona hoped that Blaze wouldn't suddenly disappear into the dense depths of the plantation, where she definitely didn't want to go.

Thankfully, although Blaze sniffed around the area where the stream emerged from the trees, he didn't head in. Instead he chose the path she'd used.

Rhona gave him an encouraging 'Good boy', hoping that perhaps Seven was in the vicinity of the trig point. She had no idea how long and far the dog, however willing, might be able to follow the scent.

Perhaps she was already demanding too much of the big collie. After all, he wasn't a police dog, no matter how well trained he was.

Blaze, despite her concerns, seemed quite clear what was expected of him. Back on that first day in the birch woods, she'd gone along with the eager dog, all the time thinking he might be leading her to a rabbit he'd killed earlier.

She'd been wrong then, as she had been later on the clifftop.

The sun, now properly up, had emerged from behind the thick cloud cover of earlier. Blaze, having circled the summit of Beinn a' Ghlinne Bhig, was now heading down the grass and heather slope towards Loch Niarsco.

Following behind him on the narrow track forged by other walkers, Rhona stopped to catch her breath and appreciate what lay before her. In the far distance was Healabhal Mhor, the southern of the two hills known as MacLeod's Tables, which she had walked to earlier in her stay on the island.

But not from here.

She wondered, as the dog continued to wend his way north-eastwards, whether he was taking her for a walk, perhaps one he'd been on with Donald, and that their path had nothing to do with Seven at all.

Soon they were skirting the lochside and Blaze, moving more swiftly ahead, came to a halt near the north end of the peaty water, very excited, it seemed. Rhona went to join him at the water's edge, where it appeared Seven's scent, if that was indeed what he was following, seemed stronger.

Rhona noted the boot prints and the stone fire ring close to the water's edge, recognizing the tell-tale signs that someone had stopped here, maybe even camped, as evidenced by a rectangle of flattened heather.

Seven had left her tent in place in the clearing, but she could have taken an emergency shelter with her, should the weather turn bad on her walk. If she had bivouacked here, then she must have set out shortly after Rhona and Alvis had encountered her in the forest.

Had they spooked her?

Something about the girl's story of not being able to make contact with the others unless in an emergency hadn't rung true. How did they alert one another if there was something wrong, if they kept their phones off all the time? Surely it was more likely they'd organized check-in times with one another?

And, if they had been involved in the incident behind A.C.E Target Sports, the best plan would have been to leave the island before anyone found out about it.

As Blaze had decided to go for a dip, Rhona took a moment to eat and drink something. When he came ashore minutes later, she realized he was much slimmer than his big shaggy coat suggested.

Once he'd given himself a good shake, Blaze indicated he was ready to move on, urging Rhona to pack up and follow him. Conscious of how far she had come from the turning circle and her vehicle, Rhona began to wonder if this trip had been a wise move at all, or just another fanciful idea she'd conjured up in her present state of mind.

Wouldn't it have been more sensible to hang about near Seven's campsite and talk to her when she returned?

The dog, however, had no qualms about the original

plan and was already setting a steady pace, following the line of the stream that ran along the lower edge of the plantation towards what was, according to Rhona's map, the A850, the road that led either back to Portree or else west to Dunvegan.

If that was where Seven was making for, it didn't look as though she was out on a survival walk after all.

Rhona switched on her mobile and three messages pinged in in succession, one each from Alvis, Sergeant MacDonald and Chrissy. As Rhona contemplated which one to read first, the mobile rang out.

'Where are you?' McNab said before she could even manage a hello.

'Out for a walk with Donald's dog.'

'Alvis says they can't reach you.'

'The signal's bad and you've reached me now.'

'The DNA from your walk in the woods is not a match for the body on the beach,' McNab declared bluntly.

Rhona didn't respond because there was nothing to say, except that she'd been wrong.

'Did you hear me?' McNab demanded.

Rhona had kept on walking and the signal had weakened so that McNab's voice had begun to break up. She could have stepped back into range, but didn't.

'Rhona? Can you hear me? The beach guy wasn't from the woods.'

'You don't have to keep telling me that,' Rhona muttered under her breath.

'But,' McNab's broken voice assumed a triumphant tone, 'I fucking know who it is.'

42

Glasgow, a little earlier

McNab cursed as the line of traffic continued to merely creep forward. He was going to be late and it wasn't strictly the fault of the current hold-up.

Had he not succumbed to Ellie's naked charms this morning – she'd had an afternoon shift at the Harley shop so wasn't in a hurry – he would have reached the hospital in good time. But, opening his eyes earlier, he'd rediscovered his delight at having her beside him and had taken advantage of her offer.

Which he didn't regret one little bit, he told himself, as his watch reminded him he was well past the arranged collection time for Prince Harry.

Even his now-inevitable late arrival couldn't douse McNab's high spirits. He'd already called Janice and told her of the success of Clean It! She'd listened in obvious amused silence, then reminded him he therefore owed her big time, which McNab had agreed with.

'And don't mess Darren around. You're not the only one who needs him in their life,' she'd told him.

'What day does he come to you?' McNab had immediately asked. 'Don't want to interfere with your arrangements.'

'You had better not. And it's a Tuesday.'

After the discussion of their domestic arrangements, McNab had explained he was headed to the hospital where Harry McArthur was due to be discharged.

'I've found him a room,' McNab had said before Janice could ask. 'In a safe house.'

'So he has something to tell us?' She'd sounded interested.

'He has,' McNab had said. 'But he's not ready yet.'

'When will he be?'

'Soon,' McNab had promised. 'Any luck locating Malky's whereabouts?'

'He's dropped off the face of the earth, apparently.'

'Worried we will find a way of charging him.'

'We could if your man gave us a statement to that effect.'

McNab had chosen to ignore the obvious dig. 'What about the knife?'

'The area between his usual spot on Argyle Street and the alley has been thoroughly searched, including the drains. No sign of it. Malky will have got rid of it far from the scene of crime or else hung on to it, for future jobs. Probably had his name carved on the handle like Glasgow villains of old.'

McNab had brought the fanciful musings of DS Clark to an end by ringing off, keen as he was not to be questioned more closely about where he planned to stash Harry. If all went well and according to plan, Harry would be at Ellie's a week at most, then social services could step in and they'd be welcome to him.

Making his way through the already-busy thoroughfare of the giant hospital, McNab entered the lift. Emerging on his requested floor, he headed for Harry's ward. Shifts had changed in the interim and he was presented with a face on the desk he didn't recognize.

Showing his ID, he introduced himself and explained he was here to collect Harry McArthur. The nurse gave his ID a cursory glance then went on her computer for what felt like five minutes.

'Mr McArthur's downstairs in the discharge lounge.'

'The arrangement was that I pick him up from the ward at nine o'clock,' McNab said.

The nurse made a point of checking her watch, knowing it was well past that now. 'His bed was required first thing, so we moved him to the discharge lounge. You can pick him up from there.'

'Is there an officer with him?'

The nurse shot him a look of confusion. 'I thought you were the officer.'

'The other uniformed officer who has been sitting outside his room since he was admitted.'

Her confusion only grew bigger at McNab's declaration.

'I've been off for three days. I don't know about the other officer.'

McNab realized he wasn't going to get the full story here, but he might get it from Harry.

'Where's the discharge lounge?'

'It's down near the exit and the taxi stance.' She gave him directions. 'According to his notes, Mr McArthur will need bed rest for at least another week. He has details of how to look after the wound with his discharge sheet. He'll be required to come back in two weeks' time.' A sudden thought crossed her mind. 'Is he going to jail?'

McNab didn't bother with an answer.

Re-entering the lift, he found himself muttering his

annoyance, much to the consternation of the other occupants.

'Are you all right, mate?' a man asked him.

'I'm a policeman,' was McNab's response, as though that explained everything.

Despite the nurse's instructions, or more likely because he hadn't listened to them properly, McNab ended up in the wrong place more than once before he finally discovered the designated discharge lounge.

Opening the door, he found himself in a spacious room containing comfortable chairs with coffee, tea and biscuits on offer. There were at least eight people in there, some behind newspapers. McNab scanned them all before facing up to the fact that none of them was Harry.

Glancing round in search of whoever was in charge, he spotted a couple of notices which indicated that no one except discharge patients should be making use of this room and its facilities.

Shouting 'Nurse!' in his loudest voice eventually resulted in a head popping round a door at the rear of the room. The male nurse gave him an instruction to keep his voice down, followed by the patently cross words, 'Please, sir, there are recovering patients in here.'

'Not the one I'm looking for. Harry McArthur.' McNab showed his ID again. 'I was told he was here.'

The man emerged and went to a book which lay open on a counter.

'If he was here, he'll have signed the book,' he said with certainty. 'Look –' he pointed with a flourish – 'H. McArthur. Signed in 9.00. Collected 9.30.'

'Collected?' McNab said, a niggling worry becoming larger by the second. 'Who by?'

'Sorry?'

'Who collected him?' McNab said, his voice staccato now.

The nurse looked bewildered. 'His emergency contact, I assume. You have to say who your emergency contact is and give their number when you're admitted.' Keen to help, he pointed at the entry again. 'He's written a number here. Could that be his emergency contact?'

McNab stared at the eight-digit number. It didn't look like a telephone number to him. Mobile numbers were eleven digits, as were landlines with their city codes. He made a note of the number anyway.

'Who was on duty here when he was collected?'

'It wasn't me. I've just come on.'

'Well who then?' McNab said, adding, 'This is a police matter.'

'I'll find out,' he said and promptly headed into the back room. Seconds later he emerged with a female about McNab's age, who looked more composed than her male counterpart.

'I was out front when Mr McArthur was picked up. A car arrived at the pick-up point outside, as is the usual case. Mr McArthur saw it through the window and said it was his ride. He signed the book, thanked us and left.'

'Did you see who was driving the car?'

She shook her head.

'Can you describe the car?'

She looked askance at him. 'It's a constant stream of folk getting picked up from the patients' lounge. If he'd been agitated I would have questioned him, but he wasn't.'

'What about CCTV?'

'You'd have to ask security about that.'

The hospital would be well covered, but checking out footage would take time. And time might be something Harry didn't have.

McNab departed before he vented any further distress or annoyance at either of the two nurses. The person it should be directed at was himself for arriving late, and the uniform who'd left his charge unattended.

Reaching the car, he called Ollie in IT and told him to check for CCTV cameras at the Death Star, in particular the nearest exit to that particular discharge lounge.

'What am I looking for?'

'Cars arriving around 9.30, one of which will pick up Harry McArthur.'

'The stabbed guy?'

'His photo's on file. I want to know who collected him from the hospital. Also,' McNab continued, 'find out what this number refers to.' He quoted the number Harry had left behind.

'Any idea what it might refer to?'

'I haven't a fucking clue, but,' McNab said, clutching at straws, 'Harry knew I was coming for him and he left that number behind. So it must mean something.'

Back in the car now, McNab headed for the station, aware the boss wasn't the only person he would have to face regarding Harry's disappearance. He was going to have to tell Ellie. And he knew which interview he feared the most.

43

On arrival at the station, McNab immediately took himself off to IT to see Ollie, hoping he'd made some headway on either of the tasks McNab had given him. Going into the boss with nothing, other than to report that Harry had been snatched from under their noses, was McNab's biggest concern at this point.

Harry played me, McNab thought as he walked along the corridor. *While all the time I thought I was playing him.*

But what if Harry had had no choice but to go?

McNab found himself a great deal more worried by that interpretation of events.

If he'd made contact with one of his junkie mates, that was a nuisance, but not a disaster. If he'd been coerced by one of Malky's mob . . .

But the nurse said he wasn't distressed when he left, McNab reminded himself. And he'd been pretty late arriving. Maybe Harry thought he'd given up on him. Or maybe he simply needed a fix of his drug of choice.

Having hated the idea of housing Harry at Ellie's even for a week, McNab found himself now wishing he had been quicker off his mark this morning and was currently installing Harry at her flat.

Ollie looked flustered as McNab appeared on his horizon and quickly pulled up a chair beside him.

'Sorry, no time to go to the canteen first,' McNab said, having arrived minus the usual offering of a burger or a sticky bun.

'You've only just called me,' Ollie said, obviously more freaked by that than the lack of a snack.

'So?' McNab demanded.

'I've talked with security at the Death Star and they said they'd send the recordings through but nothing's arrived yet.'

'And the number I gave you?' McNab tried.

Ollie's face brightened a little. 'I think I might have something on that. You said your guy was a former soldier?'

'Yes,' McNab said. 'Why?'

'Well, service numbers are eight digits long.'

McNab absorbed this. 'Why would Harry leave his service number in the discharge book? Are you sure it's not a phone number or a bank number?'

'Maybe it's not *his* service number,' Ollie said, seemingly growing exasperated. 'Maybe it's someone else's service number he wanted you to have?'

Now there was a thought.

'You don't remember Harry's number?' Ollie tried. 'You said you found his dog tag?'

McNab recalled that night in the alley, the jangle of the metal dog tag lying in Harry's blood. He remembered wiping it and the realization of what it was and that the details on it belonged to the poor bastard bleeding to death before him. 'No, I don't remember his bloody number.'

Ollie nodded in a placating manner. 'Okay, I'll check the number he left in the book against online army records. If it's a currently serving soldier, though, that'll be more difficult. They're secure. We would need a directive from above to do that.'

'Right,' McNab conceded. 'Let's try.'

Then, picking up the waves of impatience coming from Ollie, he decided it was time to go, empty-handed or not.

In a last-ditch attempt at being ahead of the game before engaging with the boss, he called Janice from the corridor.

'Where are you?' she said, her voice a conspiratorial whisper.

'In the station. Why, what's up?'

'Meet me in the cafeteria now.'

As McNab made his way as ordered, he ran over possible reasons why DS Clark should want to see him so urgently. Her tone had suggested she required them to speak alone, but why exactly?

It could be that news had already reached her about Harry going missing. Or maybe something worse, McNab's darker side suggested. For a morning that had begun so well, it was going seriously downhill now.

Arriving first, McNab purchased two coffees and found a table as far from the other customers as possible. If he was going to be given bad news or a telling-off, he preferred the whole cafeteria not to know about it and DS Clark wasn't one to mince her words.

When she did arrive, McNab tried to tell by her expression how serious it was, but that wasn't possible from the stony look she gave him. He pushed the coffee towards her.

'Harry's gone,' he said, keen to get his story in first.

'Gone where?'

From Janice's response, McNab now knew they weren't there to discuss Prince Harry.

'I'll explain later,' McNab said swiftly. 'Just tell me why you brought me here.'

Janice was eager to do just that. 'The tests came back on the beach body. There's no match with the DNA samples Dr MacLeod found in the woods.'

'Okay,' McNab said, trying not to sound too disappointed. 'I'll let Rhona know.'

'But,' Janice went on, a gleam in her eye, 'the Kilt Rock guy was on the DNA database.'

Which meant he'd been convicted for something.

McNab sprang to attention. 'Who?' he demanded.

'Paul Watson, suspected associate of one Malcolm Stevenson.'

McNab recognized the name immediately. He would have known the face too, he thought, if there had been anything left of it to view.

'If Watson was on Skye, it wasn't for the scenery,' McNab said.

'Agreed.' Janice met his look with one of her own. 'Fancy a trip to Skye?'

44

They were drawing ever closer to the main road and Blaze seemed as focused as ever on heading that way. If he was still following Seven's scent, then it appeared she'd been making her way there too.

McNab's call had of course changed everything, including Rhona's need to locate and speak to Seven about what she'd found in the woods, because it no longer mattered.

It seemed that the body on the beach had nothing to do with the group of medics. They no longer needed to be accounted for. Seven could go where she pleased, as could the others. Any search using drones, the police Twitter account and the local MRT could be called off. No more time needed to be wasted on that.

What Sergeant MacDonald and the soon-to-arrive Major Investigation Team needed now was to concentrate on what they believed was a murder enquiry. As McNab had said, Paul Watson hadn't been on Skye to view the scenery. Nor was it likely he'd fallen willingly from Kilt Rock.

The five-strong group of medics would complete their survival training and leave the island. If one of them had been the injured party from the birch woods, Rhona would never know. The thought should have pleased her, but she found it did not.

It was still a forensic mystery that she hadn't solved.

As she trudged along behind the dog, a buzzing sound from above drew Rhona's eyes skyward. The drone was clearly visible and, a few yards further ahead, the figure controlling it was already being greeted by Blaze.

So this, she presumed, would be Archie McKinnon who'd caught her earlier trip with Blaze on camera. Rhona assumed a smile and went to greet him.

'Archie?'

'Aye?'

Rhona held out her hand. 'Rhona MacLeod. You captured Blaze and myself on camera a few days ago.'

His face lit up. 'So you're Dr MacLeod. Very pleased to meet you.' He bent to rub Blaze's ears. 'Your forensic assistant and I know one another very well.' He gave her a quizzical look. 'You out on another job or still on the last one?'

Rhona didn't see any harm in telling him, now that they knew the medics were all accounted for.

'I was hoping to meet up with the female medic who was camping in the plantation. Blaze was tracking her, or I think he was.'

'Blaze doesn't get things like that wrong. What does the girl look like?'

Rhona gave him a brief description of Seven.

'Aye, she was here. Caught the 56 bus for Dunvegan and Glendale.'

'Did you speak to her?' Rhona said.

'Just passed the time of day.'

'She didn't say where she was headed exactly?'

'No, but she was dressed for walking and had a sizable backpack. Did you need to speak to her?'

Rhona dodged the question and said, 'We met up

yesterday. We were worried then about her fellow medics. They were out on survival training and there was the body on the beach.'

Archie nodded. 'Aye, I saw the Twitter messages. But they've identified the body, so they're not worried about the soldiers now.'

'I only learned that on my way here,' Rhona said in surprise. 'News travels fast on Skye.'

'Like lightning. No doubt the big boys will be over from the mainland now.'

'Why do you say that?' Rhona asked, wondering if Archie knew even more than she did.

'I heard the body on the beach was a dealer, called Paul Watson. He's been here before. If he'd still had a face, the MRT folk would have likely recognized him.' He watched Rhona as his news sank in. 'You heading back to Portree or to Glendale?'

'I left my jeep up at the turning circle near the trig point.' Rhona indicated the nearby hill.

'Then you'll be needing a lift,' Archie said.

The journey in Archie's pickup proved to be enlightening. Rhona realized her sojourn on the island had been an isolated one. Jamie had regaled her with a few stories, but Archie, it seemed, was the source of all knowledge. And Archie's take on the dead guy matched what McNab had told her.

'Although Watson wasn't the name he went by on the island,' Archie said. 'Here the kids called him the Snowman, but he didn't only visit at Christmas.'

Archie's feelings about the Snowman were obvious by his tone. 'He would arrive, spend a week pretending to be a tourist and offload his cargo, using blackmail and intimidation to do it, but never in sight of the law. Then he stopped coming and we learned he'd been jailed.' Archie hesitated, as though he wasn't sure if he wanted to say any more than that.

Then, 'My nephew was one of the ones he had in his clutches, although we didn't know it at the time. Came back in a bad way from Afghanistan. We all thought coming home to Skye would cure him. It didn't. Nightmares. Violent flashbacks. He used to hit walls with his bare knuckles. Anything to get the rage out.'

'What about help from the MOD?'

'Six months' rehabilitation. After that you're the NHS's problem.' He paused. 'For Alistair the cocaine was a way out of all that.

'So,' he continued, 'I was mightily glad when that Glasgow detective nailed Watson and put him away. That's one man I'd like to shake hands with.'

'No one's taken the Snowman's place?' Rhona said.

'If they have, I don't know about it.'

'And your nephew?'

'The SSAFA charity's Highland branch tried to help . . .'

The 'but' hung in the air unsaid between them.

Rhona didn't want to know, but was compelled to ask.

'Ali died a year ago. Exposure, up on the Cuillin.' Archie turned to Rhona. 'Some bad memories don't go away.'

They drew into the turning circle where Rhona's jeep was parked.

'But,' Archie met her eye, 'there were a few folk, myself included, who might have cheerfully considered nudging the Snowman off Kilt Rock if they'd known he was back in business on the island.'

It was clear Archie was worried that someone local had done exactly that.

'Will you be working with the Major Investigation Team when it arrives from Glasgow?' he asked.

'There's one on the way?' Rhona said.

'By helicopter, later today, according to Lee.'

Chrissy would be pleased about that, Rhona thought, since it might extend her time here a little.

She thanked Archie for the lift. 'One other thing. Is there a bus back from Glendale later today?'

'You mean one the lassie might catch?'

Rhona nodded.

'If she was planning a walk to Healabhal Bheag, she wouldn't make the return bus. I told her that,' he added. 'She didn't seem bothered, so I guess she planned to camp out. I did warn her the weather's closing in again. More snow and high winds forecast for tonight. She said she was used to storms, although in Afghanistan it was sand rather than snow that caused them.'

So Seven must have been intent on deserting her campsite in the plantation, after saying she was staying put. Folk were of course entitled to change their minds. But why then would she leave her tent and supplies behind? The Duirinish peninsula was a wild overnight stay without the proper equipment.

But it was Archie's final remark that caused Rhona the most concern.

'She'd already had an accident during the lightning storm. Had a dressing on the back of her head. Said a branch broke off and hit her.' At this point Archie looked pointedly at Rhona's bruised knuckles. 'Looks like you had an argument with something too.'

*

The late rising sun was already contemplating its return below the horizon. Rhona switched on the jeep's lights and, as it bounced down the rough track towards the tarred road, contemplated her next move.

When Archie had expressed his desire to shake the hand of the detective who'd locked up Watson, what she hadn't told him was that she knew who his hero was.

Detective Sergeant Michael Joseph McNab.

45

The incident room was a hive of activity. McNab made his way through the throng, taking a quick dekko at the board as he passed. The Sandman investigation was ongoing, but as far as he could see, nothing new had presented itself in the last few hours, apart from a dead drug dealer on Skye being identified.

Bracing himself, he knocked on the boss's door.

He had gone over his story about the loss of Harry in his head. It hadn't sounded good then, and it wouldn't when said out loud, but it was the only one he had.

Detective Inspector Wilson was on the phone even as he'd shouted to McNab to come in. McNab stood to attention just inside the door and awaited the conclusion of the conversation, where the boss appeared to be using the words 'Yes, sir' too frequently for McNab's liking.

When the conversation came to its conclusion, the manner in which the boss put down the phone didn't bode well for what McNab was about to report.

'Well, Detective Sergeant?'

The boss, like Rhona, had an ability to suss out a lie, or even a half-truth, much like a bloodhound catching a scent. McNab suspected DI Wilson had already caught a suspicious smell and was currently pursuing it, and he, McNab, was on the trail he was following.

When he didn't immediately answer, DI Wilson said, 'Rumour has it that our stab victim has been collected from the hospital and not by us. Is this correct?'

'It is, sir,' McNab said after a moment's hesitation.

'Would you like to fill me in on what's happened, Detective Sergeant, or shall I believe the reports I've had?'

McNab found himself clearing his throat like a recalcitrant schoolboy.

'I arrived at the hospital to pick McArthur up, sir,' he said. 'He'd been sent to the discharge lounge. When I got there, he'd signed himself out.'

There was a moment's silence that seemed to last an eternity to McNab.

'You missed out the bit where you were late, and the officer on duty had been recalled, since you were definitely going to be there. He checked McArthur into the discharge lounge for safety's sake and reported back to the station.' The boss paused here like the calm before the storm. 'Where the hell were you, Detective Sergeant?'

At this point McNab decided honesty wasn't the best policy. 'I slept in, sir.' Even as he gave his weak excuse, he was squirming at the recall of what he had actually been doing.

The boss's steely stare suggested he didn't believe him. As DI Wilson opened his mouth to make this plain, McNab decided to come clean, in as minimal a way as possible.

'Ellie was there,' McNab muttered under his breath. He hurried on, 'And I lost track of the time, sir. Sorry, sir.'

DI Wilson was regarded as mild-mannered. That was not strictly true. His outward manner was not gung-ho, but underneath there was a steel which McNab both admired and would have liked to emulate. In truth, DI Wilson had been a substitute father to him within the force and was the sole reason why he'd not yet been chucked out on the streets to find another profession.

A short silence followed McNab's confession, which he hoped was a good thing.

'And just where were you planning to put McArthur if you had collected him from the hospital?' his mentor said, changing the subject, much to McNab's relief.

A number of fibs presented themselves to McNab at that moment, all of which he managed to avoid uttering.

'Where, Sergeant?'

'Ellie knew him already, sir. She offered him a place to stay, with support from social services,' he added, as though it made the arrangement okay.

As DI Wilson appeared to contemplate this, McNab had a strong feeling that the boss already knew the whole story – who from, he had no idea, although the thought did strike him that it might have been from Ellie herself.

'And when were you getting round to telling me this?'

McNab hummed and hawed in silence for a moment. Eventually he found some words.

'That's why I'm here, sir, to tell you what happened. Harry left me a message when he signed out of the discharge lounge. An eight-digit number. We think it's a service personnel identification, which might be a lead to the Sandman's operations.'

This pronouncement, which had come out of his mouth unexpectedly and which he had never intended to make, now hung in the air between them.

The boss, who never reacted without thinking, said nothing for a moment, then, 'You think the Sandman may have a service personnel set-up?'

'It's a possibility, sir,' McNab said, although the thought had only just entered his head. 'McArthur was a serving soldier, probably discharged for using while in Afghanistan. What if he was doing more than just using when out there?' McNab said, warming to his theme.

The boss had already moved to the window and was looking out over his beloved Glasgow.

'So, the Sandman could be bringing it in via army personnel.' He began to think out loud. 'It's happened in the USA. Returning troops bringing in drugs and money from war zones, hidden in returning equipment and vehicles. The mess in Afghanistan has been going on under the radar forever. Never on the news. Too embarrassing for the government to admit or reveal. It's as big as, or even bigger than, the human trafficking we're having to deal with.'

'Yes, sir,' McNab felt obliged to say.

'And the Skye victim?'

'Paul Watson, probable associate of Malcolm Stevenson. Previously jailed for dealing, sir.'

'By you, when you were a DI,' the boss reminded him.

McNab was sorry he'd let the boss down, but the truth was he was glad he wasn't a DI any more. No more focusing on the rules. If he hadn't dropped down a rank, he'd have probably left the force altogether. Under a cloud, no doubt.

Which I might yet manage to do.

'As I recall, he had a foothold in Skye? So why was he back there?'

It was a question McNab had been asking himself since Janice had revealed the DNA results. McNab had a sudden thought that he might indeed be on his way to Skye. In that, however, he was to be proved wrong.

'Find out who owns that service number, Detective.'

'If it's a serving soldier, we'll need MOD permission to access their records,' McNab said.

'Which you will have.' DI Wilson eyed him from the other side of his desk. 'Locate Harry McArthur and bring him in. DS Clark will go with the MIT to Skye.'

McNab felt a distinct and probably obvious relief that he wasn't heading for that helicopter ride, although the downside of not going to Skye was not seeing Rhona again. Glancing up, he found the boss's eyes squarely upon him.

'I would have liked you to report back on Rhona's progress, but we must rely on Chrissy to do that for the moment.'

Although it was obvious by the final nod that he was being dismissed, there was one more question McNab felt compelled to ask.

'I wondered, sir . . .' He hesitated.

'You wondered what, Sergeant?'

Was that an amused glint in the boss's eye or merely the dawning of an icy rage?

'I wondered if Ellie was in touch with you directly about her offer of a place to McArthur?'

'She was not. Now go, Sergeant.'

A few pairs of eyes followed him as he made his way to his desk, wondering what the interchange they'd no doubt viewed through the glass had been all about.

McNab sat for a moment, pondering his next move. He hadn't yet told Ellie of Harry's disappearance and since she hadn't contacted the boss directly, chances were she didn't know about it . . . yet.

He'd already contemplated spinning Ellie the yarn that

they were keeping Harry in hospital for another couple of days. Then she wouldn't worry while he was trying to locate him.

That would be the easy way out.

But if anything bad happened to Harry in the interim, it would, McNab acknowledged, be a difficult place to extract himself from with Ellie.

At the onset of their relationship, they'd promised to be honest with each other. Or at least Ellie had, regarding in particular whether she might choose to have sex with someone else. Even recalling that conversation made McNab squirm a little in his seat. He'd agreed to it, pretty sure that he would not seek sex elsewhere when he had Ellie in tow. However, as a policeman and a detective, he couldn't see how he could be frank in every answer he gave Ellie, in particular when the question had anything to do with police business.

And Prince Harry fell into that category, without a doubt.

But, if he was truthful, the real reason he didn't want to admit that Harry had gone missing from the hospital was because it was his fault entirely. Although McNab feared she wouldn't let him take full responsibility for that, since she'd been as keen this morning as he had. Ellie, he knew, would likely take some of the blame on herself. And that blame would be linked in her mind with the sex. Added to that, if Harry wasn't staying in her flat, then she would undoubtedly move back there.

McNab's final thought before he phoned Ollie rested on Rhona. Word had come to him about what had happened in the forest. The PTSD psychosis Rhona had likely been experiencing, McNab knew only too well. He'd punched a few walls in his time and there were marks in the flat to prove it.

But somehow he'd never imagined Rhona doing the same. Alvis had been unapologetic about telling him.

'Does Chrissy know?' McNab had immediately asked.

'I thought it better not to tell her. With Chrissy, Rhona performs at her most natural. I think this is because she knows that Chrissy believes in her, and does not doubt that engaging with work is her route back to well-being.' Alvis had paused there, before finally offering, 'I head home soon, so . . .'

'I'll keep on Skyping her,' McNab had assured the Norwegian detective. 'Whether she likes it or not.'

46

The sky had grown increasingly heavy, signalling what the old man in Skeabost had told her. Snow was on its way again. When he'd said this, she'd had to stop herself from smiling. Snow, she would welcome. She would survive a snowstorm just as she had the sandstorms.

She would huddle in her emergency shelter like she had inside the blue prison. But out here there would be no guards to visit her, no one thrust into her cell, head encased in a sack. No black scorpion waiting in a stone wall.

The story *he*'d concocted about that night in the birch woods had been almost believable, even to her. And the guys had swallowed it without question. Or maybe that's just what they wanted to believe, because it removed the guilt from them and anchored it onto her.

She'd been suppressing the memory, but it surged up on her now with a vengeance. The darkness, the smell, her decision not to wait, as Sugarboy had instructed, but to turn and run from *him*. That had been a mistake, a terrible mistake. She sank to the boggy ground, curling up, making herself as small as possible, her eyes closed.

And she was running again in the dark, ducking through the trees and into the clearing. She'd barely stopped to catch her breath and *he* was on her. In her panic, she'd lost

Sugarboy, and the plan so carefully nurtured had become something else entirely.

When she opened her eyes again, she found herself staring into a glistening spider's web, spun between the winter heather. And there she was, the little fly struggling to free itself, while ever closer the spider came. Reaching out, she broke the cobweb, scattering the threads, freeing the fluttering fly. Then rising, she checked out exactly where she was.

The light was fading fast. She would have to make a night stop soon, but she wanted to be well away from the nearest road and any evidence of civilization before she set up camp.

47

As soon as she was in range of Portree, Rhona pulled into a passing place and gave Chrissy a call.

'You haven't lost the dog?' Chrissy said immediately, only partly in jest, Rhona thought.

'As if,' Rhona retorted. 'And we're on our way into Portree now. Lights were out at Target Sports, so I assume Donald's in Portree too?'

'Donald's at work in the Isles and I'm at the station, awaiting an update on the MIT's arrival.' Chrissy's voice held a note of excitement.

'Do we know who they're sending?' Rhona said a little guardedly.

'Not McNab,' Chrissy promptly offered, 'although I thought it would be him, seeing as the dead guy was a catch of his. They're sending DS Clark.'

Rhona was pleased to hear that. She liked Janice Clark and thought her a steady partner for the wayward McNab.

'So why not McNab?' she found herself asking.

'Not sure, but Janice will tell all when she arrives. So,' Chrissy added, 'where did you go for your doggie walk?'

Was that suspicion Rhona heard in Chrissy's voice? If it wasn't, it would be a first.

'Can we meet in the production room?' Rhona said. 'There's something I want to show you.'

By the time Rhona drew up in the square, the promised snow had arrived, light swirling flakes that immediately melted on the warm windscreen. Blaze jumped out, and with a goodbye lick, headed for the Isles. Rhona waited until the collie was safely inside before crossing to the police station.

'So,' Chrissy said, closing the production room door behind them. 'What do you want to show me?'

Rhona brought up the image on her mobile that she'd taken of the contents of Seven's bag.

'What am I looking at?' Chrissy said, interested.

'Mementos of Afghanistan, I think.'

Chrissy's questioning look grew more serious as she studied the photograph Rhona had taken in the tent.

'Fuck's sake,' she muttered. 'Is that a real scorpion?'

'I believe so. They're pretty common in some Afghan provinces. Worth lots of money now to those who catch them.'

'And the metal disc. Is it a service tag?'

'No service details so not a human tag. I wondered if it might have come from a combat dog called Rex.'

'I suppose that's a possibility.' Chrissy made a face. 'That looks like dried blood on it.'

'I believe it is.

Chrissy had moved to study the blue mesh. Expanding the image, she suggested, 'Could that possibly be the eye window of a burka?'

'You're right,' Rhona said, realizing that was the answer that had eluded her.

'All of these things,' Chrissy said, 'look like bad memories. Things that must haunt her. Why keep them with her all the time?'

'Maybe she keeps them to remind her of her own survival?' Rhona said quietly.

Chrissy reached out and took Rhona's hand, and in that light squeeze Rhona knew she was being reminded that she too was a survivor.

Rhona cleared her throat. 'There's something else in the picture.'

'What am I missing?'

'Take a look at the chain attached to the tag.'

Chrissy expanded the image.

'Recognize it?' Rhona said.

Chrissy shook her head. 'No. Should I?'

Rhona brought up an image of the necklace they'd found on the clifftop to compare it to and Chrissy's eyes opened in surprise. 'The pattern does look similar, but that doesn't mean it's from the same chain.'

Rhona nodded. 'I know. If I could have brought it in, we could have compared them properly.'

There was a moment's silence while Chrissy considered how all this had come about.

'You went looking for the Seven girl again? And, by the looks of these pictures, you rifled through her belongings, since I can't imagine her spreading them out on her groundsheet for you to admire.'

That pretty well summed it up, so Rhona nodded.

'She'd gone, heading I think for MacLeod's Tables, although she left the campsite as though she was still staying there. Her food and cooking gear, her sleeping bag and these items were all inside the tent.'

A light dawned in Chrissy's eye.

'That's why you took the dog, in case you needed to

follow her scent,' she said with the hint of an accusation in her voice.

'Blaze trailed her to the road near Skeabost, where the guy, Archie, who caught me on his drone camera, saw her board the bus for Glendale.'

'So? She said they were planning on doing survival stuff.'

'The camp was set up as though she was coming back,' Rhona said.

'Well then, she will be. Tomorrow most like.'

Chrissy was talking sense, yet to Rhona's mind it didn't ring true.

'Blaze knew her. I mean really knew her that first time. He was protective of her even then.'

'Okay. What are you saying?' Chrissy said.

'I wondered if that was because she'd been in the clearing he took me to. That it was her blood Blaze detected.'

As Chrissy absorbed this line of reasoning, Rhona quickly added, 'And Archie said she had an injury to the back of her head, which she said she'd got from a falling branch during the lightning storm.'

Chrissy waited, sensing there was more to come.

'The location of the blood and scalp residue on the birch trunk was at her height,' Rhona said.

'So you think she was the one injured in the woods?'

Rhona did think that, in fact was beginning to be sure of it.

'Assuming that's true, there is still nothing to suggest that what happened in the woods has anything to do with the body on the beach,' Chrissy challenged her.

True, and yet . . .

'Jen Mackie detected cocaine in the soil sample we sent.'

Chrissy considered that, and Rhona knew her forensic assistant was playing devil's advocate, which was what she wanted.

'Donald saw the guy in the toilet, remember? He was high and so probably were the others.'

'For cocaine residue to be detected in the soil . . .'

'There was likely more than just a little in the vicinity,' Chrissy finished for her. 'And you wondered at the onset if there might have been a stash there.'

Rhona changed tack. 'Paul Watson was known here as the Snowman.' She repeated what Archie had told her.

'Jeez. If the locals hated him that much . . .' Chrissy said in a worried tone.

'Maybe someone did help him over the edge,' Rhona finished for her. 'The footsteps you found . . .'

'And we're back with the necklace,' Chrissy said. 'Are you going to tell Lee about the chain?'

If she did, she would have to tell him she'd been going through Seven's private things, which sounded more like something McNab would do and which she would admonish him for. Maybe the sin-eater case had changed her in more ways than just the flashbacks.

'Apart from the possibility of the Afghan necklace, there is no direct link between the medics and Paul Watson, and Lee will be focusing on the reason why Watson was here on Skye in the first place.'

'True, but . . .' Chrissy didn't look convinced.

'But what?'

'You don't usually give up that easily. If the necklace does belong to the girl, it would place her on that clifftop, which means she may know something without even realizing it.'

48

This time, McNab did go by the cafeteria and, catching sight of Maria serving, waited until she was free.

'What? Am no pretty enough fur ye?' Derek, who also worked behind the counter, challenged him.

McNab made a point of looking him up and down. 'Naw, you're not.'

'Fair do's,' Derek grinned.

Maria, who'd heard the interchange, now presented herself in front of McNab. 'Buying for Ollie, I take it?'

'What's his current favourite?' McNab said. 'Apart from yourself.'

She gave him the eye. 'Are you saying he's soft on me?'

'Don't tell me you don't know that?'

'He's never said anything. Just helps me with my phone and social media stuff.'

'He's shy. You'll have to help him.'

She pondered that for a moment. 'I like him,' she said. 'You can tell him that from me. So is it ring doughnuts again? He's been buying the jam ones.'

'Two jam ones it is then, and two coffees, mine is—'

Maria cut him off, 'I know, extra strong.'

As McNab made his way to IT, he considered the possible pairing he was taking a hand in managing.

'If only I was as successful in managing my own love life,' he muttered to himself.

He hadn't been in touch with Ellie yet regarding Harry, and was saving it up for when they both got home later. If, however, Ellie took it upon herself to check her flat before then . . .

McNab had the horrible feeling that's exactly what Ellie might choose to do.

Ollie didn't catch his approach until the scent of the coffee reached his nostrils. McNab was glad to note that Ollie looked more welcoming than earlier.

Maybe he'd found something.

McNab set down the doughnuts and told Ollie the news on the Maria front.

'She said that?' Ollie's big-eyed look got even bigger.

'Tell him I said I like him,' McNab repeated for maximum impact. 'She also says she likes going to the Grosvenor cinema in Ashton Lane. I think she wants you to take her there.'

Ollie's delight at this was a pleasure to behold.

'But be careful which picture you take her to see,' McNab said, suddenly envisaging a horror or, even worse, a Japanese cartoon. 'Probably better to check what she likes first.'

Listen to me, giving out the dating advice.

'So,' McNab said. 'Any luck, apart from a date with the delicious Maria?'

'The number you gave me is, or could be, a service number. It fits the pattern.' At this point Ollie went off into a ramble about service numbers before, during and after both world wars, and how they weren't consistent.

'This is post those wars, I take it?' McNab interrupted him.

Ollie nodded. 'Yes, when the numbering became more consistent.'

'The boss says he'll make sure you have permission to access the records of serving personnel,' McNab promptly told him.

'Well, I haven't as yet,' Ollie said, apologetically.

'Bugger it,' McNab muttered under his breath. 'What about the CCTV footage?'

'That, I do have,' Ollie said. 'Want to see it?'

McNab cast him a look that suggested that was exactly the reason he was here.

A few minutes later he was viewing the exit next to the discharge lounge where three taxis stood in a row. Checking the time clock above, he noted that it was this morning, just before nine o'clock.

With his eyes fixed on the screen, McNab watched as the seconds ticked by and, one after another, patients exited the lounge. None of them was Harry.

Time moved on, and more patients came out and got into a selection of cars or black cabs. One emerged to climb on the back of a motorbike.

No sign of Harry. Although there were males whose faces were obscured.

The clock now said 9.40.

McNab glanced at Ollie. 'You're the super recognizer. Is there a chance Harry is one of those guys whose faces we can't see properly?'

Ollie shook his head.

'He signed out at 9.30,' McNab muttered. 'At least that's the time he wrote in the book.'

'Are you certain he was picked up?' Ollie said.

'The nurse said Harry told her his ride was there.

Thanked her, signed the book and left,' McNab said irritably.

'Maybe he didn't leave from that particular exit?' Ollie suggested.

McNab imagined Harry sitting there waiting for him to turn up. Taking fright and making a run for it. If that had been the case, where would he go?

He'd had no mobile on him when McNab had taken him to hospital the night he was stabbed. McNab would have been overjoyed if that had not been the case. A mobile would at least have given them some clues as to Harry's contacts.

Ollie eventually took pity on him. 'I'll get all the exit footage around that time and go through it.'

'He must be pretty sore still,' McNab said, remembering his own exit from hospital after the shooting. 'Even if they gave him a supply of strong painkillers, it won't be enough.' McNab halted there, before he could say, *for a junkie like Harry*.

'Then you'll find him in his old haunts,' Ollie said.

Or dead.

He rose. 'You'll contact me as soon as you find out who owns that service number?' McNab tried to lighten his voice. 'But first, I suggest you head for the cafe and ask the lovely Maria out.'

By the dreamy look on Ollie's face, it appeared he might just do that.

After leaving Ollie, and despite the hour, McNab decided he wasn't ready to go home just yet.

He didn't want to open the door on an empty flat. Neither did he want to open it to find Ellie there waiting for him, eager for news. Plus what Ollie had said had rung true. If Harry was desperate for a fix, he would have headed for his old haunts. McNab wasn't sure where exactly these were, except for the places he'd seen Harry himself.

Old habits were hard to break. Old paths rarely abandoned. If Harry was sore and had nowhere to go, wouldn't he go back to his usual spot?

It was worth a try. It was also an ugly night to be sleeping rough. The predicted snow sweeping in from the west had now reached Glasgow. Never going to lie for long, it had nevertheless formed a thin surface of slush underfoot.

The flakes melting on his face, McNab walked on, each step making him wish even harder that he'd turned up on time this morning at the hospital and Harry was now safely ensconced in the comfort of Ellie's flat.

He fleetingly wondered if Harry might have made it out of Glasgow. Maybe gone home to wherever he'd come from originally. His accent didn't belong to the city, although he'd adopted a Weegie way of asking for money.

Where had Harry come from?

Fife, Dundee maybe? Plenty of soldier boys were recruited in the Kingdom of Fife. In fact anywhere where poverty or lack of work made joining up a likely proposition.

He caught the underground at Govan and got off at St Enoch's, retracing his steps of the other night. Approaching House of Fraser's, his heart leapt a little at the sight of a human bundle on the steps, but it wasn't Harry, and the girl huddled under a plastic sheet didn't even try to answer McNab's questions.

Breaking the habit of a lifetime, McNab dropped some money into her cup.

Walking on, he reached the alleyway at the back of the Rock Cafe, knowing Harry wouldn't be there, but compelled to look anyway. The scene of the stabbing was just the same, apart from the unbloodied slush melting into the gutter.

He was wasting his time and knew it.

Heading for the front door, McNab went inside. The place was as busy as normal and the bustle of noise and music enveloped him. He knew Ellie wasn't working tonight, but he went downstairs anyway.

Their plan had been to eat together at his place later, but McNab couldn't contemplate going back there yet, despite a little voice urging him to do so. Approaching the bar, he ordered a double whisky and a packet of crisps, kidding himself the combination would stave off the hunger.

He didn't bother to savour the whisky, drinking it down in two swallows. The sudden shock of it on his system was dramatic, aided by an empty stomach.

He ordered another and went to sit near the fire exit.

This time he sat the whisky in front of him. No point in drinking it until the warm glow had dissipated.

'Hey,' a voice said, 'you looking for Ellie? She's not in tonight.'

McNab, recognizing the waiter from his earlier visit, said, 'I know, thanks.'

Sitting there, he replayed his previous visit, watching it rerun before him. Taking Ellie into the corridor. Kissing her to make up for whatever mistake he'd made or was yet to make. Then following Stevenson outside.

He stopped there, not keen to rerun the next scene in Harry's story, or review the image of Ellie's small hand on his own as they'd desperately tried to keep Harry alive.

Why?

Because McNab's gut told him that something similar had probably played out today, but this time with a very different ending.

49

Lee had listened carefully to Rhona's description of her walk with the dog. His discomfort during the first few minutes of this had been obvious, and Rhona knew he'd been recalling the conversation he'd had with Alvis concerning her current state of mind, which she'd overheard.

Alvis, she was almost relieved to note, wasn't at the station. According to Lee, he had gone to Raasay for his final walk before heading back to Norway. So it was just the three of them, and Chrissy's determined input during the interview with Lee had definitely swung the balance in Rhona's favour.

'We'll see if we can locate the girl in the morning,' Lee had promised. 'Hopefully weather conditions will have improved by then and we'll have the MIT here as well.'

Rhona had left Archie's part in the story until last, concerned about telling Lee exactly what Archie had said regarding the Snowman.

'People were pretty riled up back then,' Lee said. 'Trouble was, those buying were too scared to come forward and their friends and relatives, if they knew about it, didn't want to get them into trouble. It was a mess,' he admitted. 'Did Archie tell you what happened to Ali?'

Rhona nodded.

'If folk believed Watson was here to set the ball rolling

again . . .' Lee sighed. 'We'll have to speak to everyone he was involved with last time, although not all of them are still on the island.'

Sergeant MacDonald looks weary, Rhona thought, *as am I.*

'Are you planning to stay in town tonight? It won't be a pleasant drive back.'

Up to that moment she hadn't considered what she would do next.

'She'll stay at Jamie's,' Chrissy answered for her.

Rhona didn't argue until they were outside.

'Jamie's on a call-out, but he said you can stay any time, remember?' Chrissy told her. 'He left a key behind the bar in case you might need it.' She raised her eyebrows and smiled.

'Stop it,' Rhona said.

'Stop what?' Chrissy's face was all innocence. 'So food first at the Isles?'

'I'm a bit muddy,' Rhona said.

'They're used to walkers, and we can eat in the bar.'

All eyes turned towards them as they entered, covered as they were in snow from the short walk across the square. Blaze, spotting Rhona, came to greet her. Settled by the fire, Rhona ruffled the dog's ears.

'Thanks, boy, for your help today.'

The dog looked up at her, a little whine signifying his answer.

'Food order's in,' Chrissy said on her return from the bar. She set down two large glasses of white wine and handed Rhona a key. 'Jamie is still out with the MRT. It sounds like he'll be late back.'

Rhona relaxed at the news, realizing she could eat, then head back to Jamie's for a hot bath, and if Jamie was out with the rescuers, she wouldn't have to discuss where she'd been again tonight.

Jamie's, unlike the cottage, had central heating as well as an open fire, and Rhona was met with warmth at the front door. Taking off her muddy boots, she immediately headed upstairs to run a longed-for bath. The shower would have been quicker, but her aching muscles demanded immersion.

Before stepping into the water, Rhona selected one of the array of bath oils on display, deciding they definitely hadn't all been brought here by Jamie's sister.

Soaking in the scented water, with flurries of snow melting against the dormer window above, Rhona thought of Seven somewhere on the soggy bog marsh that constituted most of the area around the flat-topped Healabhal Bheag. Being out in the open tonight would certainly be a test of endurance.

But that's not why she went there.

If it had been, she would have gone prepared for the conditions.

The girl's manner, her nervousness, didn't speak to Rhona of soldiering bravado. It reminded her too much of herself for that.

Sliding down to lay her head against the rim, she raised her hands above the water and examined her knuckles. Bruising always got worse before it got better, she reminded herself, recalling the state of her body when she'd come here to Skye.

The bruising had gone from her torso, yet to her eye it still lingered below the surface of the skin. Just the way it loitered in her mind, bubbling up at times, to explode in a fierce anger, which even she couldn't pacify.

Those mementos in the bag weren't there to remind Seven of something good that had happened. They were harsh, stinging memories. Perhaps imprisoning them in the drawstring bag rather than in her mind was Seven's answer to the problem.

Her mobile rang as she climbed out of the bath. It was McNab's name on the screen. When she didn't answer, the call ended and a message pinged in seconds later.

I have news. Call me.

Dressed now, the fire lit, and having helped herself to a measure from Jamie's whisky bottle, Rhona did as asked.

'Why'd you take so long?' McNab said on picking up.

The tone of his voice warned Rhona that he had probably been drinking. It was an edge she hadn't heard in a while, and it unnerved her.

'What is it?' she said tersely.

McNab took off like a rocket. 'Harry McArthur disappeared from the hospital because I arrived late to collect him. Ellie had offered him a place to stay until he recovered. I don't know where he is, and I'll have to tell Ellie I lost him. She wanted to help him, because of her brother.'

'McNab. Slow down,' Rhona ordered when she got a moment to interrupt his litany of despair. 'I don't know who Harry McArthur is.'

He halted, as though considering this. 'Harry's an Afghanistan veteran. On the streets now. Buying from Malcolm Stevenson.'

'Okay. Now go on,' Rhona said, hoping her calm manner might dictate his own.

'He left me a service number in the sign-out book. It's a live one. We had to get clearance to access the details.'

'And?' Rhona said as he fell silent.

'It belongs to a guy from the medical corps, name of Peter Galbraith, currently on leave from Afghanistan.'

50

Afghanistan

The girl is too young to bear a child, thin and underdeveloped, her breasts only just visible. I place her at twelve or thirteen, although it's difficult to determine out here. Men become boys as soon as a gun or a grenade is thrust into their hands.

The girl-children are permitted to play bareheaded in the dirt until when? Probably when they bleed for the first time, then freedom is over and they are covered from head to toe in blue, brown or green burkas. Even the shuttlecocks, as they're also called, have a lineage. In the Kabul area they are definitely blue, although there are different shades.

Blue fireworks, I think suddenly, are the most chemically difficult to make. I have always found that odd. The colour of the sky, the colour of the sea. As natural a colour as that, yet to make things explode with a blue light is difficult and expensive.

As my mind races, seeking any thought but the one I know I must have, a hand slips into mine. Warm and comforting, it brings tears to my eyes. No one has held my hand like this since the medical tent. Then I was the one to reach for an injured man's hand and whisper, 'It's okay, soldier. I'm here.'

I realize then that the hand is accompanied by a soft voice that keeps repeating those Pashto words: *Please help. Nurse. Please help.*

I am a nurse, I remind myself, although that world seems so very far away and belonging to someone else.

I am led closer to the raised platform where she lies, then the hand releases mine.

I look down and see hips so narrow, the bones so prominent, that it makes my heart pound to imagine what could possibly pass between them.

If she dies in childbirth, am I to suffer the same fate?

All these thoughts go through my head as I kneel beside her, the other women crouching round us, their eyes wide with fear. Maybe they think that I might bring evil to her. And yet.

Her eyes, wide, liquid brown and heavily lashed, stare up at me, pleading and helpless. I think of the boy, not much younger than her, who had hidden the means of death from me. Who'd smiled shyly as I'd washed the blood from his face. Who'd planned the murder of my comrades and wished for me the horror I live in now.

But how many children and women have we killed with our drone hits?

I have no conception of what they truly think of us, the invading army, until, despite all our attempts at saving their injured as well as our own, they turn against us.

So why trust me to help now?

Even as I feel the baby move beneath my fingers, I know the reason why it cannot escape. Instinctively, I begin to massage the bulging stomach, urging the small body inside to turn. If it does, could it even then pass through the gates of its prison?

The alternative is to spare her the agony of breeching such a narrow canal. I could cut her and lift the infant out. That might be the only way to save the baby, who is alive and growing more desperate by the minute, and the child that is its mother.

I look up at the circle of desperate female faces and frantically search for a way to make them understand what has to be done here.

51

McNab had hoped she would be asleep, so he wouldn't have to explain. Tonight at least. He made a big effort with the lock and slipped his shoes off once inside. It reminded him of creeping in late at night as a teenager, smelling of drink and worse, keen not to be confronted by his mother.

A side light was still on in the sitting room and he hesitated for a moment, imagining a shadow might be Ellie, sitting in a dark corner, *nursing her wrath to keep it warm*. Then he spotted the laid table, the open wine, one glass used, and the partially eaten meal.

McNab hated himself in that moment.

He had messaged her, told her he had to work late, promised he would be home as soon as he could. *As soon as he could face her.*

He'd never considered himself a coward, not when he was confronted with evil, but when he was confronted by good, and had to somehow live up to it, that was the problem.

The bedroom was in darkness. He contemplated lying down on the couch. He wasn't drunk exactly, but doing that would look as though he was. He would, he decided, get undressed and climb in beside her. If she wakened, he would tell her he'd explain in the morning. They would talk about it then.

McNab went into the bathroom to undress. Stepping briefly under the shower, he rubbed himself dry then cleaned his teeth. Finally he braced himself and walked silently through.

A street light seeped round the blind, giving the room a strip of light that led towards the bed. The soft mound that was Ellie lay perfectly still as he slid in beside her. Normally he would wrap himself around her, but fearing the cool of his body would wake her, McNab stayed six inches away.

But still he wanted to touch her to feel her breathing.

He reached out, only to discover the soft shape beside him to be nothing more than the heaped shape of the duvet.

'Ellie?' he said stupidly. 'Ellie?'

Her name echoed round the room, drifting out of the door to meet the other empty rooms.

Ellie wasn't here, his still-inebriated brain told him. The ruffled bed was not Ellie.

McNab swung his feet to the floor and switched on the light.

Now he could see that the bag she'd brought her clothes in was missing. He went back to the bathroom, looking for the stuff she'd put in there, wondering why he hadn't noticed its absence when he'd showered.

Because I was pissed and pretending not to be.

McNab rummaged for his phone in the strewn clothes he'd thrown down earlier. It was well after midnight. Too late to call her?

He did it anyway. Her voice answered with the usual funny message, asked him to state his business and she'd get back to him. McNab, tongue-tied, hung up instead.

He lifted his clothes as though considering putting them

on again, then brought them through and sat down on the bed, undecided.

Should he go round to her place and check on her? He couldn't ride the bike or drive, not in his state, but he could call a taxi. And he had a key, one that he'd been supposed to give to Harry. So he could get in without disturbing her.

A thought suddenly struck him. Was this about Harry? Had Ellie found out that he'd disappeared?

McNab registered that his last moment of clarity had been when he'd spoken to Rhona to tell her about the tracing of the service number, which he'd then used as an excuse to order another drink, telling himself although he'd lost one soldier, he'd found another.

He moved to the kitchen and went through the motions of making real coffee, as strong as possible. Two shots later, his brain began to break through the fog. The trouble with not drinking regularly was this mind fog when you did.

Last night he'd concentrated on personal matters. Even worse, it was where his personal life impacted on his professional world. That was why he hadn't wanted Harry staying at Ellie's, and he'd been right. He'd known it would end badly.

McNab allowed himself a moment of righteous resentment that Ellie had put him in such a position. He should never have okayed it. He recalled Ellie's face at this point, her voice as she'd told him, in no uncertain terms, that she didn't need his permission.

And she didn't. If Ellie wanted to be kind-hearted, it wasn't his place to dissuade her.

But look how it had turned out. And it could have been worse. Harry could have had dealers turning up at her door. Invited his mates to squat there. Brought bad things down on her for her kindness.

He stopped his negative ramblings there and tried the alternative.

There was always a chance her help might have set Harry on a different path and helped Ellie lay the ghost of her brother to rest.

McNab dressed and, grabbing his jacket, left the flat.

The snow was still falling, light and wet, melting swiftly underfoot. Walking would help him think, he decided, and it was better than sitting brooding in the flat so close to the whisky.

They had misplaced Harry, but he had a lot to thank the guy for. He'd obviously decided when he'd left that he wasn't planning on seeing McNab again, but Harry hadn't left him with nothing. He'd left him with a lead to follow and it seemed that the lead led to the Isle of Skye.

52

Rhona heard the key turn in the lock and realized her solitude was over. A blast of cold air heralded Jamie's entrance, his face reddened by wind, his hair tousled.

'Rhona.' He gave her a wide smile. 'I was hoping when I saw the light on that it might be you. And thank you for lighting the fire,' he said, heading there to warm his hands.

'Can I get you something hot, or something strong?' Rhona offered.

'Black coffee would be good with a decent measure of whisky added.'

When Rhona returned with a large mug as requested, Jamie thanked her and quickly took a mouthful.

'How'd it go?' she said, already concerned by the look in his eyes.

'We found him.'

'That's good,' Rhona said hopefully.

Jamie met her eye and shook his head. 'He was already dead.'

Rhona waited, not sure what to say next. Deaths on Highland hills were fairly common, but that didn't make dealing with them any easier.

'I'm sorry,' she said, putting her hand on his arm.

'It looks like he got caught in a rockfall on a scree slope below Sgurr nan Gobhar. He was partly buried by the rocks and had fallen a fair bit, by the state of the body, in particular his face.'

'He was climbing the Cuillin in this weather?' Rhona said, glancing at the window.

'We think he's been lying up there a while, but there's no sign of an abandoned vehicle left at the Fairy Pools' car park, or further down near the Youth Hostel.'

'So how did he get there?'

'From the gear, he was equipped to stay out in the open for some time, so he could have simply walked in – from where, we don't know.'

'Any idea who he was?' Rhona said.

'Despite the gear, he had no ID, no mobile or wallet on him.'

'Isn't that strange?'

'Some folk leave their valuables back where they're staying or in their car. And a serious walker knows there's no mobile signal where they're going.'

'Was he reported missing?'

'No. It looks like a lone climber. That's not unusual. And neither is the absence of a car. Some folk make a point of not bringing a vehicle, relying on the island bus service. Feels more authentic that way.'

'Then how did you know to look for him?'

'A drone image.' He took another mouthful of the whisky coffee. 'We had to carry him out. That's why it took so long. Bristow don't lift dead bodies and even if they did, the visibility was down to nothing, so no night flying.'

'God, you must be starving,' Rhona said, suddenly realizing just how long he'd been out. 'I'm not much of a cook, but I can make you a fry-up?'

'Thanks, we had rations with us, and now I'm way past

eating. I just need a shower and bed, with another Talisker to send me to sleep.' He swallowed the remains of the coffee.

Rhona hesitated. 'There's no chance he might be one of the medics? Alvis and I spoke to the girl yesterday, and she said the four men were out on survival training but couldn't tell us where. Lee's keen to locate them.'

Jamie looked taken aback by this. 'I'll speak to Lee in the morning. The body's in the mortuary at Broadford. No post-mortem or police facilities, but you could take a look tomorrow, before he's shipped off to Glasgow.'

'I'll do that,' Rhona said.

'So, any news regarding the beach body?' Jamie said cautiously.

'You haven't heard?'

'Heard what?'

'It's Paul Watson, better known on Skye as—'

'The Snowman,' Jamie finished for her. 'Jesus. That's bad, very bad.' He looked at her. 'You know why?'

'Archie told me.'

'His nephew and quite a few others were buying from him.' Jamie hesitated, his face darkening. 'God, I hope no one local is involved in him going over the cliff.' He hesitated. 'Any evidence of a connection between the Snowman and your scene in the woods?'

'No. DNA doesn't match,' Rhona said. 'But—' She stopped herself before she mentioned McNab's phone call. 'Nothing. It'll keep until tomorrow. Get some sleep.'

He rose with a groan. 'I'm glad there's no one due to be buried tomorrow,' he said with a half-smile, 'otherwise I would likely fall into the grave with them. Will you bank up the fire? It's going to be a cold one.'

He bent and kissed her lightly on the cheek. 'Goodnight and sleep well. If you get cold there's extra blankets in the cupboard.'

Rhona watched Jamie trudge wearily upstairs, realizing she'd almost revealed McNab's startling revelation from earlier, because it had been very much on her mind.

If there was a link between current serving army personnel and the delivery of heroin and cocaine on the streets of Glasgow, as McNab had suggested, it would blow the Sandman investigation wide open . . . provided the MOD permitted this to happen, of course.

She recalled her own run-in with the MOD after a severed foot had been discovered in the nearby Raasay Sound, a favourite route for their submarines, the presence of which had proved a danger to local fishing vessels by snagging their nets. How swiftly the MOD had moved to deny and cover any involvement, even to the point of removing the foot from the fridge at her lab before she'd completed her study of it.

But there were also other issues to consider.

If Harry McArthur's contact was with the same Pete Galbraith who was one of the group of medics currently on Skye, could there have been any significance to their trip other than to play games at A.C.E Target Sports, get drunk and take themselves off into the wilds to do survival training?

If their presence was linked in some way to Watson's sojourn on the island, then her sense of a connection between the scene in the birch woods and the beach might have been right all along.

And now another unidentified body, partly buried in scree, with a damaged face and no identification.

Rhona thought of the mementos from Afghanistan hanging in Seven's tent. The bag she'd left behind. What had happened there to bind the group together? And what had brought them here?

She glanced at the window where a rising wind was whipping the snow against the glass in a frenzied dance, and thought of Seven, wherever she might be this night.

53

McNab had listened to the boss's early morning call through a thick head, caused not by too much alcohol, but by too little sleep.

He'd walked all the way to Ellie's flat in the sleet and had stood looking up at her window. He'd opened the street door with her key and climbed the stairs. He'd stood outside her door and listened for what seemed an age.

Then he'd taken out his notebook and written her a note explaining what had happened in the hospital. That he was sorry Harry had gone before he'd arrived, but Harry had left a positive message for him in the sign-out book and assured the nurse in charge that all was well.

He apologized for coming home late and promised he'd be in touch again soon. And he was looking for Harry to make sure he was okay. He signed it 'Michael' and posted it through her letter box. Then he'd walked home and fallen into bed to be wakened by a call from the station that said DI Wilson was coming on the line.

'The team didn't make it to Skye last night due to bad weather. Get yourself down there, Detective Sergeant, and go with them.'

'But, sir, you said I was to look for Harry McArthur.'

'Someone else can do that now we have the lead on

Peter Galbraith being on Skye. Find him and bring him back with you.'

McNab muttered his agreement, hung up and headed for the shower, standing under a tepid spray to help himself wake up. He had no desire to travel in a helicopter again and hadn't done so since the Sanday case. Neither did he like the idea of going back to Skye, which he'd seen very little of when he'd deposited Rhona there what seemed like months ago.

Then again, he would rather follow up the lead Harry had left him than look for Harry himself. And when he returned, things might have cooled down on the Ellie front. But not too cool, McNab hoped.

Emerging from the shower, he checked the wardrobe for clothes suitable for a cold, wet and possibly snowy Skye, cursing the fact he was going there and at the same time wearing a smile because he would see Rhona in the flesh again as opposed to just Skyping her.

Surely between himself and Chrissy they would succeed in bringing her home?

'You're late,' Janice told him on arrival at the helicopter station. 'There is a window of opportunity, according to the pilot, and we need to take it.'

'Aren't you pleased I'm coming with you?'

DS Clark dismissed his desire for a response with a raised eyebrow and a silently mouthed expletive.

'I feel the same way about you,' McNab assured her with a smile.

The skies above Glasgow had cleared, the streets below barely recognizable from McNab's wet midnight tramp about town. To keep his mind off the fact that he was up in the air, McNab concentrated on the view he had of the city. The heliport was close to the Death Star and from the fly-past he could even identify the exit near the discharge lounge . . . or at least he tortured himself with that thought.

After the city faded from view, McNab focused on the meandering ribbon of the Clyde for as long as possible, but as they made their way north and west into what he would term 'the wilderness' he stopped looking and, since conversation wasn't really possible, retreated into his thoughts on the email Ollie had sent first thing.

It was a report on Peter Galbraith's information gleaned from his service records.

Galbraith had served in Iraq, then Afghanistan for the last four years as a combat medical technician in the Royal Army Medical Corps. He was currently on leave, due to return for a further posting to Afghanistan shortly. Ollie's email continued:

> The information I was allowed to access was basic stuff. His service record for the previous five years. When he was out there, when he was back here.
>
> There's an oddity, though. Something happened to him, I think. Injured maybe? Anyway, for a period of a month he was declared unfit for work, but didn't come home. The language used in the record refers to a hostile incident but doesn't give any details.

McNab had written back:

> Find out. Get the boss to insist. We have to know everything about his time here and in Afghanistan. What he gets up to

when he's back on leave in Glasgow. Has he got a girlfriend, boyfriend? Who he served with. All personal details.

'Look,' Janice ordered, pointing at a line of rock pinnacles, rising like grey teeth from the surrounding hillside. 'The Old Man of Storr . . .' Her excited voice was drowned by the chopper blades, the view swiftly changing as they made a turn towards a spread of brightly painted buildings clustered round a small harbour.

'Portree ahead,' the pilot informed them. 'That's where we're putting down.'

As they started to do exactly that, McNab chose to shut his eyes and await his possible death. But if his card had been taken out of the box and examined, it had then been put back in, for shortly afterwards the chopper touched down and the noise from the blades dissipated.

McNab opened his eyes again, hoping Janice hadn't noticed they'd been closed, only to be proved wrong.

'You missed everything,' she said dismissively.

'I was watching my entire life flash before me,' McNab declared. 'Anyway, I've been here before, remember? And the only way to travel to Skye is by motorbike.'

Urged out, McNab found his feet on terra firma, albeit a decidedly wet terra firma, and following Janice's lead, he made his way towards a couple of parked police vehicles.

Minutes later he was being greeted by Sergeant Lee MacDonald, whom he'd been in touch with since Rhona had come back to the island.

'Detective Sergeant McNab, it's good to finally meet you.'

McNab took the firm handshake offered, while ignoring the questioning look being thrown at him by Janice as to how they were already acquainted.

'And this is?'

Janice, having regained her composure, introduced herself.

'Let me welcome you both to Skye,' the sergeant said, as he ushered them towards his vehicle, 'although I wish it was under different circumstances. Have you been here before?' he asked Janice as she and McNab settled themselves in the back seat.

'No, always wanted to, though. The scenery's pretty magnificent.'

'A top-ranking worldwide destination now that folk have seen some of the images posted online.'

'And in the movies,' Janice said.

'We like the visitors, but they can cause problems at some of the most popular spots, and they don't know how to drive on single-track roads.'

'McNab knows all about that,' Janice said. 'He headed up a team to Sanday in Orkney for a while.'

'Really?' the sergeant looked surprised. 'With the nearest police station being an hour and a half away by ferry in Kirkwall, that couldn't have been easy.'

When McNab didn't respond, he continued, 'The conference room at the station's to be your base, and we've booked you both accommodation at the Isles hotel, just across from us in Somerled Square. You'll have a vehicle, of course, and as much help as we can spare.'

'And Dr MacLeod?' Janice asked, with a sideways look at McNab.

'Rhona was staying in town last night at Jamie McColl's place, five minutes away from the station. So she's likely there now. Chrissy might take a little longer to arrive.'

'Where's Chrissy then?' McNab said, finding himself slightly peeved by the first-name basis of the conversation.

Sergeant MacDonald smiled at them via the overhead mirror.

'She's been staying out at A.C.E Target Sports with Donald and Blaze.'

'That's her new forensic assistant, or so I hear?' Janice said.

'Aye, Blaze makes a fine police dog, although he's not one of our own.' Sergeant MacDonald hesitated. 'Before we arrive, I think I should fill you in on the background of Paul Watson and Skye.'

'I've read a fair bit about his dealings here,' Janice immediately said. 'And Detective Sergeant McNab brought his case to court.'

'I understand that, but we'll have to tread carefully locally. There were a lot of folk here whose families were damaged by that man. And many will be privately celebrating his demise.'

'Enough to organize it?' McNab butted in.

Sergeant MacDonald went quiet for a moment, before saying, 'I used to work in Edinburgh before coming here fifteen years ago. Policing has to match the people we work with. You wouldn't want me to come to Glasgow and work as though I was on Skye, would you?'

McNab didn't answer, despite being prodded, so Janice did. 'You're the SIO on this, Sergeant, we'll take your advice, of course.'

There was a minute's tense silence until Sergeant MacDonald broke it with a question directed at McNab. 'I understand you're here primarily to locate one of the male medics currently somewhere on the island, Detective Sergeant? To do with the Sandman case?'

'A case we suspect may also involve Watson,' McNab said.

'Well, Dr MacLeod has been leading the interest in the soldier group since she first found evidence of a possible crime scene in the woods behind A.C.E Target Sports. So she's the authority on that.'

The car drew into a small square and parked alongside the police station.

'The district court's next door, so that's handy, although there are plenty visits north to Inverness court, which is a fair drive away. Distance is everything here on Skye. Folk think because it's an island, it must be small. It isn't, so a lot of time is spent in getting to wherever we're required. Rhona's discovered that. It's an hour between her cottage and Portree, which is why she's been staying in town recently.'

McNab found he didn't want to be told about Rhona's sleeping arrangements, so interrupted. 'What about Inspector Olsen?'

'Alvis is on Raasay at present, our neighbouring island, although I believe he intends coming back here before heading home to Norway.'

Olsen had kept McNab posted on Rhona, including reporting the scene of her meltdown in the plantation, which he knew the sergeant was also aware of. McNab realized things would have to change now that he was here himself, having no wish to discuss Rhona's state of mind with either of them now that he could speak to her in person.

At the thought of seeing Rhona again, his heart lifted, but, he reminded himself, he would have to watch his step when he met her. Both for her sake and his own. The last time they'd seen one another in person had been an emotional one, although travelling here on the Harley had been infinitely preferable to coming by car.

In a car there would have been an empty silence between them for hours, full of all the things neither of them wanted to say, or even remember.

As it was, on the bike, they could concentrate on the road and the surroundings. McNab had never been so enamoured by scenery before. He'd even stopped to take photographs, for God's sake.

And that had made her laugh.

Sergeant MacDonald was ushering them through the building and up the stairs, introducing them to colleagues en route. McNab made no attempt to register the names or even the faces, intent on seeing only one.

She was standing at the window looking out over the rooftops, with the sea beyond. She turned on their entry, hesitated for only a moment before coming forward. McNab hung back, letting Janice greet her first with an affectionate hug.

She looked better, he thought, better than the last time he'd seen her in the flesh, but still fragile. A word he never thought he'd use to describe Rhona MacLeod. When he'd carried her here, her hands round his waist as they rode together, he had thought her too thin, the delicate bones in her face too prominent. The hug she'd given him just before he'd ridden off leaving her here had betrayed how thin she was beneath the clothes.

She looks less thin now, he thought as she moved from Janice to him.

'McNab,' she said. 'Back on Skye. I never thought I'd see the day.' She neither hugged him, like she had Janice, nor shook his hand.

A look was all they exchanged, but it was a look McNab knew well.

Someone brought in coffee at that point, something McNab had craved as much as seeing Rhona again.

'If you'd like to take a seat,' Sergeant MacDonald said, 'we'll invite the rest of the team in and bring everyone up to date.'

54

Afghanistan

The girl believes she is going to die. I can see that in her eyes and the way she holds my hand. If they hadn't brought me here she most likely would have. The baby too.

I suspect some of the women understand what is wrong but are too frightened to do what has to be done. If I do it and it doesn't work, then her death will be appeased by my own.

I can, I decide, leave the girl to suffer the agonies of trying to bear a child that will not, cannot emerge. Or I can help her.

I have been expecting death from the moment I was thrust into my cell. At times I would have welcomed it, which is why I don't fear the presence of the black scorpion in the walls of my prison. He is my insurance for when I no longer want to survive.

But here is an opportunity to be a medic, a nurse again.

I begin making slicing movements against the girl's stomach, indicating that I want the child to emerge that way. And for that I need a knife. A sharp knife. I murmur phrases I know, praising Allah and anything I can remember about children and love.

My attempts at explaining bring a babble of excited chatter. Only one woman, her face lined with age, stays silent, observing me.

Then the knife appears and is presented to me.

I want to sterilize it first, but how to make them understand?

A fire burns in a stone chimney, cooking utensils close by. I take the knife there and hold it to the flames until it glows red. I point at the water jug and then the cooking pot and indicate I want them to boil water.

If I cut the girl open, I will have to close her, but with what? I motion as though I am sewing something. The faces, so intent, watch my movements and in at least a couple of them a light dawns.

There are patterned cushions in the room, and intricate embroidered garments, including the detailed work round the eye mesh of the blue burkas. It isn't possible to do that without needle and thread.

Having amassed everything beside me on a white cloth, they now wait for me to do whatever I have decided.

In that moment I am back in the medical tent, helping the boy up onto the bed, examining his wounds, his eyes observing me just as the girl on the bed is doing now.

What if it isn't just me who will die if I fail? What if the others will face death too?

She will have to bite down on something hard. The same old woman who has been watching me hands me an intricately carved piece of wood to place in the girl's mouth.

We are ready. I say that because I am not alone in my endeavour. If I fail, the women will not be able to prevent my death; but if I succeed, they will, I think, looking round the faces, try to set me free.

55

During the briefing, McNab had announced to the assembled company that he was here specifically to establish the whereabouts of Peter Galbraith with respect to the ongoing Sandman case in Glasgow.

'I will therefore be accompanying Dr MacLeod to view the body in the mortuary in Broadford before it is sent on to Glasgow.'

This had been news to Rhona, at least the part about McNab accompanying her. As they hadn't been alone together since he'd deposited her at the cottage in what seemed a lifetime ago, she feared a probing conversation, or a definite attempt to get her to return to Glasgow, during the trip. Neither of which she wanted to deal with at the moment.

Emerging from the station, Rhona headed for Jamie's jeep.

'Why aren't we using a police vehicle?' McNab immediately said.

'They're all needed, especially with DS Clark and the others here. The jeep's Jamie's. I've been using it since I got here.'

The last item of information was, she knew, a jibe, but McNab didn't rise to it, merely installing himself in the passenger seat without comment. The sky was clear of cloud, but after the snow there had been a sharp drop in the overnight temperature and in places frost glistened. McNab had been silent since their departure from Portree, and remained so, staring out of the window at what Rhona regarded as the magnificence of the Black Cuillin against a blue sky, but which she knew he definitely wasn't admiring.

Rhona had seen him like this before. He was either deep in thought or nursing a grievance.

His silence, she now decided, was more unnerving than the expected interrogation.

Eventually he did speak, only to ask, 'Who is this guy Chrissy's hanging about with, anyway?'

Chrissy had been late arriving at the conference room and the strategy meeting had been in full swing. She'd managed a few words with McNab when they'd stopped for coffee, but her cheerful countenance had obviously perturbed or annoyed him.

'Donald McKay,' Rhona told him. 'Owner of Blaze, my—'

He cut her off. 'Okay, I know. Your new forensic assistant. Chrissy's not thinking of staying on out here, is she?'

'What a good idea,' Rhona said to irritate him further, 'I'll have to suggest it.'

After the prolonged silence which followed her response, Rhona asked if McNab had a photograph of the medic Peter Galbraith.

'I do. Plus the info that the MOD released, which isn't much and probably not enough to make a formal identification.' He looked at her. 'That's what you think, isn't it? That the body is one of the medics and not some lone climber?'

'I have no idea how many lone climbers are on the hills at present. I do know, however, that there are four male medics out there, according to Seven.'

'Seven?' McNab said.

'She said the guys call her that. Maybe she's their lucky mascot.'

McNab snorted. 'Aye, right. More like her fuckable score when in the deserts of Afghanistan.'

'They looked like a close-knit bunch,' Rhona said, ignoring his remark. 'According to reports from the Isles bar.'

'When you've faced a whole pile of shit together . . .' McNab threw Rhona a look she didn't need to interpret.

They had reached the steep brae that curved down into Sligachan, the campsite at the head of the neighbouring loch still sporting a few big camper vans.

'Jesus, some folk need their heads looked at, camping in Scotland in the winter.'

'The vans are well equipped,' Rhona countered. 'Also the Sligachan Hotel's a real draw. Donald says the beer's good.' She pointed at the road leading west. 'That takes you to Glenbrittle and the Fairy Pools. A big attraction whatever the time of year. If you decide you want a look at the area they found him in, that's the way we would go.'

'Fairy Pools, Fairy Glen, what is it with all the fey stuff?'

Rhona knew McNab didn't want an answer so didn't give him one. Instead she asked, 'Why did you choose to come with me? You could have spoken to Jamie and talked to him about the circumstances he found the body in. Plus you could have watched zone footage being taken of possible places the medics may have gone.'

This time it was McNab who didn't answer her question. Instead, pointing ahead, he asked if the island now visible at the end of the loch was Raasay where Alvis was.

Surprised by this, Rhona said yes.

'You were involved with something out there, before I came on the scene?'

'I was.'

'Why would Alvis go there?'

'Dun Caan, probably,' Rhona said.

'Duncan who?'

'The flat-topped mountain. He'll be climbing it.'

McNab made a face that suggested, *Why the fuck would he want to do that?*

'For the same reason you ride a Harley,' Rhona answered the unasked question.

'To get his rocks off, you mean?' McNab said with a grin. 'Come on, you have to admit it, Dr MacLeod, riding pillion with me on a Harley through the Highlands is way better than climbing a fucking mountain in the freezing cold.'

His declaration followed by Rhona's laugh seemed to clear the air.

McNab relaxed now into his seat and, reviewing the interchange, Rhona decided he'd been gauging her state of mind, rather than choosing to ask her outright.

And it seemed he was now reasonably reassured by her response.

She drew into the car park, carefully avoiding a way-ward sheep standing just outside the pillared entrance to the hospital grounds, gazing at what looked like better grass available on the other side of the wall.

'They know we're coming. Lee called ahead,' she said as McNab gave the sheep a wide berth in order to follow her.

'What's with all the first-name stuff?' McNab said. 'You always refer to me as McNab.'

'I use your first name, Michael, when you've pissed me off,' Rhona reminded him as they entered and made for the reception desk.

Rhona introduced herself, adding, 'And this is Detective Sergeant McNab. Sergeant MacDonald said we would be coming to view the body the MRT brought down from the hill last night?'

'Oh yes,' the woman said in the musical lilt of a native. She gave them directions to the mortuary. 'Are you okay to find your own way there? Or will I get Kirsty to take you?' She indicated a dark-haired girl seated in front of a computer.

'We can manage,' Rhona assured her.

'Duncan's on duty down there. He'll give you every assistance we can, although we're not equipped for a police-led post-mortem.'

'I understand, thank you.'

As they went through the swing doors, McNab said, 'I thought you told me Duncan was a mountain?'

Rhona ignored McNab's attempt at a joke. 'Are you sure you're up for this? I know how you don't like mortuaries.'

'As long as there are no electric saws and disembowelling, I'm fine.'

The mortuary was for storage only, with a small viewing room. Duncan, who proved to be a mountain of a man, much to McNab's amusement, brought out the body and the bagged clothes, then departed.

Exposed, it showed all the signs of a fall onto rocks, much like the one on the shore. The face too had taken a beating, making it difficult to discern the features beneath. One thing was still obvious. The climber had, by his torso, been a fit guy.

'Well?' she said as McNab brought up the photo of a handsome army medic in full uniform and attempted to compare it to the body before them. 'Could that be him?'

'Height- and weight-wise, hair and eye colour, yes. We have his blood type too, which we can compare,' McNab said.

Rhona gave him the good news.

'All British military personnel deployed to Iraq or Afghanistan were given the chance to store their DNA in a secure armed forces repository,' she said. 'If Peter Galbraith took up that option, then we can establish for sure if this is him.'

McNab nodded, obviously encouraged by that.

'So, how long would you say he's been dead?'

When Rhona shot him a look, McNab qualified his question. 'An estimate only, of course.'

'Well, it's been consistently cold on the Cuillin over the last few days which hinders decomposition. Rigor mortis has come and gone. He was, according to Jamie, semi-buried by a rockfall, so there's not the usual infestation of someone above or below ground.'

Rhona continued, 'Insects prefer injuries inflicted prior to death, because they bleed profusely, which suggests the face wound happened before he died. All of which puts the death in the time frame of the previous few days.'

'When the medics were out on the hills.'

Rhona raised the body a little to examine the underside. 'One oddity, though . . .'

'What?'

'See here, post-mortem lividity suggests he probably died on his back, but was later turned on his front.'

McNab waited, obviously expecting an explanation for this.

Rhona attempted to give him one. 'He fell, landing on his back initially, then later rolled further down the scree and ended up on his front.'

'How did the earlier wound to his face come about, d'you think?'

Rhona shook her head. 'Something that happened during the climb, I presume. He wasn't wearing a climbing helmet, or there wasn't one found nearby. That's why you need to talk to Jamie. Even better, attend the post-mortem in Glasgow. Electric saws notwithstanding.'

McNab, she noted, didn't look enthusiastic about either suggestion. Although why talking to Jamie featured equally with the smell and noise of a PM, she had no idea.

'So what do you plan to do now?' he said.

'Take some photographs and samples. Examine his clothing,' Rhona told him. 'And write up my findings in my notebook, as usual.'

'In here?' he said, aghast.

Rhona pointed at a nearby chair. 'Over there.'

'I forgot about your creepy side, Dr MacLeod.'

'Why don't you get yourself a coffee and check back with Portree?' Rhona suggested. 'I'll text you Jamie's number and you can ask him what you want to know.'

Now alone, Rhona set about her task. Assuming Peter Galbraith had agreed to the voluntary collection of his DNA, there shouldn't be much difficulty in getting the MOD to allow them to check it against the climber, since the whole idea for storing the DNA of personnel was to allow the identification of remains.

What they couldn't do was use the MOD database for interrogation purposes with respect to a crime.

Alvis had viewed the group in the pub, but for the most part from a distance. Donald had briefly encountered one of them in the toilet. Bringing Alvis with them this morning would have been useful, but any attempts she'd made to contact him on Raasay had been unsuccessful so far. As for Donald, she could at least show him the image of Private Peter Galbraith and establish that he had been one of the medics that had stayed in the hotel.

If they could only locate all the members of the team, she thought, then the mystery could be solved. From the silence since they'd departed Portree, that obviously hadn't happened yet.

Seven might be somewhere on the Duirinish Peninsula, because of Archie's sighting of her getting on the bus for Glendale. Although she may have switched buses at Dunvegan and headed east instead. As for the others . . .

Rhona finished what she was doing and, leaving the mortuary, went to look for McNab. Reporting that she'd finished and that the body could now be sent to Glasgow, Rhona asked if the dark-haired girl had any idea where Detective Sergeant McNab was.

Smiling prettily, she said that the detective had left a message to say he would meet Dr MacLeod in the first coffee shop he came to. 'He'll send you a text when he gets there,' she added.

By the young woman's star-struck expression, Rhona had to assume that McNab had played the charm card during their exchange. Once outside, Rhona checked her mobile to find McNab was just down the road in Cafe Sia.

By his expression on entry, McNab's earlier mood had definitely brightened.

'Good news?' Rhona said.

'Ellie hasn't dumped me.'

'And she was planning to?'

'It's a long story,' McNab told her, 'and not a pretty one.'

Rhona listened in silence. She'd been aware that Ellie had been with McNab when Harry McArthur had been stabbed. What she hadn't known about was Ellie's determination to give Harry house room for his recovery.

'That was very good of her,' she told McNab at this point. 'But, I take it, not what you wanted?'

'Don't mix business with pleasure,' McNab said wryly. 'The plan did have its positives, however, since it meant Ellie staying with me for a while.'

'But not once you lost Harry?'

McNab nodded.

'So, what's changed?'

'I don't know,' McNab said, 'but at least we're in contact.'

'So, any word from Portree?' Rhona went on.

'Not on the whereabouts of the soldiers, but they've started questioning locals who were involved with Watson before.' He hesitated. 'You do realize that all five medics may already have departed the island?'

Rhona had contemplated that. 'I did ask Seven to inform the station before they left. Whether she will or not . . . But if they're a unit and due to be posted back to Afghanistan, I assume the MOD will tell us when or if they return to the fold.'

As they discussed this, McNab's mobile indicated an incoming email.

'It's from Ollie,' he said, checking the screen. 'He has some info on what happened to Private Galbraith in Afghanistan.'

56

She wondered as she walked whether the others would leave the island without her. If they did, and duly reported for duty, she would be classed as going AWOL.

The alternative would be that *he* would alert the authorities on Skye that she hadn't turned up at the meeting point. Then they would begin a search for her.

But he *wouldn't want to do that because of Sugarboy.*

Better for those remaining to leave the island without involving the police at all. And to do that, *he* needed to find her.

Seven imagined him arriving at her campsite in the plantation. She thought of the bag hanging from the roof of the tent, and, as she imagined him going inside, an overwhelming feeling of invasion almost swamped her and she had to turn and spit her nausea into the heather.

She pictured him emptying out its contents and finding the fragment from her blue prison, the black scorpion and Rex's name tag. He would know why she'd kept them and he would see them as possible evidence of her intention to tell the true story of their imprisonment. Something he did not want.

So, he wouldn't wait around but come looking for her.

She had left the flat-topped hills of Healabhal Mhor and Healabhal Bheag behind, and now, turning towards the sea, she passed An Dubh Loch. Following the stream that exited its dark waters, she soon left the heather-covered slopes to find herself in a green valley where the stream joined a faster-flowing burn as it made its way to the sea.

She had arrived, it seemed, at the south-western end of the peninsula.

At first view, this hidden valley felt like the end of the world. Yet people had lived here once, as evidenced by the broken-down walls of crofts and holdings. Counting the mounds of fallen houses, she realized that the valley must have held up to ten families at one time. The occupants, she'd learned from a book on Skye, had been burned out of their homes and forcibly sent to Nova Scotia. It was either that or imprisonment.

What had been done here wasn't that different from Afghanistan, she thought. The powerful in both lands, whether warlords or landowners, were always the ones to decide who should live and who should die. She thought of the wrecked Afghan villages the team had visited, of the broken walls and shattered lives, never sure which side had done such damage. They'd duly set up their field clinic among the ruins and waited for the survivors to bring out their crying children and injured.

He'd been dismissive about the wounded men, insisting they were helping them only to have to fight them again. But even he was moved by the traumatized and broken children. It was hard to reconcile that version of him with the man that he'd ultimately become.

Did war change him or had he always been like that and being in a war zone had simply given him the opportunity to be his true self?

The truth of everything that had happened had become

opaque since her return, mainly due to his voice constantly retelling the tale, altering her perception of it. The others had accepted his version, or been happier with it. A story that now cast her as their saviour, and not a victim.

She'd wondered at times whether she'd imagined it all – her prison, the visits – until Sugarboy would remind her, whispering the truth in her ear.

But Sugarboy couldn't remind her of the truth any more in Afghanistan, or here on Skye.

She sank to her knees, her eyes closed, desperately trying to discover his voice in her head, to smell again his presence in the darkness and hear his laughter. But couldn't.

Eventually opening her eyes again, she caught the distant sound of waves as they met the jagged edge of the peninsula.

What would Sugarboy urge her to do now?

A decision would soon have to be made whether she went west or east along the deserted coastline. Both routes were exposed and, she knew, would prove trickier than climbing either of the two hills that now lay behind her.

But she didn't care how difficult the path she chose might be. What was required was to find a place to hide among the cliffs, inlets and caves that lined the coast.

And await his arrival.

57

On their return journey to Portree, Rhona showed McNab the images she'd taken in Seven's tent.

'What's the blue cloth?'

'Chrissy and I thought it might be from a burka,' Rhona told him.

'And you think the disc is from a dog collar?'

When Rhona nodded, he said, 'I'll send these photos to Ollie. See if he can find out if there is, or was, a sniffer dog called Rex out there. Folk bring back weird mementos from war zones. I have a pal that brought back a bit of the IED that killed his mate in front of his eyes. I swear he would have brought back a piece of his mate if there had been anything left of him.'

Ollie's email had indicated that Peter Galbraith had been involved in a hostile incident involving an attack on the medical centre, when two of the team he'd been working with had died.

'That must have been why he was off-duty for a month,' Rhona said. 'I wonder why they didn't just send him home? Was he serving with the same group he came here with?'

'I have no idea. Getting information out of the MOD is literally like getting blood out of a stone,' McNab said. 'And a junkie giving me a service number doesn't constitute a criminal investigation. Until we have a reason to accuse

Private Galbraith of breaking the law in some way, the barriers will stay up and we will learn only what they want us to know.'

'What about the Sandman enquiry?' Rhona said. 'Can't you use that as a way in?'

'The MOD don't want that to come anywhere near them. In fact they'll fight to keep it away.'

'So you have to establish a link between Private Galbraith and the Sandman before they'll release the whole story?' Rhona said.

'Or discover a link between him and Paul Watson.'

The weather had stayed reasonably bright for the trip south, but by the time they set off back to Portree, a further front had swept in, bringing heavy rain with gusts of wind that hit the jeep from the west.

'How can anyone live here with this weather?' McNab declared as the windscreen wipers fought to keep up with the onslaught.

'And it never rains in Glasgow?' Rhona said with a laugh.

'Yeah, but you can escape it by stepping into a building. Out here, though?' McNab gestured at the emptiness caught in the headlights.

'A drop of rain never hurt anyone,' Rhona said, quoting her mother.

At that, McNab flung her a look that would have curdled milk. Another one of her late mum's favourite expressions.

The rain passed them on the way to Portree, and was there to greet them on arrival. By then it was coming down in sheets and demanded a quick sprint to the front door of the police station, where they found they weren't the only ones shaking themselves off.

'Sergeant MacDonald is upstairs with members of the MRT,' they were told on entry.

The conference room was a hive of activity, reminding Rhona of the many incident rooms she'd been in, in Glasgow. A coffee machine had been installed and McNab, spotting its presence, immediately headed there.

'How'd it go?' Lee asked Rhona.

'I've taken a DNA sample, which I'll transfer to the production room fridge. We can check it against Peter Galbraith's, which we hope is being held by the MOD,' Rhona said. 'There are soil samples from his boots, and I taped his clothes.'

'The MOD aren't inclined to co-operate unless they have to.'

'When it's a case of identification of remains, they can hardly refuse,' Rhona said. 'I think we should run the photo of Private Galbraith past Donald. See if he thinks it might be the guy he met in the Gents.'

'Do that,' Lee said.

'Where's DS Clark?' McNab interrupted their exchange.

'We gave her an interview room. She's working her way through the list of folk that knew Watson from before. Chrissy's in the production room with all the swabs she's been taking.'

As McNab headed off, Rhona reminded him that he should talk to Jamie, then excused herself and went in search of her assistant.

The production room turned out to be the only quiet place in the station, 'apart from the cells', Chrissy told her.

They exchanged stories as they labelled and stored Rhona's evidence samples.

'So there have been no sightings yet of the soldiers?' Rhona said.

'The word is definitely out there, but any walkers and climbers that have been spotted have been accounted for. If your medics were on survival training, their aim, I assume, was not to be seen.'

'What about the Duirinish peninsula?' Rhona said. 'That's where Seven might be headed.'

'Jamie says no sightings there, but they rely on folk being spotted by sight or drone, and that's a pretty inaccessible spot and not the most popular this time of year.' She paused as a gust of rain hit the window. 'You said they were all due to head back to Glasgow shortly?'

'So Seven said, and she promised to check in with the station before they left.'

'You'll have to hope they do,' Chrissy said. 'Archie wants to talk to you. He's over at the Isles. I'll be across shortly, or so my stomach informs me.'

Raising her hood, Rhona made the short but wet journey across Somerled Square to the Isles where she found Archie seated next to the fire with Blaze at his feet. When the big collie spotted her, he immediately came over.

Rhona, as pleased to see Blaze as he was to see her, took some time telling him so.

Archie made room for Rhona beside him on the window seat. 'You've got a friend for life there.'

'Best canine assistant I've ever worked with. Can I get you a drink, Archie?' Rhona offered.

'I'll get you one, lass. You've had a harder day than me. What will you have?'

Rhona delighted him by ordering a whisky.

'Thought you'd go for that fizzy wine that's all the rage and tastes like water.'

'You've tried prosecco then?' Rhona laughed.

'My granddaughter persuaded me. It won't happen again.'

Archie headed for the bar, returning shortly afterwards with two nips of Talisker.

'So,' Rhona said, once he was settled, 'I heard you wanted to speak to me?'

'Aye, lass.' He eyed her intently. 'You can decide if you want to pass this on, mind. Or if it doesn't matter.'

'What is it?' Rhona said, unnerved by the seriousness of his voice.

'After you asked about the lassie, a big bloke with a backpack appeared and asked the same question.'

'Really?' Rhona said. 'And you didn't know or recognize him?'

Archie shook his head. 'He told me he was a pal and keen to catch up with her. I said the lassie had caught the bus to Glendale and would likely be back later, for she was camped up in the plantation. I figured he'd hang around and wait for her so I directed him to the pub. Turns out I was wrong, because I saw him head off in a jeep, a Wrangler, I think, a wee while after that, heading out on the Dunvegan road.'

'Did you tell Lee about this?'

Archie shook his head. 'You can tell him if you think it's important. I'm a suspect in another crime,' he said with a wry smile.

'I can't believe that.'

'You'd better believe it. That detective lassie from Glasgow had us in one by one, asking questions about the death of that bastard on the beach. I had plenty to say about him. Probably enough to get myself jailed.'

'Archie, no,' Rhona said.

'I told her I'd wished him dead plenty of times. Prayed for it even. Probably better that I didn't know he was back here. If I had, who's to say what I might have done?'

58

McNab peered in the window to find Janice alone in the interview room. Taking his chance, he headed in with two coffees.

'So you're back,' Janice said. 'How did it go at the mortuary?'

'We couldn't identify the victim from the handsome Private Galbraith's photograph. However, Dr MacLeod processed him and plans to check his DNA against army records.'

Janice looked askance at that. 'I've never had much luck with the MOD. They prefer to keep everything in-house and under wraps for serving personnel.'

'I know,' McNab said. 'What about your interviews with the locals?'

'The ones Lee asked along showed up. According to him they're keen to help. However, they all said the same thing. They didn't know Watson was out of prison or that he was back on the island.'

'Well, he didn't come here for the scenery,' McNab said.

'Chrissy has part moulds, she reckons, of three sets of matching footprints found on the clifftop where we think he went over, bearing in mind the area is open to the public so there's no guarantee that any prints we find there have something to do with the fall. However, we could use them to check the locals' footwear if required. The dog also led them to this.' Janice offered McNab a photo of a blue-green stone set in a metal casing, which he immediately recognized.

'I know these. They're semi-precious stones from Afghanistan. The squaddies bring them back. Have them made into rings and necklaces for their girlfriends.' He fell silent for a moment. 'Is there anyone local who's served in Afghanistan recently, apart from our visiting vets?'

'Archie McKinnon's nephew Alistair was out there,' Janice said. 'He apparently came back in a bad way with PTSD and that's when he started buying from Watson.'

'Can we bring in Alistair?'

Janice shook her head. 'Ali McKinnon was found dead on the Cuillin from exposure a year ago.'

From the way she said it, McNab knew it had to be suicide. It looked like the conflict in Afghanistan had left a trail of disaster behind it, and not just out there.

'You've spoken to this Archie?'

'Yes. And he didn't mince his words. He hated Watson, but didn't know that he was back on the island. And he'd wished him dead on several occasions. Which is, incidentally, the same story they all gave, almost word for word.'

'I am Spartacus,' McNab said. 'They're bandying together. Forming a united front.' *Like the locals did on Sanday*, he thought.

'Which the MOD will also do,' Janice reminded him. 'So what's next for you?'

'Rhona wants me to talk to Jamie McColl from the MRT about where they found the second body.'

Janice gave him a wide-eyed look. 'The handsome Jamie? I've heard all about him from Chrissy.'

McNab ignored that and asked, 'Have you checked in at the hotel yet?'

Janice nodded. '*And* I have a room with a four-poster bed.'

'But no one to share it with,' McNab reminded her.

'Maybe Jamie could be persuaded to help me with that,' Janice said with a dreamy smile. 'If he can only drag himself away from Dr MacLeod.'

Fuck's sake, McNab thought as he headed for the main entrance. *Have all my female colleagues lost the plot on Jamie McColl?*

Just as he was about to exit, a male voice called out his name. Turning, McNab was met by, he suspected, the man of the moment. McNab gave him the once over, immediately deciding he didn't like what he saw.

'Rhona said you wanted a word regarding where we found the climber?'

Nor did he like his voice.

'I'm on my way to the hotel to drop off my luggage,' McNab said curtly.

'May I walk across with you?'

McNab figured he couldn't prevent that, so didn't try.

The rain had eased and it was definitely getting colder. As they crossed the square, McNab felt the crunch of ice underfoot.

'The forecast's for a big drop in temperature later,' Jamie told him. 'Down to minus five.'

McNab didn't respond, but secretly wondered if he had in fact packed enough warm clothes.

'Rhona spoke of you often,' McColl was saying. 'You've

worked together a lot, I understand? In particular on the case prior to her coming to Skye?'

McNab cut him off. 'I don't discuss work with people outside the job.'

McColl, obviously taken aback by McNab's sharp response, said, 'Rhona has never spoken of any of the cases she's worked on. I only know a little about the sin-eater case because of what I read in the newspapers.'

'The newspapers are full of shite,' McNab said. 'I have to dump my bags, then I'd like to see the images taken at the locus.'

'Of course.'

They were at the hotel now. McNab pushed open the door and was assailed by the warm fugginess of a bar, complete with laughter and chatter.

Jamie indicated that Rhona was already there, over by the fire. 'That's Donald she's with, and Blaze of course.'

McNab wasn't a dog lover, but this one, he had to admit, was a magnificent specimen, the intelligent eyes appraising him from afar even as he studied it.

Climbing the narrow stairs to the first floor, key in hand, McNab decided that it wasn't so much the countryside he disliked, but the familiarity of its inhabitants with one another. Sanday had been the same, he recalled. Since, by the nature of his calling, he believed everyone guilty until proved innocent, this friendly intermingling between the police and the public was not something he approved of.

Unlocking his room door, he registered that he didn't have a four-poster, but he did have a double. This thought brought Ellie to mind and he checked his mobile in the hope that there was some further correspondence from her.

There wasn't.

There was, however, a text message from Ollie.

Call me, it's about Harry.

McNab pulled up Ollie's number and listened to it ringing out. Eventually Ollie's breathless voice answered.

'Detective Sergeant McNab?'

'Fuck's sake, Ollie. My name's on the screen.'

There was a brief silence before Ollie said, 'I'm about to send a short video from the CCTV footage I retrieved from the Death Star. Can you please take a look?'

'Okay,' McNab said cautiously.

He waited impatiently as the video took what seemed like an eternity to download, sensing that what he was about to see wasn't something he would welcome.

Eventually it was ready to run. McNab pressed the play button and concentrated on the screen, his heart already skipping a beat.

It hadn't been captured in the area near to the discharge lounge he'd visited. It was somewhere else entirely, but McNab recognized Harry right away from the footage. He emerged from the building and stood, hesitant, looking about him expectantly.

A black cab drew up alongside, but Harry didn't approach it. Instead a woman appeared in a wheelchair and was helped into the vehicle by the driver. As this scene played out, Harry walked part way out of the picture.

McNab swore, thinking they were about to lose him altogether. But no. As the taxi drew away, it was replaced by the sudden arrival of a motorbike. A Harley-Davidson, the rider's outfit sporting a blood-red splash. He murmured more expletives into the air, already aware of the significance of this.

He watched as a few words were exchanged, before Harry climbed on behind the figure McNab suspected, by the outfit, to be Ellie's best mate, Izzy. Above them on the screen the recording gave McNab the time of the pick-up.

The timing was crucial. Replaying that morning's coupling in his head, he realized it had to have been part of the plan. Ellie had encouraged him to have sex, to delay his arrival at the hospital, having already arranged that Izzy should collect Harry.

The question was how had she been in touch with Harry to arrange it? And why had she done this behind his back?

The first question was easy to answer. Ellie had made another visit to Harry to arrange it. Or they had been in touch another way. Harry hadn't had a phone when he'd been admitted to hospital, but Ellie could have easily supplied him with a pay-as-you-go model.

The answer to the second question, McNab realized, was equally obvious. Ellie hadn't trusted him to keep his word to deliver Harry to her flat. So she'd organized that delivery herself, just to be sure.

McNab thought back to his delaying tactics, his staying-out-late routine, the consumption of whisky, all to avoid facing Ellie.

He recalled the spoiled meal waiting for him when he'd eventually returned to the flat to discover Ellie wasn't there. If he had gone home as promised, was her plan to tell him the truth?

McNab suspected that's exactly what Ellie would have done.

But he hadn't given her the chance.

59

Rhona passed Donald the photograph of the uniformed Private Peter Galbraith and watched as he studied it closely.

'Yep,' he eventually came back. 'I'd say that was the guy in the toilet that night.'

'You're sure?' Rhona said.

'Pretty sure. He was high, and definitely not as smart-looking, but I would say it's the same guy.' Donald hesitated. 'Would it help if I also took a look at Jamie's shots of the mountain casualty? See if I think it might be the same bloke? I've helped recover quite a few bodies on the hills over the years, and I'm not squeamish.'

'He's right,' Jamie intervened. 'And he's the only one to get up close to Galbraith that night in the bar.'

Rhona considered this. Had Donald been out with the team he would have already viewed the body, so she didn't see there was a problem letting him take a look at it now.

'Good idea,' she said.

Jamie brought up an image on his mobile and passed the phone to Donald.

After a few moments, Donald responded. 'The face is the problem,' he said. 'It's unrecognizable. Height and build are similar, hair colour, but we could probably say that about two of the three guys currently standing at the bar.'

Donald was right, Rhona thought, glancing at a party of male climbers who'd just come in.

'You don't happen to have a close-up of the back of his neck?' Donald said, prompted, it seemed, by a sudden thought. 'Army personnel are allowed tattoos on the back of the neck, but not on the front where it's visible in an official photograph. The guy in the toilet had a tattoo of the Scottish flag there. I remember because I fancied getting one done just like it.'

Jamie shook his head. 'What about you, Rhona?'

There had been a number of tattoos on the body. Had there been a small flag on the nape of the neck or had post-mortem lividity hidden it? Rhona was already going through her own shots just to be sure. She had definitely photographed enough of the underside of the body to give evidence to its having been turned after death. But had she captured the nape of the neck well enough to identify a possible saltire?

'Look,' Rhona said. 'There.' She expanded the partial image to reveal part of the white cross on a blue background.

It wasn't definitive evidence, they would need the DNA results for that, but it brought them closer to identifying the climbing casualty as that of Private Peter Galbraith.

As they took this in, Rhona spotted McNab's arrival in the bar and waved him over. McNab's scowl, Rhona noted, suggested he wasn't keen on joining the party, but he came anyway.

Ignoring a pointed look that indicated he would prefer to speak to her alone, Rhona passed McNab her mobile.

'Donald spotted the flag tattoo on his neck when he encountered him in the Gents,' she said. 'Which suggests the dead climber may well be your soldier.'

Her declaration was followed by an extended silence on McNab's part, after which he said pointedly, 'Can we speak alone, Dr MacLeod?'

Jamie and Donald glanced at one another. 'We'll let you two talk,' Jamie said as they rose.

'What's going on?' Rhona demanded as soon as the two men were out of earshot.

'You've been off the job far too long, Dr MacLeod,' McNab said. 'Sharing evidence with the general public—'

Rhona cut him off right there. 'I was not sharing evidence, I was gathering evidence.'

'Who's to say either of those men might not end up as a suspect?'

'A suspect in what?' Rhona said.

'Your other *friend* Archie McKinnon and his mates all gave the exact same story to DS Clark regarding Paul Watson. Looks like the locals may not all be telling the truth.'

'Donald has no reason to lie about the tattoo,' Rhona countered.

'Donald saw someone snorting cocaine in the Gents. Didn't mention it to anyone until he got in tow with Chrissy, which might be considered a convenient coupling, particularly if you wanted to get close to the action?'

'Chrissy would never discuss the case with him.'

'It seems to me that everyone is openly discussing the case, at every opportunity. Like you, here in the pub with those two.'

There was an element of truth in what McNab was saying, but he was still wrong. 'Things work differently in an island community,' Rhona said. 'I thought you'd learned that on Sanday.'

When McNab didn't respond, Rhona continued, 'I suggest you take Jamie to the police station after this and record what he says about the locus, which I had, if you recall, suggested you do in the first place. As for showing Donald the photograph of Private Galbraith, Sergeant MacDonald had already okayed that.'

When McNab still didn't respond, she added, her ire up, 'Maybe you'd like to interrogate the dog too, while you're at it? After all, it was Blaze that led me to the scene in the woods in the first place.'

McNab had the grace to look momentarily abashed, but Rhona knew it wouldn't last long, so she waved the two men back over. Once they were seated, she directed her next comment at Jamie. 'The wound to the face most likely occurred when he was still alive. Any thought on how that wound might have happened?'

'You mean with respect to the terrain?'

'Exactly,' Rhona said.

Jamie brought up a series of images to illustrate his explanation. 'Okay. From where we found him, we think he may have been tackling the An Dorus twins, Sgurr a Mhadaidh and Sgurr a Ghreadaidh. The ascent of An Dorus is over steep scree and involves tricky scrambling. Considering the weather, he should have had an ice axe with him. We didn't find one. After the scree there's a steep and narrow gully. If it was icy that could have proved very tricky. If a mist comes down, An Dorus can seem unrecognizable from what you've seen on the way up. Pretty scary.'

Jamie continued, 'He should also have been wearing a helmet. We searched for one, but if he lost it further up, it could have landed anywhere. Without protection you're open to boulder falls. And remember what he looked like when we found him.'

He shared the image again.

The body lay on its front, two-thirds of it obscured by a mound of rock debris.

'The scree was very loose. We struggled to reach him, and even more when trying to bring him down.'

McNab was staring at the image intently. 'How far is this spot from a road?'

Jamie, with a glance at Rhona, brought up an Ordnance Survey map and showed McNab.

'There was no vehicle abandoned at the usual parking place.' Jamie pointed to the location. 'So we're assuming he walked in.'

'You believe he was alive when he arrived at the scree slope?' McNab said.

Jamie looked taken aback by the question. 'How else could he have got there?'

By Jamie's tone, Rhona wondered whether the two men had already had words before they'd got to the Isles. That might then account for McNab's belligerence and Jamie's response.

McNab had fallen silent after Jamie's question, but Rhona could almost hear his thoughts, they were so loud.

'You're suggesting foul play?' she said.

'Everything that's happened here in the last few days strikes me as foul,' McNab said pointedly.

Rhona brought an end to the war of words. 'We need to bring Lee up to date with this, plus there's been a development on the Seven front,' she said. 'Courtesy of Archie McKinnon.' She directed this at McNab. 'Shall we head over there now?'

The way back across proved to be a sheet of black ice. Rhona's boots coped, as did those of Donald and Jamie. McNab, however, was visibly struggling.

'I can lend you grips,' Jamie offered as McNab just saved himself from going his length for the second time.

It was kindly said but, Rhona thought, by McNab's face, it only added insult to injury.

On entry to the station, it was clear that something had happened while they were at the Isles. The explanation seemed to be the sudden drop in temperature which had seen at least three cars leave the road round the island and all available police vehicles and personnel sent out to deal with the situation, including Lee.

'The Sleat road is apparently one of the ones affected,' Jamie told her. 'Best if you don't tackle it tonight.'

Rhona had no intention of doing so. 'I'll stay at yours again, if that's all right?'

'Of course,' Jamie said. 'I'm going to check in, see if the MRT's required. I'll be home later.'

Donald left with him, leaving Rhona and McNab alone.

'I suggest we locate Chrissy, then get some food together,' Rhona suggested.

By his expression, McNab liked that idea, but the sarcasm wasn't over yet. 'Won't Chrissy be headed home with the bold Donald?'

'Let's find out,' Rhona said.

60

'At last,' McNab said, toasting them with his pint of Skye Gold. 'The team back together again.'

Chrissy glanced at Rhona, who, smiling a little, didn't comment.

'What are we eating then?' Chrissy said. 'I fancy the macaroni cheese.'

'No contest,' McNab said. 'I'm having the steak pie.'

Rhona contemplated her favourite fish and chips, but instead when the waitress arrived plumped for haggis, neeps and tatties.

'So,' McNab tried again when she'd departed with their order. 'Isn't this good?'

'Stop it,' Rhona warned.

McNab made a face. 'Stop what?'

'Trying to persuade me. It's never worked before and it won't now.'

Chrissy must have kicked McNab under the table, because he gave a yelp.

Rhona now brought up the subject she'd intended discussing all along.

'I think Seven is the key to a lot of this,' she said. 'And I suspect she was the one injured in the woods that night behind A.C.E Target Sports. The question is how, and more importantly, why.'

'We can't confirm that without her DNA,' Chrissy reminded her. 'Pity you didn't collect some from the tent.'

'Which wasn't a crime scene and therefore inadmissible.' Rhona stated what they were all aware of. 'Blaze's instinct in the plantation was to protect. He'd met her before at A.C.E and in the pub, but it wasn't just familiarity, I think he knew she was frightened.'

She continued, 'Jen Mackie found traces of cocaine in the soil sample from there that I sent. What if Lee's original thought that a consignment of drugs had been buried there was correct? Could that have been why Watson was back on the island? To retrieve it?'

The food arrived at this point and they fell silent.

'There was no link, as far as we know, between the beach body and the clearing,' Chrissy reminded them after the waitress departed.

'We haven't had anything back yet on the soil samples I sent from Watson's boots,' Rhona said. 'According to the soil map of Skye, the soil structure is different in the area of the clearing from that above Kilt Rock. The vegetation too. If we could place Watson in the area of the clearing—'

'We could link the soldiers to the Snowman,' McNab said, his eyes lighting up at such a prospect.

'Have you heard anything back from Ollie about the dog tag?' Rhona said, switching her train of thought.

McNab pulled out his mobile and scrolled through his messages, selecting one of them to read.

'Well?' demanded Chrissy.

'There's nothing on the dog, but . . .' McNab's face betrayed his amazement at what he'd just viewed.

'But what?' Chrissy said impatiently.

'It's from Ellie. Harry McArthur's asked her to contact

me. He wants to come in and give a statement,' McNab said quietly.

'How did Ellie know where he was?' Chrissy demanded.

'I'll explain later,' Rhona promised her. 'So,' she said, focusing on McNab, 'you'll head back to Glasgow tomorrow for the post-mortem on what we believe is Private Galbraith's body.'

'And we find out why Harry gave you Galbraith's service number in the first place,' Chrissy said.

McNab didn't respond, his demeanour suggesting he was still dumbfounded at the latest development.

'Okay,' Rhona roused McNab, 'let's bring Lee up to date.'

They discovered DS Clark in residence at the station, although DS MacDonald and the other officers were still out all over the island.

'A couple of road accidents,' Janice said. 'It's apparently like a skating rink out there.'

'So I've noticed,' McNab said.

'Donald MacKay's been by and given his statement about Private Galbraith and the saltire tattoo. Plus Jamie McColl has handed in his shots of the location of the dead climber and details about the terrain,' Janice said. 'Is there anything else?'

Rhona explained about her interview with Archie. 'We'll need that recorded too.'

'So he thinks someone is following the girl?' Janice said. 'Should we be concerned by that?'

Rhona wasn't sure and said so. 'Something's not right between the group, but it may have nothing to do with any of this.'

'You don't believe that?'

'No,' Rhona admitted, 'but until we get any return on the various forensic evidence we've submitted, we can't be sure of anything.'

McNab came in then. 'I'm headed back tomorrow with the body. Harry has made contact and wants to give a statement.'

'When did you hear that?' Janice said, surprised but obviously delighted.

'Just a few minutes ago. It seems Ellie persuaded him.'

'Well, well,' Janice said, wide-eyed. 'So we'll find out why he pointed us in the medic's direction. That's good news.'

'We need to make the MOD give out further information on Private Galbraith and the team he was with in Afghanistan,' Rhona said, 'in case the repercussions of it may be playing out here on Skye. The girl told us they had another seventy-two hours on the island before they headed for Glasgow. Of course, she may have been lying. We need to find out from the MOD when Private Galbraith was due to report for duty.'

'I've already spoken to DI Wilson about that.' Janice suddenly remembered something. 'Oh, and Alvis is back from Raasay. He heard the news on the death of the climber and wanted to know if it was linked to the case. He's asked for a few days' extra leave to see if he can help.'

Rhona found herself more than a little pleased to hear this. 'Has he viewed the photo of Private Galbraith?'

'He has and confirmed the same physical features, but he didn't get a close-up like Donald. And the face is unrecognizable.'

'So he didn't spot the neck tattoo?' McNab said.

'No.'

'Then we'll have to rely on the MOD for a DNA response?'

'The boss is on it,' Janice assured him.

'Where's Alvis staying?' Rhona asked.

'At MacNab's,' Janice told her. 'The Isles is full with our lot.'

'MacNab's?' McNab's own face was a picture at this.

'The Royal Hotel near the harbour. Their pub's called MacNab's.'

'You have your own pub on Skye,' Chrissy said, impressed. 'You should be staying there.'

'I'll stick where I am,' McNab said suspiciously.

Rhona wondered if his response could have anything to do with Alvis being there and smiled at Chrissy, who couldn't resist it. 'I hear there's an excellent whisky bar at MacNab's. You could share one with Alvis.'

McNab chose not to respond. Probably a wise move.

Emerging from the station, Rhona sought a moment alone with Chrissy.

'Are you headed back with Donald tonight?'

'I am,' Chrissy said.

'Can you get him to call me? I want to ask his advice.'

'About what?' Chrissy said, her curiosity awakened.

Rhona shook her head. 'If it's worth anything, you'll be the first to know.'

She smiled as she watched the ever-gallous Chrissy pointedly overtake the more cautious McNab en route to the Isles. Seeing them both safely inside, Rhona set off in the opposite direction.

McNab might not want to encounter Alvis again, but Rhona was keen to see the Norwegian inspector.

61

The last time she'd seen Alvis, he'd had difficulty disguising his concern for her. Who could blame him after seeing her meltdown in the plantation?

Rhona wanted him to see that things were different now. That working this case had restored some of her faith in her own abilities. Not that she imagined for a moment that meant the flashbacks would suddenly stop. She was well aware that it didn't work that way.

But I won't let them define me. Not any more.

The devastating thing about the sin-eater case was that she'd missed the signs, which, looking back, seemed so obvious now. The question of how she could have been so blind was what had made her question if she could rely on her own judgement ever again.

But that too had changed.

Sitting high above the harbour, the Royal held an enviable spot in Portree. Despite it being a quiet time of year for holidaymakers, it still looked busy, as did MacNab's bar. Rhona had messaged Alvis on her way over, suggesting they take a walk to the harbour and the Pier Hotel pub, which she'd visited with Jamie.

Blaze, she knew, was often a visitor there with Donald, although not tonight, and with luck she and Alvis might find a seat in the tiny bar.

'Rhona.' Alvis emerged from the main door. 'I hope I haven't kept you waiting in the cold.'

Rhona gave him a quick hug. 'I'm glad you came back before heading home.'

'Things have developed, I understand?'

The sky was clear and covered in stars, and reaching the quayside, they could just make out the distant outline of the northern part of Raasay. The sight of the island brought a surge of memory for Rhona. During her sojourn there, she had travelled to the wild and most northern tip of Raasay and looked across the water to the twinkling lights of Portree Harbour and what appeared to her to be its safety. Something she'd craved at the time.

'You've been on Raasay before, I hear?' Alvis said.

When Rhona looked surprised that he might be aware of that, Alvis explained that Lee had told him the tale of her last brush with the MOD over human remains retrieved from Raasay Sound.

'It's a local legend,' he said.

Without responding to that, Rhona said, 'How was the island?'

'Like Skye, a special place for me, having been there with Marita. I think she would like to know I returned and walked out to the memorial to Sorley MacLean, a favourite poet of hers.' Alvis changed the subject. 'I hear Detective Sergeant McNab is on the Skye team now?'

'Only briefly.' Rhona explained about the possible identification of Private Galbraith, and McNab's return to Glasgow with the body. 'I think he'll be glad to get back to the city.'

'He's not fond of wild open spaces, as I recall,' Alvis said with a smile.

Rhona laughed. 'That's the understatement of the year.'

They'd reached the Pier Hotel which sat on the south side of the harbour. Alvis held open the door to the little room, where luckily one of the few tables was free. After the frosty air, the place was snug and warm, which made Rhona suddenly think of Seven somewhere out there on a frozen hillside.

'What'll it be?' Alvis said. 'I'm having a dram,' he added by way of encouragement.

'That's fine for me.'

Settled with their drinks, Alvis broke the silence. 'How are your knuckles?'

'You saw me,' Rhona said, 'punching the tree?'

He nodded. 'I thought you might have been aware of that.'

Rhona contemplated deflection but only briefly. If she was to succeed in convincing Alvis that things had changed, she would have to be honest, so she was.

'I get flashbacks from the sin-eater case. An exacerbated claustrophobia. The plantation, the closeness of the trees . . .' She ground to a halt.

'Were like your prison,' Alvis nodded. 'I understand.'

'It passed. They all pass, but working within a confined space, which I have to do at times, might prove difficult or maybe even impossible,' Rhona voiced her fears.

There was a moment's silence before Alvis responded. 'After the boat with the children, I experienced a similar response. Almost every time I heard a child cry,' he said, his voice strained. 'I found myself avoiding places where children might be. Even Marita's grave, because it lies next to a child's with an image of the boy on the gravestone.'

'I didn't realize,' Rhona said.

'No one likes to admit to their failings.'

'I distrusted my own judgement. I missed so much that I should have spotted.'

'Blaming yourself for what you didn't see. What you didn't do. A feeling we have in common. McNab suffers from it too, I believe. Who doesn't who works on the front line? The line between life and death. The what might have been.' Alvis took a sip of his whisky. 'So, you trust your judgement a little better now?'

'The girl in the plantation—' Rhona began.

'May prove to be the key to all of this,' Alvis finished for her.

'You think that too?'

'When I was out on Raasay, I found myself replaying that scene in the clearing many times, and every time I did, I was even more convinced that she was afraid. That's why the dog reacted the way that he did.'

Rhona passed Alvis her mobile with the image of the mementos.

'She had these hanging from the tent roof almost like a talisman.'

Alvis studied them, his face serious. 'Then I was right to do what I did.'

'Which was what?'

'I have some contacts in the Norwegian military. DI Wilson spoke to me after your MOD's limited help on information regarding Private Galbraith and the missing month.'

'And?' Rhona said.

'What I have is not much, and unconfirmed, but it appears that a British helicopter delivering an injured soldier and his sniffer dog to a medical camp in Helmand province was blown up by a grenade and two medics on the ground were killed. This happened around the time we're interested in.'

'Rex?' Rhona said. 'Was that the dog's name?'

'Now that I have a name,' Alvis said, 'I might be able to find that out.'

'So they may all have been present at the incident? Not just Private Galbraith?'

'It's a possibility.'

'And when Private Galbraith was off-duty for a month, but not sent home?'

'According to my sources, he may have gone missing at that time,' Alvis said.

'Gone AWOL, you mean?'

'Or he was captured by the Taliban.'

'And Seven and the others?'

Alvis shook his head. 'That I don't know.'

'Is your source still available?'

'It's delicate,' Alvis said. 'Norway was one of the first countries to join the USA and the so-called war on terror and we played an active part in the war in Afghanistan, but not everyone was happy about that. The Brits were – are – our allies. If the British Army buried this story, then they had a reason. A reason my contacts may feel they should not make public.' Seeing Rhona's disappointment, he added, 'That doesn't mean I will stop trying to find out.'

'They were a close team. You said that when you watched them in the pub.'

Alvis nodded. 'Although the girl did appear to be on the fringes of the group. Despite that, she had, I think, a special bond with Private Galbraith. That I did notice. And she and Private Galbraith together made a big fuss of the dog.'

'And now Private Galbraith may be dead.' Rhona wondered if there was any way Seven might know this, and that had prompted her lonely odyssey.

'Assuming the body is that of the soldier, does the probable time of death match when she said they all left to pursue their own survival activities?' Alvis said.

'It's a possibility,' Rhona said. 'I'm hoping we'll learn more from the post-mortem.'

Alvis was studying her closely. 'You're worried about the girl?' he said.

Rhona was worried about Seven. Something about the girl seemed to echo her own state of mind. Rhona had had the feeling that the girl, much like herself, had been dwelling on death. She recalled her conversation with Archie about his nephew and how Ali had returned from the front line a changed person. Just as she had, and perhaps Seven too?

'I am,' Rhona confirmed with a wan smile, 'and I can't explain why.' Taking refuge in the practical, she told Alvis about tracking Seven with Blaze and where she might have headed. 'Archie, the drone operator, spoke to someone who was also looking for her. It might have been one of her comrades-in-arms.'

Alvis contemplated this. 'She told us they were all planning to meet up and yet she went off without breaking camp, and almost immediately after we visited her?'

'Leaving her mementos behind,' Rhona added.

'You think she went onto the Duirinish peninsula?'

'It's an assumption only. I've been trying to make contact with the driver of the bus she boarded, to see if they recalled when she got off, but I've had no luck as yet. She may have switched buses at Dunvegan and headed east instead. Maybe she was on her way to meet the others.'

'Then why not take her belongings with her?' Alvis said.

'She wanted to travel light?' Rhona voiced her current and most disturbing thought: 'Or she didn't need them any more?'

62

Afghanistan

A birth in blood. So much blood.

I quickly hand the baby boy to the old woman, while I try to stem the stream from its semi-conscious mother. Once the women had accepted a normal birth wasn't possible, they'd produced the poppy juice to mask the pain.

Now they bring me cloth after cloth to stem the flow of blood. I fear they're not sterile or even clean, but I have no choice but to use them.

I forget the child until I hear its cry and the associated exclamation from the women. I'm relieved that the child is alive, but now I must save the mother.

At last the flow eases and I can begin to close her up. I thank God she is still asleep, and any movement that suggests otherwise sees someone drip a little more of the milky opium liquid between her lips.

The stitching isn't pretty, but the wound is closed now. Looking at my hands, I suddenly register their trembling and wonder how I managed to thread the needle through the skin at all.

I step back, fear at what I've done threatening to overwhelm me. Someone leads me by the arm to the fire and other hands gently wash my own in the warm water ready and waiting.

The baby gives a louder cry and a young woman lifts the swaddled bundle from its cushion and brings it to the semi-conscious mother, holding it to her exposed breast, encouraging it to find the nipple. For a moment there is a concentrated silence in the room, then as it begins to suck, the women's voices resound in joy.

I want to say that it isn't over yet, that they must keep the wound clean. She has lost a lot of blood. But my Pashto is scarce, unlike that of Sugarboy . . . and *him*, both of whom have made a big effort to learn. They said they did it to help them acquire a supply of opium to treat the wounded. Not our injured, but the locals, the men *he* wanted to leave to die.

A male voice shouts from the outer room and the women fall silent.

The older woman lifts the child and, holding back the curtain, steps through. In that brief moment I see the father's face, the young man who had led me here from my cell. His delight explodes in a torrent of words as he takes his baby son in his arms and walks from the shadowed outer room into the glaring sunlight, his boy held high.

The curtain falls back, leaving us with only the jubilant sounds from outside as the new father shows off his son. A volley of shots peppers the air, and I find myself covering my head with my hands. The women, unafraid, merely add their voices to the explosion of gunfire.

When the noise eventually dies and the baby is returned to its young mother, the women busily prepare the traditional tea (*chai*). My language may be limited but this is not the first time I have been involved in a tea ceremony with the women of a village.

The first cup of hospitality will be served sweet (*chai shireen*). The one they hand me in the small handleless porcelain cup is heavily sugared, which I know is a great compliment, their way of saying thank you for delivering the child.

I drink it quickly, my body craving the sweetness. The cup is swiftly refilled and the second unsweetened cup (*chai talkh*) is flavoured with crushed cardamom seeds.

After four refills, I turn my cup over to show that I have had enough.

The mother's eyes are open, the drug wearing off. She sees me and reaches out, encouraging me to come to her. I touch her brow, looking for signs of fever, but although her colour is high, her skin is cool. It is happiness, I realize, that flushes her face.

The baby stirs and pulls at the nipple, and the girl-child is swiftly turned into a mother. She touches the mop of glossy black hair and smiles up at me.

I wonder how much longer I have with these women and whether, by my actions, I have brought death closer or sent it further away.

63

McNab shut his eyes as the helicopter took off, opening them again when they were magically in the air. Morning sunlight caught the neighbouring large island that Rhona had called Raasay and the flat-topped mountain named Dun Caan.

McNab wondered idly why both names required a double 'a' and decided it must be something to do with the Gaelic.

He also considered how apt it seemed to be sharing the helicopter with a body. He had always thought he might meet death in a plane crash. That's why he didn't get into a plane or chopper unless he was forced to.

But, he mused, *maybe simply sharing one with someone already dead might be enough to satisfy that premonition.*

He knew Rhona wasn't keen on flying either, but she had somehow convinced herself of its viability via science.

Science didn't work for McNab.

Skye dropped beneath him and, the day being clear, he had a full dose of what he was leaving behind. Having seen the Cuillin ridge outlined on an Ordnance Survey map, courtesy of Jamie McColl, McNab now saw it in all its stark reality.

Why the fuck would anyone want to climb that?

The peninsula where Rhona thought the girl, Seven,

had headed, with its twin flat tables, looked to McNab like a lunar landscape, while round its edges the sea beat its power against huge cliffs and shattered coves.

As the co-pilot pointed out all the relevant locations, McNab said nothing, seeking only the bridge that led to the mainland, while reminding himself of the motorbike trip with Rhona he'd taken to get there.

Gradually all talk ceased and, ignoring the windows, McNab contemplated instead the body bag he was bringing home. Rhona had called him after her chat with the Norwegian and he had learned another piece of the mystery that seemed to surround Private Peter Galbraith, if it was indeed him zipped up inside the body bag.

The post-mortem had been arranged to swiftly follow their arrival. McNab preferred the idea of interviewing Harry first, but apparently that had been organized for the afternoon, Harry's presence at 2 p.m. being guaranteed by Ellie.

So the PM it was.

Although McNab disliked the mortuary and all that happened therein, he was curious to find out whether the estimated time of death might fall into the timeline of Watson's own demise. If the pathologist turned out to be Sissons, he wouldn't make life easy for McNab, but the acerbic doctor's caustic remarks could be dealt with if there was something interesting to learn from them.

As they approached the River Clyde and the signs of human habitation became more marked, McNab found himself relaxing. The cloud grew thicker as they neared Glasgow, and when the rain began to hit the windscreen, he decided that civilization, however damp, was very welcome.

At touchdown they were met by both an ambulance and a police car. McNab, thinking he'd spent enough travelling time with a corpse, opted for a trip to the morgue in the police vehicle instead.

'DI Wilson wants you back at the station,' he was informed as he climbed inside.

'But I was told McArthur wasn't coming in until this afternoon?'

'Change of plan,' his driver told him. 'He's at the station now.'

'Any idea why?'

The driver shook his head. 'Although I hear he's pretty jittery.'

McNab wondered if that was caused by a lack of heroin or a fear of reprisal – or maybe both.

He brought up Ellie's number and listened as it rang out. When there was no response, he left a message. 'I'm on my way to the station to see Harry. Be there shortly.'

'Did Ellie Macmillan bring him in?' McNab asked.

The driver shot him a look that suggested he knew all about DS McNab and his biker chick Ellie Macmillan. 'Can't say. Wasn't there when he arrived. My job was to pick you up and get you there. How was Skye?'

'Cold and wet,' was all McNab could manage.

'Much the same as Glasgow,' came the reply.

Oh no, it bloody well isn't, McNab thought, gazing fondly on his home turf.

On entry to the station, the desk sergeant told him he was wanted in DI Wilson's office. Expecting nothing less, McNab headed there, although he would have dearly liked to take a look at Harry McArthur first.

He didn't get time for the statutory knock. The boss,

expecting him, opened the door on his approach. He tried to gauge the mood by the boss's expression, but as always it was impenetrable.

'DS McNab, welcome back. How was your visit to Skye?'

'Short,' McNab said.

'You think you've found Private Galbraith?'

'It looks like that, sir. Although we still need DNA confirmation from the MOD to be certain.'

'A delicate operation, but we're working on it. I expect they're as keen to know whether they've lost a serving officer to the Cuillin of Skye as we are.'

'Do we know when he was due to report for duty, sir?'

'We don't, yet. Nor have we been given the names of the other medics who were on Skye with him.'

'Why the obstruction, sir?'

'The MOD would see it as a cautious evaluation of the situation.'

'Can I ask if they know about Harry McArthur, sir?'

The boss shook his head. 'Former soldiers living on the streets are not high up on their priorities, I suspect. Although should such a former soldier give us information regarding the supply line of heroin from Afghanistan, that will have to change.'

'I understand Inspector Olsen has some information regarding Private Galbraith's last stint out there?'

The boss scrutinized him. 'He has. And perhaps we'll get more from that source. But our hope lies with Harry.' He paused. 'I've had the full story of his removal from the hospital in advance of your arrangement to pick him up.'

McNab wondered just what the full story entailed. Ellie, he knew, wasn't one to spare the details, maybe even the morning sex.

'She did it, she says, because she feared you had other plans for Harry, rather than the ones you'd agreed on.'

McNab wasn't sure if that was a question, but decided he probably had to give some sort of response.

'I had deep reservations about Ellie giving him house room, but I couldn't forbid—'

As the boss raised an eyebrow at the word *forbid*, McNab quickly amended it to *dissuade her*.

'Indeed. And she did not break any law by picking him up at the hospital. Harry was a victim of a crime, not a perpetrator.'

McNab thought of the wasted hours he'd spent imagining someone like Malky picking Harry up and, worse still, Harry's body deposited somewhere around Glasgow.

'If you had gone straight home as planned that night, you would have learned where he was, Detective Sergeant.'

It sounded like a telling-off, and McNab wondered if he'd been spotted in an inebriated state and word had got back to the boss.

'I did go home, sir, but by then Ellie had gone.'

'So you went round to her place in the middle of the night and—'

It was obvious Ellie hadn't spared any of the details, so McNab finished the sentence for him, 'and posted a note through her letter box.'

The boss was looking at him with what might be the ghost of a smile.

'I learned many years ago from Margaret that it was better to tell her the bad stuff. Not full details, of course, but enough so that we were honest with each other.'

McNab, taken aback at the mention of the boss's recently

deceased wife, someone he had truly admired, muttered a 'sorry, sir'.

'Sorry for what, Detective? That my wife is dead or that you can't find it in yourself to be straight with your current partner?'

'Both, sir,' McNab said honestly.

'So. How does your professional partner, DS Clark, fare on Skye?'

McNab, relieved to move to another topic, explained where they'd got to on interviewing the locals.

'You suspect it might be an inside job?'

'They hated Watson. No doubt about that. He messed with them once before. Screwed up a few lives. They weren't happy to see him out of jail and back on the island.'

'A vigilante killing on Skye?' DI Wilson didn't look convinced. 'Any direct link between this Snowman character and the medics?'

'None, sir. And no one's come forward to report a sighting of Watson anywhere on the island, prior to his body being found on the foreshore at Kilt Rock. The medics, or at least Galbraith, was suspected of taking cocaine in the toilet of the Isles bar the last night the group was seen together.'

'And the question of a stash in the woods behind A.C.E Target Sports?'

McNab was seriously impressed by the grasp the boss had of all the threads in the case, some of which he was struggling with.

'Rhona treated it as a crime scene, and the soil did contain evidence of that as a possibility.'

'Right,' the boss said. 'It's time you talked to Harry.'

64

Rhona listened in disbelief.

'Someone's reported seeing Archie with Watson?' She repeated Lee's announcement to make certain she'd heard him correctly. 'How did they know it was Archie?' she said.

'The description matches Archie perfectly. Down to the drone. He's a distinctive figure,' Lee said.

'And Watson?'

'Same. Even down to the facial features which we now know.'

'And Archie was alone with Watson? On the clifftop?' Chrissy said.

'Yes. According to the witness, a tourist, who's now left Skye.'

'How did he know Archie?' Rhona said.

'Met him when he was working his drone, got talking to him about the scenic images he took. Was following the police Twitter feed and saw the call-out for any sightings of Watson in the area near Kilt Rock.'

Rhona fell silent. Archie had been honest about his hatred of the so-called Snowman. Even to the point of wishing the drug pusher dead. Why do that if he'd met him on the cliffs? It didn't make sense.

'You'll bring Archie in?' Chrissy asked.

'Have to,' Lee said, his concern at this showing.

'Is there any footage of this meeting?'

'The tourist says no.'

'Who is this guy?' Chrissy demanded. 'Can he be brought in for questioning?'

'We'll have to find him first.'

'It's too convenient,' Rhona came in then. 'We still don't know the names of the other medics and now we don't know the identity of a possible witness.' She looked to Janice. 'Everyone associated with this case is like a cipher.'

'True, but an anonymous call doesn't mean a witness is lying,' Janice said. 'Most folk want to help the police. They just don't want to get involved and end up having to go to court.'

'When exactly did this tourist see them together?' Rhona said.

'Mid-afternoon on the day we think he went over the edge,' Lee said. 'Archie was using his drone to take footage of the cliffs, apparently.'

'And Archie never mentioned this in his interview?'

Lee shook his head.

Whatever way Rhona looked at the scenario, it didn't ring true. Though, if they'd already written Archie out of the equation, then they would dismiss a sighting like this. There was a danger in only paying attention to evidence which matched the current interpretation of events.

'Can we trace that call at all?'

'We can try,' Lee said doubtfully.

'We should also check Archie's footprints against those Chrissy collected from the clifftop,' Rhona said.

'Agreed.' Lee looked to Janice. 'I called Archie as soon as the message came in. He'll be here shortly.'

Rhona thought of McNab's fury yesterday when he'd spotted her comparing notes with Donald and Jamie. His annoyance at how close the police and the public had become on the case. How he'd pointed out that either man might yet turn out to be a suspect. Something Rhona had immediately dismissed.

Lee rose. 'I think you should interview Archie about this,' he told Janice. 'It's better to come from an outsider. Plus there's a report of another vehicle going off the bend on the way out of Uig last night. It's been sighted well down the hill, so I'm headed there with the MRT.' He turned to Rhona. 'DS McNab's landed in Glasgow. Hopefully we'll hear back from him soon on Private Galbraith.'

Rhona and Chrissy adjourned to the production room.

'Did you speak to Donald?' Chrissy said.

'I did, and I'm borrowing Blaze again.'

'You're going looking for Seven?'

'Alvis and I, and the dog.'

'Why not get Jamie to look?'

'Because I have no definite proof she's gone in the direction I think she has, plus the MRT are stretched enough as it is,' Rhona added.

Chrissy was giving her the eye. 'What is it about this girl that's bugging you so much?' When Rhona didn't answer, Chrissy did it for her. 'You think she's a casualty of war. Much like yourself.' Chrissy reached out and touched Rhona's arm in support. 'Then you need to find her. I take it you have something of hers for Blaze to follow?'

'I do.'

Chrissy smiled. 'I thought as much. Okay. When do I start worrying about you?'

Rhona handed her a map. 'I've marked our proposed route. I'll keep in touch for as long as I have a signal.'

Alvis was waiting for her, their intention having been to leave at first light until Lee had called her in for the meeting. She already knew about the vehicle off the ridge road north-west of Uig, Jamie having wakened her to tell her what was happening. When she'd informed him of her own plans with Alvis, he'd looked pleased.

'We'll take any help we can get, and Alvis knows the island as well as you. Are you heading for the coast?'

'We're not sure where we're heading. We're hoping Blaze will help us with that.'

'You have something to help him track?'

'I have,' Rhona had said, without saying what.

Jamie had nodded. 'From our drone image, the vehicle that went off the C1225, the Staffin to Uig road, looks like a dark-coloured jeep.'

'A Wrangler?'

'Could be – why?'

'Archie said the vehicle looking for Seven was a dark-coloured Wrangler jeep.'

'There's probably a few on Skye,' Jamie had said. 'But we've had no missing people reported as yet.'

'We have seven hours of winter daylight,' Alvis told her as they exited Portree.

'If necessary, we can make camp. Donald was fine about that.' Rhona glanced in the back where Blaze was sitting erect, watching the world go by.

'I assume you have something from the tent for him to follow?' Alvis said.

'Unofficially, yes.'

'But you couldn't use it to check for her DNA?'

'You and I both know the answer to that. As for helping locate a missing person, that would be different.'

'The favoured way into the Tables is via Orbost, which means she would have got off the bus at the junction of the B884,' Alvis said.

'She did,' Rhona told him. 'I phoned the bus company again as I was leaving the station and they finally put me in touch with the driver who drove the bus Seven got on. He was off work the first time I called. He remembered Seven, though she didn't say much, even when he spoke directly to her. Apparently he tried to tell her the times he would be back along the road, but she didn't seem too interested.'

'So she wasn't planning to come back that day?'

'Doesn't look like it.'

'And what about us?' Alvis said.

Rhona shot him a look. 'We don't turn back until we're sure.'

'Of what?'

'That she's okay,' was all Rhona could offer.

They passed the car journey in silence, each deep in their thoughts. Rhona's were partly about McNab and his impending interview with Harry McArthur, of the post-mortem and what it might reveal; but they were mostly about what had happened to Private Galbraith in Afghanistan and what had really brought the group to Skye.

Had it been, like her, to try and forget? To forge new memories together so that whenever they looked at one another they didn't only remember a shared horror?

PTSD did that to sufferers, replaying past scenes vividly

– the sights, the sounds, the smells. Anything could trigger the sudden recall. For her it was confined places and suffocating darkness which brought soil into her mouth to choke her.

And what of Alvis, reliving the sights and sounds of caged children? Something, thankfully, she didn't have to endure.

They parked the vehicle on the grass verge at the beginning of the designated path. Once across the stream, Rhona produced what she'd taken from the tent. The last time she'd trailed Seven she'd been able to let Blaze smell a few items of Seven's clothing, plus the trainers, but fearful that wouldn't be enough, she'd also taken the anklet sock.

Alvis made no comment as she produced this from an evidence bag and offered it to the dog.

65

McNab observed the scarred face of the man across the table from him. 'I thought you were fucking dead.'

The pale lips assumed the ghost of smile.

'You could have been, leaving without me,' McNab went on. 'If wee Malky was having the hospital watched . . .'

'Then he would have seen me leave with you. Not a good move. Your bird was wiser, bringing me out the back way. Having her mate pick me up. Nice bike too, by the way.'

'You stayed at Ellie's?' McNab made himself say.

Harry laughed. 'Man, you got that fucking wrong. She was waiting at your place to tell you so. Fucked up there, mate.'

McNab wasn't going to argue that particular point.

'Did Ellie get you to come into the station?'

Harry met his eye. 'She asked me where I wanted to be most in the world.' He gave a little laugh. 'I told her back with my mates.'

'In Afghanistan?'

'I'd rather die out there with them than in a Glasgow alley alone.'

Registering Harry's expression as he said that, McNab had a fleeting glimpse of what he might be like if the police force ever threw him out. It wasn't an image he liked.

'Why did you leave me that service number in the sign-out book?' McNab said.

Harry twitched a little at the mention of that, and for a moment McNab imagined him clamming up and this whole interview becoming a waste of time. It wouldn't be the first time someone had offered a statement only to change their mind.

'You found Sugarboy then?' Harry said cautiously.

'Private Peter Galbraith, a medic who served in Afghanistan?'

Harry nodded. 'Bastard saved my life.' He pointed at his face. 'When this happened.'

McNab had no idea where this conversation was going, but it didn't seem like the path led to the Sandman. He decided to shake things up a little.

'Then I'm sorry to have to tell you that Private Galbraith is dead.'

'What the fuck did you just say?' Harry sat to attention.

'The medic Private Peter Galbraith, who you call Sugarboy, is dead.'

A look of abject fear crossed Harry's face. 'But I just saw him.'

'Where?' McNab demanded.

'He came looking for me. He always does when he's home on leave.'

'When did he do that, Harry?'

'Before it happened. Before I was in hospital.' Harry's face was working through his memories, trying to make sense of them.

'Did Malky see you with him?' McNab said.

'Malky?' Harry looked at him stupidly. 'I don't think so.'

He swayed in his seat as though the shock at what he'd just heard had suddenly hit him.

McNab, thinking for a moment he might meet the floor, jumped up and came round the table to prevent that from happening.

A horrifying thought seemed to strike Harry. 'Did you lot have something to do with it? Fuck you, you bastard. Ah should never have given you his number.'

That they might lose Harry if he thought the police had anything to do with Galbraith's death prompted McNab to tell him the truth, or the truth as they currently imagined it to be.

'Private Galbraith was with a party of his fellow medics on Skye. He fell off a mountain.' He stopped himself from admitting to the fact that Galbraith had not yet been formally identified.

Harry struggled to comprehend this. 'The others were on Skye with him?' he said as though he knew of their existence.

'The girl, Seven, was there.' McNab halted at this point, hoping Harry might fill in some of the other names.

When he didn't, McNab said, 'He was alone when the Mountain Rescue Team found him. They had split up to do survival stuff, Seven said.'

'Seven knows Sugarboy's dead?'

'We can't locate her or any of the others to tell them.'

'Seven . . .' Harry began, then halted, a catch in his throat. 'They were mates. Good mates.'

Harry fell silent, which wasn't what McNab wanted, so he tried another tack.

'Did Sugarboy know Paul Watson, the Snowman, as the islanders called him?'

Harry glanced up at him. 'That bastard's inside.'

'Not any more,' McNab said. 'His body was found at the foot of Kilt Rock on Skye four days ago. Looks like he fell off the cliff.'

Both relief and horror crossed Harry's face at this news.

'So it's started,' he said.

'What's started?'

'The fucking war.'

Harry covered his head as though bombs were about to fall. Standing by his side, McNab spotted the saltire tattoo on the nape of his neck for the first time.

'Why did you point me in Sugarboy's direction?' McNab said quietly.

'They were after him. I wanted you to get to him first.'

DI Wilson laid the statement down. He had read it through twice already, and no doubt would again.

'Will you share this with the MOD, sir?'

Harry's treatise on how they'd got the consignments out of Helmand province and onto the streets of Glasgow made for interesting reading. Even writing it down would mean his death warrant from the Sandman side, although that warrant had, McNab suspected, already been issued. Hence Malky's attack on Harry in the alleyway.

And the other thing Harry had told him . . .

'It all began because they were sourcing the opiates locally to treat the Afghans caught up in the fighting. Sugarboy can . . . could speak the local lingo,' Harry had said, 'like a fucking native.

'They'd officially run out of morphine when I came in, burning like a fucking candle. I wanted someone to shoot me. I begged them to shoot me. Sugarboy told me he was going to take the pain away, and he did.'

He'd looked at McNab then and given him a haunted smile. 'I'm still taking that pain away.'

'What happened to Sugarboy when he disappeared for a month?'

'They all disappeared. Taken by the Taliban. It didn't make the news. The MOD smothered it, but we knew. Story is, the girl, Seven, got them out.'

'How?'

Harry had shaken his head. 'I was back in Glasgow by then and out of the army. And I'm not the only Afghan veteran littering the streets. Then Sugarboy turns up. Said he'd been looking for me. Gave me money and some snow. Told me he was getting out of the arrangement. He had a plan.'

What that plan was, Harry didn't know. 'But he said it involved the Scorpion.'

'Is that a person?' McNab had said.

Harry had shrugged. 'Some bastard's nickname, I think. Sugarboy didn't say. A link in the chain, I suppose. But definitely one he was afraid of.'

The boss had risen from his desk now and was at his customary thinking place by the window.

'Is it possible that Private Galbraith didn't fall from that mountain?'

'Anything's possible, sir. The PM's this morning. Maybe the pathologist can interpret the wounds enough to give us a clearer picture of when and how he died.'

The boss shook his head. 'The facial injuries on both Watson and the possible Galbraith, coupled with the fact neither men had identification on them, seems just a little convenient, don't you think, Detective Sergeant?'

It had certainly delayed identification, and had given

anyone involved a window to get well away before either body was found. McNab said so. 'Plus the possible fall or suicide angle,' he added.

'Find out if Harry disclosed anything else to Ellie. He seems to have trusted her enough to agree to come in here. If they talked there could have been something said in the passing which turns out to be important.'

'Will do, sir.'

The boss picked up the statement again. 'So we find Malcolm Stevenson, bring him in and charge him for the knife attack on McArthur, and I tackle Her Majesty's Ministry of Defence on their part of the proceedings.'

McNab didn't say that the boss's declaration sounded a bit like a wish list, but he thought it nonetheless.

66

Afghanistan

They bathe me, murmuring at the scratches and bruises that pepper my body. I am kept fed, given sweet tea to drink and urged to consume some of the milky liquid given to the new mother in her extremity. When I refuse, they point to a cushioned bed and mime sleep.

Eventually, to please, I accept the porcelain cup and drink.

I have lost track of how long I've been in what feels like an Afghan version of heaven. At least twice the father has come to the outer room and the older woman has spoken with him. I can make out only scattered words and phrases, but I suspect he's being told that his wife and baby still need me, the nurse.

He accepts, I think, because he cannot bear to deny his wife and child anything that will aid their survival.

The sun finds the window and moves across the floor. I lie, eyes half open, enjoying its warmth. Unlike my cell, the dirt floor here is covered with brightly coloured rugs. I cannot imagine spiders or scorpions daring to enter this rainbow heaven filled with chatter and laughter.

It will end soon, I know, but perhaps I can store up the memory for when they take me back to my cell.

The women point to items in the room, requesting my words for them. They try them out, smiling when I correct them. I do the same and they smother laughter at my attempts to reproduce their sounds.

I ask about the others, all the time using the word 'nurse', but my questions only cause consternation, although I suspect the elderly woman knows what I'm asking. Her jet-black eyes seem to me to contain the entire world in their deep darkness.

I have finally decided that when they take me back to my prison, I will seek out my friend, the black scorpion, and accept the escape route he offers, because the sweet memories of being here with the women will be too hard to bear.

And eventually that time comes.

I am given a clean blue burka to put on over my undergarment and sandals for my feet. As this is done, I am patted and fussed over like a child. When they believe me ready, I am handed the baby to say goodbye.

I kiss the soft hair on his head and am happy that he is obviously thriving. The mother takes my hand. I know she is thanking me, but I cannot speak.

The older woman leads me to the doorway and, pulling back the curtain, takes me into the outer room. My fear threatens to overwhelm me, but I still allow myself to be steered outside.

When my eyes adjust to the bright light, through the mesh I view the empty compound. Which of the buildings is my jail? And where are the others being held?

As the baby's father appears, the old woman is dismissed. Her final words tell me to praise Allah. I believe in that moment that I have been washed and dressed ahead of my execution.

But perhaps not.

I am led to a building larger than my previous cell, and encouraged to enter, after which the door is closed behind me. I wait for my eyes to adjust to the dimness, but in the gloom I sense – no, smell – a presence other than my own.

'Sugarboy?' I say, searching for him among the shadows.

Then the other scents hit. Sugarboy, if he exists in here at all, is not alone.

'Seven,' a voice says.

Can this be real?

I make out the others now, emerging like wraiths from the darkness, and believe the opiate the women have encouraged me to drink is giving me hallucinations.

I catch all their scents now, even *his*.

He comes towards me, and though I recoil, he takes my hand.

'They're going to free us. The baby is the grandson of their leader. When you saved him, you saved us all.'

67

Blaze had accepted the sock, sniffing it eagerly, his excitement suggesting he relished the game beginning again. Running from side to side, he eventually found a match and set off with a determined air.

Initially there appeared to be a path, but Rhona knew that wouldn't last. The mix of boggy ground, grass and heather involved finding your own route through to the closest hill.

And Rhona didn't think Seven had come this way to conquer the Tables. It was more likely that she'd been intent on getting off the beaten track. This became obvious when Blaze's trail began to bypass Healabhal Bheag.

They walked in silence, picking their way through the mix of energy-sapping bog and heather, swerving this way and that to avoid the worst patches. Blaze, on the other hand, seemed to have no problems in deciding where he should place his paws.

Eventually the dog led them to a hidden valley through which a burn ran rapidly towards the distant sea. A valley Rhona recognized from photographs only.

'Do you know this place?' Alvis said, taking in the striking image of lush pastureland after the rough moorland and bog they'd just crossed.

'It's called Lorgill. Once a thriving community as you

can see by the number of buildings, until the local factor for the estate decided he wanted the land for himself and forced the people to leave. It was imprisonment or a ship to Nova Scotia. I know about it because distant relatives of my adopted parents came from here.'

'You come across places like this all over the Highlands,' Alvis said. 'The sadness never seems to go away.'

Checking for Blaze, they noted he appeared to be working his way through the tumbledown ruins of the cottages, eventually focusing on an area behind a wall.

'Looks like he's found something,' Alvis said.

Approaching, it was obvious by the flattened grass that someone had recently rested there. Provided Blaze was indeed following Seven's scent, then his excitement at this point suggested it may well have been her.

The light was already beginning to fade, although it had just turned midday.

'Shall we take a break or just keep going?' Alvis said.

Rhona didn't want to stop here and not only for reasons of time. Some of Skye's cleared glens had found life enter them again, but not this one. Just as Alvis had said earlier, the broken hearts of the exiled inhabitants seemed to Rhona to linger here still.

'Is rural Norway like this?' she said as they followed Blaze through the abandoned township.

'No. We have our own history of exile, but for different reasons, and the preservation and support for rural life are part of the government's remit. Land is owned locally and most Norwegians have a rural hut they use to get back to nature. So no abandoned villages like this one.'

They followed Blaze and the river down to the shore,

where he began running about trying to pick up Seven's scent again.

Looking eastward, Rhona searched for MacLeod's Maidens, the group of rocks that rose like teeth out of the grey waves.

'I think we'd have to be higher to see them,' Alvis said, anticipating her search. 'Maybe from Hoe Point.' He pointed in the opposite direction.

To the west were the highest cliffs on Skye, more spectacular than the much-visited and photographed Kilt Rock. The entire coastline, Rhona knew, was dotted with arches, caves and hidden bays.

'If you wanted to hide, you're spoilt for choice in either direction,' Alvis said, consulting the map. 'But it would likely involve descending a cliff face or finding a gorge.'

'She's an experienced soldier, and the group apparently came here to climb. If she's capable of climbing a mountain, then she's likely capable of scaling cliffs.'

Rhona was watching the dog who, having scoured the foreshore, now seemed perplexed as to where his quarry had ventured next.

'There's no chance she may have taken to the water?' Alvis offered.

Rhona was already contemplating this possibility, and if Blaze failed to pick up Seven's scent again on land, that might well be their conclusion. Or – and this dark thought was growing – Seven hadn't left by boat, but simply continued walking into the sea.

Rhona turned to find Alvis studying her.

'Do you have any reason to think that Seven may have been suicidal?' he asked as though reading her mind.

'You said she and Private Galbraith had a special rapport. If Seven found out that he was dead,' Rhona said, 'might that be why she abandoned her camp, leaving everything behind including the mementos?'

'You think this walk might be a suicide mission?' Alvis said.

Rhona didn't want to think that, but it couldn't be ruled out. If Seven had found out that Private Galbraith was dead, and that had happened shortly after they'd met her, how would she have reacted? And how was she told? By mobile or a visit to the camp? Both of which could only have happened if the other soldiers already knew their fellow soldier was dead.

Rhona thought of McNab's theory that Galbraith hadn't fallen from An Dorus, but had died elsewhere. Was that even a possibility?

Eventually Rhona registered that Alvis was calling her name and, coming out of her reverie, heard the flurry of barks from Blaze. Having retraced their steps, the collie had now apparently picked up Seven's scent again, and was heading for the Hoe.

'Looks like the cliffs won,' Alvis said.

'Or she's heading for Ramasaig or Waterstein and civilization?' Rhona said, her hopes rising.

'There's a lot of coastline before we get to there,' Alvis said. He glanced at Blaze, now back on the job in earnest. 'And we'll be close to the cliff edge in places. What about the dog?'

'I checked with Donald, he says Blaze is completely reliable near cliffs.'

'Let's hope we prove to be as well trained,' Alvis said with a wry smile.

The two great precipices of Ramasaig Cliff and Waterstein Head dominated the view ahead as they made their way nearer to the beak-like cliffs of Gob na Hoe rising 600 feet from the sea. Bog had given way to grass underfoot and there was even the trace of a path, which Blaze was very interested in following.

Had they been there for any reason other than the one that drove them on, Rhona would have been constantly stopping to admire the views. The weather had remained cold but the sky was clear and the low light from a winter sun created an eerily beautiful landscape.

Looking back, they could now make out the sharp silhouette of MacLeod's Maidens rising in jagged pinnacles from the sea and, beyond them, the snow-topped wonder of the Cuillin.

But the winter light would soon run out. The dog, Rhona knew, wouldn't be put off by a lack of daylight, but she and Alvis increased their chances of an accident on the rough ground, even using their head torches.

'We'll have to make camp soon,' Alvis suggested. 'We should probably look for some shelter too. We're pretty exposed up here.'

'We're not that far from Ramasaig,' Rhona said. 'If we don't locate her before, we'll camp in the bay.'

Her hopes of locating Seven today were fading, despite the efforts of Blaze. She checked her mobile, but there was still no signal, although there might be a chance of one when they reached the tiny township.

Somehow Rhona didn't think Seven would have chosen to camp anywhere near the suggestion of civilization, however meagre it might be, so the fact she appeared to be heading in that direction seemed odd.

Her thoughts were proved correct shortly afterwards, when Blaze left the path and made his way towards the cliff edge.

Her heart skipped a beat and despite Donald's assurances that Blaze was surefooted, she shouted, 'Blaze, here to me.'

It was at this point that, instead of responding, Blaze suddenly dropped from sight.

68

The downtown traffic was light and, having chosen to visit the Harley shop by bike, easy to negotiate. McNab didn't exactly have a smile on his face, but inside he was mightily pleased. Harry had come up trumps and maybe, just maybe, this whole business was beginning to unravel.

Plus, he and Ellie were bound to be back on good terms, if he managed to explain his stupid actions the other night.

Parking up, he stowed his helmet and entered the big glass-fronted building. The new Harley headquarters on the outskirts of Edinburgh he knew to be grand, but there was no matching the Glasgow shop. He entered and headed for the desk, but before he got a chance to ask for Ellie, he'd already been spotted and someone was ringing through to the customizing area where she worked.

'Ellie says to go to the cafe and she'll see you there.'

McNab didn't need to be told twice to get himself a caffeine fix, so he headed for the cafe as ordered. Settled with a double espresso, he sent Rhona and Chrissy a message that Harry had given a full statement and that it looked like the medics were caught up in some way with the shipments of heroin from Afghanistan.

Harry's in custody for his own safety, and we're bringing in Malky and charging him with the knife attack . . . as soon as we find him.

Having sent the text, McNab looked up to find Ellie standing before him, causing, as usual, his heart to skip a couple of beats. He tried to read her expression, but it seemed neutral, which might be good, but then again, it might not be. He was never sure of his ability to read women, having failed on numerous occasions with Rhona, and now with Ellie.

'Can I get you a coffee?' he offered.

She nodded an okay, and he felt his anxiety lessen a little. When he arrived back she had settled herself at the table.

'How's Harry?' she immediately asked.

Glad to be on positive ground, McNab told her as much as he was allowed. 'He asked to stay overnight at the station.'

'I told him to come back to my place,' Ellie said sharply.

'It's too dangerous for that now, Ellie. We'll put him in a safe house until we break this thing open.'

She thought about that for a moment, then accepted his reasoning with a quick nod. When the silence extended a little too long, she broke it with the question he'd been anticipating.

'Are you planning to say anything about why you didn't come back that night?'

'I am,' McNab said, sitting back in the chair and meeting her questioning gaze head-on. 'I didn't come back because I'm an arse, and having lost Harry, I couldn't face you. Of course, had I come home as promised, I would have discovered that I hadn't lost Harry.'

His honesty appeared to be working because he thought he saw a relieved smile twitch at the corner of her mouth.

'I wasn't sure you would bring Harry to my place,' she said, with the hint of an apology. 'You'd made it plain that you didn't want him there. I was worried that . . .'

Any anger he'd nursed about being tricked had dissipated. 'I've let you down before. So I can see why you might think that.' McNab reached out and covered her hand with his own, and was pleased when she allowed it to stay there.

'So?' he said. 'We're okay?'

She gave an almost imperceptible nod, which allowed McNab to finally relax.

'And they can't get at Harry when you have him in custody?'

'He's safer with us than anywhere else,' McNab said, hoping that was true, yet suspicious that the Sandman's influence was a spider's web, seemingly invisible but remarkably far-reaching.

When Ellie appeared to accept his assurances and now took time to drink her own coffee, McNab decided it was time to carry out the boss's orders.

'DI Wilson was very pleased that you managed to persuade Harry to come in and give a statement. He sends his thanks. He also gave me advice on appreciating my partner better, which I will try to follow.'

That gained him an actual smile.

'He asked me to chat to you about the time Harry spent at your place and what you talked about.'

When Ellie looked a little perturbed by this, McNab added, 'Just in case Harry said anything else which might turn out to be important.'

'Like what?' Ellie demanded.

'His time in Afghanistan,' McNab prompted. 'There was a guy there who saved his life. He called him Sugarboy.'

He watched as she considered this. 'He told me he wanted to be back there with his mates.'

McNab nodded. 'He told me that too.'

Her face darkened. 'He has nightmares. I heard him in the night. It sounded . . .' She stumbled as though what was in her head couldn't be repeated. 'He was trying to get out of somewhere. I think it was a tank on fire.'

McNab didn't respond, because what could he say, except that he was sorry she'd had to hear that.

'I would take drugs if I was haunted by something like that,' Ellie challenged him.

'I probably would too,' McNab agreed.

It didn't seem the right moment to ask another question, so McNab didn't, not immediately. Eventually when Ellie went back to her coffee, and her shoulders relaxed again, he carried on.

'The guy we're really searching for is known, we think, as the Sandman. Did Harry mention that name at all?'

Ellie looked puzzled. 'Didn't you ask him that at the interview?'

'Yes, he acted as though he didn't recognize the name.'

'He never mentioned that name to me,' Ellie said.

Names sometimes emerged during an investigation, often coined because they had no idea who was at the centre of it all. Perhaps there was no single boss of the operation, and the Sandman was merely their creation.

Ellie came back in, breaking McNab's train of thought.

'Harry wants to get clean. Get his life back. He's got skills. The army should help get him into work again.

They owe him that at least,' she said in a determined manner.

They did and they ought to, but judging by what was about to blow up in their faces, McNab didn't think saving an ex-soldier and drug addict would be high on their list of priorities. More likely as much of this as was possible would be swept under the carpet, with MOD law prevailing and no leakage to the press.

'We'll get him help,' McNab heard himself say. 'I'll make sure of it.'

The look Ellie gave him was worth the grief such an offer would bring.

'When do you finish here?' McNab said, his mind already on what might come after.

'Six,' she said.

'I have a job to do now, but what if we ditch the bikes after work and I'll meet you at the Rock Cafe for a drink and some food?'

She made a face. 'Yes to meeting up, but could we eat somewhere else?'

'What about Italian?' McNab suggested.

'Better.' Her face lit up in a smile.

Having settled things with Ellie, McNab now turned his attention to the second and arguably less pleasant job he'd been given by the boss.

Since his sharp exchange in the Isles bar with the ladies' favourite, Jamie McColl, the idea that Private Galbraith had died somewhere other than the mountain had been growing.

At the time, he'd come out with it just to be thrawn, but ever since then, the suspicion that it might not have been a fall that had massacred the soldier's face hadn't gone away. One unrecognizable victim was possible; two, who were more than likely linked, McNab didn't buy.

And neither did Rhona.

Parking the bike as close to the morgue as possible, McNab steeled himself to enter. A post-mortem could take up to five hours, during which time many smells, none of them pleasant, were known to accumulate. And a mask, as far as McNab was concerned, offered little protection from the stench.

He did hope, however, that arriving late might mean he'd missed most of the messy bits.

The viewing room was vacant, and glancing through the glass, McNab established they were indeed nearing the end of the proceedings. There was no sign of Dr Sissons, who'd apparently departed, leaving his second-in-command to finish up.

That suited McNab fine. Entering, he raised a friendly eyebrow to the SOCOs in attendance and winked at the mortuary assistant, whom he recognized. The blue eyes of Dr Walker acknowledged his arrival.

'We're almost done here, Detective Sergeant,' he said.

'Apologies for that, had a lead to follow on this guy first.'

'And that took long enough to avoid some of your favourite parts of this procedure?'

'Luckily, yes.'

'So what do you want to know?' Dr Walker said, coming straight to the point.

'Was he moved after death and how did his face get in such a state?' McNab said.

*

McNab extracted himself from the suit and tossed it in the bin.

Dr Walker, of a different nature to his superior, Dr Sissons, had been happy to discuss their findings. It appeared that the body had indeed been moved after death. The victim had been subjected to blunt-force trauma about the face, which may have come from falling down the scree.

'But the deep wound in the right eye was made earlier.'

'The weapon?' McNab had immediately asked.

'A blade of some description, maybe that tomahawk Dr MacLeod asked us to look out for. We found fragments of wood in the wound, together with traces of vegetation.'

'So, he didn't die from a fall on the mountain?'

'In our opinion he died from the earlier head injury. Location was woodland rather than hillside. The other facial injuries came later, when he was likely beaten about the face with rocks, giving the impression he'd died on the scree.'

69

Chrissy heard the message come in and, surprised that she suddenly had a signal, quickly opened and read it.

Taking her chance, she called and waited impatiently for McNab to answer. Eventually he did.

'Chrissy. You got the text?'

'Any evidence of where he died?' she immediately asked.

'The wound contained wood fragments possibly from the handle of the weapon used. Plus—' He waited a second for impact.

'Fuck it, McNab. What?'

'There was vegetation. Doc said he'd been lying in woodland.'

'Rhona was right,' Chrissy said.

'If the DNA's a match.'

They both fell silent, before McNab came back in. 'Is Rhona about?'

Chrissy told him about the search party for Seven. 'And, McNab, a jeep went off the Uig road last night and caught fire. Two fatalities. Rhona said the guy looking for Seven was driving a dark-coloured jeep. Thing is, the bodies I'm looking at don't belong to fit guys like soldiers. Too much blubber.'

'Have you run the number plate?'

'Lee's tracing it now.'

Chrissy could almost hear McNab's brain turning over this new information. Eventually she couldn't wait any longer and demanded he tell her his thoughts.

'When I told Harry that Galbraith had been found dead on Skye, he said "the fucking war's started".'

When McNab rang off, Chrissy tried Rhona again, without success.

During her call with McNab, the team had sectioned off the area around the burnt-out jeep, and she could make out a search team going over the ground between the wreck and the road.

It wasn't the first time a vehicle had come off the road at this spot, Lee had told her. Visitors to the island often drove too fast on the steep and winding roads, never anticipating what lay beyond the next bend. Add to that the sudden drop in temperature after the rain, turning road surfaces into a skating rink, and it was easy to see why the jeep had left the road.

What wasn't so obvious was why it had caught fire, seemingly trapping both occupants inside. Contrary to popular opinion, due mostly to watching Hollywood movies, cars did not suddenly burst into flames, even when they plunged down a hillside.

Chrissy, having stepped back from the remains of the vehicle, now re-entered its radius.

She'd already collected DNA samples from the bodies. They would be checked against the DNA database of known criminals, and also with the MOD, to be sure the victims weren't in fact the serving soldiers.

Approaching the burnt-out vehicle again, Chrissy raised her mask. She had been at numerous scenes of crime, but the overpowering smell of burnt human flesh was very particular. She was reminded of a scene she and Rhona had dealt with in a skip on the outskirts of Glasgow. The body they'd examined there had burned above the waistline, the intensity of the fire in the metal container exploding the brain. The lower half had been left unmarked, protected from the flames by the compression of the closely packed cardboard that had served as a blanket for the former soldier, gone AWOL and living rough.

As Chrissy stood, such thoughts playing out in her head, she spotted Donald waving to her from outside the perimeter tape. He was concerned, she knew, that having allowed Rhona to take his dog, he couldn't now make contact with them.

Chrissy went over, to at least reassure him.

'Rhona told me she would be off-grid. We don't have to worry yet,' she said.

Donald didn't look convinced. 'Have you any idea where on the peninsula she's heading?'

'No. Why?' Chrissy said.

'I know this sounds weird, but I've lost Blaze in my head. That's not a good thing.'

When Chrissy didn't immediately respond, he added, 'You've got a kid. You would know when he was in danger, yes?'

Chrissy thought about wee Michael. How he was always in the back of her mind, until she thought something was wrong, and immediately he consumed all of her thoughts.

'What do you think's wrong?' she said.

'I think my dog's injured. Or dead,' Donald said, his face too pale for comfort.

'Don't,' Chrissy said, thinking of Rhona, rather than the dog.

Donald gestured to the burnt-out vehicle. 'This isn't normal on Skye. It's like we're in a war and not of our making. I'm going to head out to Duirinish and make sure they're all right.'

'Okay,' Chrissy said cautiously. 'You'll keep in touch?'

Donald shrugged, indicating how likely that would be.

In that moment, Chrissy longed to be back on the mainland. Preferably in Glasgow where shit happened, but at least they knew where and when it had.

'I'm sorry,' she said, as though it was all her fault.

'I'll see you when I get back?' It sounded almost like a plea.

Chrissy nodded.

She watched as he climbed the hill towards the road, no Blaze at his heels. It was difficult not to assume that they had brought as many problems to the island as those they were intent on resolving.

Lee's approach, his expression grim, did nothing to allay Chrissy's concerns.

'No response from Rhona?' he said.

Chrissy shook her head.

'I think we should bring in Search and Rescue. We need Dr MacLeod here, and it's the quickest way to locate her. Although with the failing light, we're running out of time.'

With fewer than eight hours of daylight, wherever Rhona was, she would already be considering making camp for the night, assuming of course that she, Alvis and Blaze were okay.

'Donald's worried about Blaze, which makes me concerned for Rhona,' Chrissy said.

'And you have no idea where she might be?' Lee tried.

'Rhona thought that Seven would most likely head for the coast,' Chrissy told him. 'She thought she was avoiding civilization.'

'That's easy enough in Duirinish.'

'But it all depends on where Blaze leads them.'

'Okay. We'll send the chopper to check the coastline, although in truth we have a limited time before the weather sets in again. For this too.' He gestured at the burnt-out jeep. 'There's heavy rain and sleet forecast.'

'Can't we raise a tent?'

'No tent will stay put in what's coming our way. I'd advise you to get as much evidence as you can in the next two hours.'

As Lee walked away, Chrissy, raising her mask, turned her attention back to the wreck and what it contained. There were two bodies in the jeep, a driver and one in the front passenger seat. From observation, both were male, both of medium height. Both overweight, which suggested it was unlikely to be two of the medics. Lee's search on the partial from the number plate would hopefully produce a result as to who owned the vehicle.

The worst of the fire had apparently occurred at the front of the jeep, and by the concentration of intense localized burning and trail lines, Chrissy suspected the fire hadn't happened spontaneously.

The wind had picked up since she'd arrived, and despite the protection of the forensic suit, Chrissy was beginning to register the cold. She stood for a moment, running mentally through all the tasks Rhona would have set her had she been here, while at the same time wishing she was.

'Okay. This time it's up to me,' Chrissy mouthed. 'But please come back soon, Rhona.'

She'd completed two-thirds of what she thought necessary by the time Lee's predictions began to be realized. The wind she was experiencing when not in the shelter of the vehicle was now strong enough to remove a forensic tent, and the occasional flake of snow had become a thick flurry.

'Chrissy?' Lee's voice brought her out of the vehicle. 'Start making your way up to the road and a patrol car will take you back to Portree. We'll cover the vehicle with a tarpaulin and try and lift it out tomorrow, depending on the weather.'

'You'll remove the bodies first?'

'We'll bag them and send them to Glasgow. The car we'll try to lift out whole. Heavy equipment is on its way from Fort Augustus. And we'll have more SOCOs here by tomorrow.'

Chrissy nodded. It was obvious this wasn't the first time Lee and his team had had to deal with a difficult road accident recovery on Skye.

'What about the chopper?'

'It'll have to wait until tomorrow when conditions should improve. Rhona and Alvis were prepared for an overnight stay,' he assured her. 'They'll be okay. Plus Donald and Jamie and two more of the MRT are already headed into Duirinish.'

Chrissy nodded, hoping Lee's words weren't just said to make her feel better.

70

McNab, having drawn into the side of the road to answer Chrissy's call, now re-entered the line of traffic and began weaving his way to the front.

What he'd just learned had necessitated a return visit to the station, and hopefully a full report from Janice, who was, as far as he could gather, still at Portree police headquarters, focusing on the Kilt Rock victim. A death that now appeared to be linked in some way to the medics' trip to Skye.

On the way McNab went over again all that Chrissy had said, and married it to what he currently knew himself, then made a mental note to call in on Ollie and see if he'd gleaned anything further about the group and Afghanistan in particular.

On entry, however, he was informed that everyone had been called to the incident room, and he was required to join them there, so it looked like either DS MacDonald or DS Clark had already been in touch with the boss regarding the latest developments on Skye.

McNab felt the frisson of excitement that often accompanied a breakthrough in a case as convoluted as this one, and only wished that Rhona had been here to experience it. That took his thoughts west again to whatever godforsaken location Rhona had found herself in. With that thought came a stab of fear. If the medic group were part of this, then so too was Seven. And it was Seven whom Rhona sought on Duirinish.

The incident room was packed. The Sandman enquiry was a major investigation, one in which the former soldier, Harry McArthur, had suddenly become a part. Harry's face was up on the board along with the other already known or suspected characters.

Also added to the rogues' gallery was the dead Watson, and the photographs of the burnt-out jeep on an improbably steep hillside outside the village of Uig, together with images of the remains of the victims found inside.

Although the number plate had been replaced, the jeep was suspected as having been the one reported as stolen from the drive of a villa in Bearsden the previous week.

The boss registered McNab's entry before he continued drawing the various strands together.

'The MOD have *reluctantly,*' he emphasized the word, 'confirmed that the DNA of the dead climber is that of serving medic Private Peter Galbraith, who was currently on leave and due to return to Afghanistan forty-eight hours from now. They have not however released details regarding the rest of the team. The post-mortem conclusions on Galbraith suggest foul play, so I believe the military police will also now be involved. Maybe then they will be more co-operative.' His expression suggested that as being unlikely.

'Harry McArthur is still with us and his statement refers to a link between serving personnel in Afghanistan and the local Sandman network helping to bring heroin shipments into Scotland and Glasgow in particular.'

He continued, 'Harry McArthur's testimony is proving to be valuable to the investigation, lifting a lid on the entire organization, which was probably why there was an attempt on his life. Fortunately, DS McNab, who was following the assailant at the time, confirmed as being Malcolm Stevenson, succeeded in getting McArthur to hospital in time to save his life.

'Harry has since confirmed the identity of his attacker, and we have been searching for Stevenson. He also identified Private Galbraith, who he knew as Sugarboy. They met in Afghanistan when the medic saved Harry's life after he was trapped in a tank fire. Harry states that Galbraith sought him out, gave him money and drugs, and told him he had a plan to get out of the business. This plan may have led to Private Galbraith's death and the turf war now apparently playing out here and on Skye.'

McNab's focus as he'd listened to much of what he was aware of already had been on the grisly images of the most recent victims on Skye. There were multiple shots of both occupants of the burnt-out vehicle, none of them pleasant to look at. Yet his eyes refused to be drawn away from one photograph in particular.

From experience, he knew he was looking at a picture that held some meaning for him. What it was, he had no idea. *Something he should perhaps recognize?*

McNab moved forward, his eyes drawn to a closer observation of the board. As he approached, his gaze intent, the place fell silent, DI Wilson's words dying on his lips.

McNab halted before the photograph showing the remains of the driver's burnt hands still attached to the wheel.

'Detective Sergeant McNab?'

McNab stabbed at the photograph as the memory his brain had been searching for suddenly presented itself.

'The fucking ring, sir. There.' He jabbed again at the image. 'Wee Malky wore a ring like that. The driver of the stolen jeep is a fried version of Malcolm Stevenson . . . sir.'

Harry was still safely in his holding cell. When McNab arrived, he found the door standing open and Harry deep in a book. McNab stood for a moment, taking in this surprising image, before Harry registered his presence and looked up.

The face before him still had the gaunt look of a heroin user, but McNab was pleased to note that it had more colour and Harry looked less jittery than the last time they'd spoken.

'I see they're feeding you.' McNab gestured at the nearby tray. 'And providing ways to pass the time.'

'You thought I couldn't fucking read, Detective?'

'I never doubted it,' McNab responded. 'What's the book?'

Harry showed its cover. 'The sergeant loaned me it.'

The title McNab recognized from a TV adaptation of a fantasy world where folk fought one another for a mythical crown and the undead marched down from the north.

'Do the goodies win in the end?' he said.

'You tell me, Detective Sergeant.'

McNab handed Harry the photograph from upstairs, without telling him why.

Harry grued a little at the image, then checked McNab's expression, and took a second and closer look.

Harry checked with him. 'Is that fucking Malky?'

'Why'd you think that?' McNab said.

'The fucking ring, that's why. It was his trademark. How'd this happen?'

'A jeep came off a road on Skye, caught on fire and took whoever this is, plus one other, to the promised land.'

A smile caught at Harry's lips and the faint colour on his cheeks blossomed still further. 'Sugarboy got him,' he said with a smile.

'The MOD confirmed that the dead climber on Skye was definitely Sugarboy, so it couldn't have been him.'

A dark cloud passed over Harry's eyes. 'Then someone else in the squad did it.'

'Seven?' McNab tried.

Harry thought about that. 'She must have been in on whatever plan Sugarboy had, but there were seven of them together in Afghanistan.'

'Names?' McNab demanded.

'Fuck, I don't know. Sugarboy mentioned someone called the Scorpion. By the way he said it, he hated him. But five of them got captured together.'

'Sugarboy didn't mention any names other than the Scorpion?' McNab persisted.

Harry was trying hard, his forehead creased by the effort. 'A sniffer dog got brought in. Sugarboy said the handler begged him to save it.' He waited, his brain trying to recall whatever Sugarboy had told him. 'The two guys who carried in the stretcher – Ben and Charlie, Mountain and Chucky, that's what Sugarboy called them,' he said triumphantly.

Harry smiled and in that moment McNab saw what Ellie probably saw, the Harry he'd been before he'd been imprisoned and his face cooked in a burning tank.

'The MOD should fucking tell you the names.'

'True,' McNab agreed. 'But they're not inclined to tell us anything that makes them look bad.'

Harry pointed to his face. 'Which is why I'm not on a recruitment poster.'

McNab left Harry to his book as the sergeant who'd recommended it appeared with a mug of tea for his prisoner.

'Hope he's not giving you any lip, Sergeant?' McNab said.

'A star pupil,' the sergeant said, 'as long as he gets his methadone.'

71

Don't try and hide from the enemy. Lead him to you and then you have the advantage. But make it subtle. Your enemy knows you, too well in fact. But he also underestimates you.

The air in the caves was damp, but the wind couldn't reach her, or the snow that had begun falling again.

And in the deepest recesses of the cave, the sand was dry, and inside her survival bag she was warm and comfortable. As for army rations, she had sufficient to see her task out. The required water she got from a tributary of the waterfall that cascaded down the cliff face, unless the wind was too high and forced it upwards again.

She sat now consuming the contents of one of the three ration bags remaining, preparing herself for what was sure to happen.

He would follow her here. She knew that without a doubt. And she had made it possible for him to do that. Even though he might suspect this, he would still come, because what else could he do? He couldn't leave her alive, not with Sugarboy gone. And what of the other two? Who had they decided to back, now that Sugarboy was dead?

That word conjured up an image, one that she'd been trying hard to suppress. Despite her efforts, it blossomed and grew, and with it came the smells and the sounds.

He had anticipated their decision and had moved to

thwart it, the outcome of which had left Sugarboy dead at her feet.

She felt again the crack of her skull against the birch tree, causing her world to swim out of focus. The trickle of warm blood on her neck. The fear like a knife in her heart as the scenario played out again in her head.

Ben and Charlie had known nothing of the plan to eliminate *him*, so it had been easy to put the blame for Sugarboy's accidental death on her.

But you did strike the fatal blow, a small voice reminded her.

Did I? Did I really?

Sugarboy told me not to run, but I couldn't stop myself. It was my fault. I thought *he* was behind me, not Sugarboy. I thought I could smell the bastard, but I was wrong.

She stopped there, the unbearable image of Sugarboy lying on the ground, startled eyes staring up at her. She'd dropped to her knees, hugging him to her, begging him to live. For a moment, there was life in those eyes, and his mouth moved in answer.

Desperate, she'd leaned in closer, trying to hear the mouthed words.

Then *he* was there with the others, the words *What the fuck have you done, Seven?* ringing in her ears.

The wave of memory was retreating. She braced herself, not permitting the backwash to take her into the darkness with it.

She knew what Sugarboy wanted her to do. She'd heard his final words.

Finish it.

She had deliberately chosen an uncomfortable section of the rock to lean against, to prevent herself from falling into anything but a fitful doze. The distant and only entrance required watching.

Time-wise, he should be here shortly, if he was coming at all.

Although there had been other things for him to think about, bar herself. The fallout from Watson's death being one of them. The mashing of his face would only deter the authorities for as long as it took to run a DNA profile. Watson was a convicted drug dealer who would be on the police database.

The fact that there had been a forensic expert on the island when the body had been found had been unforeseen. Had the woman she'd met in the plantation not been so readily available, then it would have delayed things still further. They might all have got away and back to Afghanistan and be free again.

But he would never have permitted that to happen. He didn't want the arrangement to end. He wanted to make sure *he* was in charge of it again by the time they returned to the source.

Turf wars didn't just erupt on the streets of Glasgow.

The only way to end it was for him to go. That's what Sugarboy had said. *Remember that night in prison? Remember what I said?* His voice echoed in her brain.

'You'd kill any bastard that would rape me.' She mouthed the words as though Sugarboy was still in the darkness with her.

The sound of rushing water warned her that the tide was coming in and there wasn't much time before the entrance to the cave would become inaccessible. She'd imagined that the speed with which he would follow would result in him being here by now.

Perhaps she'd been wrong about that?

Seven trickled the sand through her fingers, feeling its soft caress. The stone walls of the cave reminded her of her cell. The sand on which she sat, a different colour, but still sand. She thought of her fellow prisoners back then. The spider and the black scorpion, the latter offering her a way out, if she should so choose.

Perhaps that was also true about what was about to happen here, with the human version, equally deadly. That thought didn't distress her. Sugarboy was dead, and inside so was she. Nothing *he* could do to her now would change that.

Seven felt in her pocket for the crumpled paper the woman had given her in the clearing. She didn't need light to know what was written there.

Maybe I should have called her? Told her everything? That would have answered the question in her eyes. All the questions.

If Sugarboy hadn't died, maybe she would have.

The sound was barely distinguishable, but when you'd spent so much time alone in captivity, you discerned and evaluated every noise.

He was here.

Relief swamped her because it meant that it was nearly over and oh how she longed for it to be over.

'Seven?' his voice called. 'Are you okay?'

She remained silent, listening for his footfall on the sand, counting the steps until he met what she had prepared for him.

He'd halted, believing her to be there, but not yet sure of his approach. His voice was his greatest asset and he would use it, to cajole and reassure her of his intentions, just as he had when in a combat zone, and after the Taliban had released them, when he'd revealed how much that release had been down to her saving the baby.

Later of course the story had changed. It had been 'the Scorpion' who had really saved them, with his ability to speak the language and his proposition that they were of much more use to the Taliban alive rather than dead. He had become the hero of the tale.

All wars needed money to endure, he'd told them. And money far outweighed the birth of one baby, even a male.

She tried to envisage how far into the cave he had come. If he stood long enough, he might notice that something was wrong, and then what she had planned, like in the woods, would fail.

But his confidence in what he was capable of was as strong as ever.

'Seven,' he called, 'I know you're in there. I can smell you.'

She smiled as he stepped forward confidently into the trap she had laid for him.

72

'Blaze. Here to me. Here to me.'

Rhona knew her voice sounded desperate, because she was.

It had been a self-indulgent move to come here and bring the dog. Trying to prove herself right. Trying to pretend she was back on the job. That her decisions were logical and properly thought through.

'Blaze,' she tried again.

'There,' Alvis said. 'Quiet, Rhona, listen.'

She did. Nothing at first, then . . .

'He's barking.' Alvis confirmed what Rhona thought she'd heard. 'He's below us somewhere.'

They were at least a couple of yards from the edge. Because of the ins and outs of the rock face, you could be well back, then suddenly much closer, and in the fading light it had been getting more difficult to make the necessary judgements, even with their head torches.

'We should get down flat,' Alvis urged. 'There's a gully. I think Blaze is down there.'

Rhona removed her backpack and lay flat. The surface was grassy, wet and no doubt slippery. She could hear the sound of falling water above the rising wind. Somewhere out ahead of them, she spotted the lights of a boat.

The barking had become fainter or the dog had stopped

alerting them to his presence. Rhona, trying not to imagine why that might be, crept ever closer to the edge. Now her torch picked out the gully Alvis had suggested was there. It dropped swiftly and deeply, as an underground stream emerged to find itself suddenly exposed to the air, before it plunged over the cliff face.

In the moving circle of her head torch, Rhona couldn't identify anything that looked like the big collie.

He's black, with only a little white, she told herself. *It doesn't mean he's not there.*

Swinging round, her torch now found Alvis much closer to the edge than she was comfortable with.

'Can you see him?' she said.

'I think he's maybe reached the beach,' Alvis told her. 'He's not on the ledge, and if he's as sure-footed as Donald says, he will have found a way down.'

Alvis sounded surer than Rhona could persuade herself to believe.

'What do we do now?'

'There's nothing we can do,' Alvis said, 'until it's light. I can lower you down there as soon as we can see well enough to do that.'

'But what if Blaze is hurt?'

Alvis didn't respond, because it was a question he couldn't answer. Not in any way that would make either of them feel any better.

Instead he said, 'Let's get the tent up, and we need to get back from the edge unless we want to be blown over.'

The wind was steadily rising, and snow clouds scurried past the moon. Rhona suddenly registered how cold it had become. How cold she had become, although it seemed the ice-like wind was inside her body, encasing her heart.

73

Alvis had the map spread out between them and directed his head torch on where he thought they were.

'Okay. There's the gully. Note the contours. There's a sharp drop, then it gets more shallow. With ledges, a sure-footed dog like Blaze could manage going down, although getting back up might be more difficult.'

'So he's stuck on the foreshore?'

'Unless he can make his way along to the bay and not be trapped by the tide.'

'But if he went down there on purpose, it must be because he was tracking Seven,' Rhona said.

'I suspect as much,' Alvis agreed.

'If we head for the bay, can we come in from that direction?'

'Possibly, but there's no guarantee.'

'For us or the dog,' Rhona said. 'So, as soon as we get the light, you help me down.'

Alvis didn't look enamoured by the prospect of Rhona being the one, but he was the better anchor for the rope.

'Help could be here by daybreak,' Alvis said cautiously.

'We both stressed that we were equipped for an overnight stay, and that there was no reason to worry about us because we were offline.' Rhona halted there. 'Besides, this isn't about finding Seven now. This is about Blaze.'

Alvis, noting her distress, nodded his agreement.

'Okay, we go as soon as we have enough light. I suggest you try and get some sleep.'

Rhona nodded, not because she imagined she would get any, but because she knew he wouldn't agree to her taking the first watch.

Rhona lay down, her brain going into overtime. How could she have let this happen? She should never have borrowed Blaze in the first place. He wasn't a police dog. She should have acknowledged that. She had promised to keep him safe and she hadn't.

Time ticked past, second by what seemed endless second. The wind hurtled around them, plucking at the tent, which thankfully stayed anchored there in a shallow dip, only, she thought, because of Alvis's bulk and weight.

If I'd been alone, I would have been plucked off the grass by now and tossed over the cliff to meet Blaze at the bottom.

She shook her head to dispel that thought, not because of her own possible demise, but of what she might encounter at the foot of the gully.

She must have eventually dozed off, because Alvis's voice woke her.

'Rhona. Come out here and see this.'

Opening her eyes, Rhona found the tent dancing with light. It was extraordinary. She'd experienced the northern lights before now, but by the brightness in the tent, they must be filling the sky.

Crawling out of the tent to join Alvis, Rhona realized that the snow had ceased, leaving a white reflective film over the landscape. Above her the dancing lights vied with countless stars for attention, with the moon's creamy colour adding to the show.

'Let's go,' Alvis said. 'With our torches and this display, I think we can see well enough to get you down to the shore.'

As they crept towards the gully, the sky above them continued its display of greens and pinks, the colours swirling like the skirts of an exotic dancer. Skye had always seemed like a fairy tale to Rhona with its strange rock formations, its dark demonic moods and shining beauty. Now it was putting on its best display just when they needed it.

'There's a big rock here where we can secure the rope,' Alvis said. He tossed Rhona the other end. 'But first we need to attach it to you.'

Once he was happy she was secure, he explained once again the path she should take.

'I'll be watching you all the way, and remember, I can see what's coming up whereas you'll be facing the rock. So take your time and listen.'

Rhona could sense his disquiet that she should be the one to descend and he be the one to wait behind. Alvis had, she suspected, more experience than she had on the hills. And he'd had to watch Marita fall, and hadn't been able to save her.

Letting Rhona go down the gully was going to be as hard on him as it was on her. Or even worse.

'I'll be fine,' Rhona assured him. 'Jamie and I scrambled about Skye when we were teenagers.'

They had, and they hadn't always been roped up, she recalled. But back then death had never seemed a possibility.

Turning onto her front, Rhona eased herself over the edge, feeling for and finding the first foothold Alvis had described for her.

Here goes, she thought, wishing she was back safely ensconced in Jamie's safe grip on Kilt Rock. Having done that descent once she'd had no wish to do it again.

Yet here she was and without the safety of Jamie's arms about her.

But I do have a harness of sorts, and Alvis as my anchor.

Alvis's concise and repeated instructions eventually brought her safely to the ledge they believed the dog had jumped down to.

Finding herself breathless with exertion and the rush of adrenaline that had fed her determination, Rhona heeded Alvis's shouted advice that she take a rest before tackling the lower slope. She settled her back against the rock and took steady breaths, still hearing the fast beat of her heart in her ears. Having turned now to face the sea, she watched as the fairy dance played out over the water, its reflection like the lights of Atlantis below the waves.

'You okay to go?' Alvis's voice came from above.

Rhona shouted in the affirmative, then instead of turning back towards the rock, she decided instead to ease her way down by the seat of her pants. That way if she slipped surely she would just slide on down.

'Rhona. I think you should turn and keep looking up at me. I've got you, so you don't need to worry about falling.'

The ground had been getting wetter. Her walking trousers were supposedly waterproof but there was only so much wet they could cope with, and a sudden spring appearing from the rock wasn't helping.

As Rhona turned to follow Alvis's orders, she began to slide. It happened so quickly that she could do nothing to prevent it, despite grabbing at the nearby tufts of grass.

Her sudden and rapid descent had also caught Alvis off

guard and literally pulled the rope from his grasp. Then her boot met a rock, which momentarily halted her descent, before momentum propelled her over it head first and she rolled the rest of the way to land on soft wet sand that sunk beneath her weight like a cushion.

Winded but essentially unhurt, Rhona called up to a no-doubt horrified Alvis, 'I'm okay, Alvis, and I'm on the beach.'

Alvis mouthed words in Norwegian that Rhona interpreted as 'Thank God'.

As she detached the rope, the dancing ladies ended their display and deserted her, leaving Rhona only the light of the moon and the stars.

74

'We can talk about this, Seven.'

'My name isn't Seven,' she said just loud enough for him to hear.

There was a moment's silence while he considered how to deal with this aspect of her rebellion. Eventually he decided not to even acknowledge it.

'We have the stash. Watson and his mates are dead. Ben and Charlie saw to that. The war's over.'

'My name isn't Seven,' she repeated.

He tried a different tack. 'That was Sugarboy's name for you.' He laughed. 'A tidy Seven, he used to say after he came back from his visits. You served us all well in that hellhole. Kept us alive.'

She knew what he was doing. She knew to ignore the words. But yet still they wormed their way into her brain. Just as they had always done, even before the attack on the camp. He knew how to play her. He knew how to play them all. He was the voice of reason, of common sense, or that's what he had persuaded them to believe.

But there was one weakness and she had to remember that. His lies were always believable as long as he didn't go too far.

Sensing her softening perhaps, and warming to his chosen theme, he couldn't stop himself from embellishing.

'We always talked about it when they brought us back. We told each other everything. That way we were all with you, not just one at a time.'

Despite her best efforts, she could imagine that scene, listen to what they might have said about her.

Sugarboy would never have done that, another voice told her. *Sugarboy never touched you, even when they beat him to make him.*

When she didn't respond, and unable to see her expression to read it, he now took a bigger step.

'Sugarboy was the favourite though, wasn't he? And yet you killed him. Remember? That night in the woods. The knife through the eye and into his brain. Why would you do that?'

As he spoke the words, she relived the scene. She couldn't stop herself, which was of course why he'd said it. The air fled her lungs and they filled with blood, Sugarboy's blood.

She coughed, choking on it.

He waited, sensing he was winding his way into her psyche again, reclaiming it as his own, then after waiting for a response, which didn't materialize, he came back with the next reminder.

'But we took care of that, didn't we, Seven, because the ones left alive, we're a team, and we'll do anything to help one another. Anything,' he emphasized.

The darkness swallowed his carefully considered words, while she imagined them buried forever, and not in her mind.

Having played what he felt were the required cards, he was awaiting her response, just as he always had.

She decided not to give him one, but thought again how

this place reminded her of the stone-walled prison cell when he'd been in there with her. Only back then, she had been the powerless one.

She smiled a little to herself, although a small shiver of fear had entered her brain.

The deep hole she'd dug just inside the entrance had caught him unawares, but that alone wouldn't have stopped him. It was the netting that had neutralized his initial attempts to climb out.

He was immobilized for the moment, but how long that would last she had no idea. He would have his knife with him, and at this very moment might be cutting himself free.

'I thought it was you in the woods,' she said to stall for time. 'It was you I was trying to kill.'

'Where would you be now if it had been me? Trussed up somewhere in Glasgow with the fuckers all taking a shot at you. Sugarboy couldn't save you in Afghanistan, and he couldn't save you here.'

He laughed then, and that sound drowned her in unbearable memories.

She had heard enough.

The net encased him but it didn't shut out his voice, and that's what she wanted to do now, more than anything.

She snatched at the canvas bag she'd brought with her and, creeping towards him, dropped it over his head.

'What the fuck, Seven!'

He was writhing madly now like a spider caught in a giant web and she knew that he hadn't freed his hands, hadn't reached his knife, wherever it was.

'Time to shut up, Jack.'

She'd diverted her water source, giving it another escape

route. Now she released it, hearing it return to its preferred path. To encourage what was about to happen, she upended the plastic container she'd already filled, over his hood. He must have anticipated what was about to come, because it took a few moments before he was forced to open his mouth and the coughing and choking began.

Seven poured some more and felt a rush of pleasure at his increasingly frantic attempts at breathing in with his waterlogged lungs.

The incoming tide had found the hole now and was rushing in to meet the running stream.

She thought she heard a 'Please, Seven' among the ever-more strangled coughs.

'My name isn't Seven,' she said quietly.

75

The conference room, she knew, was still heaving with people. Chrissy was beginning to wonder if the entire population of Portree was either in the police station or outside in the square.

The weather had cleared but there had been no change on the plans to use the chopper. Looking for personnel, even if they were showing a light, was an almost impossible task. Better to wait for daylight, especially searching such a wild coastline.

Chrissy knew all the sane and sensible reasons why Search and Rescue didn't normally go out in the dark, but it didn't make any difference. Their absence just felt like a failure.

But Donald's out there looking with Jamie, and they have radios. They'll tell us as soon as they locate Rhona, she reminded herself.

And what of Blaze?

Donald would be worried sick. She knew that. He had been more than kind about loaning the services of his dog, but maybe, just maybe, Rhona had gone too far this time? The split loyalty of such a thought only served to increase Chrissy's fears for both Rhona and the dog, forcing her to concentrate on what she could affect.

Her samples from the burnt-out vehicle and her report

and photographs were no doubt already being discussed in Glasgow. McNab would have seen to that. There was also, according to McNab, the likelihood that the body in the stolen jeep had been Malcolm Stevenson. The ring that might identify him was sitting before her in an evidence bag, ready to be sent in the morning.

As if on cue, her mobile drilled, McNab's name on the screen.

When she answered, McNab immediately asked if there was any word on Rhona.

'Not yet,' Chrissy told him with a heavy heart. 'But she's with Alvis, so she'll be all right.'

'What about the other soldiers?'

'Nothing there either.'

They lapsed into silence at that point before McNab changed the subject, making Chrissy wonder if what he was about to say was the real reason for the call.

'I plan to drop in on Maguire. Bring him up to date on what's happening there with Rhona.'

'Is that wise?' Chrissy said.

'Why? Has Rhona said something about being in touch with him herself?' McNab asked.

Chrissy only wished she had done.

'Is she coming home when this is over?' McNab asked the question that Chrissy realized probably lay behind all of this.

Chrissy decided to tell him the truth. 'She mentioned she might spend Christmas on Skye. Said she hadn't had a Christmas here since she was a teenager.'

When McNab didn't immediately respond, Chrissy rushed on, 'And she's been invited to Jamie's pal's wedding. They're having his stag do up at A.C.E Target Sports where this all began,' she added, as though that explained it all.

'And she's going with Jamie boy, no doubt?'

When Chrissy didn't respond, another expletive was voiced.

'She'll have to come back for the sin-eater trial,' Chrissy said. 'And once Rhona comes home, she'll stay.'

An ominous silence followed her declaration.

'What's wrong?' she demanded.

'He's changed his plea to guilty, so there will be no trial,' McNab said.

Chrissy wondered if that was the news Rhona wanted to hear. Now she wouldn't have to give evidence. Wouldn't have to face her nemesis again in court. Yet, that would have brought her back. Chrissy realized she had been clinging to that thought, believing that once Rhona did return to Glasgow, she would be persuaded that she belonged there.

Plus, Rhona may have feared her demons, but, knowing her, she would have also relished facing up to them during the trial, maybe finally conquering them, which would no longer happen.

'He didn't want his forensic knowledge disputed in court,' Chrissy said. 'This way it won't be. He thinks he's won already.'

'So we can't bring her back that way.'

'Maybe it's up to Sean now,' Chrissy said.

Ringing off, she found Janice at the open door of the production room.

'They've found them?' Chrissy asked eagerly.

Janice shook her head. 'They've found a tent near Ramasaig Bay, but it's empty.'

'Is it Rhona's?'

'Unconfirmed, although likely. There is some good news, though,' she said, seeing Chrissy's woeful expression. 'Archie's been sent home. The number that called here to implicate him has been traced. The owner said a guy asked to borrow his mobile, said his had run out, and he had some information for the police.'

'Who was it?'

'He gave us a description. We ran it past Archie before we told him what it was about.'

'And?'

'He said it sounded like the guy who was looking for the female medic.'

That made sense, Chrissy thought, if the soldiers were involved in Watson's death – and knowing what they knew now, that looked increasingly likely.

'What do we do?'

'The only thing we can do. We wait.'

76

Looking upwards, Rhona realized her view of the top was impeded, which more than likely meant Alvis couldn't see her either. Even the waving light of her torch. She would have to rely on the hope that he had heard her shout that she'd reached the beach safely.

Before he'd lowered her down, they'd made the decision that Alvis would go west, heading into the bay at the first opportunity. From there, he would attempt to make his way back along the shoreline to reach her.

Rhona was already beginning to doubt that as a possibility, aware as she was of an encroaching tide. The sand at the foot of the gully had been wet, but more because of the stream that had helped her slide to the bottom. Alvis had checked the tide tables while they still had a signal. High tide along the Duirinish peninsula was scheduled for shortly after 4 a.m., and they were getting perilously close to that now.

Like Kilt Rock, there would no doubt be areas of foreshore, but not necessarily the entire way along, and the cliffs here were peppered by caves, arches and stacks, which only served to illustrate the continuing force of the sea against the basalt rocks.

She was taking a chance even being down here. And yet Blaze, having been set the task of finding Seven, hadn't hesitated. Rhona thought of Donald's description of his dog's sure-footedness: 'He's cautious too, though. He only attempts what he knows he can do.'

Rhona prayed that Donald was right, while wishing she could claim the same for herself.

So in what direction had the dog gone exactly?

Any call she'd made to Blaze had remained unanswered, but the relief of not finding an injured dog at the bottom of the cliff face had given her a measure of hope at least.

Training her head torch on the surrounding sand, Rhona searched for paw prints. Luckily, the tide had not yet reached the area she stood in. Blaze had barked to them from where she now stood at the foot of the gully. Where had he gone after that?

Eventually she made her decision. Her tracing of what looked like paw prints in the damp sand, plus the thought that Seven was unlikely to have descended the gully only to head for the bay, prompted Rhona to begin to make her way in an easterly direction, keeping close to the rock face.

The strip of foreshore moved between sand and rough stones. Sometimes wide, with the sea sufficiently far away. At other times too narrow for comfort, the rocks slippery underfoot with seaweed. Each time she picked her way across a stony part she swiftly searched for paw print evidence on reaching the other side. Those moments were the most frightening.

The sea, when it reached here, if given the slightest chance, could sweep anyone off their feet, including the determined collie.

On each of these occasions, Rhona called out the 'here to me' command Donald had taught her, then waited, hoping against hope that the collie would hear her and respond. He never did and eventually the stony foreshore took over completely, and with it the trail she was following.

She stood for a moment, trying to gather her thoughts. The dog had come this far, that she was certain of. So where had Blaze gone now?

Standing there, she felt the first brush of the incoming tide around her feet like a warning of what was to come.

The foreshore had to all intents and purposes disappeared and before her stood an arch on its way to becoming a stack, like one of MacLeod's Maidens. To get through the arch would involve getting wet, very wet. And with no knowledge of how deep the water was and how rough it would be underfoot.

The dog, having arrived here some time before her, might well have found the going easier, with the ability to walk beneath the arch before the incoming tide had reached here. Alternatively, the sure-footed dog may have chosen a different route, and climbed over the rocky outcrop.

Having studied both possible ways in the moonlight, Rhona had to admit that there was little chance of her being able to climb the rock and descend the other side. Her main option seemed therefore to lie in negotiating a passage through the arch, regardless of how wet that would make her.

The one thing she could not imagine doing was giving up.

In the end, however, the decision was made for her.

A sound she thought she might never experience again, she now thought she'd heard. Rhona stood stock-still and strained to listen through the crash of the waves against the outer region of the arch.

'Blaze?' she said, hardly daring to hope.

The bark was partially drowned out by the surge of the sea against the rocks, but it was definitely there. And it hadn't come from above, but rather from further along the shore.

Bracing herself, Rhona stepped under the arch and into the water.

77

The waterboarding had silenced him, perhaps even killed him. She considered this. How she felt about *him* being dead. She'd thought – no, imagined it for such a long time. The last breath he took symbolized for her the first breath she might take of her new life.

Or so she had believed.

Her previous life rushed up to meet these thoughts. She was a medic. She was there to save lives, not take them. All the bodies she had tended, all the terrified eyes that had looked into her own. All the trembling hands she had held.

It's okay, soldier. I'm here. Her internal voice reminded her of her words of comfort.

But she and Sugarboy had decided that the only way to get out of this was for *him* to die. It was the only way to be free. *He* was the prison she carried with her. Even thinking of *him* brought back the smell and the horror of what had been done to her there.

The problem was she'd always assumed that Sugarboy would be here with her. And Sugarboy was dead.

The horror of that hit her again. Sugarboy was gone and that meant the decision had to be hers and hers alone.

A spluttered cough from below brought her abruptly back to the present, and the reality that he wasn't dead. Not yet. She took her torch and directed it into the hole. The sand had shifted and re-formed round him, just as it had done round their camp in Afghanistan. Running the torch over his hooded head, she saw him flinch, but he said nothing.

She had vowed to shut him up, and it appeared she had. Where was his cajoling voice, his psychological manipulation of her thinking, her very being?

Fear reappeared, surging through her like electricity.

Her plan had worked up to this point, but what would happen now? Her imagined success, she acknowledged, had unnerved her, making her query her actions.

That's what always happened in his presence. He had been the unquestioned leader of their enterprise. How had that happened? Even Sugarboy, after they'd been released, had willingly gone along with the plan he put into action.

But that was before I told Sugarboy what he'd done. Told him in detail. Every word, every time he'd forced me to do what he wanted.

She was wet from the relentless creep of the incoming tide and the constant spray from the running water above. But she wasn't shivering because she was cold, she was shivering because she was afraid. Afraid of what she was capable of. Of what she was incapable of.

He moaned a little, as though in sympathy.

Why had he not fought his way out of the net? Where was his knife and why had he not used it? One cough turned to three as he struggled to raise himself up.

She thought she heard the word 'please', followed by her name. Her real name.

This is his next move, she thought. His next attempt to soften me up. He'd done that in her prison. Called her by her real name, as though that meant he could pretend what was happening was consensual.

'I'm sorry,' he called out suddenly. 'What I did was wrong. They threatened to kill us if we didn't. Even worse, they threatened to kill you.'

'Sugarboy didn't do it,' she said. 'They almost killed him, but he still wouldn't. Ben and Charlie pretended to. But you . . .'

The truth annoyed him. His wheedling tone changed to anger.

'We were in a fucking war. Remember the helicopter? Remember the kid you took in? You never searched him and he had a grenade. He blew up our fucking friends because of you. But we never punished you for that. We forgave you.'

Had they forgiven her? Had she forgiven herself?

They were all unreliable narrators, she thought. *We all have our versions of the same story, although in his there is never any doubt, because the route he chooses is always the right one. What he does, what he did, is always justified.*

'And remember, we will never give you up for Pete's death. Never.' He hurried on, sensing perhaps that she might be coming round to his way of thinking. 'Just as we will never tell them that he killed Watson.' He paused, but only briefly. 'We can get out of this scot-free. Get back to being a team again.'

At his words, she felt something collapse inside herself. There was no escape from all of this. How could Sugarboy have imagined there would be?

Perhaps sensing this, he made his promise. 'Let me out of here and we'll go meet with the guys. We can be off this island and back out to Afghanistan, just as planned. Sugarboy was never going back. You know that, don't you?'

Unleashed now, the truth came flooding back. The

reason why they'd come on this last trip together, pretending they were still one big happy team. They weren't, because Sugarboy was never going back and neither was she.

In that moment, she wanted nothing more of this – or him. Drawing her knife, she reached into his cell.

78

Alvis, having walked on until he could easily access the shore, spotted the dancing lights on the clifftop and instantly knew that a team had been sent out to look for them, which meant something had happened in their absence or else Donald had been too concerned for his dog to hang around until morning to check on their whereabouts.

Four sets of lights dotted the hilltop close to where they'd pitched their tent. Shortly following this, two set off in the direction Alvis himself had followed and were, he thought, heading for the bay.

The decision therefore had to be made as to whether he should await their arrival or keep going. Alvis made his mind up immediately. The likelihood was that if those approaching were part of the Mountain Rescue Team, then they would be equipped with radios, which meant what had happened up to now could be related back to headquarters.

Alvis took off his head torch and waved it, indicating where he was. Being professionals, they would likely reach here much quicker than he had.

He was right. In fact, according to his own estimate, they'd taken less than half the time he had in negotiating the route. As he waited on the beach, the two lights bounced towards him. He heard Donald's voice first and it was Rhona's name he called.

Alvis answered in as positive a way as he dared.

'She's on ahead, with Blaze.'

Donald's face appeared in the light of his head torch. 'Blaze is okay?'

The last bark he'd heard suggested that was true, so Alvis answered in the positive.

Alvis gestured to where he had come from. 'Blaze followed Seven's trail to a gully up there where we pitched our tent, and went down it.' When Donald had seemingly absorbed this information, Alvis quickly added, 'He gave us an answering bark when he reached the bottom, so I lowered Rhona down when we had enough light.'

'The northern lights sped us on our way,' Donald said, obviously relieved by the news of Blaze's well-being. 'So the girl is somewhere east of here?'

'Rhona followed Blaze, who she thought was headed that way.'

'Okay.' Donald nodded, then introduced Allan, the MRT member who'd accompanied him to the beach.

'We'd better get a move on then, if we want to walk there. The tide isn't on our side.'

Alvis didn't need to be reminded of that. He'd checked the tables the day before, but never imagined they would be down on the beach at this hour, if ever.

'You know this part of the coast?' Alvis asked as the three men walked together. Alvis expected Donald to respond but found that the answer came from Allan.

'This is my part of the world. My family's from Orbost. My father has a boat. We came round this coast often.'

'Is there anywhere the girl might choose to hide?'

'It depends how frightened she is and who's after her.'

They tramped on in silence apart from the crackling of the radio. At one point Alvis heard Chrissy's voice on the line and her desperate desire to know what had happened to Rhona, but also her obvious concern for the dog, and Donald.

Donald's response had been positive, although Alvis wasn't sure how honest he'd been. After discussing the coastline in some detail with Allan, all three men were aware of what Rhona and the dog had faced when they'd descended that gully earlier.

And it wasn't as straightforward as perhaps she'd hoped.

'There's an arch ahead,' Allan told them. 'We have maybe twenty minutes before high tide and the word from the coastguard is that the sea is choppy. We'll have to be quick.'

79

'No, Seven, don't do it!'

He was frightened of her. The intensity of the feeling that brought almost overwhelmed her. She felt a rush of emotion, almost sexual in nature. It was both exhilarating and powerful. This was the feeling he'd experienced when he'd visited her in her cell, she realized. In the Taliban world where he controlled nothing, he could at least control her. Force her to his will.

Did this mean, when given the opportunity, she was like him?

Such a notion sickened her so much that she gagged. She thought of Sugarboy. What made the two men so different that Sugarboy would not rape her despite the torture that brought in return?

Jack, in contrast, had ignored her calls when she'd asked – no, begged – him not to rape her. Why did he think she would respond differently if given power over him?

Because we are not the same. What happened in the woods taught me that.

Then again, if she weakened and spared him, he would play the role of winner, before he set about what he had really come here to do.

And that, she suspected, was to dispense with her once and for all.

He would put *her* in the hole. Let the rising tide flow over her, as she had planned for him.

Or drown her out there in the ocean.

He need only hold her head under the water long enough to give the impression of suicide. A troubled returning female veteran, captured by the Taliban. Abused and raped. He would have the story all worked out to tell the authorities. Her comrades had tried to help her, Sugarboy in particular, but in her traumatized situation, she had sadly killed him.

She moved from his imagined explanation of her state of mind to that which he might not be able to explain so easily. How had Sugarboy's body got onto the mountain? Perhaps the story Jack had concocted about that wasn't as good as he'd thought. Would the forensic scientist who'd questioned her in the plantation buy the story of the wounds on Sugarboy's face having come from a fall?

She wasn't as sure as Jack was about that.

He was talking again, trying to focus her decision on his plan.

'So,' he was saying, 'we'll stay here until it's light, then meet up with the guys and leave Skye together.'

There was a moment's silence before she responded.

'No,' she said.

The certainty in her voice surprised her even more than him.

'No,' she repeated for emphasis.

She stood up as the next wave entered the cave, climbing the rock wall as it did so, pouring into the pit.

'Seven,' he tried to shout through the waterlogged canvas.

'My name isn't Seven,' she repeated like a mantra as she waited for the surge of water to retreat.

'That's enough, Seven. Cut me fucking free. That's an order.'

There were so many orders that he had issued and all of them she had carried out. But not this one.

'You're a soldier. Cut yourself free . . . sir,' she spat back at him.

The explosion of anger that followed her as she waded towards the entrance made her smile. Much like she had done with Sugarboy in their darkest moments.

Hearing his frantic attempts to free himself, she fought back the pity that threatened to engulf her.

She couldn't soften now.

Outside, she registered that they were fast approaching high tide, when the cave would be almost fully underwater, judging by the marks on the wall. The earlier aurora show had disappeared, leaving only the brightness of the moon and stars. She thought how often she had stargazed from the tiny opening of her cell in Afghanistan, imagining herself back somewhere in Scotland, where the air was sharp and clean.

Trying not to think about Jack, she focused instead on her memory of what had happened that night in the woods and on the headland.

Watson had been fit, but he'd been unprepared. He thought they were on the same side. Soldiers in the pay of his governor, the Sandman. Making money together via Afghanistan's bounty.

'The fucking MOD don't care if you die or not out there. We do,' he'd told them.

As long as we delivered the goods.

Any thought that the supply chain might come to an end, or cost more, had changed his mind.

Jack had outlined exactly what was required for them to keep working together. Watson hadn't liked that. Not one little bit.

Take it or leave it, Jack had told him. *There are plenty of others keen to get our supply line.*

Watson had made a big mistake when he'd pulled the gun. Never threaten a serving soldier. Watson thought he was a tough guy, but he'd never served in a war. A real war. Nor did he know that you never challenged a black scorpion. Not if you wanted to live.

She had learned that at least.

And so had Watson. And, it appeared, the other two members of the team who had apparently come to Skye with him.

Jack had declared the war over, and the safest place for the four of them remaining was back in that other war.

Only there weren't going to be four of them to go back.

Seven slid to the ground and set herself against the rock face, knowing it would all soon be over. The nightmares, the fear, the hate that had filled her very soul.

Closing her eyes, she prepared herself. In that moment, she recalled Sugarboy's explanation for the war and its deaths. For the cruelties, big and small. And for the love such as she'd experienced among the women of Afghanistan as they'd washed and fed her and made her tea.

Surely Sugarboy had been right: *All the Gods, the Heavens and the Hells are within us.*

'Get the fuck up,' Jack ordered, dragging her to her feet.

His anger broke over her like a menacing wave. Grabbing her hair, he yanked her through the rising water.

'Thought you would fucking drown me?' He caught her

arm and twisted it hard. The snap of breaking bone was unmistakable and she screamed in pain.

'I'll do worse than that, you evil slut.'

He dragged her along what was left of the foreshore.

'You fucking tried to kill me. You little shit. You started all of this. The explosion was your fault. Mitch and Gordo would be alive today but for you. Sugarboy too.'

He was right about the grenade, but not about Pete. She knew that now. Was sure of it.

'You killed Pete,' she said. 'Not me. I hit him, but it was an accident. You were the one who killed him.'

He laughed at that and a deep sense of the end of everything came over her.

She had made the choice to sit on the beach and let the sea take her. She had been ready for that, because he would go too. But he wasn't going to die. The bastard wasn't going to die.

Seven fought back now, twisting in his arms, trying to break free of him. They had sparred in training and she knew his moves, but out here, with one arm useless, she didn't stand a chance, not unless she got him into the water.

The next wave reached them. Knocked slightly off balance, he loosened his grip for a second and Seven launched herself into the undertow of the retreating wave.

Righting himself, he saw her go and threw himself into the water to follow her.

If I go down, so does he, Seven promised herself.

80

Rhona clawed at the rock face as the water tried to drag her feet from under her. The insistent barking of the dog, suggesting that Blaze had found something, served to spur her on. That and the bobbing lights behind her which had to be Alvis and hopefully members of a search team.

Having timed the waves, she'd tried to estimate how long she had before the next one hit. If she was lucky, chances were she could reach halfway through the arch and cling on to what looked like a good handhold before the retreating wave could drag her out to sea.

She had discarded her gloves, keen to get a better grip on the rock's surface. In the poor light, she could make out the battered remnants of her fight with the tree in the plantation, which seemed a lifetime ago.

As the wave retracted, Rhona stumbled her way across the seaweed-strewn boulders and launched herself at the handhold, which wasn't as solid as she'd assumed. Grabbing it dislodged a shower of loose gravel before she found a part firm enough to hang on to.

As the wave approached, she felt the strength of it slam her knees against the rock, then the powerful suck as it desperately tried to take her back with it into the swell. Her fingers torn and bleeding, she hung on determinedly until eventually, as the water retreated, she emerged on the other side of the arch, soaked but triumphant.

'Blaze,' she shouted. 'Here to me, Blaze.'

She searched the distance for the small flash of white amongst the shaggy black coat which would signal the dog's advance, but it never appeared. Plus the barking had stopped. Rhona made her way as swiftly as she could, stumbling over the rocks that scattered the sand.

According to the map they'd studied in the tent, there was a series of caves this side of the archway, which could be where Seven had taken refuge.

Rhona came on the first one by chance. Shielded by a covering stone, it would have been easy to miss the small entrance, especially now as the tide was working hard to reclaim it. A flash of her torch picked out a semi-filled hole in the sandy floor, which she may well have stumbled into, had the water been deeper. Floating alongside was a wad of plastic netting.

Towards the back, the beam rested on the remains of a camp.

So it looked like Seven had been here. If so, where was she now?

Rhona waded back out, and continued east along the shore. There was a second gully in this direction, one they'd bypassed on the way along the clifftop because Blaze had shown no interest in it, even though it had looked accessible.

Was Seven heading there, with Blaze now following her?

Rhona stepped back into the water to try and get a view of the cliff summit. Were any of the team still up there or had all those who'd followed made their way to the beach?

Looking back the way she'd come, she found the promontory now blocked her view of the bay beyond the archway, so she had no idea where Alvis had reached.

A sudden and piercing human cry was almost immediately followed by the barking of a dog. Not any dog, though.

It was Blaze. Definitely Blaze.

Swivelling round, Rhona searched desperately along the line of the breaking waves.

Then she saw them.

Two figures in the water, the dog frantically running back and forth along the shore east of where she stood. They appeared to be struggling together, one definitely having the upper hand. Then suddenly there was only one, the other swallowed by the waves. Too tall to be Seven, the remaining figure turned and began wading towards the beach.

Rhona knew in that moment that the dog was in as much danger as the body left behind in the water, and shouted frantically for Blaze to come to her.

Blaze ignored her call and, instead, dodging the approaching figure of the man, jumped into the water and began to swim towards the bobbing body of what had to be Seven.

Rhona ran along the water's edge, certain that if she didn't get out there in time, both Seven and her rescuer were liable to be swept away in the insistent swell of the incoming tide.

But she was wrong.

She knew from Donald that Blaze was a keen swimmer. She'd also seen him in action in the loch near the plantation. But keeping himself afloat was one thing. Helping Seven stay above the surface of the choppy water was another.

She drew nearer and, with the aid of the dawning light, saw what the dog was trying to do. He had something in his mouth, likely the hood of Seven's jacket, and was slowly but surely pulling her body towards the shore.

As Rhona waded out to meet Blaze, she saw the dancing lights of three torches emerge from beneath the arch and head quickly towards them across the sand.

Then Donald's voice resounded across the intervening water.

'Here to me, Blaze. Here to me.'

The girl was alive.

The three men had carried her to shore where Rhona had removed her wet clothes and wrapped her in a sleeping bag Donald had given her, and then inside a survival bag. Blaze, having seemingly satisfied himself that Seven was okay, then took off, despite Donald's instruction to the contrary.

'Blaze doesn't give up easily,' Donald said with a shake of his head.

'He reminds me of Chrissy, my other forensic assistant,' Rhona smiled, her heart lifting because, despite the cold and the wet, Seven was safe.

Donald, answering a radio call, told her that the helicopter was on its way.

'What about her attacker?' Rhona said as another call came through.

'Currently climbing the gully. Not sure if he realizes Blaze will be right behind him, with Jamie and Scott at the top awaiting his arrival.'

'I'm sorry I put your dog in danger,' Rhona said.

'Don't be. I know Blaze and he can do that all by himself,' he said. 'I'll go wait for Search and Rescue. There's a spot further along they can hover, then they'll get you and the girl out of here.'

Seven's eyes opened. Confused at first, they gradually cleared and immediately fastened on Rhona.

'Where's Blaze?' she demanded. 'He saved my life.'

'Blaze is fine and about to apprehend your attacker along with Skye and Lochaber Mountain Rescue.'

A wash of emotion crossed her face, from remembered horror to relief.

'There was a dog in Afghanistan,' Rhona said. 'Called Rex?'

'You know about that?'

'I went into your tent in the plantation.' Rhona paused. 'I'm sorry for messing with your things, but I wanted – no, needed – to know where you'd gone.'

'And you found Rex's tag?'

'Yes.'

'And the other stuff? The burka mesh and the remains of the necklace?'

Rhona expected Seven to be angry at the violation of her privacy, but instead she seemed relieved, as though finding the mementos of Afghanistan released her from them in some way.

'You came back to the plantation looking for me?'

Rhona nodded. 'With Blaze. He got your scent and we followed it to the road. Archie said you'd taken the Glendale bus. Blaze picked up your scent again, leading us here.'

Seven shook her head in amazement.

'Why would you do that? Why would you look for me?'

Rhona wasn't sure what to say. How could she explain that she saw her troubled self in the girl? So she spoke in certainties instead, explaining about the scene in the woods behind A.C.E Target Sports.

'Blaze led me to the clearing. He knew, as did I, that something bad had happened there. The way he sought to protect you suggested . . .' Rhona halted.

'That what happened there might have involved me,' Seven finished for her.

'What's your real name?' Rhona said.

'Lexi. My name is Lexi. Private Lexi Forbes.'

'And the man who tried to drown you?'

'Corporal Jack Dempsey. My superior officer.' She halted there as though the memory was too much. 'Did you find Ben and Charlie?' she asked quickly.

'Not yet, but we did find Private Peter Galbraith's body,' Rhona said.

Lexi's face crumpled. 'They took him into the hills. That's all they told me. He didn't die there. But I expect you know that?' There were tears in her eyes.

'Where did he die?' Rhona asked quietly.

'In the woods, that night.' She looked horror-stricken at the memory. 'I thought he was Corporal Dempsey and hit out at him. I didn't kill him. Corporal Dempsey did. I know that now.'

'And Ben and Charlie? Where are they?'

'Jack said we were going to meet them.'

'Did he say where?'

Lexi shook her head. 'I think he was lying anyway.' She collapsed back, coughing, her breathing suddenly sounding laboured.

Rhona, fearful there was still water in her lungs, motioned to Donald.

'Any word on the chopper?'

'They're on their way. Is she okay?' he added, seeing Rhona's concerned expression.

'Her breathing's not good and she's coughing.'

He nodded, knowing the dangers of secondary drowning. 'We'll get her to the hospital in Portree. Did she tell you anything?'

Rhona nodded. 'But I get the impression there's much more to come.'

81

'Detective Sergeant. You're wanted upstairs.'

McNab's eyes sprang open to the sight of the police cell he'd spent the night in. Or at least a few hours of the night.

He swung his feet to the ground and sat upright.

'What is it?' he managed, attempting to force his brain back into action.

'They're bringing in the prisoner. The helicopter just landed.'

He'd grabbed a couple of hours' sleep after receiving the news that Rhona had been picked up, together with the girl they called Seven and the leader of the medics group, Corporal Jack Dempsey.

Knowing Rhona was safe had been the most important part of the message for him, but he had to admit the initial unravelling of what had been happening on Skye had played a big part in the pleasure he'd taken from the news.

Stretching, he took himself off to the coffee machine and two double espressos later presented himself, rumpled but otherwise awake, in the boss's office. Despite the early hour, DI Wilson looked fresh, or perhaps his expression was simply enhanced by the news of the latest arrest.

'I want you and DS Clark to question Dempsey.'

'DS Clark's here?' McNab said, surprised but pleased that his partner was back.

'She came in with the suspect,' the boss said. 'You'll hear this from DS Clark but in a conversation with Private Lexi Forbes, Rhona was told that Private Galbraith died in the woods and was taken up to the hill to cover that, just as Rhona suspected.'

So all the time they'd been questioning her state of mind, Rhona had been right that it was all connected.

'How did he die?' McNab said.

'The girl said it was an accident and it was her fault.'

'Is the girl here too?'

'She's been transferred to the Queen Elizabeth hospital to be monitored after the attempted drowning. We'll have her in once she's been given the all clear.' DI Wilson went on, 'If Corporal Dempsey is the lead player in all of this, then he may know the identity of the Sandman.'

McNab nodded.

'However, I suspect your time with Corporal Dempsey will be limited, Detective Sergeant.'

'How so, sir?' McNab said, genuinely puzzled.

'Sergeant MacDonald followed protocol and informed the MOD that Corporal Dempsey had been arrested in Portree after a suspected attempt on a fellow soldier's life.'

McNab swore under his breath, knowing the MOD would be all over this now like a rash.

'His quick transfer here was in the hope that we might get a statement before the MOD come for him. So get what you can before that happens, Detective Sergeant.'

McNab stood unseen behind the glass and observed the man Seven had referred to as the Scorpion. A call to Rhona as he awaited the arrival of the prisoner had furnished him with considerable detail on this man's activities, both here and in Afghanistan.

If what Seven – McNab mentally corrected himself – what Lexi had told Rhona was true, it was obvious why Corporal Dempsey had believed her to be a risk to both his smuggling enterprise and his freedom. Hence his attempt on her life.

'She wouldn't talk about her captivity in Afghanistan, but something terrible happened there that changed everything for her, and in particular how she viewed her commanding officer.'

Rhona had ground to a halt then, her voice heavy with emotion, and McNab suspected that if anyone could have any inkling about what it felt like to be held against their will, it was Rhona.

McNab had changed the subject at that point, asking about the two remaining soldiers.

'Lexi said they would have carried out Dempsey's orders, left the island and reported for duty.'

'The burnt-out jeep?'

'I would suspect so,' Rhona had said. 'Lexi didn't know the details.'

'So the MOD will have them by now?' McNab had sworn under his breath.

Rhona repeated what the boss had just said. 'They'll come for Dempsey and Lexi too. It's only a matter of time.'

Dempsey didn't look up as McNab and Janice entered and introduced themselves, but waited until they'd taken their seats opposite him at the table. McNab took time to study the face more closely now. The stillness, the direct eye engagement, the almost bored attitude suggested they were unlikely to be offered anything of interest from Corporal Dempsey. He was right.

'You are required to inform the MOD of my arrest.'

McNab shrugged his shoulders as though he didn't give a damn about such niceties and asked a question instead. 'What do you know of the Sandman?'

'The Sandman?' Dempsey repeated, a smirk playing the corners of his mouth.

'The Scorpion and the Sandman.' McNab feigned surprise. 'Looks like you're the one who got stung. And you a soldier, too.' McNab sat back, arms folded, and smiled. 'Now a woman, that's a much easier target, don't you think? Fuck them and kill them. Easy-peasy.'

Dempsey's face darkened and McNab wondered for a moment if he'd hit home, so he took another shot.

'Seven told us what you did to her in Afghanistan. MOD will really like to hear that story.'

'She's a fucking liar. I got her out of that hellhole. I got them all out.'

'Oh, we know how that worked and we don't care. That's the MOD's concern now. We just want what you want. To fuck the Sandman.'

Dempsey was definitely considering this, the muscles of his face rippling with undisguised wrath.

McNab laid it on a little thicker. 'If we don't, then he gets what you lose. All of it. And guess what? The Sandman wins the war.'

McNab rose at this point and nodded at Janice to follow.

'Wait,' Dempsey called as they reached the door. 'I'll give you the bastard.'

82

'So you're both coming to the wedding party?' Jamie said for the second time.

'Assuming your groom is alive after the stag do at A.C.E Target Sports.' Chrissy pulled a face. 'Too soon for that joke, d'you think?' she added, looking to Rhona.

Rhona apologized to Jamie. 'Gallows humour,' she said, 'but hey, you know all about that in your line of work.'

'I certainly do,' Jamie agreed. 'But if you're definitely up for it, it'll be at the Gathering Place, the big old building on the hill above the harbour. And of course you're welcome to stay over at my place afterwards.'

'I've got my B&B booked, thank you,' said Chrissy, as though he'd been addressing her. 'Plus we need to be back at Donald's after, because of the new arrival.'

'What new arrival?' Rhona demanded.

'Ah. Just you wait and see,' Chrissy said with a smile.

'Now that I've given a full statement to Lee, I'm going to head for the cottage,' Rhona told Jamie. 'But I'll be back in time for the party tomorrow. Have fun tonight and stay safe.'

'You bet,' Jamie said with a grin.

'And can I still use the jeep?'

'For as long as you need it.'

Chrissy's elbow in her ribs showed that she too had spotted the smitten look he'd given Rhona.

As soon as Jamie had gone, Chrissy gave Rhona the full force of her thoughts on the matter.

'You've made a conquest there, Dr MacLeod. And he's pretty tasty. DS Clark definitely thought so.'

'Jamie is a good friend, that's all. And you're one to talk about being smitten,' Rhona admonished her.

At this, Chrissy's face fell a little. 'It was good while it lasted,' she said.

'And it's not going to last any longer, you and Donald?'

'Long-distance relationships rarely do.' Chrissy gave Rhona a pointed look, which she read as *When are you going home?*

Rhona didn't want to be quizzed on Sean or on whether she was going home. Not yet, anyway.

'I think I'll be back,' Chrissy said. 'But we'll just have to wait and see. Anyway, I intend enjoying my last couple of days before I head back to Glasgow. As should you.'

Rhona, non-committal, indicated she was heading off now, and would see Chrissy tomorrow.

For once, Chrissy let her have the last word.

The forecast was for settled weather over the next few days. It seemed the gods had decided that Skye needed a respite from the storm, both physical and emotional, that had raged over it for the previous week.

As she headed towards Sligachan, the view of the Cuillin, still snow-topped, its image like something from a fairy tale, brought a gasp of wonder. No matter the number of times Rhona viewed these hills, or from where she caught their outline, each image seemed unique in colour and light.

But now, for a while at least, whenever she saw the

Cuillin she would think of the scree slope at An Dorus and the body of Private Pete Galbraith, or Sugarboy as his friend Lexi called him.

They'd talked a great deal during the wait for the helicopter, then later when Lexi had been admitted to Portree hospital, waiting for her transfer to the Queen Elizabeth. Rhona thought she knew most of the story by now and had written a full statement of everything the girl had said during those hours and given it to Lee.

The incident that had started it all, the child with the hidden grenade. Lexi's failure to search him resulting in the death of two of the team – Mitch and Gordo, she'd called them, breaking down in tears.

A description of their capture had followed. About the conditions of her imprisonment she said very little until, prompted by Rhona, she revealed the truth about Dempsey's actions during her incarceration. At that point Rhona's horror must have shown on her face, because Lexi had drawn away from her, retreating into herself again.

One thing that had been obvious was Seven's tortured mental state. It was as though as Lexi she was one person, but becoming Seven had made her another. Or maybe the connotations of that nickname had an even darker side than Rhona could imagine.

What had been obvious was the power Corporal Dempsey had had, and still had, over Lexi. The hole in the cave had been dug by her to trap him. She'd admitted that she'd planned to kill him.

'I couldn't do it. Not directly. Even though I knew his intention was to kill me. So I left it to fate and the tide.' She'd seemed bemused by that decision. Rhona, on the other hand, wasn't.

She knew what it felt like to have a life there for the taking. And by taking it, save your own. She believed it was a decision no one should have to take, because she'd experienced it herself.

But Lexi's biggest regret had been Sugarboy's death.

'I didn't know it was Sugarboy. I thought it was *him* coming to get me.'

Her strange use of *him* rather than Dempsey's name made the soldier sound like a character out of a horror story. A horror story that Lexi, Rhona suspected, had had a starring role in.

'And with Sugarboy gone, who will believe me anyway?'

'I believe you,' Rhona had assured her. 'You must tell the MOD everything that happened here on Skye and out in Afghanistan.'

'They'd already discharged Sugarboy. They suspected him of smuggling heroin, but they didn't have the proof. Plus they don't want any of what's happening out there becoming public knowledge. Besides, I knew about the smuggling. I was as complicit as the others. Sugarboy wanted out. So did I. He died trying to make that happen.'

'What about telling the police?' Rhona suggested.

She'd laughed then, a hollow and disbelieving sound. 'I've told you. That's enough.'

It seemed like a lifetime ago that she'd last driven the road to the cottage. Despite the frenetic nature of the last few days, Rhona found herself more at ease than the previous time she'd passed this way.

Then she was questioning every thought, with no faith in her own instincts.

Trauma did that, even to her . . . something she'd denied

ever since she'd left Glasgow and come to Skye. You can't escape trauma by running away from it. Seeing what it had done to Lexi had made her face up to that.

So what should she do?

Talk to someone, the way that Lexi talked to you.

It was such a simple thought, but it had taken a long time for her to allow herself to even consider it. She hadn't taken Lexi's trauma away, but she had freed her voice for a little while at least.

She would do as DI Wilson wanted, she decided. She would go to Castlebrae and tell someone her story. Everything she'd done and not done as a captive. Maybe then she would be able to go back to her old life.

Turning into the drive to the cottage, she halted for a moment, as the setting sun found the blue door and brought it alive with light. The cottage had been her refuge; it would always be her refuge, when she needed it. But she couldn't stay here any longer.

It was time to go back.

McNab Skyped her at the usual time, just as she'd anticipated.

'Where are you?' he demanded, then spotted the familiar layout of the cottage kitchen behind her. He looked pleased, but she knew that was only because it wasn't Jamie's place.

'How are things your end?' Rhona asked.

'The MOD removed Private Forbes from the Death Star before I got to talk to her, so good job you got her statement in Portree. Janice and I managed a quick interview with Corporal Dempsey and he was very co-operative on the subject of the Sandman. We're following up on that now. Both men in the burnt-out car have been identified.

I was right about Stevenson. The other one was McNulty, who we pulled in recently for a domestic. That's one less woman walking into doors.'

'You're pleased,' Rhona said.

'I'll be more pleased if or when we get the Sandman, seeing as we won't have the opportunity to prosecute Dempsey.'

'So what happens to him?'

'Like Lexi, he disappeared into the arms of the MOD. Who knows where they'll end up.'

Rhona broke the silence that followed. 'How's Ellie?' she said.

'I didn't get home last night, but I'm hoping what I planned for then will happen tonight instead.' He paused and she could tell by his expression that he wasn't sure if he should say what was now on his mind.

'What is it?' she demanded.

'I think you should give Maguire a call. I had to tell him when you went missing.'

There was no point in berating McNab for something he'd had to do.

'Okay,' she said.

He broke into a grin. 'Right, Dr MacLeod. I'm signing off now. Got things to do and people to see.'

Rhona watched as he disengaged and the screen went blank, then she took herself outside and walked down to the shore to a place she knew she would have an uninterrupted mobile signal to make the necessary call.

83

'This is the new arrival?'

Rhona couldn't believe the face that peeped out at her from the back seat of Donald's 4x4. It was a collie puppy, mostly white with a touch of black. But it was the eyes that were extraordinary. One blue and one brown.

'It's a rescue dog. No one wanted it, and the rescue centre got in touch with me and asked if I'd take it,' Donald explained.

'And what does Blaze make of the new arrival?'

'You know Blaze. He has the patience of a saint, and I suspect he'll need it,' Donald said.

'What his name?' Rhona said.

'Laoch. It means hero in Gaelic.'

'I thought there was only one hero around here,' Rhona said, ruffling Blaze's thick shaggy coat. 'It's a big name to live up to, but I guess Blaze will make a fine teacher.'

They were outside the Gathering Place which was bright with music and the sounds of a party. Rhona had come as promised, but as much to keep Alvis company as to be part of the wedding.

He, like Chrissy and Rhona, was heading out tomorrow morning. He was pleased to hear that she was going home.

'I'm looking forward to getting back to work myself,' he said. 'You'll keep in touch?'

'Of course. And let me know the next time you have a forensic science conference in Stavanger.'

'Better still, you come for a holiday. Climb some Norwegian hills with me. I've covered a few with you now in Scotland.'

Chrissy shouted a goodnight as she headed off with Donald. 'See you for the helicopter ride back tomorrow.'

When Alvis went back inside, Rhona stayed looking down at the little harbour and then over to the darkly edged shore of Raasay. She'd intended, she remembered, to take a trip out to the island, but had never managed to.

Still, there would be a next time, she was sure of that.

'Dr MacLeod. I thought you'd gone home,' Jamie said as he appeared, carrying two glasses. 'But just in case you were still here, I brought a couple of drams out with me.'

He handed her a glass.

'A dram is the measure of whisky acceptable to both the pourer and the drinker. As you can see, the groom is a generous pourer. It's Talisker, by the way.'

Rhona accepted the glass and, chinking it against Jamie's, gave the appropriate toast.

Slange Var.

After a few moments' silence, Jamie said, 'I won't say I'm sorry to see you leave, but I'm glad that you came back and stayed for as long as you did.'

'So am I,' Rhona said.

'And you'll return, do you think?'

'That I can promise.'

84

So it was that a day later Rhona stood at the door to her flat, listening, catching the sound of music being played inside. It was a female voice, and after a few moments she realized it was Ella Fitzgerald singing 'Summertime'.

The song was a favourite of Sean's. In fact everything Ella sang was a favourite with Sean.

She hesitated, not knowing if, despite getting this far, she was capable of going inside. In that moment, she wished she was back on Skye about to open the blue door to the cottage, even relishing the knowledge that it would be cold on entry and that she would have to light the stove.

On the other hand, if she opened this door, she would be met with warmth and the bounding figure of Tom coming to greet her. If the cat remembered her at all, considering the amount of time she'd been absent.

Rhona counted to three, then slipped the key in the lock and, turning it, pushed the door open before she could change her mind.

She had been right about the warmth. It immediately enveloped her, as did the glorious smell of cooking. She could hear Sean moving about the kitchen, humming along with the music. It was this above everything that almost overwhelmed her.

The warmth, the promise of food, even the cat that had

not yet discovered her presence – none of these demanded anything of her.

Seeing Sean again did.

Her stomach turned over and she was briefly in that place of darkness once more, the walls closing in on her so swiftly that she turned towards the door again, prepared for flight. Then Tom appeared, like a guardian angel, racing towards her, wrapping himself around and between her legs, mewing loudly.

Whether it was that sound that brought Sean into the hall, she didn't know, but his face when he looked at her changed everything. She thought she was dreading seeing him again, yet his appearance had the opposite effect.

'Rhona, you're home. Good.'

He came towards her and in a moment she was wrapped in his welcoming arms.

'I hope you're hungry,' he said as he led her into the kitchen.

Rhona halted briefly at the door, waiting on recall to change her favourite room in the flat into her worst memory. Then she realized it had been transformed.

'You've painted it,' she said in amazement.

'You were talking about it, remember? Even chose a few possible colours. I just had to make a decision as to which one. Is it okay?' he said, his voice a little anxious.

'It's beautiful,' she said honestly. 'And the fridge. That's new and very stylish.'

'The other one conked out. This one sort of matches the new look,' he said, a question in his voice.

My fridge didn't die, she thought. *Sean knew what I would think about every time I opened its door.*

'Thank you,' she said.

He ushered her to the table. 'It's boeuf bourguignon. Red or white wine?'

'I think it's time I tried to acquire a taste for red,' Rhona said with a smile.

Eventually they talked properly, after the food, the wine and the coffee. During the meal, Sean had posed no questions about Skye or how she was. It was one of the things she liked about him, she remembered. He didn't try to be a part of her life, until asked.

Rhona did question him briefly about the jazz club, and told him some funny stories about Chrissy, and of course her romance with Blaze's owner.

'Do you think it'll last?' Sean had said.

'Who knows with Chrissy? And Skye's not exactly nearby. But she seems keen. She's been talking about taking wee Michael out for a holiday. And the dogs are a big draw.'

'Dogs? I thought there was just one. The famous Blaze, dog detective.'

'He has a younger brother now. Laoch, a rescue puppy. One blue eye and one brown.' Rhona showed Sean a photo on her mobile. 'From first impressions, Donald thinks he might be a little harder to train than Blaze.'

Eventually, the time came for Rhona to tell Sean what he deserved to know. As she began in a halting fashion, Sean intervened.

'You don't have to explain anything to me.'

'But I do.' Rhona stopped there, unsure exactly how to do that. 'When I was in the tunnel, I made a promise . . .' She hesitated. 'To myself. No, to our unborn child.'

Sean waited, his face growing pale.

'I promised that she, or he, would live. That we would

escape together.' She stumbled then as that moment in the tunnel came sweeping back to drown her again.

Her face must have shown her anguish, because Sean reached out and took her hand.

'I'm truly sorry I failed.'

The enormity of her decision to keep the child, and its tragic outcome, hung in the air between them. Rhona wondered if it would ever go away.

'Bad things happen sometimes,' Sean said, cradling her hand in both of his.

And nothing more needed to be said.

Rhona rose and went to the window. Below, the garden of the convent was bathed in light and the Virgin Mary gazed out over the glistening, frosted grass.

She was home.

Epilogue

There is a photograph of fully kitted-out soldiers, on patrol, wearing sunglasses, guns at the ready. They are walking through a field of flowering poppies.

This photograph, with its juxtaposition of flowers and guns, symbolizes more than anything else the failure of the war in Afghanistan.

The illicit harvest of the pretty Afghan poppy produces over 90 per cent of the world's heroin. Heroin that is responsible for multiple deaths around the world.

And into this theatre of war, soldiers are sent. What do we expect them to achieve? This is not a war between ideologies. It is not about women and children being allowed an education. It was only ever about resources, and about the global wealth of heroin. Something the West craves in all its forms.

Wars require money, a great deal of money, and the Taliban always knew where it could make the money it sought for the struggle. In the West, which craved its most prodigious product.

Such a war can have no end.

Acknowledgements

My thanks to all the kind people who made this book possible.

Firstly, Blaze's Dad, Steve Millar, who introduced me to Blaze and Laoch and A.C.E Target Sports, and who allowed me to make Blaze my forensic assistant for a time. When asked if I might borrow Blaze for a weekend, Steve said, 'Only if I can borrow Chrissy.' I've tried my best to make his wish come true. Without Steve's knowledge of walking and climbing on Skye, this story couldn't have happened: www.blaze-walks.com

BLAZE'n'TRAILS

@Blazespage

Matt Harrison at A.C.E Target Sports for my visit in February 2018, when this story was conceived. (I threw an axe as successfully as Rhona due to his excellent instructions!) I'd greatly recommend a visit: www.ace-skye.com

Sergeant Andrew Shaw of Lochaber and Skye Police, Portree, who kindly answered all my questions regarding policing on Skye. Any errors are of course my own.

Professor Lorna Dawson of the James Hutton Institute for inspiring the creation of soil scientist Dr Jen Mackie and advising me on the soils of Skye.

Dr James H. K. Grieve, Emeritus Professor of Forensic Pathology at Aberdeen University, who is more than generous in answering my queries about modes of death.

Gerry Ackroyd who helped me with information regarding Skye and Lochaber Mountain Rescue.

And last but certainly not least, my excellent editor Alex Saunders, and all at Pan Macmillan.

Driftnet

By Lin Anderson

Go back to where it all began with the thrilling first novel in the Rhona MacLeod series. Turn over for an extract now . . .

I

THE BOY DIDN'T expect to die.

When the guy put the tasselled cord round his neck, grinning at him, he thought it was just part of the usual game. The guy was excited, a dribble of saliva slithering down his chin and falling onto the boy's bare shoulder. He nodded his agreement. He was past feeling sick at their antics. He lay back down, turning his head sideways to the greyish pillow that smelt of other games, closed his eyes and shifted his thoughts to something else. There was a goal he liked to play out in his head.

On the right, the Frenchman, arrogant, the ball licking his feet, thrusting forward. The opposition starts to group and there's a scuffle. Bastards. But no worry 'cos the Frenchman's through and running, the ball anchored to him, like a child to its mother. The crowd breathes in. Time stretches like an elastic band. Then the ball's away, curving through the air.

Wham! It's in the net.

The boy can usually go home now. Not this time. This time, before the ball reaches the net, his head is pulled back, then up. The intense pressure bulges his eyes, bursting a myriad of tiny blood vessels to pattern the white. His body spasms as the cord bites deeper, slicing through skin, cutting the blood supply to his brain. At the moment of death his penis erupts, scattering silver strands of semen over the multicoloured cover.

2

SEAN WAS ALREADY asleep beside her. Rhona liked that about him. His baby sleep. His face lying smooth and untroubled against the pillow, his lips opened just enough to let the breath escape in soft noiseless puffs. No one, she thinks, should look that good after a bottle of red wine and three malt whiskies.

Rhona has given up watching Sean drink. It is too irritating, knowing the next morning he won't have a hangover. Instead he'll throw back the duvet (letting a draught enter the warm tent that had enclosed their bodies), slip out of bed and head for the kitchen. From the bed she will watch (a little guiltily), as he moves about; a glimpse of thigh, an arm reaching up, his penis swinging soft and vulnerable. He'll whistle while he makes the coffee and forever in her mind Rhona will match the bitter sweet smell of fresh coffee with the high clear notes of an Irish tune.

They have been together for seven months. The first night Rhona brought Sean home they never reached the bedroom. He held her against the front door, just looking at her. Then he began to unwrap her, piece by piece, peeling her like ripe fruit, his lips not meeting hers but close, so close that her mouth stretched up of its own accord, and her body with it. Then, with a flick of his tongue, he entered her life.

When the phone rang, Sean barely moved. Rhona knew once it rang four times the ansaphone would cut in. The caller would listen to Sean's amiable Irish voice and change their view of answering machines, thinking they might be human after all. Rhona lifted the receiver on the third ring. It would be an emergency or they wouldn't phone so late. When she suggested to the voice on the other end that she would need a taxi, the Sergeant told her that a police car was already on its way. Rhona grabbed last night's clothes from the end of the bed.

Constable William McGonigle had never been at a murder scene before. He had stretched the yellow tape across the tenement entrance like the Sergeant told him and chased away two drunks who thought that police activity constituted a better bit of entertainment than staggering home to hump the wife. Constable McGonigle didn't agree.

'Go home,' he told them. 'There's nothing to see here.'

He was peering up the stairwell, wondering how much longer he would have to stand there freezing his balls off when he heard the sound of high heels clipping the tarmac. A woman leaned over the tape and stared into the dimly lit stair.

'Sorry, Miss. You can't come in here.'

'Where's Detective Inspector Wilson?'

Constable McGonigle was surprised.

'Upstairs, Miss.'

'Good,' she said.

Her fair hair shone white in the darkness and Constable McGonigle could smell her perfume. She lifted a silken leg and straddled his yellow tape.

'I'd better go on up then,' she said.

The click of Rhona's heels echoed round the grimy stairwell, but if she was disturbing any of the residents, they didn't show it by opening their doors. No one here wanted to be seen. If there was a fire they might come out, she thought, in the unlikely event they weren't completely comatose.

A door on the second landing stood ajar. She could hear DI Wilson's voice inside. If Bill was here at least she wouldn't have to explain who she was. She could just get on with the job, go home and crawl back into bed.

The narrow hall was a fetid mix of damp and heat. The sound of her heels died in a dark mottled carpet, curled at the edge like some withered vegetable. She paused. Three doors, all half open. On her right a kitchen, on her left a bathroom. She caught a glimpse of a white suit and heard the whirr of a camera. The Scene of Crime Officers were already at work.

The end door opened fully and Detective Inspector Bill Wilson looked out.

'Bill.'

'Dr MacLeod.'

He nodded. 'It's in here.'

He allowed himself a tight smile. The two other men in the room turned and stared out at her. Dr MacLeod was not what either of them had expected.

Rhona looked down at her black dress and high-heeled sandals. 'I came out in a bit of a hurry.'

'McSween will get you some kit.'

Bill nodded to one of the men, who went out and came back minutes later with a plastic bag.

Rhona pulled out the scene suit and mask, put her coat into the bag and handed it to the officer. She took one shoe off at a time and, hitching up her skirt, slipped her feet into the suit. Only then did she step inside.

Rhona took in the small room at a glance. The hideous nicotine-stained curtains stretched tightly across the window. A wooden chair with a pair of jeans and a tee-shirt thrown over it. Two glasses on a formica table. A pair of trainers on the floor beside the bed. A divan, three-quarters width, no headboard but covered with heavy silken brocade in an expensive burst of swirling colours.

The boy's naked body lay face down across it, his head turned stiffly towards her, eyes bulging, tongue protruding slightly between blue lips. The dark silk cord knotted round the neck looked like a bow tie the wrong way round. The body showed signs of hypostasis, and the combination of dark purple patches and pale translucence reminded Rhona of marble. Below the hips blood soaked into the bedclothes.

'I turned the gas fire off when I arrived,' Bill said. 'The smell nearly finished off our young Constable, so I put him on duty outside for some fresh air.'

'Did anyone take the room temperature?'

'McSween has it.'

Rhona took a deep breath before she put on the mask. The smell of a crime scene was important. It might mean she would look for traces of a substance she would otherwise have missed. Here the nauseating odour of violent death mixed with stale sex and sweat masked something else, something fainter. She got it. An expensive men's cologne.

'McSween and Johnstone have covered the rest of the room. The photographer is working on the kitchen and bathroom.'

'What about a pathologist?'

'Dr Sissons came and certified death. Then suggested I get a decent forensic to take samples and bag the body because he needed to get back to his dinner party.'

'Important guests?'

'He did mention a "Sir" somewhere in the list.'

Rhona smiled. Dr Sissons preferred analysing death in the comfort of his mortuary. Taking samples of bodily fluids in the middle of the night he regarded as her territory.

'That's some bedcover!'

'We think it might be a curtain, but we'll get a better look once we take the body away.'

'Did the doctor turn him over?'

'Just enough to tell if he's been moved. He said the left side of the face, the upper chest and hips had been compressed since death occurred. He's lying where he was killed.'

Rhona opened her case and took out her gloves. She knelt down beside the bed.

'There's a lot of blood under the body.'

Bill nodded grimly. 'You'd better take a look underneath.'

Rhona lifted the right arm and rolled the body a little. The genitals had been gnawed, the penis severed by a jagged gash that ran from the left hand tip to halfway up the right side. One testicle was mashed and hanging by a thin strip of skin.

'This must have been done after he died or the blood would be all over the place.'

'That's what Sissons said.'

Rhona let the body roll back down. The boy's head nestled back into the dirty pillow.

'Any sign of a weapon?'

Bill shook his head. 'Maybe it wasn't a weapon.'

'A biter? Did Dr Sissons check for other bite marks?'

'He muttered something about bruising on the nipples and the shoulder.'

'I'll take some swabs.'

'How long do you think he's been dead?' Bill said.

Rhona pressed one of the deepening purple patches, and watched it slowly blanch under her finger. 'Maybe six, seven hours. Depends on the temperature of the room.'

Bill risked a satisfied smile.

'Matches the Doc.'

Rhona raised her eyebrows a little. She and Dr Sissons didn't usually agree. He had a habit of disagreeing with her on points like the exact time of death.

It was almost a matter of principle. Rhona had done three years' medicine before she switched to forensic science. She liked to practise now and again.

'How did you find him?'

'An anonymous phone call.'

'The murderer?'

'A young male voice. Very frightened. Maybe another rent boy came here to meet a client?'

'Alive, this one would have been pretty,' Rhona said.

Bill nodded. 'Not the usual type for this area,' he said. 'A bit more class, but rented all the same. I'll leave you to it? Just shout if you need anything.'

She was nearly an hour taking samples of everything that might prove useful later on. After she'd finished with the surrounds, she concentrated on the body, under the fingernails, the hair, the mouth. Dr Sissons would take the anal and penile swabs.

The skin felt cold through her gloves, but with the blond hair flopped over the empty eyes, he might have been any teenager fast asleep. Rhona lifted the hair and studied the face, trying to imagine what the boy would have looked like in life. There were none of the tell-tale signs of poor diet and drug abuse. This one had been healthy. So how did he end up here?

'Finished?' Bill's timing was immaculate. 'Mortuary boys are here.' He looked at her face. 'Go home and have a hot toddy,' he said.

A hot toddy was Bill's answer to almost any ailment.

Rhona got up from the bed and unwrapped her hands. 'Any idea who he is?' she said.

'Not yet. But I don't think he was Scottish.' He pointed to the hall. Behind the door hung a leather jacket and a football scarf. 'Manchester United,' he said in mock disgust.

'There are people up here who support Man U,' Rhona suggested cheekily, knowing Bill was a Celtic man.

'Yes, but they wouldn't flaunt it. Not in Glasgow anyway.'

Rhona laughed.

'All right then?'

'Yes.' She began to pack her samples in the case.

'The Sergeant will run you home.'

He walked with her to the front door.

'How's that Irishman of yours these days? Still playing at the club?'

'Yes, he is.'

'Must get down and hear him again soon. Good jazz player. You'll ring me as soon as you've got anything?'

'Of course.'

Sean was still asleep when Rhona got back. With the heavy curtains drawn the room was dark, although outside dawn was already touching the university rooftops. She had stopped at the lab on her way home and checked the swabs for saliva. It was there all right.

She left a note on the bench for Chrissy in case she got there first, giving her a brief history of the night's events, then she headed home for a few hours' sleep.

Rhona pulled her dress over her head, kicked off her shoes and slid under the duvet. She wrapped her chilled body round Sean's. He grunted and moved his arm over to take her hand.

'Okay?' he mumbled.

'Okay,' she said, but he was already back asleep.

Rhona closed her eyes and tried to relax into his warmth. She had been at many murder scenes, some more horrible than the one tonight. Death didn't scare her, not when it was reduced to tests and samples. But tonight was different. There was something about that particular boy. Something she hadn't been able to put her finger on. Not until the Sergeant had put it into words for her, coming back in the car.

The boy who had been abused and strangled in that hideous little room looked so like her, he could have been her brother.

3

WHEN SHE GOT to the lab the next morning, there was a delicious smell of fresh coffee. Someone had been to the Deli, because there were two croissants on a plate next to the machine.

'So you finally decided to come in?' Chrissy's red head appeared round the door of the cupboard. 'Thought I was going to have to do all the work myself.'

'You got my note?'

'I found it,' said Chrissy grimly. 'The samples you brought back are logged, and the bags of clothing and bedclothes arrived about half an hour ago.'

'The croissants look good,' Rhona said, picking one up.

'I thought lover boy made the breakfast,' Chrissy observed tartly.

'I made him stay in bed. It was too early for sane people to be up.'

'You have a man who thinks it's his job to make the breakfast and you stop him doing it.' Chrissy shook her head in disbelief. 'Try getting one of my brothers to do anything in the kitchen.'

'What about Patrick?'

'Patrick was different,' she said flatly. 'That's why he left.'

They sat at the lab table while Chrissy made notes on what was to be done. Rhona had already filled in the background, at least the stuff Chrissy needed to know. She didn't know why she was always so careful of Chrissy's feelings. She might be young but she'd seen plenty in her life, if her tales of her brothers were anything to go by.

Chrissy looked up from her list. 'We're going to be pushed to do all this with Tony away.'

'Unless they draft in some help, we'll just have to put the regular work on hold. Murder has priority,' Rhona said.

'They never gave us any help for the last one.' Chrissy's voice was wearily resigned. 'Have they any idea who the boy was, or do we have to identify him as well?'

'He had no ID on him. We'll profile him on what we have and see what Bill comes up with.'

'I'll start on the clothing then?'

Rhona nodded. 'The cover looks as though it has been used before. I circled areas to be tested.'

'Semen?'

'Probably. Oh, and there was a smell in the room.'

'I bet there was!'

'No. I mean a nice smell. Like a man's cologne. Subtle, probably expensive.'

'Definitely not Brut then?'

'Definitely not your average aftershave. It's a long shot, but maybe there's some on the boy's tee-shirt or that cover.'

'There was plenty of blood.'

'Yes.' Rhona wasn't going to elaborate.

'It's okay. The photos arrived first thing. I've already had a look. Poor guy. Nice looking too.'

She gave Rhona an odd stare. Rhona remembered what the Sergeant had said the night before. But if that was what Chrissy was thinking, she didn't say it.

'That's the problem nowadays, all the nice looking ones are gay.' Chrissy grinned. 'Except your Sean, of course.'

'If you could stop thinking about Sean, we could get started.'

Rhona was trying to pull rank but it was water off a duck's back. Her Scientific Officer gave her a look that said, 'So you didn't get it last night.'

'By the way. There was a phone call for you, Rhona. A bloke. Sounded sexy. Wouldn't give his name. Just said he'd try later.'

Death always involved relationships. Death because they loved you. Death because they didn't. Death because no one loved them. Love and hate. Hate and love.

And what about this death? Why had the boy died? It looked as though he had come to the room for sex. There was no sign of a struggle, not until the noose had tightened round his neck and even then, only when the perpetrator had gone too far.

Dr Sissons had confirmed that death was by asphyxiation during anal sex. The ligature had probably been used to restrict oxygen to the brain to promote orgasm, he said.

'The death wasn't premeditated then?' Rhona asked.

'There's some evidence to suggest the boy has been involved in this sort of activity before. Earlier bruises in the same area, though less pronounced. There was probably a pad placed between the ligature and the neck.'

'But not this time?'

'No. This time, the ligature was tightened to unconsciousness and beyond. Whatever the boy agreed to do, I can't believe he wanted to die.'

'And the mutilation?'

'After death definitely, and probably by biting. The gash on the penis is elliptical. I took the liberty of calling in the Odontology Unit. Hope that's okay?'

Dr Sissons liked to believe there was rivalry between the various forensic departments. Even if there was, Rhona wasn't going to encourage him.

'I located saliva on the nipples and the shoulder,' she said.

'Good. There was also semen on the anal swab. What about the curtain?'

'We're working on that. It looks as though it's been used more than once. We'll take our time and go over all of it. There might be fibres or old blood,' Rhona said. 'Oh, and I combed two head hairs from the pubic region.'

'Not the boy's?'

'I've still to check, but one's dark, so it's unlikely.' Rhona paused. 'I take it you don't know who the boy is yet?'

'No. The post mortem suggests he was in his late

teens, say between sixteen and twenty. Good health. No evidence of drug abuse. Non-smoker. Well nourished. Your forensic biologists are enjoying the dubious pleasure of examining his stomach contents, so we'll know soon what he'd been eating before he died. With a bit of luck it will be curry and the police can start checking all the Glasgow curry houses to see if they recognise him. And Dr MacLeod?' Dr Sissons' voice was thoughtful.

'Yes?'

'You aren't missing a member of your family, are you? The boy bore an uncanny resemblance to you.'

Rhona assured him that as far as she knew, her family was fully accounted for and rang off.

Rhona lifted her head from the microscope. A smirr of rain was touching the window, but here and there the sun was breaking through the cloudy skies. The park below the laboratory was quiet, just a few mums and kids at the swings and a couple walking, arm in arm. As she watched, the boy stopped beside a clump of trees, bent down and picked a bluebell and handed it to the girl. They began to kiss.

Six months before, Rhona had stepped over another yellow tape just where the couple were standing now. It had turned out to be a student, murdered on his way home from a dance at the Students' Union. Last night's murder, she thought, made four in one year. All young men.

The first two had been violent assaults with no evidence of sexual activity, but the one in the park had been different. It had all the hallmarks of queer bashing. The student was gay and was in a known cruising area. His chest and arms were covered with kick marks and his head had been caved in by a blunt instrument, which was never found. The area had been scoured for traces of the killer – or killers. It had been useless. Heavy overnight rain had washed the place clean of clues.

One thing connected that murder to this one. The victim had been wearing a thin leather neck band with a Celtic cross on it. At the post mortem the pathologist had found bruising round the neck, consistent with the neck band being pulled during the assault. What if tightening the neck band had been part of a violent sexual assault?

When Sean found out what her job was, he had laughingly called her Lady Death. Rhona didn't care. She loved her work. She loved the functions and the structures and the painstaking carefulness of it all. She had forsaken medicine because she found it too depressing. So many sick people and, if she was honest, so little she could do to help them. Forensic Science was different. Here she could help, as long as she was prepared to look for the truth. That was the fascination. The truth hid from her, until she found just the right question to ask. At the end of the day, it wasn't what had happened but why it had happened that held the truth.

Maybe that's why we couldn't find the killer, she thought. Maybe we got the 'why' bit of the jigsaw wrong.

The couple had moved off towards the Art Gallery and were climbing the steps to get under the ornate portico, out of the rain. Rhona went back to the microscope, not wanting to think about the Gallery. Not since last Friday when she'd taken her lunch there and spotted the familiar long blue raincoat and dark hair.

She tried to concentrate on the next slide, ignoring the knot in her stomach.

'Fancy coming out for some lunch?' Chrissy was standing in the doorway.

Rhona shook her head.

'Right. I'll bring you back a sandwich then.' Chrissy wasn't asking. She was telling. It was like having your mother working for you.

Rhona watched Chrissy emerge below. A bloke on the other side of the street crossed to meet her, his shaved head bowed and his hands in his pockets. It looked as if Chrissy was giving him a right mouthful. The latest in a long line of boyfriends or one of Chrissy's brothers on the scrounge, Rhona thought.

Bill Wilson contacted her halfway through the afternoon and asked how things were going. She told him what she'd told Dr Sissons.

'I'm working on the hairs just now,' she said. 'It'll take us a while to examine the cover thoroughly, but you can have the whisky glasses back. I've finished with them.'

'Thanks, although I don't hold out much hope of finding our suspect's prints on file.' Bill sounded resigned. 'By the way, the story's splashed all over the evening paper.'

'Right.'

She heard a short 'mmm' of displeasure.

'If anyone pesters you for info?'

'I don't have any. Oh, and Bill.' She hesitated. 'Were you right?' she asked.

'About what?'

'The English connection.'

'We haven't found out who the boy was or where he came from. But you can read that in the *Glasgow News*. They always know more than us anyway.'

Rhona stopped work at five o'clock. Her eyes were tired from peering down the microscope and the lunchtime sandwich had long since been eaten. Chrissy had left at four, pleading a 'domestic' to sort out. One look at Chrissy's face convinced Rhona not to ask any questions.

Now, all she wanted was something substantial to eat and a long hot soak in the bath. But that meant facing Sean. She started to tidy the lab, methodically filing away her notes and storing the samples, putting off the moment when she would have to go home.

Outside, the rain had moved off north towards the Campsie Hills. The sky had cleared to a dull blue. She was a twenty minute walk from the flat and as long as the evening was fine there was no point in taking a bus. It would just sit in traffic anyway. She headed for Byres Road.

She knew Sean would have already bought something for tea but she stopped at the pasta shop anyway. Mr Margiotta welcomed her with his usual patter and persuaded her to try the spinach and ricotta cannelloni, adding an extra dollop of tomato and basil sauce for good measure.

'Love food,' he promised with a wicked grin.

Just what she didn't need.

Rhona allowed herself five minutes to decide what she was going to do, before she put her key in the lock. Part of her wished she could just forget what she'd seen in the Art Gallery, but it was like a forensic clue and she couldn't let it go. Like one of those semen samples. She had to know whose it was.

When she opened the door of the flat she was greeted by the rich scents of garlic and olive oil.

'Hi,' Sean called from the kitchen. He was chopping vegetables next to the cooker. He turned and smiled, wiping his hands on a tea towel. 'You look tired,' he said. 'Coffee? A drink?'

'A bath.'

He came towards her and she forced herself to smile.

'Come on,' he said.

She wanted to be in the bathroom alone with the door locked, but Sean led her in, turned on the taps and began to undress her. Behind Rhona the water pounded into the tub, hot and cold, like her thoughts. He sat on the chair and pulled her onto his knee, stroking the back of her neck with one hand while his other tested the water. When it was right, he turned off the taps.

'Get in. It's fine.' She stepped into the water like an obedient child. 'I'll give you a shout when tea's ready.'

He left the door open when he went out. She leaned over to shut it properly.

'Don't lock it!' he called. 'I'll bring you in a glass of wine.'

Rhona sat down defeated, leaned back and closed her eyes.

Sean came in twice. First with the wine as promised and again with the bottle to refill her glass. Rhona kept her eyes closed the second time, although he knelt beside the bath so that she could feel his warm breath on her face. Then the water parted with her knees, hitting the sides of the bath in a wave of emotion, as he ran his hand slowly up her thigh.

This was what it was like, she thought. To be primed. Made ready. Sean was good at that. She pushed herself up and opened her eyes.

'Okay now?' He was smiling at her, the dark blue eyes full of confidence.

She stood up and he handed her a towel, then the dressing gown.

'Don't bother getting dressed,' he said.

Sean liked women. He was comfortable in their company. But most of all he liked to take them to bed. He played his saxophone with the same sensual concentration he gave to sex. He would cradle it, stroke it, press the right buttons and blow into it until it squealed with pleasure. Recently Rhona had noticed a difference. She had begun to suspect that Sean was not playing her any more, he was playing with her, an entirely different thing.

'Good?' Sean said.

'Delicious.'

'I put the pasta in the fridge. It'll do for tomorrow night.'

Sean played a regular gig in a club in the centre of town every Friday night. The Ultimate Jazz Club was dark and intimate. On Fridays it was always packed. The gig started at ten o'clock and didn't finish till two. Sean often stayed there jamming until sunrise. Rhona had loved to watch him play, ever since the night they met. He'd been booked to play at a police function at the club. At the interval he'd come over to her table and asked if he could talk to her. He was so straightforward, she couldn't refuse. Besides, she'd been having erotic thoughts about him all evening. She stayed on till late, till the band wound down, playing soft soul music while the crowd drifted off. After he'd packed up his gear, they'd left together and they'd been together ever since.

I can't go back to the club, she thought. Not now I know.

Sean was up, whistling as he rattled cups and spooned freshly ground coffee into the machine.

'I went to the Art Gallery on Friday,' Rhona heard herself say in a detached voice.

Sean didn't answer at first and she wondered whether he had been listening. Often when he whistled he was miles away, planning a tune in his head. Not this time. This time he heard her.

He brought the cafetière over to the table and poured the coffee. He was whistling again, bringing the notes to a proper end before he spoke.

'Ordinary people go to art galleries here. I like that. It reminds me of Dublin.'

His voice was unperturbed and soothing. He was not going to be drawn into a sparring match. They lapsed into silence. Rhona fingered her cup.

'You were in the Gallery on Friday,' she said.

'I was.'

(Was that a question or an answer?)

'You were with a woman,' she said.

'I was.'

He took a sip of coffee then placed his cup gently back on the saucer. He did everything like that, his big hands moving in firm gentle ways.

'Who was she?' Rhona tried to make her voice as if she didn't care.

Sean studied her carefully, his eyes catching hers.

'A woman I know who likes art galleries,' he said.

'Like me.'

'No,' he shook his head, 'not like you.' He ran his fingers through his hair.

I've got to him, she thought. She waited for him to say something else, then interrupted him when he tried.

'Rhona . . .'

'Are you fucking her?'

'Fucking her?' He repeated the words so lightly they no longer seemed important. 'It doesn't matter if I am.'

'It matters to me,' she said angrily.

He didn't answer. In the distance Rhona heard a church clock chime. She counted eight before he spoke.

'That's because you make it matter,' he said quietly.

Sean was never outright angry. When he was ruffled or irritated he always gave the impression he couldn't understand what all the fuss was about. Sometimes Rhona wished he would argue with her, let it out. But he never did and she was always left yapping at his heels like a terrier.

'If I tell you I'm not, will you believe me?' he said.

She had known this would happen.

'Listen.' He reached over the table and lifted her chin and made her look at him. 'I will not cook for her or play for her or stroke the back of her neck when she's tired,' and he ran his hand tenderly down the curve of her face.

They left the table without clearing it and moved through to the living room. Sean lit the gas fire and closed the curtains. He sat on the couch and made a place for her in the crook of his arm. Rhona allowed herself to slip close against him, laying her head on his chest; already thinking of what her life would be like without him.

When the phone rang, Sean was the one who got up and answered it.

'It's for you,' he said. 'A man. Didn't give his name.' Sean's face betrayed nothing.

She took the receiver and Sean left the room. From the bedroom she heard a trickle of notes.

'Hello?'

'Rhona? It's Edward. Edward Stewart.' The repetition was unnecessary. As if Rhona wouldn't know that voice anywhere, at any time.

There was the sound of a throat being cleared.

'Would it be possible to speak to you about some business?'

'No.'

'Rhona, this is difficult for me . . .'

Things were always difficult for him, never for anyone else.

'Fuck off, Edward,' she said and began to put the phone down.

'Rhona, wait, please. It's important.'

There was something in his voice that stopped her.

'Could we meet?' he was asking.

Rhona heard herself agree.

'Tomorrow. Half ten?'

Edward was confident again as he said good-bye. He's got what he wanted, she thought. What sort of business could he possibly want to discuss? Business, as in his law firm, or business as in the by-election he's hoping to win next month? And why now, she asked herself. We haven't spoken in three years, and then only across a bench in court. He hadn't been pleased when her evidence put his client away. Edward didn't like losing.

Sean was still playing his saxophone but now he'd moved to a tune that Rhona had come to think of as theirs. The tune he'd been playing, he said, when he fell in love with her.

She knew he meant it now as a peace offering.

Sean wouldn't ask her who the man on the phone was. He wouldn't ask her if she'd slept with him in the past or was sleeping with him in the present. He wouldn't ask because it wouldn't make any difference to the way he felt about her.

Rhona only wished she could feel the same.

Torch

By Lin Anderson

Torch *is the second book in Lin Anderson's Rhona MacLeod series.*

It's Edinburgh, Scotland, days before the biggest New Year's party in the world. When Karen, a young homeless girl, dies in a case of suspected arson, her friend Jaz sets out to avenge her death.

Faced with similar cases in Glasgow, Dr Rhona MacLeod heads to the capital to establish whether the string of attacks are linked. Arriving as festivities begin to get under way, Rhona starts her investigation and is confronted by combative Severino MacRae, the city's chief fire investigator.

As the attacks escalate, it becomes clear a ruthless individual is behind the fires and has threatened to strike again at Hogmanay. While Jaz begins to uncover what happened to his friend, Rhona and MacRae must work together in a desperate attempt to locate the fire starter before any more people die . . .

'Forensic scientist Rhona MacLeod has become one of the most satisfying characters in modern crime fiction – honourable, inquisitive and yet plagued by doubts and, sometimes, fears' *Daily Mail*

Deadly Code

By Lin Anderson

Deadly Code *is the third book in Lin Anderson's Rhona MacLeod series.*

Following a grisly discovery made on Scotland's Isle of Skye, forensic scientist Rhona MacLeod is sent over to investigate. It's there she finds a decomposing foot, caught in a net by a local fisherman, and there are key questions which remain unanswered: Where is the rest of the body? Who was the dead man? And why does the Ministry of Defence want the discovery to be kept out of the media?

Returning to her island roots, Rhona soon becomes embroiled in a conspiracy that stretches far beyond the beautiful and remote Western Isles. For there are deadly international forces at play, controlled by powerful people who are willing to do anything to protect their interests and will silence anyone who threatens to expose them . . .

'Chills the blood . . . would make Ian Rankin's old man Rebus choke on his whisky chaser' *Big Issue*

Dark Flight

By Lin Anderson

Dark Flight *is the fourth book in Lin Anderson's Rhona MacLeod series.*

Six-year-old Stephen Devlin has vanished, his mother and grandmother horrifically murdered. At the scene of the devastating crime, forensic scientist Rhona MacLeod finds a chilling African talisman, made from the bones of a child.

Working with DS Michael McNab, Rhona joins a task force that has been formed in a desperate attempt to track down the missing child before it's too late. As the case builds momentum, it becomes clear the killer's motive was linked to the fact that the boy and his mother had recently returned from Nigeria.

When further victims are found, Rhona realizes she must decipher the talisman's meaning if they are to have any hope of finding Stephen before he becomes the next link in the killer's chain . . .

'Lin Anderson is one of Scotland's national treasures; don't be fooled by comparisons, her writing is unique, bringing warmth and depth to even the seediest parts of Glasgow. Lin's Rhona MacLeod is a complex and compelling heroine who just gets better with every outing'

Stuart MacBride

Easy Kill

By Lin Anderson

Easy Kill *is the fifth book*
in Lin Anderson's Rhona MacLeod series.

A vulnerable young woman has been brutally slain and left on a grave in Glasgow's sprawling cemetery, the Necropolis. Upon examining the body, forensic scientist Rhona MacLeod has no doubt that the depraved killer's motives were sexual in nature.

The case takes on an even more disturbing dimension when the removal of the girl's body reveals a second victim, who has recently been buried in a shallow grave underneath. When yet another sex worker is reported missing, there are fears that a serial killer is at large in the city.

This man has killed before – and will again unless Rhona can break the chain and track him down before any more lives are lost . . .

'Definitely a cut above the average: vivid and atmospheric'
Guardian

Final Cut

By Lin Anderson

Final Cut *is the sixth book in Lin Anderson's Rhona MacLeod series.*

When Claire regains consciousness after a stranger causes her car to crash in a snowstorm, she is frantic to discover that her nine-year-old daughter Emma is missing from the back seat. Then Emma is found in the woods nearby, unharmed but cradling a child's skull. She claims it 'called' to her – and she can hear another voice nearby . . .

Meanwhile, forensic scientist Rhona MacLeod is trying to discover the identity of a corpse found badly burnt in a skip. The body is wearing a soldier's ID tag, but DNA tests show it's not him. When DS Michael McNab asks for her help identifying the remains Emma found, they discover the two cases are linked in ways they could never have imagined . . .

'Inventive, compelling, genuinely scary and beautifully written, as always' Denzil Meyrick

The Reborn

By Lin Anderson

The Reborn *is the seventh book in Lin Anderson's Rhona MacLeod series.*

When the body of a pregnant teenager is found at a Glasgow funfair, her unborn baby surgically removed, forensic scientist Rhona MacLeod is called in to assist the police. Suspecting the baby may still be alive, finding the killer becomes paramount.

Delving deeper into the twisted case shines suspicion on Jeff Coulter, a psychotic inmate at a nearby hospital whose hobby is making Reborns – chillingly realistic baby dolls intended for bereaved parents. But how could he have orchestrated the murder from a secure psychiatric facility?

With time running out, the investigation soon leads to four of the girl's friends, who have mysteriously all fallen pregnant at the same time, calling themselves the Daisy Chain. It becomes clear that something much more sinister is at play than Rhona could ever have imagined. A killer is out there, watching, waiting and ready to strike again . . .

'Anderson clearly knows what her readers want and how to keep them coming back for more' *Sunday Herald*

Picture Her Dead

By Lin Anderson

Picture Her Dead *is the eighth book in Lin Anderson's Rhona MacLeod series.*

When art student Jude Evans disappears on a trip to photograph one of Glasgow's many derelict cinemas, her friend Liam reports her missing to the local police. Unable to get the authorities to take him seriously, he enlists the help of his mother, forensic scientist Rhona MacLeod, in his search for the missing girl.

In an attempt to retrace the last known steps of Jude, they begin working through the list of cinemas she had intended to visit. Their efforts lead them to make a grisly discovery, hidden behind one of the cinema's crumbling walls, and soon a murder hunt is under way.

Dealing with personal trauma arising from the unknown fate of a close friend, Rhona must maintain focus as the investigation gains momentum. Fearing the girl's disappearance could be linked with something she wasn't supposed to see at the ruined picture house, time is running out, and if she's not found soon it could be too late . . .

'This brilliantly creepy novel is a must-read for crime fans'

Bella

TH 27-08-2020